Her breath came out in a soft rush, and with it came a debilitating flash of intuition. Even as he kissed her, she was shattered by a sense of loss. This would end. She would be alone again.

Chad raised his head just long enough to catch a flicker of something across her face.

"Darling, what's the matter?"

She shrugged, lifting both shoulders off the chaise in a way that seemed as if she were getting set to run.

"We're in this together," he told her. With the backs of his knuckles he caressed her cheek.

His eyes searched her face as if there was nothing—or no one—more precious on earth. Her dread eased, and she allowed her tears to flow out of her like a receding tide.

Live in the moment. All you have is here and now.

MERYL SAWYER

BETTER OFF DEAD

HQN™

ISBN 0-373-77024-3

BETTER OFF DEAD

The best way to love anything is as if it might be lost.
—G. K. Chesterton

This book is dedicated to Sheila Field.

BETTER
OFF
DEAD

PROLOGUE

"YOU CAN RUN, sweetheart, but you can't hide—not from me."

Brock Hardesty muttered those words to himself after his top field agent delivered the news he'd been waiting for months to hear. They'd found Samantha Robbins.

He dropped the telephone receiver into its cradle and grinned at the high-tech device he held in the palm of his other hand. With the reverse ID he could monitor what phone number anyone in the building had dialed. The gadget electronically recorded the number and length of each call from his underground bunker beneath Obelisk Enterprise's top secret headquarters.

At his convenience, Brock could check out any call his people made. If he discovered anything—anything—suspicious, he had a listening device installed in their office or assigned an operative to investigate. No one was beyond his reach.

Certainly not Samantha Robbins. It had taken a little longer than he'd expected, but he'd found the bitch. Disappearing was a lot more difficult than people believed. There was always a trail, a way of finding someone.

In this case, the key had been cold, hard cash. Money wasn't his first love, but without it, he couldn't indulge his true passion. Money often provided a trail or made a good trap, when he was after someone. He'd patiently waited until Samantha Robbins bought her condo with cash.

Brock gave himself full credit for finding Samantha. He

knew that the Witness Protection Program—WITSEC—relocated witnesses in a place where they had no family, no friends, and little chance of running into someone who might recognize them. Contrary to what most people thought, WITSEC did not fabricate credit histories for their witnesses.

WITSEC created new identities, but it was up to each witness to establish credit. Getting a credit card was a no-brainer. So many offers arrived in the mail that it was a joke, but it would take several years and a clean payment record for a witness to parlay a good credit card track record into a home loan.

Samantha was different. She had enough money to buy a place.

He'd made a list of the states where Samantha had connections and eliminated them. His agents tracked homes purchased for cash in the remaining states. Without a credit history, she would have to pay cash for a place to live.

Of course, there was always the possibility that she would rent, but the psychologist he'd consulted insisted Samantha Robbins was the type who liked control. She wanted to run things, own things. The shrink had been right.

As Director of Security at Obelisk Enterprises, it was Brock's job to make certain the group's interests were protected—at all times. This woman was a threat. He'd said so from the day he and the Obelisk brass made a secret visit to the CFO at PowerTec. As the CFO's assistant, she'd asked too many insightful questions.

Samantha Robbins had been suspicious about PowerTec's dealings and should have been eliminated immediately. His superiors had insisted he allow the dumb-fucks at PowerTec to handle their employee.

What happened? Just what Brock said would happen. The snoopy bitch had notified the FBI, and the Feebies had sent an undercover agent to work at PowerTec. Brock had been forced to have the agent killed.

Even the Federal Marshals who ran the WITSEC program

knew security should never be taken lightly. Not with this much at stake. Too many powerful, important people had everything to lose. They relied on Brock to make certain nothing went wrong.

Dominating one wall of his office was a world map on a liquid plasma television screen. The weather satellite displayed the cloud formations and used green Doppler striations to indicate where it was raining. Points of colored light, each the size of a thumb tack, continuously moved to reveal the positions of the satellites orbiting overhead.

Using the EPA satellite nearest to where his operatives had located the Robbins woman, Brock punched a few keys on the computer. From space the super-magnified camera could focus all the way down to a single pine needle, and that lone needle would fill the entire screen. With a few keystrokes, Brock used the satellite's camera to inspect the area where she was working.

"Yeah, sweet cheeks. You can run, but you can't hide."

If Brock wanted to find someone, he would. Then that person would find out the bitter truth.

"You're better off dead."

CHAPTER ONE

LINDSEY WALLACE walked across the plaza that was the heart of Santa Fe's historic district. She pretended to be casually walking her retriever, but she was checking to see if anyone was following her. Only a handful of people strolled on the streets bracketing the square. None of them seemed to notice her.

Things aren't always what they appear to be.

A good operative wouldn't be easy to spot. According to what she'd been told, operatives often traveled in pairs. Frequently they seemed to be ordinary couples.

From behind her shades, she scanned the people in the area. Two disappeared into buildings. Another rounded the corner, heading toward La Fonda Hotel. Satisfied no one was interested in her, Lindsey moved on.

There was a thin line between caution and paranoia, she told herself. Maybe, just maybe, she'd crossed over the line.

No, she wasn't being neurotic.

She'd been safe for almost a year, but she would be foolish to let down her guard. One woman—an experienced FBI agent—had already been murdered.

She reached Palace Avenue, but stayed on the south side of the street with Zach beside her. She could have crossed to walk under the shady adobe portico of the Palace of the Governors, but she didn't.

Native American women were setting up their wares in front of the building that dated back to missionary days. On well-worn Navajo rugs, they arranged row after row of silver jewelry that had been manufactured in Malaysia. There was a smattering of pottery and rugs to entice tourists. Little of it was made at the pueblos, most of it not even produced in this country. Their once proud heritage was being lost.

In Navajo she greeted an older woman, lugging her goods to the palace. *"Yaa' eh t' eeh."*

She smiled slightly and responded in Navajo, *"Yaa'eh t'eeh."*

Like the women assembled under the portico, the elderly lady wore the traditional velvet blouse with Concho-style silver buttons and a long skirt that swept across her squaw boots. Her pewter-gray hair was pulled back into the traditional figure eight bun worn by women from the reservation.

Seeing Native America's arts being lost forever bothered Lindsey. Some of her best artists, like Ben Tallchief, came from the reservation. She supposed they were the future of pueblo art—unique, individual pieces, not tribal art passed down from generation to generation.

Most of the people on the reservation had little to do except hawk trinkets to tourists. From what she could tell, their situation bordered on hopeless, and it was a downer. Depression was her enemy, she warned herself. Not her foremost enemy, but an enemy nevertheless.

The hardest part of being in the Witness Protection Program wasn't knowing someone would do anything to kill you, the way she'd originally thought. It was not seeing your family, your friends.

The love of your life.

It was not knowing if you ever would see any of them again. Even after the trial, it might not be safe to return home.

"Count your blessings," she said under her breath.

Until they found work, most people in WITSEC had no money and were forced to rely on the monthly stipend doled out by the Federal Marshals who ran the program. Because she'd been a successful executive with considerable savings, her field contact had arranged to have her funds transferred to the Bank of Santa Fe.

With that money, she'd opened the Dreamcatcher Gallery,

which specialized in Southwestern jewelry in contemporary settings. She'd been able to buy the small condo where she and Zach lived. She had a pet, someone to talk to, someone to care about.

Still, the past tore at something deep inside her. *You never appreciate what you have until you lose it.* Those words had seemed trite. Now she knew how true they were. She forced herself to live in the moment, to appreciate what she had— not what she'd lost.

"Good boy, Zach."

The golden retriever looked up at her, his soulful eyes full of love. His honey-blond tail whipped from side to side. Canine solace, she thought, the best medicine on earth. She had a home, a gallery, a pet—and a friend. After months of isolation and loneliness, she'd made a friend. Not that she'd expended any effort.

She'd been afraid to get to know someone. What would she say about her past? You never realize how much you talk about your past until you don't have a previous life to talk about.

With Romero, her past hadn't mattered. He owned the Crazy Horse Gallery next door to hers in Sena Plaza. He'd blown into her life like a whirling dervish. Romero listened and jabbered nonstop, but he'd never asked questions about her past.

She'd had almost a year—and coaching from Derek—to get used to her new name and come up with a cover story. She'd used the story once on Romero and again when she'd joined the Chamber of Commerce. But because she kept to herself, rarely socializing with anyone except Romero, she hadn't had to paint herself into a corner with lies.

"You're late," Romero called out from his gallery as she unlocked the heavy plank door to the Dreamcatcher Gallery.

"Hey! It's one minute after ten. Lighten up."

Every morning when she arrived, she experienced a small thrill at having found this unique spot in a two-story building that had been divided into shops and galleries. Dating back to the seventeenth century, Sena Plaza was a rectangular adobe structure with a lovely interior courtyard. Built in the Spanish Colonial era, it featured the original hand-hewn beams and trusses, black Andalusian iron, and plank floors burnished smooth over centuries by countless soles.

She stepped inside what—in only one of many incarnations—had been a shoe store before she'd leased it. Before that, it had been part of Romero's larger gallery, and between them was an adjoining door. They kept it open during the day. When business was slow, they talked and helped each other with displays.

She hadn't realized how much she'd missed having someone intelligent to talk to. Romero was well-read, cosmopolitan, and never failed to make her smile. In many ways, he reminded her of her long-dead father. Hollow emptiness welled up inside her, the way it often did when she recalled her parents' deaths. Since she'd met Romero, it had lessened. She didn't want to regress, so she tamped down the thoughts.

Lindsey unhooked Zach's leash and put it in the second drawer of her sleek chrome and glass desk, and opened the connecting door. Zach trotted along behind her.

"Is coffee ready?" she asked, although she knew Romero made it a point to arrive an hour before he opened and brew a pot of Kona coffee. The fragrant scent hovered in the summer air that was still cool thanks to the building's thick adobe walls.

"Sure. Pour yourself a cup."

She walked over to the Southwestern style hutch in the alcove where Romero kept the coffee. She'd decorated her gallery in contemporary fashion, aiming for a stark contrast with the ancient building. Romero, on the other hand, had used antiques from the Spanish colonial period, when Sena Plaza had been constructed by the Conquistadors.

"It's going to be a warm day," he commented, and she nodded.

Romero had a full head of white hair that made his complexion seem darker than it was. He was a tall man in his late fifties and slightly stooped, the way some older men are. He proudly traced his ancestors back to one of the original Spanish land grant families. She doubted anyone knew local history as well as Romero did. Certainly, no one could talk about it so colorfully.

She poured herself a mug of coffee and added a splash of milk before taking a sip. "You make great coffee."

"I'm a good cook, too. I'm making blue corn enchiladas tonight. Join me for dinner?"

"I'd love to. What can I bring?"

"Nothing. Just close up the gallery for me. I'll need to leave around six. Enchiladas taste better if they set for an hour or so before you eat them."

"No problem. I'll lock up." In the summer, they closed at eight to take advantage of the tourists who lingered in the historic area.

"You know, I was thinking."

Something in the timbre of Romero's voice brought up her guard, and she tried for a joke. "Thinking? That's a first."

A beat of silence.

She plunged on, her instincts telling her to change the subject. "I heard a good one. What do you call a woman who knows where her husband is at night?" She paused. "A widow."

Romero didn't crack a smile. "You're very beautiful, but the way you dress...your hair."

"I like the way I dress," she fibbed. Drab clothes helped her blend in. "My hair. What can I say? God screwed up."

A total lie. She had glossy black hair and violet-blue eyes. They couldn't change her eye color as easily as they could her hair. WITSEC insisted she strip it with bleach and dye it barnyard brown. They made her cut it to chin length, and she now wore it ruler straight.

Romero studied her. She was lying and he knew it. She could almost hear him asking: Why?

He'd never gotten this personal, never asked about her past. His comment had taken her by surprise. She needed him in her life more than he would ever know, but if he breached the invisible barrier she'd put up to protect herself, she would have to back off.

The bell on the door to her shop tinkled, saving her and announcing the arrival of the first customer of the day. "Gotta go."

She quickly walked back into her gallery. A lookie-lou, she thought. The petite brunette was dressed in matching powder-blue Bermudas and twin set. She could have been in an L. L. Bean catalog.

Lindsey's experience told her the type of woman who would be interested in her jewelry dressed more adventurously. They experimented with clothes, hair.

The kind of woman she had once been.

Another lifetime, she thought, even though it had been only a little over a year. Now she didn't experiment. The last thing she wanted was to call attention to herself.

"That bracelet is by my premier artist, Ben Tallchief," she told the woman who was looking at a hammered silver cuff set with deep lavender sugilite stones. "Madonna, Julia Roberts, and lots of other famous women collect his work."

She didn't add how lucky she'd been to lure him away from the gallery where he'd been featured when it changed hands.

The woman studied the unusual piece for a moment. "Too trendy for me."

"You might try Zazobra Gallery on Canyon Road. They have a nice selection of jewelry." She didn't add that it was conservative, unimaginative and overpriced.

"Thanks. Great dog," the woman said as she headed to the door.

Lindsey sat at her desk to do some work on her computer, and Zach settled at her feet. She finished in less than ten minutes. What she was doing wasn't much of a challenge for someone who had a CPA license.

In WITSEC you weren't allowed to work in your own profession. That would make it too easy for enemies to find you. They insisted you take a job in a new, unrelated field.

Boy had she ever. If only her friends could see her now. And Tyler. What would he say, if he knew she owned a jewelry shop?

Don't go there.

Dwelling on the past only meant depression. And anger. She was entitled to a normal life.

The life that rightfully belonged to Samantha Robbins.

She shouldn't have to reinvent herself. They'd broken the law—not her. But in one of life's baffling ironies, they were free—pending trial—and she was in hiding.

A cell without walls.

That's what she'd been told in the safe house where they'd debriefed her and prepared her for a new life in WIT-SEC. They had been more right than she ever could have imagined.

Provo, Turks and Caicos Islands

SITTING IN A CABANA-style beach lounge, Chad Langston stared out at the expanse of blue water beyond Grace Bay's twelve-mile crescent of sugar-white sand. He'd just finished reviewing the coroner's report. Cause of death: drowning.

"Yeah, right," Chad said out loud, half-listening to the melodic sound of the surf gently breaking on the shore.

Robert Townsend IV had been an experienced master diver who'd come to this swank resort in the Caribbean specifically to dive "the wall" on Long Cay. The steep wall plunged seven thousand feet and was rated expert. How could he successfully complete that challenging deep water dive, then the following day go on a newbie's dive and drown?

Not only didn't it make sense, the coroner's report sucked. No tissue samples had been taken. No toxicology report. *Nada.*

Okay, okay. What in hell did he expect?

The coroner was the local mortician in the capital of Grand Turk, which wasn't surprising. Turks and Caicos Islands were a British colony half an hour southeast of the Bahamas. Once a hideaway for notorious Caribbean pirates, the eight islands were now a haven for divers and fishermen.

Serious crime was rare. They weren't geared up to investigate the way cities in the States were. The coroner had taken one look at the body and decided <u>drowning</u> was the cause of death.

Townsend had been found floating, facedown, in his scuba equipment on Iguana Key. Air was still in his tank and he was close enough to shore to have waded in.

"Go figure."

The place to start would be with Townsend's diving gear. The coroner should have spotted an obvious problem, but experience had taught Chad that even the most competent professionals overlooked things. The local mortician didn't rank high on anyone's competency list.

Townsend had been a sixty-two-year-old man with a wife thirty years younger and a considerable fortune. Fidelity Insurance had hired Chad to see if his death could be suicide. If it were, they wouldn't have to pay the five mil life insurance policy. If Townsend had killed himself, he'd used a unique method.

"Yo, Langston."

Who in hell knew him here? He peered out from under the lounge's blue canvas shade and saw Archer Danson strolling across the sand in front of Ocean Club West—all white skin that hadn't seen the sun in years and skinny legs with knock knees.

"Son of a bitch! What are you doing here?"

"Tracking you down."

Chad moved his legs to one side, and Danson sat on the end of Chad's lounge and pushed his shades to the top of his head. He always tried to be cool but ended up looking even nerdier— if that was possible. Danson's slathered-on sunscreen made him smell like a French whorehouse, overwhelming the pleasant scent of frangipani drifting through the tropical air.

Who could look down at a sweet little baby in a crib and call it Archer? They must have had a nickname for him. As Archer grew up, the kids would have teased him, Chad decided.

Chad had been lucky—if you called growing up in a small house with three sisters lucky. Being tall with dark hair and having a gift for sports meant he'd been popular. And happy.

He sensed Danson had never been happy. The man lived for his work.

"Danson, how in hell did you find me?"

With a shrug, Danson grinned. "Your secretary said you were out of town on business. I—"

"Gimme a break." He knew Danson must have hacked into the airlines' databases and seen he'd flown out of Honolulu to Turks and Caicos through Miami and the Bahamas. "What's so important?"

"We need some testing done."

Chad didn't bother to ask what Danson had developed for DARPA now. The Defense Advanced Research Projects Agency—DARPA—operated out of the Defense Department and had been credited with some of the world's most revolutionary inventions.

Global positioning, stealth technology, drones, and the mouse all had been some of their brilliant, innovative ideas. Their motto was "no idea is too wild." Well, hell some of their ideas were screwed-up. FutureMap, an online futures market to predict terrorist attacks, had left the Congress and the public reeling with disbelief.

"My testing days are over," Chad told him with just a touch of regret. "In case you haven't heard, I've been a civilian for over eight years now."

Chad managed to say this and keep a straight face. Danson headed special projects for DARPA. He had access to everyone's records. He knew *exactly* what Chad had been doing.

Not that his career was any secret. He was still in touch with most of the Delta Force guys who'd served with him in Desert Storm. Some were still in the military, while others, like him, had opted for a so-called normal life.

"I know you're an underwater forensic expert."

Danson's tone was clipped, a sure sign he was pissed. Like lots of military types, Danson was big on respect. He didn't appreciate a former subordinate giving him a ration of grief. Of course, Chad didn't give a rat's ass what Danson thought.

"Underwater forensics means—"

"I know. You're Sherlock Holmes with a scuba tank. You contract out to police departments that don't have an underwater expert, but most of your work is for insurance companies who balk at paying certain claims. Like Townsend."

Chad gazed at Danson, not surprised to learn the man knew exactly what he was doing down here.

"Look, we're prepared to pay you a bundle to test for us."

"Why not use one of your own boys?" Chad would be damned before he'd act curious, but he was. DARPA usually tested its own inventions. Why didn't they want to test this?

"Good question." Danson fiddled with the shades perched on top of his balding head. "We don't want word to leak out on this one. Too sensitive. You still have your SAP/SAR."

Why hadn't the military terminated his top secret clearance? Special Access Program/Special Access Required— SAP/SAR—was damn tough to get. The light dawned. DARPA had kept his SAP/SAR active in case they needed him.

"You could do this, Chad, make some easy dough, and still snoop around under water all you want."

"What is it that you want me to test?"

"I can't tell you until you agree to test and sign the mandatory confidentiality document."

"Then count me out until I know what it is. How else can I decide if I'll have the time or interest?"

"Christ, Langston, you're pressing your luck."

"Damn straight. You need me more than I need you or you wouldn't have flown all the way down here."

Danson stared at a knockout blonde in a hot-pink butt floss bikini who wandered past. Chad knew Danson wouldn't tell him a thing until the woman was too far away to hear them.

The first time Chad met Danson was when Chad joined Delta Force. They were being trained to be dropped behind enemy lines. Danson outfitted each member of the team with a portable multiband scanner that was supposed to scan for any available uplink to the Department of Defense satellite.

Damn things never worked reliably, but they didn't find that out until they were behind enemy lines in Desert Storm and couldn't contact the DOD satellite. Chad had taken his apart and tinkered with the mechanism and finally got it going. After the war, Danson used Chad's modifications to make a smaller—and totally reliable—scanner.

Chad had spent his last year in the service testing military devices for DARPA. He'd loved the work, but when his father died unexpectedly, Chad returned to Honolulu.

"Okay, off the record," Danson said with a huff of disgust. "We've developed a handheld infrared device that can distinguish between thermal signatures."

Chad knew all living creatures, plants and machinery gave off heat. Sophisticated infrared sensors could detect the heat and know where something was located. But what was the object?

Chad let out a low whistle. "You mean it can tell the difference between a car and a man?"

"You bet. It'll tell the difference between a gorilla and a person."

Chad was more than impressed. Satellite surveillance relied on telescopic photography during the day, and it was damn good. You could hit the magnify button and look at a drop of dew on a leaf, but at night surveillance went to infrared. Every living thing had a thermal signature that showed up as red on the screen.

Objects such as cars in use gave off enough heat to be confused with people when viewed on the screen. In populated areas, all that could be seen at night was a big red blob. Essentially satellite surveillance after dark sucked.

"Sounds promising." Chad deliberately kept his tone noncommittal. "So why isn't the military testing it?"

"It's top secret. I mean double classified. Most of the world thinks we can't track them if they move at night. We'd like to keep it that way."

Chad would bet his life there was more to it, but he was smart enough to accept what Danson told him without comment.

"You in?" Danson asked.

Chad hesitated, thinking of everything he had going on in his life. The insurance investigations, his dive boats—most of all, his family. Five years ago, his father had died and soon after, his mother. Being the only son with three sisters and a slew of nieces and nephews meant he became head of the family. He liked it, but their activities took up a lot of his time.

"I'll test it for you, if I can do it in Honolulu."

"Not a problem."

"You know I'm going to look for every flaw and report it."

"Just what we want. When you report, call me at this number." He pulled a card out of the pocket of his swimming trunks. "Use a pay phone, not a cell phone. No IMing. No e-mails."

Chad nodded. Now he knew the problem. Somewhere, the brass had a leak.

CHAPTER TWO

IT HAD BEEN SUCH A BUSY morning that Lindsey hadn't taken time to phone in her usual order for a turkey sandwich from The Basket Lady who delivered lunch to businesses. It was hard to believe she was hawking jewelry to tourists instead of working in finance. She loved numbers and always had. She had an MBA in statistics. When would she be able to work in her field again?

Until last year, what she'd known about crime, she'd learned watching DeNiro and Pacino. Hul-lo! Welcome to the real world. White collar criminals were just as deadly as the Mafia.

Looking up, she saw a couple from the Midwest pass her shop. They were slurping soda from huge plastic cups. They didn't even glance at the jewelry in the window.

She'd selected this shop not only for its historic beauty, but because it gave her a good view up the street and there was a back way out. Two, actually, if you counted the back door to Romero's gallery.

Ever-vigilant, she'd learned to memorize people's faces. If someone was following her, she would know it. At least that's what she told herself. With so many tourists swarming through the city now that summer had arrived, it was impossible to truly memorize every face.

Still, she continued to try.

She squinted against the early-afternoon sunlight at the dark-haired man striding toward the gallery. He was a head taller than most men, but even if he hadn't been, Lindsey would have been able to pick out Derek Albright, her WITSEC field contact.

The deputy marshal had square-jawed good looks and carried himself with an erect, military bearing. He'd been a Marine before joining the Federal Marshal's group that ran the witness protection program. His training showed not only in his posture but in the way he talked and acted.

What was he doing here now?

Not that he ever announced his visits. In the beginning, he'd popped in to see her several times a week. As she became acclimated, he visited her each week. Lately she was lucky to see him once a month.

Derek had appeared at her condo one night last week. It was much too soon for him to be here again. Wasn't it? Maybe something had happened to her sister, Tina or her niece, Ariel. Her stomach cramping with apprehension, she braced herself for bad news as Derek opened Dreamcatcher's door, but he greeted her with a smile.

"Hey, Lindsey."

A thought suddenly hit her. Maybe a date had been set for the trial. Perhaps an end to this nightmare was in sight. Something in her chest felt lighter—almost hopeful.

Derek's eyes were on the open door leading into Romero's gallery. "Close it."

Lindsey slipped over to the connecting door and saw Romero animatedly talking to a couple about a Kevin Red Star lithograph. Without a sound she shut the door.

"I need to talk to you," Derek said, his voice barely above a whisper. "Close the gallery. Let's go to lunch."

"Okay, but let me tell Romero. He'll watch the shop and take care of Zach."

It took her a minute to explain an old friend had dropped by and needed to talk to her. Since Romero couldn't see Derek from where he was standing, she thought he would assume it was a woman. From his wink, she decided he believed she had a boyfriend.

What a sweetie, she sighed inwardly. He genuinely cared about her. Too bad she couldn't tell him how much his friendship meant to her.

She left Zach in the gallery and walked outside with Derek. "What's going on?"

"I'll tell you all about it." He sounded happy. "I made lunch reservations at La Casa Sena."

"Really? Since when does WITSEC bankroll lunches at pricey restaurants? This must be good news."

"Good news and bad news." Suddenly the air was fraught with tension and an undercurrent of expectation. "Which do you want first?"

She'd been so battered down with bad news that she almost opted for the good first. No. This experience had taught her to face her fears and deal with them.

"The bad."

His eyes shifted, a subtle movement most people would have missed, but she knew he was checking out the people around them because that's what he'd taught her. Tourists, she decided, covertly skimming the clusters of people strolling through the area.

"Headquarters intercepted an expert hacker who was attempting to access your file."

His words beat against her temples. Fear she'd been trying too long to ignore spread through her with a mind-numbing punch.

"Don't worry. We stopped them."

THE FRAGRANT YEASTY SCENT of warm sapodillas filled the air in La Casa Sena. Ordinarily Lindsey would have been ready to fill one of the hollow centered buns with honey and gobble it down, but her mind wasn't on food. Derek had insisted on putting off telling her the good news until they had ordered lunch and wine had been served.

"Okay, now for the good news." Derek raised his glass of Pinot Noir to hers.

Lindsey clinked her goblet against his, concealing her frustration with a manufactured smile. She still held out the hope that the good news was a date had been set for the trial.

Derek grinned and took a swig of wine before, saying in a voice charged with excitement, "I've been promoted. I'm going back to headquarters in D.C."

He kept talking, but all she heard was a blur of words. This was the *good* news? Anger mushroomed inside her. What had begun as frustration morphed into something larger, darker.

Derek was her lifeline, her contact with the people who had taken control of her destiny. They weren't close—exactly— but there was an immeasurable, unseen bond between them. They'd talked for hours, particularly in those early days just after her arrival. He'd taught her how to start over, how to construct a new past, and how to protect herself.

Since she'd come to Santa Fe, Derek had been the only person she dared trust. Now, he was leaving and to him this was an occasion to be celebrated. For her it was...she couldn't quite put in words how she felt, what he'd become to her.

With everyone and everything she'd known and loved taken from her—even a field contact whose job it was to guide her—was a special person. Allowing Derek Albright to gain such importance illustrated just how screwed-up her life had become.

"Hey, Lindsey, what's the matter?"

"You jerk! This is the *good* news?"

He shrugged and tried for a smile.

"Am I supposed to be happy for you?"

"No, not really." A note of apology crept into his voice. "I thought I owed you an explanation."

"Really? I can't imagine why." Like a balloon inflating, anger was quickly becoming rage.

"I know you expected me to stay with you until after the trial." He furtively glanced around him to see if anyone was listening. No one was, but he lowered his voice and leaned even closer. "With all the pressure to increase Homeland Security, the Marshal's pool of agents has been sucked dry. They need me in D.C. It's an opportunity I can't pass up. Hell, under normal circumstances, it would take me another five...ten years to get to that level."

When she'd been on the fast track at PowerTec, she had been just as ambitious. Maybe more so. She should give him a break, but she couldn't. The head of WITSEC had assured her that her handler would be with her until the trial was over. Derek had sworn he would stay until the end.

Well, what did she expect? Close enough for government work, her father used to say. They did whatever they damn well pleased—regardless of their promises.

He waited for the server to put down their salads before saying, "My replacement will be here next week."

"When are you leaving?"

"On the five o'clock flight this evening."

Now all she had was Romero, and the way he'd been acting, she might have to distance herself from him. What a hoot! Tyler had once accused her of being "too social." Now she was alone in the world with just a dog.

"Don't worry. You'll be fine. You're the most self-sufficient witness I've ever protected. We just want you to be cautious. At about a year witnesses become careless. They think the danger has passed."

"That's why Rutherford and Ames have waited until now to find me by trying to access my file. They think WITSEC has become careless, too."

He poked at his salad with his fork. "Masterson thinks someone was testing the waters. You know, making sure the electronic security works. Yours wasn't the only file they tried to access. Could have been the FBI or CIA. Nothing to worry about."

Curt Masterson directed the WITSEC program. He was an impressive bull of a man who probably knew what he was talking about. If he were wrong, she was dead.

"Your jacket is buried so deep that no one's going to find it. Trust me, the Feds saw to it and Masterson double-checked them."

Federal Prosecutors were usually the ones who recommended witnesses for the program. It was in their interest to protect the confidential file—the jacket—on a witness.

Reese Barnaby III—three-fer to his buddies—was among the most ambitious of the federal prosecutors. His successful prosecution of the top executives of PowerTec would make him a household word in Texas without him having to spend the millions it usually took politicians to buy name recognition.

Lindsey took a bite of her salad. It was hard to swallow; life was hard to swallow. "I hope Masterson is right. I want to live to testify."

"I'm sure Masterson has taken precautions he hasn't told me about. You're a top priority. You know the 800 number you have memorized?"

"Yes." Before she left the safe house in D.C., she had to memorize the special number. Each time she met Derek, he had asked her to repeat the number she was to call in case she couldn't reach him in an emergency.

"Not every witness is given that number."

"Why not?"

"Because a lot of them are lowlifes from drug gangs. It's not safe for them to go home, but hit teams aren't looking for them."

She managed a nod, her anger barely under control.

"The number is for high risk, high priority witnesses. You call and a special task force will be mobilized to help you."

"What a joke! They're supposed to rush from D.C. in time to save me?"

"WITSEC will notify the FBI's field office here. They'll help you."

Lindsey found this somewhat reassuring. She had contacted the FBI when she'd discovered the discrepancies in

PowerTec's accounting records. The FBI had immediately responded, analyzed the situation and sent in an undercover agent to gather more information. Annette Sperling had been a top-notch accountant who easily joined PowerTec without anyone suspecting who she really was.

Annette had worked at PowerTec six months, covertly analyzing their financial transactions, before someone killed her execution style. An hour after Lindsey found her body, the FBI yanked Lindsey out of Houston and put her in protective custody.

"Any word on when those creeps will be brought to trial?" she asked.

"No. These things take a while."

"It's been almost a year."

"Don't raise your voice," he warned. "I know you're frustrated. Remember Enron. It was over a year before indictments came down. It takes time to build the kind of case they need to get convictions. Rutherford and Ames can afford counsel who'll provide the most amazing legal gymnastics imaginable."

Ted Rutherford, CEO and her boss, CFO, Jackson Ames. Thinking of them made something in her gut coil inside itself. Once she'd looked up to them, especially Jack. She'd worked with him every day—and never suspected the truth.

"Has there been any progress in the investigation of Annette's murder?" she asked, although she was certain she knew the answer. She monitored the case on SmokingGun.com. No leads. Nothing. All the signs of a professional hit.

"No, but everyone knows who's responsible."

"Rutherford and Ames."

"Annette didn't deserve to die."

She didn't say she might have bought it that night, as well. Tyler's unexpected meeting with out-of-town clients had given her some free time. She'd returned to PowerTec just after the undercover agent had been murdered. If she'd arrived a few minutes earlier, the killer would have shot her, too.

"From what I hear the Feebies thought highly of Annette. They miss her."

"Why did you come all the way here to take me to lunch and tell me you're leaving? You could have called."

Two beats of silence. "There are things I wanted to discuss with you—off the record."

An ominous premonition snaked through her. What next?

"If Masterson or anyone finds out—I'm finished."

"I won't say a word. I swear."

"Most of the witnesses I've worked with have been drug dealers or LCN. Scumbags who flipped—turned on their bosses—but they're still criminals."

She'd learned the FBI and U.S. Marshals called the Mafia by the abbreviated term for La Cosa Nostra—LCN.

"I thought less than ten percent of WITSEC people return to lives of crime."

"True, but I still have to deal with a bunch of lowlifes."

"With Worldcom and Enron and now PowerTec, it looks like white collar crime is a growth industry."

He chuckled at her lame attempt at a joke. "Be serious."

"I'm serious. Deadly serious."

He waited for the server to remove their salad plates and serve their entrées. Lindsey mustered a smile for the waiter. She sampled the veal in tequila chili sauce after Derek was served his Adobo steak.

"Like I told you earlier, you're entering the period when most witnesses let down their guard. They call people they're not authorized to call. You wouldn't believe how many of them return home to attend a funeral or a wedding."

"I know I'm in danger. I was the one to find Annette Sperling's body, remember?"

She would never forget walking into the office where the agent was working undercover. Annette had been slumped forward over her computer keyboard. A single bullet had parted the blond hair at the back of her head, leaving a neat hole and a trail of blood running down her back and pooling on the carpet.

"I remember," he said between bites of steak. "We're still worried."

We? Obviously he'd been discussing her with the boys at headquarters in DC.

"Why are you worried about me?"

"You haven't adjusted. Living here, owning a gallery isn't enough. You should have friends—"

"I have a good friend. We're having dinner tonight."

"One friend isn't enough. If all you have is one friend, you eventually confide in him. Then they tell someone, who tells someone..." His tone said he'd seen if before—too many times. "Next thing. You're compromised."

"Trust no one."

"It's not that simple. Become the new you. Build another life. You need to get out there. Date. Make a circle of friends the way you did in Houston so you're not emotionally relying on one friend. That'll help you become normal again."

"Normal? After the trial, my life can return to normal."

Derek swiped at his lips with the napkin. "Don't count on being able to go home. We're convinced the PowerTec jerks will arrange to kill you even if both of them are in jail."

How could she go on like this? Always watching her back? Listening to strange sounds in the night and wondering if they'd found her. Never seeing her sister. Her niece. The man she loved?

What choice did she have?

This was her life—part two—the sad and lonely part.

Whoever said the truth will set you free—obviously hadn't tried it. The truth had wiped out a promising career, a wonderful life.

And the truth might be the death of her.

Derek continued, "We just can't trust Rutherford or Ames not to hire someone to kill you from their prison cells."

She didn't doubt it. From what she'd been able to tell, they had a fortune socked away in offshore and Swiss accounts. Carrion eaters of the corporate world, Rutherford and Ames had taken voodoo accounting to a new level. They each had a ruthless, vengeful streak.

"Don't forget all I've taught you. Keep your eye on people around you, even those at a distance."

"Believe me, I'm getting good at it."

"You've got two cell phones, batteries charged?"

"Of course. They're in my purse. Same with the gun."

"About the gun." There was a tick of something that bordered on worry in his voice. "Witnesses aren't supposed to have guns."

"But if someone is after them—"

"Too many are former criminals. Giving them a gun is against the rules."

The light dawned. He'd broken a rule for her, and he didn't want anyone to know. This was the real reason he'd come to see her. Derek had expected to be with her through the trial. He never thought he would have to hand her over to someone who might jeopardize his career by revealing what he'd done.

"I won't say a word to the new guy."

Obviously relieved, he grinned. "Might be a woman."

They ate in silence for a few minutes, before she asked, "Why did you give me a gun?"

"Right from the first, you were different. All I'd dealt with were LCN lowlifes or drug pushers. You were a class act. Intelligent. Quick to learn." He put down his fork, his dark eyes troubled. "But I worried about you. I didn't—still don't—think you know what you're up against. I wanted to give you as much protection as I possibly could."

Lindsey was touched. Derek had been professional the entire time. She'd never suspected he'd cared one whit about her. Not only had he cared, but he'd jeopardized his career to help her.

"I'm good at self-defense. I go to the firing range once a week." She leaned over and patted his hand. "You've done the best you could. The rest is up to me. Enjoy your promotion."

She was unable to conceal the note of appreciation that had

crept into her voice. Once men had fallen all over themselves to help her. Then came the murder. Suddenly the men in her life gave her orders, not caring in the least what she thought or wanted.

"Start dating. You're too pretty, too intelligent to become a hermit."

"I'm not all that interested in—"

"Even if you did return to Houston..." He let the words drift away.

She remembered her final day there, a sunny Saturday in April. The last time she'd been with Tyler. The weather had been nice enough to have the top down on his Porsche. They'd laughed and talked as they slogged through traffic to have lunch on the patio at Zov's Bistro.

Even though the FBI investigation loomed over her, something she couldn't discuss with Tyler, she'd been happy. He knew there were problems at PowerTec and that some sort of investigation was underway. She'd naively assumed the FBI would fix the trouble. This problem was nothing more than a blip on the radar screen of life.

"Why does it take a million sperm to fertilize one egg?" she'd asked Tyler.

Accustomed to her jokes, he'd shaken his head. "I give. Why?"

"They refuse to stop and ask for directions."

His rich, husky laugh still echoed in her ears. He always laughed no matter how lame her joke. Just thinking about him made her long to go back in time. To go home.

Home. Unless you can never return home again, never see your family again, you'll never really appreciate what the word means. You have to lose everything to comprehend its significance.

"Lindsey, I gotta tell you," Derek said, intruding on her thoughts. "I don't know how to say this..."

"Tell me what?" Something in his tone warned that he'd saved the worst for last. "Just say it."

He hesitated, fiddling with the grilled zucchini he hadn't touch. "Tyler Prescott is getting married on Saturday."

The words went through her like a serrated blade. Tyler getting married? How could that be?

Of course, Tyler had gone on with his life. She'd vanished with hardly a word. She'd left a message for him at the office—in the middle of the night when he wouldn't be there—to tell him that she was being sent on an emergency overseas assignment and would contact him later.

It was a lame story, but the FBI had insisted she tell him this. She'd hoped Tyler would see through the lie. He knew a little about PowerTec's problems, but not about the FBI's involvement. She hadn't had the opportunity to discuss the murder with him, but she thought he would put two and two together. Obviously he hadn't.

What did she expect him to do? Wait forever?

He'd fallen in love with someone else. How could that happen in just a year? They'd been together almost three years. They'd spoken of marriage, but he hadn't actually proposed.

"Is he marrying anyone I know?"

Again Derek hesitated. "Skyler Holmes."

Her stomach rose, then plummeted in a sickening lurch. He'd always called Skyler the blond bimbo. It was true. Her bra size was bigger than her IQ.

Holding back tears, she quelled her emotions. Nothing was ever gained by crying, her father used to say. She deliberately directed her thoughts to the months ahead. Like a mirage, her future shimmered in the distance. Out of focus—out of reach.

CHAPTER THREE

BROCK WALKED INTO HIS OFFICE. He'd spent the morning attending a seminar conducted by the FBI. Combating Computer Assisted Crimes. What a joke! They'd shown him a few new tricks, but most of it he knew.

Booooring.

He shivered as he shrugged into the microfiber jacket in the room, hyper cooled to protect the sensitive equipment. He pulled on tight-fitting microfiber gloves with the fingers cut out.

What Brock wore didn't matter to him. Most days, no one saw him. He worked alone by choice. The company would fund all the staff he needed. He had fifty-three people working for him, but he kept them in the field. That way no one at Obelisk but him knew how to use the sophisticated equipment.

Some of the arrogant pricks he worked with, like CEO Kilmer Cassidy, thought they did, but should they try to use his equipment, they would destroy everything. Without an authorized laser fingerprint and the top secret password, on the fourth try his computers would assume unauthorized entry mode, self-format, and devour the hard drive.

He had a backup no one knew about—his personal laptop that he kept with him at all times. He'd downloaded all of Obelisk's top secret data onto it and had several of his own special programs installed, as well. It was against company rules for any of the secured info to be removed from the premises. But who was to know? He was head of security.

Brock smiled and glanced around his office to see what

was happening in his domain—the world. He had six state-of-the-art computers with twenty-seven inch flat-screen monitors evenly spaced around the U-shaped room, but he didn't rely on them the way he did his personal laptop.

Wall mounted televisions—currently on mute—were tuned to CNN, MSNBC, and FOX News. A fourth television was on Al Jazeera, the Arab news channel. The other wall was dominated by a map of the world on a liquid-plasma television screen. It was raining in California, he noticed. So who cared? Let the nuts and fruits on the West Coast drown. All the satellites were still orbiting normally, he observed, but one of Russia's wasn't functioning.

"Par for the course."

The end of the Cold War had been the death knell for Russian science. The state no longer funded research the way it once had. The Russian Mafia now ran the country, and they had no use for scientists.

The satellites and news channels helped Brock keep track of Obelisk's myriad interests overseas. They required intensive monitoring. A conflict—no matter how small—anywhere on earth was a potential for Obelisk to profit.

Normally staff would have been needed, but Brock had shown the higher-ups how security could be mastered by a single—talented—person and modern technology. Naturally they'd gone along. It was in their best interests for as few men as possible to know the truth about Obelisk's dealings.

He heard line seven ring. It was the number only his operatives in the field used. Attached to all his private lines was a special mechanism that chopped words into minute sound bites, then jumbled them so that even a state-of-the-art computer would have to spend months unscrambling the garbled noise.

He had no reason to think there was a tap on a line no one—not even the telephone company—knew existed. But various incidents at Obelisk had taught him to be extraordinarily careful. That's why he had insisted his office be in an underground bunker beneath Obelisk—away from prying eyes.

"Numero Uno," he answered.

"We're in place. Everything's set," said Operative 111.

His agents had numbers, not names. That way only Brock knew who they were. Their names weren't written down anywhere except in his mind. They were paid in cash, not by the payroll department.

They never knew his name. He was the number one operative. He always answered the special operative line with "Numero Uno."

He told Number 111, "Call me when you've made contact."

"Roger that."

Brock glanced at his Brietling. "If it's after six EST, call me on my cell."

He recited the number. He didn't like talking on cell phones. The message went out over the airwaves, and anyone listening could hear every word. But he had a life beyond this underground bunker. Tonight he was showing his '52 Gull Wing Mercedes in the Bethesda Classic Car show. To stay in contact he had to use a cell phone.

Every third day a con he knew brought him a stolen cell phone. Brock gave the man his phone, and the con resold the phone again. That way none of his cell calls could be traced back to him.

"It looks like a go for tonight," Operative 111 told him.

They hung up without another word.

"She's as good as dead," Brock said out loud.

Of course, before Samantha Robbins died, she would have to deal with him in person.

BY SEVEN-THIRTY DARKNESS had fallen on Santa Fe's historic district and customers had slowed to a trickle. Since returning from lunch with Derek, Lindsey had sold several more pieces of jewelry—including her most expensive piece.

"Lookin' good," she said to Zach before she remembered

the retriever had trotted off with Romero when he'd left earlier to make enchiladas.

She knew the tourist season was relatively short. It began in late June and went full throttle through the opera season and Indian Market, but after Labor Day, the buying slowed. She needed to make money in the summer months to tide her over during slower times. Miraculously, the way things were going, she would make a profit her first season.

Lindsey tried not to let Derek's departure bother her. Making friends was probably good advice. She didn't want to rely too much on Romero.

For a moment, her mind wandered to Houston. Tyler and Skyler. Their names even rhymed. It was probably meant to be, but that didn't make her feel any better.

"Get over it," she told herself.

Easier said than done. She'd been in love and during these long, lonely months in isolation, she'd replayed every moment she'd spent with Tyler, becoming more in love with him as each memory replayed in her mind. How could he marry—Skyler of all people—within a year after she'd last seen him?

The thought tore at something raw inside her. She'd been living with a nagging, constant anxiety, wondering if she would be killed. The whole time she'd assumed Tyler was missing her, and in time, they would be together again.

WITSEC had refused to allow her to telephone him. Masterson claimed that since they weren't officially engaged it was too dangerous. Now, she wondered if her interview with the risk assessment psychologist had somehow indicated she might try to see Tyler again while she was in protection and that was why Masterson insisted on cutting off contact.

"What does it matter?" she muttered under her breath. "It's over. Forget him."

She picked up the phone and hit autodial for Ben Tallchief's number. While it rang, she gazed at one of her cell phones concealed in the letter rack on her desk. She had another, smaller cell phone in the deep pocket of her skirt.

Derek's flight had already left. She was on her own for the next week. Now was the time to practice everything he'd taught her. Don't become careless just because nothing has happened for almost a year.

"Ben?" she said when he answered with a grunt that was supposed to pass for hello. "Guess what? I sold the Rising Sun necklace."

"No way!"

"Yes. Way. I love saying I told you so."

"I made the right decision," he said in his deep baritone, and she could almost see him fiddling with the turquoise beaded strip of leather that cinched back his sleek, black hair into a ponytail at his nape. "Your gallery shows my work—"

"Showcases your art."

He grunted again. "I'll make more money with you than I did at the other gallery."

We'll both make more money, she silently added. "I need two, three—whatever you've got—large important pieces."

"My work takes time...inspiration."

Lindsey studied the hand-hewn beams, *vigas,* that supported the ceiling in the historic building. Ben Tallchief received most of his "inspiration" in the horizontal. Not only was he a talented artist known for his inventive work with hand-forged silver, but he was a world class womanizer.

Most nights he could be found at the Pink Adobe's bar, picking up female tourists who couldn't resist a "real" Indian who was tall and drop-dead gorgeous. He'd gone to UCLA on a football scholarship and graduated with honors. He'd returned to his hometown to teach art at the Indian School where promising young artists from the pueblos studied.

From his West Coast days, Ben Tallchief had a surfer's attitude about life. Laid back. She could almost hear him telling her, "Chill, Lindsey. Chill."

Maybe he was on to something, she decided. She'd spent

her life on the fast track. Look where it had gotten her. A cell without walls.

"Get me what you can, Ben, as soon as possible."

The shop bell tinkled and a couple from the Midwest sauntered in. She smiled at them, but doubted they would buy anything. The man was in his early thirties, but he'd already lost the battle of the bulge. His stomach stretched his Ohio State T-shirt so much that the seam on one side had popped and a patch of skin showed through.

He had the worst comb-over she'd ever seen. Six or seven strands of light brown hair went from ear-to-ear. His expression told her he was "in tow" and his wife was the shopper. The plump blonde was inspecting the earring case more intently than Lindsey had expected when they'd walked through the door. Maybe Lindsey was wrong, and the woman would buy something.

It was a guessing game that Lindsey indulged in each time a customer walked through the door. Were they lookie-lou's or buyers? Could she predict what they would do? She'd kept a tally on the pad beside her telephone. She'd been right almost ninety percent of the time. Not bad, she decided, knowing probability the way she did. Actually, her predictions were phenomenally correct.

"I'm sorry. What was that?"

Ben had been talking, but something was niggling at the back of her mind and she hadn't heard him.

"Do you think I should make more sugilite pieces or turquoise?"

"Sugilite," she replied without hesitation. The stone ranged from pale lavender to deep plum and looked spectacular when set in silver. "It's unique. Most tourists seem to be drawn to those colors."

"You got it. I'm just waiting for divine inspiration."

"Hustle over to the Pink Adobe and pick up some...inspiration."

"Why don't you meet me there?"

It wasn't the first time Ben had come on to her. The last thing she needed was to become involved with one of her artists.

"Sorry. I already have plans."

"Too bad. We could discuss, you know, my work."

"I've gotta go. Customers are here looking at your jewelry."

She hung up the telephone. For practice, she reached forward and switched on her cell phone concealed in the letter rack. She pressed the autodial button that called the cell phone in her skirt pocket. That telephone was off, but anything said in the gallery would be recorded on her voice mail that was set to run for hours.

"Are you from Ohio?" she asked as she walked up to the couple.

The woman looked up from the earring case. "We live in Indianapolis. Bud went to Ohio State. He never lets you forget it."

The man smiled, his eyes cold blue marbles in his fleshy face. "What can I say? It's a great school."

A sense of unease lurked in the back of her mind. "I went to UCLA—another great school."

She was surprised at how easily the lie came from her lips. Her undergraduate studies had been at Duke, but when WITSEC created a new ID for her, they had chosen UCLA. It was so big that even if she ran into someone from her class, they wouldn't necessarily have known each other.

The man smiled again, his soft chin sinking into the fold of flab at his neck. "We just drove in from Albuquerque. Is there a good place to eat around here?"

Something in the reptilian part of her brain clicked, and a chill coursed through her, but she refused to allow her face to reflect her feelings. "You just drove in? Was there a lot of traffic?"

He chuckled. "Not compared to L.A. Right, honey?"

"Right," she replied without turning around.

A frission of alarm waltzed across the back of Lindsey's neck as she realized what had been bothering her. Hadn't she seen this couple walk past the gallery shortly before Derek arrived?

Trust your instincts.

That's what Derek had taught her. A depth charge of fear exploded in her chest. Move! Get out of here!

"You know, Casa Sena is the best restaurant in the area. I just had lunch there today. You won't get in without a reservation, but my neighbor next door is the owner's cousin." She was making this up as she went and managing to sound convincing. "I'll get you one of Romero's cards. Give it to the hostess and you'll get in without a problem."

"That would be great. Right, honey?"

"Sure. Whatever."

Lindsey walked through the connecting door into Romero's gallery. Inside, she picked up her pace and bolted out the back door. She sprinted down the alley, rounded the corner, and dashed for a dark side street. Only a breath separated her from debilitating panic.

No one was around, and the soft summer night seemed unusually quiet. In the distance, she heard the lonely wail of a coyote, urging his pack to pounce on some small animal— probably a rabbit.

I'm the rabbit, she thought.

She stood, panting, wondering what to do next. Verify. Don't panic until you know if you're imagining things or not.

She slithered behind a cluster of lilac bushes and hid in the shadows of a rambling adobe home where no lights were shining from the windows. She jerked her cell phone out of the pocket in her skirt. Maybe she'd imagined all this. She punched autodial for her voice mail.

Lindsay picked up the conversation from the point when she'd asked where the couple in the gallery was from. Their voices had a hollow ring, but just as Derek had shown her, the cell had acted as an open mike. She listened—a full minute behind real time.

"What happened to her?" Lindsey heard the woman ask after a static-filled pause.

"She probably can't find the card."

He sounded casual enough. Maybe she'd made a silly mistake. This might not be a pair of operatives—disguised as a couple from the Midwest—sent to carry out a hit. She agonized through another long silence punctuated by a low hum of static.

The woman's shrill voice came through the small cell phone. "Check on her."

A few seconds of dead air.

"She's not in there! The bitch must have gone out the back door."

"Shit," screamed the woman. "What tipped her?"

"You, stupid! You were too interested in the jewelry for a broad from Indy."

"I was just browsing like women do. I don't think I—"

"Stop sweating it. The bitch can run but where's she going to hide?"

Lindsey flipped her cell phone shut, sank down to the ground and asked herself the same question. The metallic taste of fear nearly choked her. They were coming to kill her.

CHAPTER FOUR

"EVERY INCH HAS BEEN RESTORED to its original condition," Brock told the admirers clustered around his Gull Wing in the Bethesda Sports Center where the car rally was being held.

The two doors were open and thrust upward like the majestic wings of a metallic bird, Brock thought. The lipstick-red paint glistened and the chrome was like a mirror. Hell, Brock decided, his car was *better* than it had been when it rolled off the assembly line in Stuttgart in 1952.

His baby. He had other cars, sure. A George Barris modified all steel '32 Ford and a rare '27 T Roadster, but the Gull Wing was his favorite. It was a crowd pleaser. People flipped over the unusual doors.

The show would close for the day in another twenty minutes. There were a few people wandering around looking at the other cars, but he was the only one with a crowd. He grinned, pleased with himself and the Mercedes.

He caught his distorted reflection on the chrome fender. His brown eyes were grotesquely wide as if someone were pulling taffy. His sandy hair didn't show, but he knew women found him handsome.

Brock admitted he was a tad short. Before Obelisk had lured him away from the Defense Department, a general had accused Brock of having a Napoleonic complex. The prick had a tragic fatal car accident the following week.

The cell phone clipped to his belt vibrated. He yanked it off and glanced at the screen. It was his operatives in Santa Fe, Number 111, a man, and 32, a woman.

They had the bitch!

Brock punched "talk" and walked away from the car to avoid anyone overhearing him. "Yeah?"

"I—I d-don't know what happened," the woman stammered. "She slipped out the back door."

"Unfuckingbelievable!"

"She's only been gone a minute. Well, maybe two minutes."

"The bitch can't be far. Get her!"

Brock hit the end button. Hearing how his operatives had bungled it could wait. At least they hadn't started searching before they notified him. Samantha Robbins—now Lindsey Wallace—was a black-bagger, a high risk WITSEC witness. The Federal Marshals knew she was very likely to be killed. She would have been given an emergency 800 number at the U.S. Marshal's D.C. office.

Her cover blown, the bitch would call the number. It took Brock a few seconds to get on the Internet. He always insisted the con bring him a cell phone with Internet access for emergencies like this. Trouble was no two phones worked the same.

It felt like hours, but it was less than a minute before he was online and had contacted his computer at Obelisk. He gave it instructions to dial his anonymizer. This remailer was based in Switzerland and used a super-powerful software program that buried your real e-mail address.

Within seconds—thanks to technology—the remailer had contacted the phone company in D.C. When Lindsey Wallace tried to alert WITSEC that she'd been compromised, all she would get was a busy signal.

PANTING, A STABBING ACHE in her side from running, Lindsey slumped against an adobe wall blocks from where she'd listened to the hit team over the cell phone she'd left behind in her gallery. She punched the autodial for the emergency number she'd been given.

Still busy.

How could that be? Perhaps there was a storm back East or another widespread power outage. What else could explain a constant busy signal on an emergency line?

Frozen by fear, she could hardly think. Derek had drilled her relentlessly on what to do if worse came to worst. What would he say to do now?

There was an FBI field office here somewhere. Contact them. Her fingers were trembling so much she could hardly dial, but finally she managed to call information and obtain the number.

A busy signal.

Panic curdled her blood. What was going on? She was an expert on statistics and knew the odds of the emergency line and the local FBI office both being busy were astronomical.

Someone knew what she would do and had deliberately blocked her access to those numbers. She couldn't imagine how, but she had to get away. Without her purse, she had no money, no ATM card, no credit cards. No gun.

Nothing.

She didn't dare go to her condo where she kept an emergency stash. If they were clever enough to block the phone lines, they would know where she lived.

She could phone the police, but it would take a lot of explaining and calls to the U.S. Marshal's office before her story could be verified. The hit team would expect her to do this. They might even be waiting near the station. One sniper shot and she would be in a black bag.

Out of the corner of her eye she saw a beam of light swinging back and forth. The flashlight was far down the type of narrow unpaved street that made Santa Fe so quaint. She saw the hulking shape of the man in the shop, methodically searching the bushes. If she ran, he would see her.

Her only choice was to climb the adobe wall as quietly as possible and drop down the other side onto the adjacent street. Like most adobe walls in the historic area, this one had been crudely made by the Native Americans who had been used as slave labor by the Conquistadors. Over time it had weathered and had several holes where the adobe had deteriorated.

She jammed the toe of her sandal in an indentation partway up the wall. Bracing on that leg, she boosted herself upward. She managed to grasp the top of the wall with the tips of her nails. Heaving one leg skyward, her foot caught the top of the wall.

The broomstick skirt made it nearly impossible to scramble to the top. After two tries, she was lying flat on top of the ancient adobe wall. The light was so close now that the man holding it would hear her if she dropped down the other side.

A pickup with a bad muffler and a radio blaring music from a station in Juarez rumbled up the street. *Pachucos*—bad boys—out looking for trouble. She waited until they were closer, almost upon the man with the flashlight, then she plunged off the wall.

Thump! She landed on her side and rolled. Starting at her shoulder, a sharp, punishing jolt of pain seared through her body. Shuddering in agony, she pulled her feet under her and lurched upright. The *pachucos'* music was still blaring, and she forced herself to run, knowing the noise she made couldn't be heard.

She breathed through clenched teeth. With each pump of her lungs, a stab of pain told her a rib must have broken. She couldn't lift one arm above her waist. Her shoulder might be broken. Sweat gushing from every pore, breath coming in ragged painful spurts, she willed herself into a fast walk. Running was out of the question.

It was only a few blocks to Romero's house. If he would give her some money and lend her his car, she could drive to Phoenix. There she could call WITSEC or the FBI field office. The hit team would expect her to head for the airport, but she wouldn't be that stupid.

What would she tell Romero?

Camino de las Animas—the soul's way—was an unpaved narrow street with sprawling haciendas. Romero's house was at the far end. She spotted the wrought-iron lantern shining at his front door. Like a beacon the light sent a burst of adrenaline through her. Somehow she broke into a sprint.

She charged through the arched adobe gateway and up the steps of the hacienda built almost two hundred years earlier. Cringing with pain, a wild story for Romero forming in her brain, her world suddenly pitched from side to side, then halted with a mind-numbing jolt.

The front door was wide-open.

"Romero," she cried out before she could stop herself.

What if the woman was inside? It had been a man with the flashlight. He couldn't have beaten her here. More important, how did they know about Romero?

Zachary bounded out of the house. The soft lantern light revealed fresh red blood on the retriever's paws. A suffocating wave of terror enveloped her like a vision of hell.

"Please, please," she whispered, "don't let them have hurt Romero."

Common sense said to run, but she refused to desert her friend. She tiptoed into the house and was met with dead silence. A single lamp was on in the living room Romero had so meticulously decorated with furnishings from the Spanish Colonial period.

The only sound was the *click-click* of Zachary's nails against the tile floor. The aroma of blue corn enchiladas filled the air. She inched forward. Each ragged breath brought white-hot pain from her ribs.

In the dining room, she called out, "Romero, are you there?"

No answer.

She rounded the corner into the kitchen. Sprawled on the floor in a puddle of blood and bloody pawprints, Romero's dark eyes stared up at the ceiling.

"Oh, God, no!"

She staggered forward and fell to her knees, scraping them on the tile. Someone—it had to be the woman—had slit Romero's throat. Anger like invisible lightning arced through her.

Why? Why? Why?

Why kill an innocent man? It was incomprehensible. She knew Rutherford and Ames were responsible. Corporate piranhas, they let nothing and no one get in their way.

In a heartbeat the anger drained from her. They had more money, more resources than she did. They were able to get around WITSEC. What could she possibly do?

"Come and get me," she called out. "I'm ready to die."

It was true. She'd been living in hell for over a year. Tyler had married another woman. She couldn't see her sister or niece, her only family. The way things were going her purgatory seemed endless.

Now this.

A kind, wonderful man had befriended her. He'd paid for his trouble with his life. She hoped the woman hadn't tortured him somehow before she put the blade to his throat.

Tears sparkled on her lashes, and then blurred her vision as she waited to die. Seconds passed. The house was eerily still except for the low hum of the refrigerator. She wiped at her eyes with the back of her hand. With a broad swipe of his tongue, Zach licked her face.

This could mean only one thing. The woman was searching for her elsewhere. They may have thought she had car keys in her pocket or had gotten a ride or that she had gone to the police station.

Hang on, she thought. Those bastards had money and would kill anyone who got in their way, but she had something more important. Truth was on her side. She had to get away and live to testify.

She reached over to close Romero's eyes. To his left, hidden by the shadow from the kitchen table was a message scrawled on the cabinet in blood.

Lindsey
Kill
me

"What?"

The woman must have dipped Romero's finger in his own blood. The bile rose up in the back of her throat. She prayed the poor man had been dead by then.

There was a purpose to his death, she decided. They'd slit his throat to frame her for his murder. Why, when they wanted to kill her? It took a second for her to realize the killers hadn't a clue where she was, and they wanted more manpower in finding her. What better way than to have the police after her, as well?

"I'm sorry," she told Romero's lifeless body. "I knew better than to make a friend. Forgive me."

With her fingertip she gently closed Romero's eyes. She kneeled beside him and said the Irish Blessing just as she had when each of her parents had been lowered into their graves.

May the road rise up to meet you,
May the wind always be at your back
May the sun shine upon your face
The rains fall soft upon your fields
And, until we meet again,
May God hold you in the palm of His hand.

CHAPTER FIVE

Provo, Turks and Caicos Islands

THE THATCHED ROOF BAR sloped downward, supported at the four corners by bamboo poles. The open-air bar had no walls and overlooked the beach a few feet away.

Chad wished he were with a babe. There were plenty of them around, wearing skimpy suits that would have given a statue an erection, but there you go. He was spending his time with a nerd and the sophisticated piece of equipment Danson wanted him to test.

Chad accessed the Department of Defense satellite, inputting his SAP/SAR code into a device that reminded him of a handheld GPS.

Scan Retina appeared on the screen.

"What in hell am I supposed to do?" he asked Danson.

"Hold it up to your eye," Danson replied. "The satellite will receive an image of your retina and relay it to the scanner in the DOD database."

"Won't work. I had my iris scanned when I was testing for you guys but not my retina."

Danson chuckled, obviously pleased with himself. "A scan of your iris photographs your retina, as well."

Chad held up the device to his right eye. He knew only too well that biometric sensors like fingerprint scans, voice recognition, and iris scans were popular at high-security facilities.

"What was wrong with an iris scan?" he asked.

"Too many guys work with saws or welding equipment. One tiny piece of sawdust you don't even feel gets embedded in the iris. Next thing you know that guy's scan comes up invalid. You'll only have to do this iris thing once to put yourself into the system to do the testing. In the field, it's too tricky."

"Gotcha." Too-sensitive equipment was a nuisance, especially in the field. The device now read Access Granted.

"Zoom down on us."

Chad punched in their lat/long coordinates. The satellite camera rotated, moving from central Africa to Turks and Caicos. He pressed the zoom button and two small splashes of infrared appeared on the blue screen. It was impossible to tell what the blotches were but the screen read Humans.

"I'll be damned. Seems to work." He tapped in new coordinates so the satellite's camera focused on the dog sleeping near a beach cabana.

A second later the screen read Canine.

"This will revolutionize satellite surveillance," Danson whispered.

"If it doesn't have any bugs."

"True, true. We thought the iris scan was the answer until we discovered that one tiny flaw. Test this in every situation. Let's make sure it's perfect before we go into production."

The refrigerator behind the talapa bar was now on the screen. Small Machinery.

"Okay, so where's the leak?" asked Chad.

"I might have known you'd figure it out." Danson shrugged. "If we knew, I wouldn't be here."

Honolulu
Three months later.

CHAD LANGSTON pulled a chair up beside Eddie Kukana's desk. "Any luck replacing Lori?"

"*Aole.*" No. Eddie shook his dark head. "Every woman

thinks she would make a good wedding coordinator. I've interviewed dozens. None have enough experience."

"Shelby can't handle it?"

"No way."

They were in Eddie's office in the Crockett Building overlooking the Ala Wai Boat Harbor. Chad had his office just across from Eddie's. A stately banyan tree in the center of the courtyard blocked their view of each other's offices. They were in the habit of dropping in to chat at least once a day, when Chad was in town.

They had grown up together in Turtle Bay on the North Shore of Oahu where they'd surfed the Banzai Pipeline every chance they had. Best friends since the third grade, they were what islanders called calabash cousins. They were so close they should have been related. Each had chosen very unusual professions, but both of their careers evolved from their love of the water.

After Chad left the military, he bought a scuba diving company whose main base was in Honolulu but had locations on the other islands, as well. His managers were so good that Chad devoted much of his time to his real passion, underwater forensics.

Eddie had begun his business by taking tourists on sunset catamaran cruises. He'd saved his money and bought "party" boats that were usually rented for conventions held on the island. Several years ago, he'd branched out and began having weddings onboard his boats.

It quickly became the most lucrative part of his business. Thanks to a flashy Web site, many mainlanders contacted him. They expected him to coordinate everything. Knowing little about wedding planning, Eddie had hired Lori, but she'd recently moved to Kauai. Apparently her assistant Shelby didn't have enough skills to take over.

Eddie glanced at his watch. "I have another gal coming for an interview in a few minutes. A *haole* from Chicago. She has experience."

"Sounds good."

Eddie arched one dark busy eyebrow the way he often did when he was upset. His almond eyes narrowed. "You know *malihini*. They always think they want to live in paradise. Mainlanders head home in six months."

Chad nodded. His managers were all from the islands. He encouraged them to hire divers who had been raised in Hawaii. Too many mainlanders came to the islands and took jobs away from the locals. No sooner were the *malihinis* trained than they went home.

"Look at it this way," Chad told his friend. "If this woman stays a few months, maybe Shelby will be able to take over."

Eddie snorted and slapped his thigh. "Yeah, right."

Shelby was Eddie's niece. To say the girl was a flake would be a gross understatement, but the woman who'd previously held Shelby's position had managed to embezzle a ton of money before an auditor caught her. At least Shelby was family. While she was a few beans shy of a full burrito, she could be trusted.

Trust was a real issue with Eddie, Chad realized and not for the first time. His friend trusted everyone and kept sloppy records. Anyone could take advantage of him without half trying. Aloha Yachts and Weddings would be a lot more profitable if everyone from the vendors to the deckhands didn't exploit Eddie's generosity.

Chad had offered to take care of Eddie's books in his office, but Eddie's pride wouldn't permit him to admit he needed help. In time, Eddie's son, Andy would come into the business. The kid seemed to have a knack for finance even though right now Andy was obsessed with computers and was responsible for the Web site.

BEFORE DEVON ARRIVED for her interview, she'd already checked out Aloha Yachts and Weddings. The offices were on the ground floor and had a back exit—just in case. The rear door led to two different streets, depending on which way you turned. She'd been offered dozens of jobs, but none of them suited her requirements.

The setup was as near perfect as she was going to find. The firm was small and low-profile, the type of place her new handler, Warren Martin, had told her to work. It was in the part of town that saw only a few tourists—not that WITSEC expected anyone to recognize her.

She'd escaped Santa Fe by taking the cash out of Romero's wallet and the keys to his SUV. She drove the back roads north until she and Zach were in Denver. Once there, she contacted the FBI field office.

Within the hour WITSEC had her on Con Air, the private federal airline that usually shuttled prisoners. They flew her back to the WITSEC safe site and orientation center in a secret Washington suburb. She'd arrived there with Zach in an armored vehicle with blackout windows.

This time she had been prepared for what was going to happen. Movement within the center was as controlled as it is in prison. Doors automatically bolted and could only be opened by the Federal Marshals on duty. Hallways were monitored by motion detectors and video cameras.

The compound, she'd been informed the first time she was there, could hold six families without any of them seeing each other. The typical orientation lasted two weeks, including a formal risk assessment of each witness. Her cover blown meant her risk assessment this time was sky high.

They'd spent an entire day debriefing her and trying to find out how she'd been compromised. Even Curt Masterson, head of WITSEC couldn't decide what had happened. They had wiretaps on Rutherford's and Ames's telephones, and they were under surveillance. As far as the FBI could tell neither of the men had contacted a hit team.

She suspected there was an internal leak within WITSEC. After all, Derek had warned her that someone had tried to access her file. Federal Marshals had their price, and no doubt, the ruthless executives would pay any amount of money to have her killed rather than to allow her to testify.

She had a dislocated shoulder and cracked ribs, but she had managed to outsmart the hit team. Masterson decided she needed some minor cosmetic surgery to change her appearance and green contacts to conceal her blue eyes before he was willing to relocate her.

Curt Masterson had listened to how the WITSEC 800 number and the Santa Fe FBI Field office both had busy signals. He decided whoever Rutherford and Ames had hired wasn't an ordinary hit team. They could be checking various states' DMV databanks. With sophisticated high definition computer imaging, they could compare recent drivers' license photographs to pictures of Devon when she'd been Samantha Robbins.

Armed with a new face, another name, a new birth certificate and a Social Security card, she was flown to Honolulu. Witnesses were rarely relocated in paradise, Masterson reasoned. This would be the last place her enemies would think to look for her.

It had taken a lot to convince Masterson to allow her to keep Zach. Her new handler, Warren Martin, certainly hadn't wanted to help her find accommodations that would accept a dog.

CHAD AND EDDIE were discussing how to set up an Exel spreadsheet. Chad couldn't help think that part of the reason his friend had been bilked by an employee was that Eddie didn't have a good grasp of his income and expenses. Spreadsheets were easy enough, but Eddie was resisting the change.

"Hello," called a willowy blonde from the door to the office, her figure silhouetted by the sunlight from the courtyard. She stepped forward into the office, and they could see her better. "I'm looking for Eddie Kukana."

Chad's eyes roved over her slowly. Her high full breasts flared above a narrow waist and long showgirl legs. She

60 BETTER OFF DEAD

turned her head slightly and shoulder-length blond hair rippled seductively across her shoulders. He clenched his teeth so he wouldn't be staring at her slack-jawed.

Devon gazed at both men, but it was the taller, powerfully-built man who caught her attention. Glossy chestnut hair hung across his forehead, a little longer than was currently stylish. Blue eyes filled with sparkling humor stared at her with undisguised sexual interest.

The man had a commanding presence, a way of holding himself. She instantly knew he would not be easy to manipulate. He continued to gaze at her, taking in her entire body with assessing eyes that missed nothing.

Her throat constricted and for a moment it felt as if someone were strangling her. The feeling passed—thankfully—and she drew in a deep hitching breath.

What was wrong with her? The man hadn't said a word, yet her pulse was thundering in her temples, and she suddenly felt light-headed. She must have the jitters over this interview. She pulled her eyes away from his.

For a second neither of the men said anything. Chad wasn't sure who they were expecting to arrive for the interview, but it wasn't a knockout with a mane of tawny blond hair, cat-green eyes and a killer bod. She could stop a guy's heart from a block away.

"I'm Devon Summers. I have an interview for the wedding coordinator position."

Chad found his voice first. "This is Edward. Everyone calls him Eddie."

She walked toward them, not smiling, her eyes intent. "I hope the position hasn't been filled."

"It hasn't," Eddie said, his tone gruff, a sure sign he was nervous.

Chad stood up. "You have experience as a wedding planner?"

"Coordinator," she corrected him.

Unusual green eyes, he thought. Hypnotic. Seductive.

"Ms. Summers e-mailed me her résumé." Eddie picked up a piece of paper from the top of a desk littered with brochures for his various party boat services, faxes and letters. "Impressive. Five years at the Cress Creek Country Club in Chicago."

"Napierville, actually. It's one of the more upscale suburbs." Devon wondered if her voice reflected her nervousness.

"Right. Napierville." The other man responded, grinning boyishly, his arresting blue eyes sparkling with humor.

Uh-oh, Devon thought. This man is way too sure of his own charm. Like Tyler, she thought with a pang. He's accustomed to women falling all over him. Well, not this woman.

Chad decided Devon was a total babe, but not in the way Chad might have expected had he merely seen her from afar. When she spoke she had the glint of intelligence in her eyes and a very direct manner.

What would she be like in bed?

He'd bet the ranch that she liked physical sex. She probably would insist on being on top. Worked for him. He imagined her tawny hair brushing his face, her nipples tight and swaying slightly as she rode him hard.

"Before that I worked three years at the Four Seasons in Philadelphia as the assistant coordinator."

"But you have no experience with weddings on the water," Eddie said.

Chad knew Eddie was thinking of an excuse not to hire Devon. When Eddie's wife Malaea saw this babe, she would pitch a fit. Not that Eddie was a player. Far from it, but Malaea was extremely protective.

Chad was protective, too, but for another reason. A hottie like this could easily take advantage of Eddie financially.

Devon recited the cover story she'd concocted for this interview. "I did one wedding on Lake Michigan. The club catered the event on a member's yacht. I coordinated everything."

Eddie nodded thoughtfully.

"Sounds like she's perfect for the job," Chad said. No way would he let this woman not be hired even though he'd already decided he would have to keep his eye on her so she didn't use Eddie.

Okay, so keeping his eye on her wouldn't be any problem. Keeping his eyes off her would be another matter. She chose that second to turn those cat-green eyes on him.

Their gazes locked and for a long suspended moment they gazed at each other. Seconds ticked by. Devon refused to look away and let him know how much he unnerved her.

Chad experienced an erotic charge, but quickly realized it was one-sided. The intensity of her gaze and the tight set of her full lips, confirmed her mind was not on sex. Her look was almost a challenge, almost as if she were daring him...to what? In that tiny suspended moment, he felt the full impact of her undeniable sex appeal.

Eddie broke the tension. "When can you start?"

Devon weighed her options. Her instincts told her this was a dangerous situation. She was unaccountably attracted to the taller man even though he reminded her of Tyler.

"Before I take the job, I need to know if I can bring my golden retriever with me. He's well-trained and won't be a problem."

"Goldens are great dogs," Chad said.

Eddie hesitated a moment before saying, "Bring him."

"So when can you begin?" Chad asked. Not soon enough.

"Next week."

"Tomorrow," Chad said. "A big wedding is coming up this weekend."

"All right," she agreed, but Chad heard a note of reluctance in her voice. "What time do you open?"

"Nine," Eddie replied. "Since we work weekends, you have Monday and Tuesday off."

Chad watched the knockout blonde as she filled out the employment forms Eddie had given her. He was standing close enough to get a whiff of some faint lemony scent. Perfume or perhaps shampoo.

What was her story? No wedding ring, but she was a heartbreaker. Chad could spot one a mile off.

Why had she come to Hawaii? In his experience people who relocated to Hawaii were looking for something or wanted to get away from something. They usually went home within the year.

Watching Devon Summers, Chad wondered why she hadn't applied to one of the big resort hotels or one of the larger wedding coordinators. With her credentials and looks, Devon could land a job anywhere. Why was she applying for a job with a small firm that wouldn't pay as well as one of the upscale companies?

A thought niggled at the back of his mind. Something about this woman seemed...off. What? Okay, okay, maybe it was visceral warning signals or simply his protective instincts where Eddie was concerned.

"How long have you been in Honolulu?" Chad asked.

"Less than a month." Devon didn't dare look up from the form she was filling out, fearing this man would see she was lying.

"Why did you move here?" Eddie asked.

"I've always wanted to live here." She handed Eddie the forms. "Tomorrow, I'll come a little before nine."

"Maikai."

"That means good," Chad told her.

She gazed at him for a moment, her eyes as unreadable as stone. Man, oh, man. She was one sexy lady and didn't even seem to realize it.

"What do you do here?" she asked.

"I'm Chad Langston. I don't work for Eddie." He offered his hand.

Devon's instincts told her physical contact with this man was out of the question. She mustered a businesslike smile, but didn't shake his hand.

"My office is across the courtyard. I—"

"See you tomorrow," she abruptly told Eddie and headed for the door.

Chad was right behind her. "Later," he said to Eddie.

"Do you need a ride?" he asked Devon.

"No." She wanted to get away from his disturbing presence. That's *what* she needed.

"I'll drop by tomorrow to see how you're doing."

Devon didn't dare reply. She walked through the courtyard to the entrance of the building. A shiver of anticipation coursed through her. Why? It must be a reaction to Tyler's betrayal, she decided. Her subconscious wanted to know if men still found her attractive.

An ice queen, Chad thought. Just his luck. At one point anything in panties had captured his attention.

Must be getting old.

The first woman who'd interested him in a long time was frigid. Give Devon a break. Maybe she'd moved here to put a bad relationship behind her. She could be temporarily off men—or have a boyfriend.

Thanks to three sisters, Chad had a good understanding of how a woman's mind worked. He got along with women and enjoyed them. He was even willing to go shopping, although that was a stretch.

He watched Devon disappear. He wanted to kiss her until she was breathless and begging for more. Hell, what he really wanted was to whisk her away to his place and peel that sundress off her.

Heat pooled in his groin. Chad silently cursed himself for thinking with his dick. Like a siren, Devon called to him, urging him to come closer...and be destroyed.

DEVON RUSHED OUT of the building, anxious to escape Chad Langston, but she paused to check the street. There were a few people, but none of them looked familiar. She hadn't been followed.

She should have turned down the job because she found Chad attractive, but she quite literally couldn't afford to. She'd been offered lots of jobs, but none of them met her requirements should she need to escape.

Chad Langston. Quite a hunk. Tall, sun-streaked chestnut-brown hair, blue eyes and a body to die for. No man had the right to possess so much masculine virility. He seemed to know it, she decided, remembering the aggressive boldness in his gaze.

She would just have to give him the deep freeze until he got the message. No matter how sexy the ripped bod or how adorable his smile, Devon did not need a man in her life. But she had to admit his long sensual look, as close to a caress as you could get without touching, had triggered a bittersweet sensation.

She hadn't experienced anything like it for well over a year, when she'd been forced to leave Tyler behind in Houston. She'd immediately recognized the telltale gleam in Chad's eyes for what it was—lust.

What had stunned her was her own reaction. She had been too long without a man, but she couldn't afford to get too close to anyone. The last man to help her had paid with his life.

Over and over at odd, unexpected times, she kept seeing herself closing Romero's eyes. *Until we meet again, may God keep you in the palm of His hand.*

The weight of the loss, realizing she would never see Romero again swept through her. Where would she be if not for him? Even more lost and lonely than she'd been.

Guilt had a stranglehold on her emotions. The hit team had killed something vital inside her when they'd murdered Romero. Problem was, she hadn't died yet.

Death was terrifyingly final. Knowing she'd caused his murder brought the blur of unfallen tears to her eyes. No more star-filled nights for Romero, no more artists to discover, no more walks through the historic plaza. No more anything.

She forced herself to hit the speed dial on her cell phone and called Warren. "I got the job. I don't think they checked my references."

"Doesn't matter. They're backstopped."

From her first relocation, she knew phony credentials and references were fixed so that if they were checked, they would appear to be legitimate.

"Problem is I need to become an expert at planning a wedding by tomorrow morning."

"Try the Internet."

"I plan to." She hesitated a moment before asking, "Has Masterson given the okay to call my sister yet?"

"No. I'll let you know when he does."

"Any word on selling my condo or the gallery?"

"Like I've told you before, Lindsey Wallace is wanted for murder. WITSEC can't just quietly sell your assets without attracting attention." He hung up without saying goodbye.

Warren was not a warm fuzzy guy. When Derek had been her handler, he had been much more helpful. She supposed Warren thought she knew the ropes since she'd already been relocated once.

This time she had to take the WITSEC stipend until her assets in Santa Fe could be sold and the money transferred. Meanwhile, like most other WITSEC witnesses, she had to live on the cash her handler doled out and establish credit on her own. Until she had an income stream, she had to live in an apartment the size of a broom closet.

The need for cash and the office's setup with a back door and two escape routes made Devon take the job at Aloha. Otherwise, she told herself, she would have steered clear of pushy Chad Langston. For a moment she wondered if she should have told her handler about him. No way, she decided. Warren would have made her look for another job. Except for Chad, this office was perfect.

She climbed into the temperamental Toyota that Warren had helped her buy. The rattletrap car was rusted, a common occurrence in Hawaii, and probably wouldn't last another year, but for now it was all she could afford.

Chad Langston drifted into her mind. His office was just across the courtyard. *I'll drop by tomorrow to see how you're doing.*

Oh, no, you won't.

BROCK HARDESTY STARED at the special map on the wall that he had created for Samantha Robbins/Lindsey Wallace. He'd marked every state where she had attended school or had relatives or friends. He'd tagged the spots where she had vacationed. WITSEC wouldn't relocate her in any of those places.

"She's probably in the Pacific Northwest or California," he muttered. She hadn't traveled to those places and had no friends there. But exactly where was she?

The bitch was smart. He would grant her that. Not only had she evaded his hit team, but Lindsey had been clever enough to change the license plates on Romero Zamora's car. When the APB went out, the police were looking for the blue Suburban, but they never spotted it because it had different plates.

He later learned, through a source at FBI headquarters, that she'd driven north to Denver. WITSEC had immediately evacuated her.

He'd caught hell from Kilmer Cassidy because his agents had muffed it. He reminded the scumbag CEO that he had advised him to have the bitch terminated the first time they had visited PowerTec.

He had been running checks on new licenses issued by DMVs in the Western states. Hacking into the DMV was a no-brainer. It took a badge number to get into the local police computer. No problem since badge numbers were stored with employment files.

Once Brock was into the local police computer, it was easy to springboard into the State Police computer. From there, it was a few keystrokes and you were in the DMV database. So far, nothing. He'd run hundreds of pictures of new applicants against an imaging software program with Samantha Robbins/Lindsey Wallace's photograph on it, but none of them matched the picture of the woman he was after.

His operatives—the dumb shits who'd let Lindsey Wallace get away—had a contact at the Bank of Santa Fe. The minute her condo or gallery sold and the funds were being transferred, he would know about it.

It might take years. Romero Zamora had been a popular man with a lot of influential friends. His murder was getting more attention than Brock would have thought. With the media hovering, WITSEC wouldn't dare sell her assets.

In the meantime, he would wait. And when no one at Obelisk was paying attention to Number 111 and 32, Brock would arrange for an accident. He hadn't come this far to suffer fools. He was already grooming another top-notch hit man.

Man. Like Number 32, women were too emotional. Slitting Zamora's throat was an unbelievable fuckup. Something only a woman would do.

One of his telephones rang. The caller ID said it was one of the secret sources he'd developed for Obelisk.

"Yeah?"

"I've got some interesting info on a new device the DoD is testing."

"The Defense Department is always testing something."

The source chuckled. "How many times do they test it *outside* the department?"

"Never."

"Never say never. Remember the Predator."

"Right," Brock reluctantly agreed. The Predator drone had been developed in astonishing secrecy.

"Archer Danson himself gave this prototype to some ex-military officer to test."

"No shit! What is it?"

"I'm trying to find out."

"Get back to me the minute you do."

Obelisk had an unending need for military equipment. Something phenomenal would remind them how brilliant he was.

CHAPTER SIX

SITTING ON A BEACH CHAIR with his long legs stretched out, Chad chomped on a slice of pork slathered with a barbecue sauce that was supposed to be a family secret. It was store-bought sauce doctored with Worcestershire, Tabasco, and a bit of honey. The taste depended on who made the sauce. Keke made this batch. It was loaded with Tabasco.

It was almost sunset and he was with his sisters and their families under a cluster of date palms. His three sisters had seven kids among them, and they had brought along assorted rugrats who were friends or relatives. On most family birthdays and other occasions, Chad's brothers-in-law came early in the morning to Waimanalo Beach on the west side of the island, not far from Honolulu. They'd dug an *imu* pit in the sand, lined it with dried banana leaves, and slow-roasted a kalua pig.

The waves were calmer here than in other parts of the island, and the fine sand made awesome sandcastles. Chad preferred the surf on the North shore where he'd grown up, or nearby Sandy Beach around Makapuu Point where the body surfers hung out. But for young children, this beach was perfect.

The *luau* was a Hawaiian family tradition. It had been botched by hotels that served gross food while *hula* girls and fire eaters performed. Family *luaus* usually didn't have *hula* dancing. For entertainment someone might pick up a ukulele and start playing after having a few too many Primo beers. Keke's husband Paul was sure to bring out his slack key guitar as soon as he'd had dessert.

For Hawaiians a *luau* was a chance to get together with their extended family and "talk story" while they feasted and celebrated a birthday or special occasion. Talking story was their way of passing on island lore and traditions to the young.

It was also a way of handing down family tales. Talking story meant telling the same tales over and over, but Hawaiians didn't mind. It was customary to listen intently as if hearing the story for the first time.

His sister Keke came over and sat down beside him. "You're awfully quiet. What's up?"

Keke and Chad were closer than he was to his other two sisters because they had been born fourteen months apart. With his father away constantly managing the Turtle Bay Resort, their mother had been so overwhelmed that it had been another three years before the twins, Nola and Hana had arrived.

"Come on." Keke poked him in the ribs. "Tell me."

"I met a woman."

"About time!" The blue eyes he saw every morning when he shaved sparkled with mischief, and Keke laughed. "Tell me about her."

He didn't know what to tell Keke. As much as he was attracted to Devon, something about her made him wary. It wasn't anything tangible. It was a gut feeling, a holdover from his Special Ops days with Delta Force, when he'd learned to rely on his instincts.

"Her name is Devon Summers. She's going to be the new wedding coordinator for Eddie."

Around her finger, Keke twisted a strand of dark hair wet from swimming with her kids. "Remind her that I'm on the list if she needs extra help."

Keke sometimes worked Eddie's parties to make extra money. She was exceptional at tending bar for a large number of guests and could do the work of two bartenders.

"I'm sure Eddie will tell her."

"You can't have known her very long. Malaea told me yesterday morning that Eddie was still interviewing."

Keke was very close to Eddie's wife. Once Chad would never have believed it could happen. Eddie and Keke had dated steadily throughout high school. After Eddie left the North Shore for Honolulu, he'd met Malaea.

Chad had been overseas with the Delta Force fighting Desert Storm. Nola and Hana had sent him a barrage of e-mails to tell him how upset Keke was. The first chance he'd gotten, Chad had called Eddie and found out his calabash cousin was in love but not with his sister.

A little more than a year passed and Keke met Paul Nakamura. They married and had children. With young children so close in age and being thrown together at family gatherings, the women had the opportunity to get to know each other and become friends.

"Eddie must have just hired her."

"This afternoon."

"So what's the problem?"

Chad watched his sisters' brood splashing in the surf glazed golden by the setting sun and thought how perceptive Keke was. "I think the woman took an instant dislike to me."

"No way."

"Yes. Way. I was trying to talk to her and she walked off."

"You didn't come on too strong, did you?"

Chad shrugged one shoulder. "She walked in and—wham—a guy would have to be dead not to stare at her."

"I might have guessed. Big tits."

"No, not centerfold material. She's hot, though. Slim, long legs, blond hair."

Keke *tsked.* "Looks aren't everything. Beautiful women are often conceited and looking for a rich husband. Better watch out. Playing hard-to-get is the oldest trick in the book."

"Mommie! Mommie!" screeched Keke's youngest. "Watch!"

"I'm watching."

The three-year-old leaped over an incoming wave that was six inches high at most.

Keke clapped, and yelled, "Very good."

"Way to go," Chad shouted.

He waited until he had Keke's attention again. "I don't think Devon is playing a game. I usually have a sixth sense about women from living all those years with you three."

Keke giggled. "Well, you should. Remember the time you had Eddie and the guys to the house for a sleepover? We put all our panties and bras in your room so the guys would think you were gay or a pervert."

"You're lucky I didn't strangle you."

"Mom stopped you. Otherwise I wouldn't be here today."

They both were silent for a moment. Chad was positive his sister was thinking the same thing he was. Their parents should be here today, celebrating their granddaughter's birthday, but they both had died, his father in an auto accident and his mother two years later of ovarian cancer.

"About this Devon person. Think of hyenas."

Chad groaned. Keke adored animals. Every time she could, she made a point with an example from the animal kingdom.

"Despite what people think about the law of the jungle, male hyenas who are too aggressive and try to dominate the females, don't father as many pups as those who make friends *before* mating."

"I guess I do come on too strong sometimes, but it always seems to work."

"And we sisters—the fab three—have always warned you that some women don't like it, especially if she's had a bad experience with a man."

The stupidity of allowing a brief encounter with a stranger to bug him like this made him groan inwardly. Aw, hell, he didn't know what to think. Since his first sexual experience at fourteen, he'd called the shots in his relationships with women.

Sure, a few had blown him off. It hadn't bothered him, but Devon had managed to get to him, Chad realized, perplexing emotions coursing through him.

Why her?

SHELBY SOMETHING—an unpronounceable Hawaiian last name that Devon couldn't say let alone remember—gushed wedding trivia nonstop from the office to the posh residential area near Diamondhead.

"Why do brides wear something blue?" Shelby had asked, then immediately answered her own question. "It symbolizes faithfulness."

"Who, like, thought of wedding cakes? They began in England in the Middle Ages. People would bring small cakes to weddings. They would, like, pile them up high. Soon people frosted them, like together. Get it? The tiered wedding cake."

Devon had smiled indulgently. Surely, if Shelby could remember so much trivia, the girl could be a bigger help with the details of wedding planning. No such luck. Shelby was content to be an airhead.

Devon had come in early, prepared to give Chad Langston the brush-off. She'd worked all morning and had made a lot of headway with the three upcoming weddings, thanks to her crash course on the Internet. Chad hadn't dropped by the office, even though Eddie was in and scheduling party boat cruises in a voice so loud that it was difficult to concentrate.

"Mostly we, like, do fab weddings on Eddie's yachts," Shelby explained for the second time, "but occasionally we get a request for a private home. You know, an awesome place with an ocean view like the mansion we're using Sunday evening."

Devon nodded, resisting the urge to say anything. Shelby had an overly friendly attitude, like a puppy who wanted its master's attention. She didn't want to encourage the girl to become too friendly.

She feigned interest in what was known as the Gold Coast. It ran along the shore east of Diamond Head along Kahala Beach. Most of the elegant homes were behind custom-made gates. Occasionally she caught a glimpse of lushly planted grounds.

Devon hadn't expected to fall in love with Hawaii, but from

the moment she'd stepped off the plane, she was greeted by a sky so blue, so clear it made her heart soar and momentarily forget her problems. Diamond Head stood nobly in the distance, burnished purple by the angle of the sun. The heady scent of plumeria mingled with the loamy smell of the tropics and the bracing scent of the sea.

I'm going to love it here, she'd thought.

Shelby drove her Honda through a set of open stainless gates flanked by towering, stately royal palms. In the center of the enormous circular courtyard was a huge bronze dolphin spouting water into a reflecting pool. The modern home had a curved wall of glass to view Diamondhead and the ocean.

Devon tuned out Shelby as they left the car and rang the doorbell next to towering stainless-steel doors etched with a wave pattern. She noticed how the contemporary lines of the home had been softened by banks of ferns and brilliant pink bougainvillea.

A barefoot, shirtless guy in his early twenties answered the door. His spiked hair was bleached a blinding white by the sun. His skin was as bronze as the dolphin in the courtyard.

"Hi, Rory. Aren't you, like, surfing today?" gushed Shelby.

From the looks of the home, Devon had expected a houseboy in some sort of outfit. But the rich were different. Apparently this was the owner's son.

"I surfed already. I was up at the Pipeline before dawn."

"Getting ready for the contest?" she asked in a breathy voice.

"Right."

Shelby turned to Devon. "Rory's surfing in the Rip Curl Cup. The winner, like, gets two hundred and fifty thousand dollars."

"Wow!" Devon hadn't realized there was so much money in surfing.

Rory pointed in the direction of an infinity pool visible off to the side. "He's out there."

Rory disappeared around a corner, and Devon followed

Shelby through the dramatic black marble foyer where a dust mote would have had the good sense not to land on the pristine floor. They walked through a living room the size of a hotel lobby. What must be glass doors disappeared into the walls so the room naturally flowed outside.

"Ahoy, there," Shelby called to the man on a plush chaise lounge with its back to them.

Ahoy? Sheesh, but this girl acted embarrassingly young. Devon wondered how she'd landed the job as the coordinator's assistant. Obviously she wasn't capable of taking over the coordinator position or Eddie would have promoted her.

"Ahoy? Shelby, you need to learn to be more professional," called the man.

Oh, my God! Chad Langston. What was he doing here? Sunning himself obviously and toying with a handheld video game or perhaps a GPS.

Could this be his home? The Crockett Building was a modest office complex. It didn't seem to be the type of place where a person who owned this mansion would have an office.

"I'm more professional, like, every day. Right now, I'm showing the new wedding coordinator around. Have you met Dev—"

"We met yesterday." Chad deliberately glanced at her for only a split second, then turned his attention to Shelby.

He told Shelby, "Get Devon up to speed so the wedding on Saturday goes smoothly. I'm here if you need me."

He settled back in his chair, pretending to be more interested in the gadget than her. No way was he going to hit on Devon. Let her come to him, he'd decided after his talk with Keke.

Devon told herself she wanted Chad to leave her alone, but a twinge of disappointment rippled through her. She tamped down the feeling, upset with the sensations he aroused in her.

Shelby led her across a broad sweep of diachondra that gradually dropped down to the water where a group of

chaise lounges had been placed along the shore. Like holi-
day bunting, garlands of seaweed decorated the beach, a gift
of the retreating tide. At the far end of the grounds was a
lagoon where a black swan was swimming, barely rippling
the water.

Now they were far enough away from Chad for Devon to
question Shelby. "Is this Chad's place?"

Shelby nodded and her dark hair fluttered across her shoulders. "Totally awesome, isn't it?"

"Totally. What does Chad do?" She perched her sunglasses
on top of her head.

"He owns lots of scuba diving shops and dive boats on,
like, all the islands." Shelby stepped closer and her voice
dropped to a conspiratorial whisper, "I've heard Eddie say
Chad's *real* money comes from underwater spying."

"Spying? On whom?" Devon pretended to be consulting
her notes in case Chad was watching.

"Like dead people. He goes underwater and looks for evidence. The family hired him in the Laci Peterson case."

"Not spying. That's underwater forensics."

"Whatever."

Fascinating, she thought. He would be an interesting man
to get to know, but she didn't dare.

From the chaise, Chad watched Devon, his eyes scanning
each feature of her face. None was particularly remarkable but
together, they were a stunning combination. She was pretty
in an exotic cat-eyed way. Okay, he'd dated more beautiful
women, but there was something about Devon, something
elusive that called to him. He wanted her, plain and simple.

Be a hyena. Keke's advice reverberated in his head. Be a
friend first. See where that goes. Could be, if he came to
know Devon, he wouldn't like her.

Fat chance.

Her blond hair rippled across her shoulders as she studied
a piece of paper. A full, pouty lower lip glistened with a hint

of gloss. He'd noticed her mouth yesterday. Since then all he could think about was kissing her.

Devon consulted the printout in earnest, saying to Shelby, "Lori's computer notes indicate about two hundred people are expected for the wedding. Where are we going to hold the service?"

"Here on the grass."

Devon scanned the grass and silently cursed herself for taking this job. Her Internet searches had turned up valuable information, but estimating how many chairs would fit on this lawn wasn't among them. It didn't appear to be room for two hundred chairs plus an aisle and a place for the minister to perform the service.

"Are you sure? Were you with Lori when she spoke with the couple?"

"Well, no, but it's an awesome spot. We've, like, had two other weddings on the lawn."

Devon considered asking Chad, but being near him was too risky. She flipped open her cell phone and dialed Eddie. "I'm out at Chad Langston's place. Do you know if the wedding is supposed to take place on the lawn? It doesn't look big enough."

"I have no idea. Isn't it in Lori's notes?"

"No."

"All I remember her mentioning was the ten thousand red rose petals."

"Rose petals?" She scanned the printout. Oh, my God! With two other weddings coming up, she hadn't noticed. No flowers had been ordered at all.

"The petals will cover the lagoon. We grow roses in Hawaii, sure, but most are flown in."

Eddie didn't sound terribly concerned, an attitude typical of many Hawaiians Devon had met. It took a disaster to fluster them.

"Eddie, if any flowers were ordered, even the bridal bouquet, Lori didn't make a note of it."

"I'll try to reach Lori in Kaui. If Chad's around, ask him where the service is being held."

"I will." She said goodbye and snapped her cell phone shut. "Do you know if any flowers have been ordered for this wedding?" she asked Shelby. The last thing she wanted to do was talk to Chad.

Shelby shook her head.

Devon read the printout more closely. A caterer had been hired, thank heavens. Something weird had been written on the music line.

"Is there a band called Bite Me?"

"They are, like, *the* best band in the islands."

Who would have thought? "I guess we'll have to see if Chad knows where the service will be held. Then we need to get back to the office and jump on the flower order."

Devon put on her sunglasses and marched across the grass toward Chad. His long, tanned legs were dusted with sun bleached hair. Obviously he spent a lot of time outdoors. It gave him the appearance of a surfer.

She'd always gone for smart men, not jocks. But Chad seemed to be an exception. Every time she was around him, the pull was stronger.

Chad kept tinkering with the gadget and didn't look up although he heard Shelby chattering as they approached. Devon was wearing a pale yellow sundress that hugged the lines of her slim body and emphasized the swell of her breasts. He imagined her stepping out of it and into his arms.

Get a grip!

Devon noticed Chad's still wet Hawaiian print swimming trunks. They hung low on his slim hips and molded his powerful thighs. From behind her sunglasses, Devon observed his torso and noted the hard planes of his chest and the defined contours of his arms. He was buff but not overly pumped the way some guys were. A skein of hair trailed down his chest and disappeared under the waistband of his trunks.

Her eyes dropped to his powerful thighs. At their apex, she couldn't help observing the masculine bulge barely concealed by the fabric. Nice package, she thought before she could stop herself.

No telling what he might try in bed, she decided. He had the looks and the money and the personality to attract any woman he wanted. No doubt, he'd had plenty of experience.

Plus he had charm in spades—just like Tyler.

"Excuse me, Chad. We're wondering if you know where the service is being held? On the lawn?"

Chad pushed his shades to the top of his head and looked up. His blue eyes flickered with amusement as if he got a kick out of life. Their gazes met and a sharp, unexpected jolt of excitement hit her.

"There isn't enough room out here. They're using the living room."

"Great. Thanks." She started to walk away, but stopped and asked, "What are you doing with the furniture?"

"Lori hired a moving company to pick up the stuff and store it. That's why I'm hanging around. They're supposed to be picking up the furniture this morning."

She groaned. "Bite me."

"Where?" Chad asked.

"She's talking about the band," Shelby said.

"No. I said it to avoid a four-letter word. I have this bad feeling that Lori didn't order a lot of things, including furniture removal."

CHAPTER SEVEN

IT WAS JUST AFTER FOUR that afternoon when Chad arrived at his office. He'd spent the afternoon testing the DARPA's latest widget. He'd already had the Defense Department's Advanced Research Agency's gadget for over three months, but Danson had insisted on a six month test in all types of weather conditions and varying terrain. It had a few kinks, but, so far nothing major.

The device was impressive. The damn thing would revolutionize surveillance. He'd been sitting in the blinding sun, wearing shades, and on an uplink to the DoD satellite when Devon and Shelby had arrived. He had been tracking movements of large groups of men coming over the border of Pakistan into Afghanistan.

As soon as Devon and Shelby had left, he'd driven to a pay phone and notified Danson. Chad couldn't resist asking about the leak. Danson hadn't found out who in the DoD was leaking top secret information, but he assured Chad that his best agent was zeroing in on a promising lead.

"Anything important going on?" Chad asked his assistant as he walked into his office.

"I would have called you on your cell," Ane replied without taking her eyes off the computer screen.

Ane Sephuhu was a beefy woman who could trace her ancestors back to King Kamehameha. The Nippon Bank had laid off Ane, a widow on the dark side of fifty, after nearly thirty years of service. She hadn't been able to find another job because of her age and her weight. Chad had interviewed

her and had been impressed. For the last five years, she'd handled the work of three people.

"You need to take a look at the invoice I'm sending Fidelity Insurance for the Townsend case."

Chad reluctantly took the papers from Ane's extended
hand. He'd spent a full week in Turks and Caicos, where he'd
discovered Robert Townsend IV's death hadn't been a simple drowning. Townsend's own bang stick, a weapon divers
used to kill an attacking shark, had punctured his air hose.
Why Townsend hadn't waded to shore was a mystery, but
Chad had a theory.

After interviewing the wife and the stud who was captain
of Townsend's yacht, Chad had the distinct impression the
two of them had iced the old guy. Chad had spent extra days
trying to prove it. There was no forensic evidence, but the
angle at which the bang gun had hit was a bit odd. He'd sent
Townsend's dive gear to the FBI for trajectory analysis. He'd
also suggested the insurance company put a tail on the sex-
pot the old dude had married to see if she was having an affair with the ship's captain.

He signed the invoice and wished he could have solved the
case. Aw, hell, that's pure ego talking. He'd solved numerous
cases, but no one could solve all of them. Still, he hated to
see anyone get away with murder.

"Don't worry," Ane said. "The case will be solved."

"I doubt it. Even if the FBI proves Townsend couldn't
have accidentally fired his bang stick, there's nothing to link
his wife to the crime. She has a perfect alibi. The captain says
she was on the yacht all afternoon and the two crew members confirm it."

Chad went over to his desk, booted up his computer and
scrolled through his e-mail. Nothing interesting.

"You might want to check on Eddie," Ane told him. "I
heard him screaming something about not renting linens."

Chad shook his head. Lori had really dropped the ball with
this one. Devon had four days to pull this together. Not much

time, considering most weddings were planned a year in advance.

He remembered Devon saying *Bite me.* Even in a crisis, she had a sense of humor. He would have bitten her—not a mean bite but a playful nip—anywhere on that sexy bod.

He tried not to think about her too often, but he had a helluva time getting one image out of his stupid gourd. Devon naked and on her back, her hair fanned across his pillow, a happy smile on her face for a change instead of her shuttered, distant expression.

He wouldn't force himself on her. After his talk with Keke last night, he was backing off. Let her come to him when she was ready. Hell might freeze over first, but there you go.

"Pono!" Careful! Ane's dark eyes flashed in her lined face. "Pele will disappear on Eddie."

According to ancient lore, Pele was the volcano goddess. An assortment of other lesser gods and the *menehune,* elves who loved to play tricks on people, were included in the island myths.

"What are you talking about?"

Ane smiled knowingly. "Devon. She's Pele for the new millennium."

"Lolo!" Crazy.

The island had more myths and goddamned superstitions than any place on earth. One of the most prevalent was the story of Pele's ghost appearing along the side of the road in the form of a beautiful young woman with a dog, needing help. It was considered bad luck not to help her, but no matter what you did, she disappeared as suddenly as she had appeared.

Ane was into island lore in a major way. She had what Hawaiians called "the eye," a sixth sense about things. In the time she'd worked for him, Chad had been amazed at how often she had been right.

"Why do you think Devon needs help?"

"Watch her. Da woman's on guard."

Chad had been watching—big time. Well, hell, he was just a guy. He might not have had his eyes on the right body parts.

He couldn't imagine how Ane had picked up on all this the first day Devon was on the job, but he knew better than to argue. From his sisters, he'd learned women are far more intuitive than men. In this case, he'd also felt something was strange about Devon.

Chad walked across the courtyard toward the open door of Aloha Weddings. The large office wasn't a typical cube farm. There were no cubicles at all. There was a fancy reception area off to the side where albums of wedding invitations, brochures about the boats, and photographs of floral arrangements could be inspected by clients. Since most of Eddie's wedding business came from the Internet, this area didn't have to be too large.

Behind the reception area was a work station with a high speed copy machine. Several potted palms with ferns at their bases screened the work station from the reception area.

Three desks were in the main section. A large one stood off to the side, loaded with high-tech computer equipment. From here, Eddie's oldest son updated the Web site after his high school classes were over.

On the opposite side of the room, the wedding coordinator's station had a large photograph of a sunset wedding on one of Eddie's boats. In the background, outlined against a golden sky, Diamond Head thrust out like the prow of a battleship. It was the first photo on the Web site, and no doubt had sold dozens of weddings for Eddie.

Shelby's smaller desk was in the center of the room. It never had anything on it except for a photograph of her tabby cat in a bamboo frame.

In the back corner of the large room was Eddie's desk. The louvered corner windows gave him an exceptional view of Ala Wei harbor and let in the cooling trades. Next to this area was a louvered door. It opened onto a walkway that led to two different streets, depending which way you turned.

Chad walked through the front door. Devon quickly looked up. For an instant something flickered in her eyes. With what might have been a suggestion of a smile, she went back to her computer. He couldn't interpret her shuttered expression.

He noticed Devon had moved her work station. Before, the side of her station had been to the door. Now she faced the door. Why?

Beside her desk lay a golden retriever with a mullet. There weren't many goldens in the islands—it was too hot for dogs with so much fur. Those that lived here usually had a mullet clip: their bodies and legs were sheared, leaving their ears and tails fluffy.

"Hey, what's your name?" he called to the dog.

"Zachary," Devon said without looking up. "Zach for short."

Chad squatted down. "Good boy, Zach."

The dog didn't need any more encouragement. He leaped up, mullet-like tail wagging and romped up to Chad. He petted the retriever and scratched his chest, a sure hit with dogs.

"Yo *brah.*" Eddie's voice boomed across the office. *Brah.* Pidgin for brother. Eddie spoke pidgin, the local's language, a melding of Hawaiian, Creole and English. Eddie rarely used it in a business environment. The reversion to pidgin and the deep patches of dampness on his Hawaiian shirt told Chad that Eddie was upset big time.

Chad left Zach and walked back to his friend's desk. *"Hie aha?"* What's happening?

Eddie lowered his voice, "I'm in deep shit." His voice picked up volume as he continued. "Lori had total brain fade. The wedding at your place. She didn't order tables, flowers, half of what she should have. All the good rentals are taken. Rose petals. Forget it."

"Hold on. You must have loyal vendors who'll help out—"

"The good stuff is spoken for. This close to Sunday, they've been paid in full. They can't fail to deliver now."

"There must be something—"

"No. I'm finished. It'll take years to repair my reputation. This is Inoye's niece, for Christ's sake. Everybody who's anybody will be at this wedding."

Daniel Inoye was Hawaii's revered senator who had lost his arm fighting in the Second World War. He was a very powerful, respected man with lots of influential friends. It would deal a blow to Eddie's business that would be hard to recover from. Honolulu wasn't that big when you took away the tourists. In the tight-knit community, word would spread quickly.

Eddie stood up. "Let's get outta here. I need something to eat. Didn't get lunch trying to sort out this crap. Malae's still in Maui. I'm not getting dinner tonight."

An idea came to Chad. "Let's take Devon with us and sort out this mess."

Eddie looked skeptical. "We've tried, but maybe you'll come up with something. You always were the smart one."

If there was one thing that ever came between them, it was Eddie's insecurity about his lack of education. He was ill-at-ease around people who had gone to college. Since the embezzlement had been discovered, Eddie had become even more sensitive. Chad suspected his friend was taking a hit financially, but he would be insulted if Chad offered to loan him money.

"Three heads are better than one," Chad replied. They walked over to Devon who was still concentrating on her computer screen. "Got a minute?"

She raised those compelling eyes from her computer screen. "Not really."

"We're going to get something to eat and discuss the problems with the wedding. Maybe we can think of something."

"We've already—"

Chad cut off her protest. "Bring all your notes."

As they left the building and walked the two short blocks to The Pink Gecko, Chad watched Devon out of the corner of his eye. He did his best not to notice the soft swell of her breasts just visible at the top of the scoop-neck red sundress or the provocative sway of her slim, graceful body. She looked straight ahead and listened while Chad ran his mouth to relieve the tension.

Her eyes shifted slowly, seemingly casually, taking in each person's face as they passed. His curiosity as well as his interest was aroused. He put on his shades so she couldn't see him watching her. By the time they'd reached the harbor, he'd caught her checking over her shoulder twice. What was going on here?

At the harbor side café Chad held the door for her, saying, "They have the best *hulihuli* chicken around. It's slow-roast on spit over wood."

When the hostess led them to a table, Chad didn't pull out a chair for Devon until she put her hand on one. He slid out a seat, and she slipped into it. She'd selected a seat with its back against the view windows overlooking the harbor and the boats, but from this position, Devon could watch everyone coming into the café.

"What's *saimin?*" Devon asked. "I've seen it on a lot of menus. Even McDonald's."

I'll be jiggered, he thought. Devon didn't seem like the McDonald's type. But this woman was something else.

"It's an island staple. Noodles. Try 'em."

Eddie was starving so they quickly ordered. Devon seemed adventurous enough and took his suggestion to have the *hulihuli* chicken and *saimin* even though she'd never tried, either. An interesting person, he decided.

Now that he knew what to look for, Chad couldn't help noticing Devon checking out customers coming through the door. She wasn't blatant about it. Most people wouldn't notice, but Chad did. His Delta Force training had taught him to do the same thing.

Watch your back.

The trick was to effectively use your peripheral vision, something most people didn't do. It was necessary to train yourself not to focus on a certain object. Keep your field of vision wide-open, always aware of what was off to the side. To do this took special training. Most people's vision was snared by a single object and held for a number of seconds or longer. Chad had learned to use his peripheral vision during training for covert operations.

The only way to become an expert at this was practice. Devon was so good that he decided she must have been doing this for some time. Why?

"Okay, so outline the main problem," Chad told them. "Then we think outside the box."

"Main problems," Eddie corrected with a heartfelt sigh. "Big problems."

"We can't get the furniture out of your house and onto a van that will keep it for four days without unloading it," Devon said.

"The two companies available are midnight movers," Eddie added. "They'll wreck your stuff big time or they'll steal something."

Chad nodded, thinking there were only a few reputable movers on Oahu. Most of the locals moved themselves. Chad needed to get what amounted to a house full of furniture out of his living room and into storage for just a few days. Last time, they'd arranged to have it packed into a long van and stored in the moving company's yard until it was time to return the furniture.

The waiter delivered two Primo beers and a glass of Pinot Grigio for Devon. Chad raised his glass, and they lifted theirs. As they clicked, Devon's eyes shifted to watch the couple coming through the door.

He was sitting close enough to her to get a whiff of the citrus cologne she used. It was hard to fight the thrill of anticipation he felt every time he was around her. Be a hyena, he reminded himself. Be a friend first.

"Here's to thinking *outside* the box," Chad said. "Do you have any close friends at the docks?" he asked, an idea hitting him.

"Sure. I've been running my boats around here for—what?—almost fifteen years. I know everybody."

"Is there someone who'll let us borrow a cargo container?"

Eddie gazed at him blankly for a second before his dark eyes widened. He slapped the table with the palm of his hand. *"Akamai 'oe!"* You're so smart! "Damn! Now I know why you went to Stanford and I didn't. Of course, I know several guys who'll lend me a container for a few days."

"You went to Stanford?" Devon asked.

"That's right. Where did you go to school?"

"UCLA." She took a sip of her drink. Her sensual lips were now glazed with the wine. A quick dart of her tongue brushed them clean in a way Chad found extraordinarily erotic.

"What about the shipping container?" she asked. "How are we going to move it around?"

"We'll have to rent a container truck," Chad replied. "It shouldn't be a problem. Ninety percent of the goods that come into Hawaii arrive on ships. Most of it in containers."

"Some folks go to the dock and get their stuff loaded onto their own trucks," Eddie told her. "Others, especially places on the North shore, have the container delivered."

Devon looked impressed, but her eyes drifted to the entrance. Now and then her gaze would casually scan the café.

"One problem solved." Chad liked the relieved expression on Eddie's face as he said this. "Next we have the rentals. The good stuff is already taken."

"We tried all the hotels to see if we could arrange something," Eddie said. "Either they need their tables and chairs or they don't have enough that matched."

"I have a thought," Devon said in a deceptively soft voice as if she didn't quite trust her idea. "Chairs for a wedding of this caliber aren't the usual nice white folding chairs. They have fancy slipcovers over them. Several rental companies have slipcovers, but they don't all match. I was thinking of making our own. If—"

"Not enough time," interrupted Eddie.

"If we could get yardage, the fabric could be cut with pinking shears. The roll is machine hemmed on two sides. There wouldn't be as many pinking shear cuts as you think. Instead of sewing them, drape the fabric over the chairs and use extra-wide ribbon to tie a bow at the back of the chair."

"Hey—" Eddie raised his beer "—you're onto something. Those draped chairs always have bows at the back."

"Yes, but the ribbon is sewn onto the slipcover. You just drop it over a folding chair and tie the bow. Making our own will be very labor intensive. Between the service inside and the dinner outside, we're talking over four hundred chairs alone."

Chad admired her ingenuity. "It can be done. I have three sisters who'll help. Get the fabric and ribbon ready to go. Have the tables and chairs delivered immediately. That way we'll have plenty of time to work on them."

"I'm not sure where to go to get that much fabric," she admitted.

"I'll call my sister Keke tonight. She'll help you. She sews a lot. I think she goes to Chinatown for material."

The waiter delivered the *hulihuli* chicken garnished with wedges of barbecued pineapple. Steaming bowls of *saimin* were placed beside their plates. They ate in silence for a moment.

Chad seemed powerless to resist looking at Devon. He watched as she chewed, the fine line of her jaw gently working in a way that fascinated him. At the base of her throat a pulse beat and swelled. What would it be like to kiss her there? The thought alone was a definite turn-on. Okay, so? Everything about this woman turned him on.

He had to guard against his feelings. Something was wrong with Devon. Why was she so concerned about the people around her? What was she hiding?

"Does the bride know about any of the problems?" Chad asked.

"No," Eddie replied with a grunt. "She lives in San Francisco. She's flying in tomorrow."

"We'd better solve the flower issue," Chad said.

"Notice how people no longer have problems?" Devon asked. "They have issues. People no longer tell each other anything. They share."

Eddie hooted and Chad laughed along with him. So the lady had a secret and a sense of humor.

"Okay, what about the flowers?" Chad asked.

"None were ordered. Not only are the ten thousand rose petals unavailable, the bride ordered all this exotic stuff for the house, the tables, her bridesmaids, the bouquet." Devon sighed. "You name it."

"I have a thought," Eddie said between bites. "Canna grows wild around here. Nurseries have plenty of it. Let's order red and strip the petals. Sprinkle them in the pond."

"Good thinking." Chad smiled at his friend. "The service starts at six—"

"In my experience, few brides are on time," Devon said. "The average wait, according to *Bride* magazine, is thirty-three minutes."

"Even better," Chad said. "The wedding begins later and the light in the yard will be even dimmer. I'll have the lagoon lights on low. Wanna bet no one notices Rudy isn't floating in rose petals?"

"I may be able to pull together the flower order by calling Singapore instead of distributors we usually contact in the States," Devon told them. "It may cost more to fly them in on short notice, but we'll be saving on the rose petals."

"Issues solved," Chad joked. "We're a team."

Eddie chuckled, looking relieved and happy. Devon's eyes were on the door.

CHAPTER EIGHT

KEKE STOOD OVER THE HUGE WOK in her kitchen, hoping this
time she would steam the baby bok choy the way her mother-
in-law liked it. The kids were in the family room, watching
Nickelodeon. The telephone rang. She put a lid on the wok
and grabbed the receiver.

"Did I catch you at a bad time?"

"The mother-in-law from hell is on her way. It's a bad
time."

"I forgot," Chad said. "This is the night she comes to dinner, isn't it?"

"Yeah, and you'd think Paul would come home early like
he promised. Wouldn't you?"

"I'm sorry. I'll make this quick. Could you help Eddie tomorrow?"

"I'll need a sitter. Maybe Nola or Hana, I'll have to call
later and let—"

"We need them, too. I'll pay for the sitters."

Keke smelled a rat. "It's that Devon woman, isn't it?"

A beat of silence. "I never could fool you."

Keke listened as Chad explained the need for fabric to
cover the chairs. "I know just where to go. There's a place in
Chinatown that has exquisite yardage you can't find anywhere else. It's not that expensive because the owner's son
works for a container firm. It comes in from China with containers of herbs—"

"They don't pay the import tax or duty."

"What can I say? Goes on all the time." Sometimes she

thought her brother was just a little too straight. It must have been all his military training. He'd been more hang loose growing up.

"Come by my office at nine, and I'll introduce you to Devon."

"Okay. Later."

Keke hung up. He must have it bad. She was perfectly capable of walking into Eddie's office and introducing herself, but Chad wanted to do it. This promised to be fun.

She lifted the wok's lid. The baby bok choy in miso sauce, her mother-in-law's favorite, lay soggy and wilted at the bottom of the wok. She pitched the mess in the sink, rammed it down the disposal with a wooden spoon and rinsed out the wok. A quick check of her watch told her that Mother Nakamura—a stickler for punctuality and the preparation of baby bok choy—would be here any minute.

Where *was* Paul?

He worked long hours with his uncle in the family pharmaceutical supply business. It was a good living, but they would never have been able to afford a home on Maunalua Bay near KoKo Head, if Chad hadn't given them a no interest loan for the down payment. A smaller version of Diamond Head, KoKo Head was the symbol of the Back Bay, a friendly neighborhood and a great place to raise children.

She had her brother to thank for this as much as her husband. Her two sisters lived nearby again because Chad had loaned them down payment money. His mansion in the ritzy Kahala area near Diamond Head was spectacular, but Keke found it slightly cold. Maybe this Devon woman would move into his life and warm up the place.

Chad had been away years, and the family had gotten used to the idea that he was never coming home. Then Papa had been killed in an accident a little over three years ago. Just after the funeral, their mother was diagnosed with cancer. Chad had bought a chain of dive boats and shops and returned home. He'd taken over for Papa as patriarch of the family.

Keke peered in the fridge, tired of trying to satisfy a

mother-in-law who refused to be pleased. She pulled out some stuff and was suddenly aware it had been an awfully long time since she'd heard anything from Lui and Mei. At three and five they were old enough to be alone in the next room watching television, but they were awfully quiet, a sure sign they were up to something.

She walked toward the den and heard low grunting or something. Rushing in, she saw two naked women French kissing each other, watched by a nude man who was hung like a horse.

"That does it! Uncle Nomo is never baby-sitting here again."

Paul's teenage nephew had once again fiddled with their satellite blocker to watch porn flicks. She snapped off the television and whirled around. Lui and Mei were sitting on the floor, their eyes wide, their little mouths gaping open.

Her first impulse was to scream: Time out. Go to your rooms. But this wasn't their fault. At five, Lui had already learned channel surfing from his father. Obviously Nick's program had bored them. Lui had surfed until he'd come upon the adults only station his uncle had been watching.

At three, Mei probably wouldn't have a lasting impression of what she'd seen, but Lui was a different story. Five-year-olds talked and *asked* questions.

"Lewis, May," she called them by their English names, the way she did when they were at school so they would know she meant business. At home and with family, she used the Hawaiian versions of their names. "You mustn't pay attention to movies like these. Adults play funny games sometimes."

Lui, so like Chad it was frightening, opened his mouth to ask something, but Keke didn't have time. Paul was going to have to explain this R-rated movie to his son. The doorbell rang. The mother-in-law from the Black Lagoon had arrived. "Turn on Nick and don't change the channel."

Keke rushed to the front door and swung it open. Paul's mother had already taken off her shoes and neatly placed them beside the row of shoes haphazardly lined up to the left of the door.

"Mother Nakamura," she greeted the older woman in the customary fashion that honored her status in the family.

"Is that burned baby bok choy I smell?"

"We're not having baby bok choy. Tonight we're having my favorite dish."

Mother Nakamura's dark eyes snapped, but she didn't say a word as she walked into the house. She didn't even remind Keke, the way she usually did, that the Japanese brought cleanliness to the islands like the custom of leaving street shoes outside to prevent dirt from being tracked into the house. Paul drove in that second.

Keke stood with Mother Nakamura in the doorway and waited for her husband. He was going to have to entertain his mother while she made enchiladas. Looking harried, Paul rushed up to them.

"Mother." He dutifully kissed the old witch on both cheeks.

"Sorry I'm late." He gave Keke a quick peck and slipped out of his loafers..

Lui and Mei had wandered into the room behind Keke. *Nani*—beautiful—she thought. They had the ruler-straight black hair that reflected their Japanese ancestry, pale skin, and wide blue eyes—the Langston eyes. They seemed to have Langston personalities, as well. With luck, neither of them would have Mother Nakamura's sour disposition.

Even though their grandmother came each Wednesday evening for dinner, the children hung back. They were a little intimidated by her. Once again, Keke wished her mother had lived. Then her children would have truly known a grandmother's love.

"Come to your grandmother."

Mei stood there, her blue eyes wide.

Keke tried to intercept Lui as he charged up to Paul. He dodged by her and grabbed his father around the knees and gazed up at him.

"Daddy, Daddy, is your pee-pee as long as the man's on television?"

"CHINATOWN DATES BACK to the eighteen hundreds when Chinese laborers were brought to work in the sugar cane fields," Keke explained.

Devon listened politely. Chad's sister was taking her to find material to cover the chairs and tables. Keke had Chad's eyes and shiny chestnut-colored hair, but she was petite and liked to chatter.

"The *pakes*—that's what we call the Chinese—started out dirt poor, but now many of them are among the wealthiest people on the island. They live everywhere. Very few live in Chinatown. There are a lot of Koreans, Filipinos and Vietnamese here now."

"These buildings date back to the 1800s?" Devon asked, looking at the buildings and thinking they didn't look that old.

"No. Sometime shortly before the First World War, a fire was deliberately started to control a bubonic plague epidemic. The wind whipped it out of control and wiped out all of Chinatown and the surrounding areas, too."

There were plenty of seedy dives in Chinatown, Devon noticed and not for the first time. She'd been here before. There were also plenty of noodle factories, herb shops, bakeries and jewelry stores.

She caught her reflection in a window. Finally she was beginning to get used to the way she looked. The cosmetic surgery had changed the shape of her eyes, giving them a slanted, catlike expression. Her nose had been altered slightly and it was now smaller than it had been. A chin implant had added length to her face.

WITSEC had insisted she have the surgery, but of course, they weren't paying for it. She had signed her second MOU— Memorandum of Understanding. It outlined what WITSEC would and would not do for her. Curt Masterson had specified WITSEC would be repaid for the cosmetic surgery from the sale of her condo and gallery.

"There it is," Keke said. "Tail of the Dragon. The name re-

fers to the wisp of heroin smoke as it curls upward. Chinatown. Opium dens. Get it?"

Devon eyed the ten-foot vertical banner with a menacing
black dragon fluttering in the breeze. The warehouse was up
a long, narrow street in what appeared to be the worst part of
Chinatown. This was the dark underbelly of Honolulu tourists never saw.

A place to hide.

Since Santa Fe, Devon looked at the world around her as
a dangerous place. She never knew when they would find her,
when she would be on the run again. Or when she would die.

She'd lied to Eddie and Chad, when she'd said that she'd
only been here four weeks. She and Zach had arrived a month
earlier than she'd told them. Warren had taken part of each
day to brief her. She had spent the remainder of the time cas-
ing the island.

Always search—ahead of time—for cover. Always have
more than one escape route in mind. Always have cash and
another identity stashed in a safe place.

Masterson had assured her that Hawaii was a great place
because few WITSEC people were relocated in paradise.
They wouldn't look for her here. She'd countered by saying
there was really only one way out—by air. In the end, he'd
persuaded her to go.

This time she'd taken more precautions. She'd studied the
terrain and had money and a phony ID she'd bought on the
street stashed in another place—just in case. She'd taken the
added precaution of using a private mailbox company as her
address. The home telephone number she had given was for
one of the two cell phones she kept with her at all times. No
one knew where she lived except Warren.

For a moment she thought about Chad. Yesterday at lunch,
she'd been physically closer to him than she'd ever been. Not
a good idea. There was an underlying magnetism between
them. It would only mean trouble if she allowed anything to
happen.

"I know this place looks like a rat hole," Keke said, "but it has great fabric. Trust me."

"Okay." Devon struggled to keep her tone cool. She really liked this woman and had from the moment Chad had brought her into the office. Devon forced herself to pull back and not be swept up by Keke's infectious optimism about everything.

The lucky woman had no idea how ugly life could get.

They entered a dimly lit warehouse three stories high. From floor to ceiling were bins filled with bolts of fabric. Tall ladders slid along rails from side to side. On them were husky men with weight lifters belts around their waists.

"Fabric is sorted by color. Tell them the color, and they'll bring down every bolt with that color. Since you need so much fabric, you'll tell them the color and the yardage you need."

The wizened old Chinese woman behind the counter barked at them, "Color?"

"Canna red," Keke snapped back.

"Rose petal red," Devon whispered to her.

Keke's voice was low. "This is Hawaii. Chinatown. We don't think in terms of rose petals. Canna grows here. Everyone knows that shade of red."

Devon watched, thinking that elsewhere in America they would have used forklifts. Here they had sling and rope contraptions, dating back to the early twentieth century.

"Look at this roll," Keke whispered. "Say 'take away' if you don't like it. Do *not* say you like anything. If you do, they will know you're an easy mark and charge you more."

"I'll let you handle the negotiations, if you don't mind."

Keke beamed, her smile an echo of her brother's. "I'm good at it."

They rifled through dozens and dozens of rolls of fabric. Many of them would have worked but Keke and Devon didn't find any of them to be special. A few more bolts were brought down from the uppermost reaches of the warehouse. These were dusty and had obviously been up there for a long time.

They unrolled one after another. Too intense. Too heavy. Too fussy a pattern. Devon was losing hope. All the fabric had been great, but not quite what Devon had in mind.

"Devon," Keke whispered, "check this."

She moved over to the bolt of fabric Keke had unwound and was holding up to the light of a bare bulb swinging on a long cord between racks of fabric. "Let's get several bolts to the light, but this is the one we're interested in, I think."

Keke motioned to the men standing nearby. She had them haul several bolts of fabric to the side door that opened to an alley. The odor of garbage and incense nearly choked Devon, but Keke was unfazed.

"Look at this! It's vintage material," she whispered.

Devon sucked in her breath. This was IT! A sheer red silk with the barest trace of silver woven into the fabric. The silver seemed to glint here and there, a reflection of the light rather than part of the material.

"This is perfect," Devon whispered. "I can see the silver centerpieces filled with flowers, the white china with its platinum band and the sterling silver dinnerware—all of it against this red silk."

"Okay. Here's what we do," Keke whispered. "I'll ask the prices of all of these. You pretend to be mildly interested in all of them. Let me do the bargaining."

LATE THAT AFTERNOON, Chad watched from Eddie's desk as a tall gaunt Asian woman sashayed up to Devon with the bored groom in tow. Just looking at Devon made his pulse kick up a notch.

"I'm looking for Lori Evans. I'm Phaedra Nitsu." She glanced at the man beside her. "Our wedding is Saturday."

Phaedra? A Greek name with a Japanese surname. What *were* her parents thinking? Never mind what they'd been thinking. Her parents must be rich. She was wearing enough bling-bling for a dozen women.

"I'm here to check on the arrangements for Saturday,"

Phaedra informed everyone in a raised voice. "Let's hurry. I have to be at the Halekulani spa by six."

The Halekulani—*house befitting heaven*—was the only five-star hotel on Oahu and charged accordingly. Chad knew the rehearsal dinner was being held at La Mer, the hotel's best restaurant. After a dinner there, Chad hoped the wedding caterer was really good. He hadn't wanted to worry Devon by telling her it was a new company. No one knew why Lori selected it.

That was the tricky part about destination weddings. Since the bride didn't live close, she couldn't see everything, sample every morsel of food. Off-island brides relied more heavily on the coordinator than if they had been married in their hometown.

Devon was already standing, regal in her own way. "I'm Devon Summers. I've taken Lori Evans's position."

Phaedra appeared baffled. "No one told me."

"Lori had family problems. Don't worry. I've coordinated weddings for the Cress Creek Country Club in Chicago for the last four years."

Phaedra seemed annoyed. She glanced at her fiancé. He shrugged.

"I've been with the Four Seasons, as well."

Chad grinned inwardly. That got them.

"Here is a mock-up of your tables at the dinner." She led the couple to the round table that Keke and Devon had only ten minutes ago completed setting up in the reception area. It featured the newly purchased red silk and had a complete place setting and flowers.

"Spectacular!" Phaedra turned toward her husband-to-be, "We're going to top Missy Okehu's wedding in spades!"

He kissed her, obviously more interested in the honeymoon than the ceremony. During the prolonged liplock, Chad winked at Devon. Her suggestion of a smile gave him a hot little buzz.

"Wait," cried the bride, springing from her fiancé's arms.

"I ordered plain red tablecloths. This must cost a fortune. My father will kill me. I'm *waaay* over budget already."

The groom put his arm around his fiancé. "Change it back to regular tablecloths."

Chad watched Devon put a soothing hand on Phaedra's shoulder. "There's no additional cost. We want weddings suited to each special person." She gestured toward the table. "This shouts *you!* It's sophisticated, unusual."

Chad smiled at Eddie, who was pretending to be working on his computer, while actually watching the scene. Devon was a real find. Maybe too good a find, Chad decided. Why did she "watch her back" the way Special Forces did?

He planned to get to know her a whole lot better. That would mean finding out what secret she was hiding. The place to start was a background check.

"The silk on your tables and chairs was woven almost sixty years ago for Madam Chiang Kai-Shek just before the Communists drove her from China to Taiwan. You're looking at history—not an ordinary wedding."

"Perfect," Phaedra squealed. "No ordinary wedding for me."

CHAPTER NINE

BROCK HARDESTY STUDIED the program for the Miami Classic Car show. "Unfuckingbelievable!"

Someone was showing a one-of-a-kind Gull Wing Mercedes. According to Mercedes Benz this was the only 300 SL coupe ever factory painted caper-green.

He read the owner's name out loud. "Jordan Walsh." He'd never heard of him. Brock knew everyone in the elite group of Gull Wing owners who showed. This jerk must have just gotten into it.

Brock was standing outside the Miami Convention Center where the cars were lined up to be washed before they were moved inside. Brock always arrived early with the transport crew and supervised the unloading. Even though specialized companies charged outrageous prices to shuttle cars around the show circuit, he didn't trust them not to put a scratch or a ding on his babies.

Glancing at his Rolex, he saw time was slipping away. He carried his laptop with him. He should be working on it right now, but the wash crew might show up any second.

He kept his laptop with him every minute he could. The dumb-fucks at the Pentagon didn't keep track of their computers, and several had disappeared. Who knew what happened to the top secret information on them?

To keep up with his workload and show his cars, Brock had downloaded material that was never supposed to leave Obelisk. The laptop was in the closet safe in his hotel room. He could be in his room working, but no.

He was still *waiting* for the wash crew. They had a dolly with canisters of deionized water and lint-free towels. Most owners let them wash their cars.

Not Brock. He paid them and borrowed their equipment. He loved washing his cars, loved drying them even better. The sensual feel of their curves and the smoothness of their hoods under his hands gave him a hard-on.

If there were people nearby, he didn't get an erection. Like sex, detailing his cars was best done in private. That's why he stored them in a small building outside D.C. where his cars were alone in the facility. He didn't want anyone around when he tended to his babies.

The wash crew was still nowhere in sight. Brock decided to walk down the long line to see if the rare Gull Wing had arrived. About half the cars expected for the show were in line to be washed, and crews were unloading more every minute.

There were a few owners around, but Brock didn't know them. His work consumed so much of his time that he didn't bother with anyone unless they owned a car like one of his.

Ahead he saw it. Caper-green. Shit! Capers were those greenish brown things chefs threw on fish and stuff. Looked like bird turds.

This green was nothing like that. It was a mossy-green with a radiance to it that suggested a dollop of silver had been added to the mixture.

His Gull Wing was great, but this one was fabulous. The only one in existence. How many collectors could *ever* say that? He lovingly ran his finger along the hood.

He would kill for this car.

"Isn't she beautiful?"

Brock flinched at the sound of the female voice behind him. He slowly turned around and nearly lost it. The voice belonged to a dynamite redhead with knockers that jutted out like a Bugatti's headlights.

"She?" He grinned at the broad and managed to sound

cool. "Ships and hurricanes are named after women. Automobiles are male testosterone machines."

"We now have male hurricanes."

He liked the humor in her voice. He hadn't had a date in over two years. Between his cars and Obelisk, he couldn't find the time. A quickie at the auto show would get his rocks off. He'd be set for another two years.

"This Gull Wing's female. I'm positive."

"What makes you so sure?" he asked as he calculated how long it would take him to wash his three cars. Afterward they could meet for dinner. He'd taken a suite at the Delano where all the rich car owners stayed. He'd bet the redhead would be impressed enough to hop in the sack with him.

"She's my car. She told me so."

Brock blinked to let the words register. "Your car?"

She offered her hand. "Yes. I'm Jordan Walsh."

"Brock Hardesty." He barely croaked out the words. A woman owned this priceless classic. Unfuckingbelievable.

"I know you." The answer had a purring sound to it that resonated in Brock's groin.

"Really? How?"

"I've loved Gull Wings forever. I've seen yours at shows."

"Really?" He must be losing it. Hundreds even thousands of pretty women had admired his car, but surely he would have remembered a knockout redhead with Bugatti tits.

"Yes. I always wanted a car to show, but I didn't have the money. In the last couple of years, things changed. My XtremeX Web site paid off."

He didn't give a flying fuck about her Web site. "Where did you find this car?"

She let out a little squeak of excitement and bounced on the ice-pick heels she was wearing. The Bugattis jiggled and heat rushed to his pecker. "You're not going to believe it!"

"Try me."

"My brother sells custom wheels in Sioux City. Some farmer brought—" she pointed to the car's gleaming wheels with the caper green hubcaps "—her wheels in. He wanted fifty bucks for the set."

All the air was siphoned from his lungs. A jewel, the only one on the planet had been languishing, unloved, unappreciated with some stupid-ass farmer who didn't know each wheel on *any* Gull Wing was worth more than the average farmer made in a year.

"Of course, Danny—he's my brother—asked about the car. The farmer had it in his barn. In the *barn*. Can you imagine?"

"Actually, I can. Lots of classic cars have turned up in odd places with people who hadn't a clue what they were worth. May I ask what you paid for it?"

She winked at him, and he decided she was just his type. A sense of humor. Classy. She had a major set of Bugattis, but she didn't flaunt them. Her black turtleneck sweater covered her and wasn't too tight.

"Brock, this is where the story gets good. The farmer wanted five hundred dollars for it. You know, being a Mercedes and all."

Brock thought he might upchuck. "You paid five—"

"No, silly," she replied with another sexy wink. "I couldn't cheat that dear old guy. I paid him twenty-five thousand dollars for it."

Brock roared. This was one smart broad. If she'd paid him the measly amount he'd wanted and he'd later found out the Gull Wing's true value, he would have had grounds for a lawsuit.

"I put it on a truck and shipped it back to Falls Church where I had it restored."

"You live in Falls Church?" When she bobbed her head, he added, "I live in D.C."

"Oh, my! We're neighbors."

This just kept getting better and better.

The light dawned. The fucking Bugattis had distracted him. Restored in Falls Church. The Gull Wing had languished in a barn. It had to be repainted. Trust a broad to add silver to the green. If this wasn't the original paint, it wasn't one-of-a-kind. It was *merely* another restored 300 SL.

This realization cheered him so much that he chuckled. He could hardly wait to report this infraction of the strict rules to the attention of the committee chairman, Gilbert Everhardt. He was a tight ass bent on upholding even the most minor rule.

"What's so funny?"

"I thought this was the original paint. Caper-green. I've never seen a caper this color. No wonder. It's been repainted. Whoever did the blending was a little off."

"You're wrong about that."

Brock resisted a cutting remark. After all he intended to screw this broad's brains out.

"The car hadn't been properly cared for. The paint was beyond restoration. I might not have bought it." She smiled sweetly. "You see, I didn't want just another Gull Wing. So I called Germany, and guess what? They still had the original paint."

Fuck. Double fuck. Trust the Nazis to keep paint for fifty years, and it would still be good. His cell phone chose that moment to vibrate. He pulled it off his belt. It was his source at the DoD.

"Excuse me," he told her. "I'll be right back."

He walked out of hearing range. "Yeah."

"I just heard from the vet."

That was their code for finding out something about the Defense Department's top secret project.

"Give me your number."

He memorized it and went to find a pay phone. His operative was already at a pay phone. He hated leaving the Gull Wing and the broad, but this was business. A bank of pay phones lined the side wall of the convention center.

He found one not in use, dialed the number and his operative picked up before the first ring was over. "I know the location of the device they're testing."

"What is it? I'm not wasting money sending one of my guys after it until I know if it's worth it. The DoD tests lots of crap that's just a waste of taxpayer dollars like thousand dollar toilet seats."

"It's worth it. Believe me."

Brock listened to the description of the handheld device that could use thermal imaging to track people even at night.

If Brock brought this device to Obelisk, he could leave the bunker and take over the CEO's job. This technology, provided it worked, would revolutionize surveillance.

"I'll see you get a bonus."

He hung up without another word and called Operative 777, a new man he'd put in the field after the debacle in Santa Fe. This agent wouldn't hesitate to kill if necessary, but he wouldn't muff it.

Excited, Brock hurried back to the broad's Gull Wing. It was still there, but Jordan Walsh was gone.

KEKE SNUGGLED into the crook of Paul's arm. They'd finally gotten Lui to sleep, and they were down the hall in their own bed. The plantation style shutters were wide-open. Fragrant plumeria scented the darkness, mingling with the loamy earthy smell of the tropics.

"Lui's just like Chad was," Keke told Paul. "He never needed sleep like other little boys. There would be noise in the middle of the night, and we would find Chad in the kitchen playing with his Erector set. That was the best case scenario. Often he was getting into things. Once he wanted to learn how to use the electric can opener. He opened *every* can in the pantry and had them displayed on the kitchen table when we got up. He couldn't understand why my parents were upset."

Paul kissed her forehead. "Look on the up side. If we can survive Lui's youth, he'll make millions and support us in his old age, the way Chad helps everyone in the family now."

Keke peeled back the sheet. Lordy, was it warm tonight. Where were the trades when you needed them?

"Hey, speaking of Chad, how did your day with what's-her-name go?"

They made a pact not to discuss things in front of the children. Lui was too likely to repeat anything he heard—or saw. She hadn't told Paul about today's foray into Chinatown.

"Her name is Devon Summers. As you might expect, knowing my brother, she's smart and very attractive."

"Blond, no doubt."

"You know Chad has a weakness for blondes. But this woman is different. I can't explain it exactly. She's nice but not too friendly. I asked her a few questions about where she came from. You know, normal stuff. She answered, but it was almost as if...I don't know exactly, but I had the feeling she would rather live in the moment."

"What a surprise. How many people move here to get away from something? Thousands every year."

"Devon is different. I can feel it."

"Sweetie...mind your own business." He ran his hand up the curve of her thigh, and she knew he wanted sex.

"I am. I haven't said anything to either one of them about the other, but I am worried about Chad. I think he's in over his head with this woman."

"Hul-lo! They haven't even had a date. How could a Delta Force guy who specialized in Black Ops be in over his head anyway?"

"I don't know but I have this feeling. Ane told me—"

"That old crone? Gimme a break."

Paul's heritage was Japanese. He didn't understand about women like Ane. She reminded Keke of her own mother. They clung to the traditions and customs of old Hawaii, a time whose sunset was fast approaching.

"I know you don't believe in the tales of the past, but one of the most widely held beliefs is that Pele, the goddess—"

"I know. Her ghost takes the guise of a young woman who is found along the side of the road—"

"With a dog. Devon has a golden retriever named Zachary."

"So? She wasn't found along side of the road." Paul sounded exasperated and she knew his cultural background made it difficult to appreciate Hawaiian lore.

"I know, I know. It's bad luck not to help her."

Kids on Hawaii, of any ancestry, knew the myth, but those with native Hawaiian blood were notoriously superstitious. There had always been a cultural divide between Paul and Keke. His father had accepted her, but he'd died shortly after their wedding. His mother was never going to forgive her for not being at least part Japanese.

"I was raised with these stories, Paul. There's a kernel of truth in them."

"Show me the kernel in the Pele's ghost myth."

"It's bad luck to turn your back on someone who needs your help."

Paul heaved a sigh. "God save us from women."

"Oh, save yourself—" she slipped on top of him "—if you can."

"I love you."

Keke smiled, her warm belly against his. "I've never loved you more than when Lui asked about your pee-pee, and your mother wanted to know what show they'd been watching. You think on your feet. I would never have thought to say it was a Jockey commercial."

He ran has hands over her bare bottom. "I'm good at other things, too. Wanna see?"

"You're not having lurid thoughts, are you?"

CHAPTER TEN

BROCK CONGRATULATED himself as he walked away from the front desk at the Delano. Jordan Walsh had checked in as he thought she would. The Web site for 300 SL Coupes owners—GullWings.com—had announced the group would be staying here.

Each year when the show came to Miami, the group stayed at the Delano. Why? Brock didn't have a clue. Every friggin' room was white. White walls, pillows, chair, sheets. Nothing but white.

Some idiot had put a bed in the lobby. People sat on it instead of chairs. Made no sense to Brock. At the prices they charged, the hotel could afford a few comfortable sofas like the Four Seasons.

A young punk with tattooed biceps and a diamond stud in his nose lay sprawled on the lobby bed. Chattering groupies surrounded him. Some rock star, Brock decided as he walked by. The place was always crawling with butt-ugly punks who made megabucks with music that fractured eardrums.

He figured they stayed here because the place was as weird as they were, and Madonna owned the hotel's Blue Door restaurant. The food was good, but the view of the palm-lined pool with nearly naked babes everywhere was the best thing about the place.

He left the lobby and walked toward the martini bar. It was a long narrow table set at an odd angle, tall barstools lining both sides. Tiny glass halogen bulbs dangled from filament wires to give the bar a touch of light while leaving the surrounding area in shadows.

He spotted Jordan Walsh sitting alone at the far end of the bar. She had changed into a black dress with a V-neck. It showed off enough of her Bugatti tits to be sexy but not slutty. Her red hair provocatively brushed her shoulders and glistened in the glow of the halogens.

"What are you drinking?" he asked as he walked up and saw her with a Martini glass full of black liquid.

"A Black Dahlia Martini. Vodka with Chambord. It's yummy."

Looked and sounded gross but he kept it to himself. "I'm a single malt guy."

He slipped onto the barstool beside her, and sneaked a look at the swell of those Bugattis just visible along her neckline. Soft, creamy white skin, the kind a true redhead would have. No doubt she had a flaming pussy, too.

"Which is your favorite?" she asked.

"Knockando," he replied without hesitation. The waitress drifted by them and he ordered the Scotch on the rocks.

"Ah, a Speyside malt."

Startled, Brock stared at her. Few women knew much about the great scotch distilleries.

"I've traveled extensively in Scotland," she told him. "I'm familiar with the Highland malts, the Lowland malts, the Island malts. Speyside is in the heartland of whiskey distilling. Glenfiddich, Glenlivet, and Macallan are better known, but Knockando is right up there."

He bristled a little, wondering if she were implying he'd selected a great malt but one that was inferior to the *really* big single malt names. He hadn't begun drinking single malts until he'd come to Obelisk where Kilmer Cassidy guzzled it. He'd taken to drinking Knockando because it was a little offbeat.

He refused to be one of the herd. Those other single malts could be found in any supermarket. You had to look a little harder to find Knockando. Of course a five-star hotel like the Delano would have it.

"This my first show," Jordan told him. "I'm nervous."

"People will ask a lot of dumb questions," he replied, deciding he was being too sensitive. Jordan didn't disapprove of his taste in liquor. "Just remember not to let them touch the car. Oil from their hands will ruin the paint."

She took a tiny sip of her martini. He couldn't help noticing her delicious red lips. He imagined that succulent mouth around his cock. He had a woodie in half a second.

"Do you have dinner plans?" he asked, his mind actually on getting her up to his room after eating.

"I'm having dinner with Horst at Nemo's."

Shit! Horst Trensen IV was the Gull Wing Association's president. The cocksucker had never worked a day in his life. He'd made his money the old-fashioned way—he'd inherited it. Well, one day soon Brock was going to be just as rich. He would leave Obelisk and devote himself to collecting cars.

Maybe Jordan would be willing to sell hers. The glamour of the show circuit would wear off after a few shows. If she refused to sell, there were other ways to take care of the problem. It was one of the perks of his job.

"I'm free tomorrow night," Jordan said.

"Great. I'll make reservations at Tuscan Steak for eight o'clock."

The waitress delivered his scotch, and he asked, "Would you like another martini?"

Jordan shook her head. "More than one and I do crazy things."

Brock would have to remember that. He scribbled his room number on the tab and added a five percent tip. He saw no reason to overtip cocktail waitresses for doing basically nothing.

"There's Horst. He's early."

Brock saw Horst swaggering toward them. Picking up his drink, he said, "I'm taking this up to my room. I've got work to do."

"Really? What do you do?"

"I'm at the Pentagon. Top secret stuff. If I tell you, I'll have to kill you."

She laughed, a mellow tinkling sound. "Go on. You don't mean it."

Brock chuckled. The broad had no idea just how much he did mean it. He would allow her a little fun with the car and himself time to have fun in the sack with her. But if she didn't sell him the car, he would kill her.

CHAD STOOD in his empty living room and watched Keke, Hana, and Nola drape folding chairs with the red fabric and tie it in place with big bows. Off to the side, Devon was covering a table. His sisters were chattering about their children, but Devon had hardly said a word.

He'd checked the references she'd listed on the employment form Eddie had given her. Both the Cress Creek Country Club and the Four Seasons had called him back with the information. Devon had been an excellent employee and was welcome to return at any time.

He'd Googled her, but came up with nothing, which seemed a bit odd. Most people had their name in the paper occasionally, and it went onto Google's database. He'd originally told himself that he was doing this to protect Eddie, but he wasn't fooling himself now. The mysterious Devon Summers must be up to something.

He walked up to her asking, "Where's Zach?"

She glanced briefly at him just long enough to be polite. "I left him at the office. I didn't want him shedding on your beautiful floors."

"Don't worry about it."

Her back was to him and she was bending over. Great buns. Every time he got close to her his pulse rate spiked. He was undeniably attracted to her, but she didn't seem to feel a thing for him.

"Zach's welcome any time. Bring him tomorrow."

"Thank you. I will."

There was a smoldering quality to her remarkable eyes. This close he could see it, feel it. Her subtle yet provocative citrus scent conjured up X-rated images.

Shelby drifted in, late as usual. "Hi, there. Tell me what to do," she said to Devon.

"Start draping chairs. Keke will show you how."

"I found, like, this amazing, awesome tip," Shelby responded. "Diamond engagement rings should be cleaned with vodka."

"Shelby, what do you get when you cross a Labrador and a Bloodhound?" Devon asked.

"I give. What?"

"A Blabador."

Shelby giggled, and Chad decided Devon's jokes were her way of counteracting Shelby's obsession with wedding trivia.

"Now get to work," Devon told the girl.

Chad said goodbye to his sisters and left for the office. On the way there he decided to drive by Devon's place. Call it morbid curiosity, but he wanted to see where she lived.

The area wasn't exactly the best part of town, but it was probably all Devon could afford. The street she lived on was more commercial than Chad had anticipated. He couldn't remember the last time he'd driven along it. There were one or two rat trap apartment buildings, but it was mostly businesses.

He slowed down his Porsche and double-checked the number Devon had given as her address. Son of a bitch! It was Mailboxes in Paradise, a chain of mail delivery stores that also sold office supplies.

He parked his car and walked down to the Stop N Go Minimart. By using a pay phone, his caller ID wouldn't show up on Devon's telephone. That was assuming she'd given Eddie her correct home phone number.

On the second ring, Devon answered, "Hello...hello."

Chad immediately realized she'd put down her cell phone number. Maybe she couldn't afford another phone. Still it didn't explain why she hadn't given her home address.

"Hello? Hello?" Chad was about to hang up, when she said, "Warren is that you? We have a bad connection."

Chad hung up and stood staring at the pay phone. Who in hell was Warren? He walked back to his car, trying to think of some reasonable explanation for her behavior.

Devon was definitely up to something, he decided. She didn't seem to be the dishonest type. Kicking himself mentally, he shoved the key in the ignition. How in hell did he know? The woman barely talked, to him or anyone else.

By the time he'd reached his office, Chad had come up with a plan. It would be easy to hack into the databases of the water and power companies. He breezed by Ane, who had a few messages but nothing important, and went to his computer.

The firewall was so outdated that it took him less than three minutes to access the power company's files. Devon Summers's name did not exist in their database. She didn't exist in the water or gas company records, either.

What in hell was going on?

Maybe she had a roommate, he thought, or perhaps she rented a room from someone. That would explain not having accounts in her name. Somehow he saw Devon as a loner. He couldn't imagine her renting a room, especially with a dog, and he couldn't see her sharing quarters with another person.

His gut instinct, fine-tuned during his years with Special Ops, told him Devon lived alone. He was right about this. He knew he was.

DEVON HAD WALKED OUTSIDE Chad's living room to answer her cell phone. The only person who had the number was Warren. When the connection malfunctioned, she tried calling Warren back, but was transferred to his pager. She IMed him to call her back ASAP.

She walked across the yard to make certain no one could overhear her conversation with her handler. She'd never called him before, but she knew he was supposed to be available 24/7. Her phone rang less than a minute later.

"Is there trouble?" Warren asked.

"No. I thought you called me."

"Get back to me on a secure line." Warren hung up.

Devon knew how paranoid WITSEC was about using cell phones. What went out over the airwaves could easily be monitored by anyone with a cheap scanner from Radio Shack. She wasn't sure where the nearest pay phone was but none were close. A big house like Chad's had lots of telephones and a local call surely wouldn't be noticed.

She found a sleek black telephone in the kitchen and phoned Warren. She asked, "Did you call me about something?"

"No."

"I guess it was a wrong number then. Someone called and hung up. I thought it was a bad connection."

Two beats of silence. "Probably was a wrong number."

"That's it. Nothing else to report. I—"

"How's the job going?"

"Great. We're really busy with a big wedding. We're holding it at Chad Langston's beachfront home in the Kahala area. Do you know him?"

"No. Should I run a check on him?"

Devon told herself she didn't want to know anything more about Chad. It was difficult enough to keep her mind off him as it was. "No."

"Your boss checked your references."

Puzzled, Devon asked, "After he'd hired me?"

"A little strange but..."

"I'm doing a good job—"

"Don't worry about it," Warren told her. "The Cress Creek Country Club and the Four Seasons forwarded the inquiry, and our people called back."

Eddie seemed too harried by the snafu with Inoye's niece's wedding to suddenly check her references, she decided. "Do you know what telephone number they called?"

"I could find out. What's going on?"

"Nothing. I just wondered."

After a moment of silence, he said, "I'll get back to you with the number."

"Okay." Devon stared around the enormous kitchen with the white lacquered cabinets and sleek black granite counters. It was hard to imagine Chad preparing a meal in here. "Is it safe to call my sister yet?"

"This Saturday."

Relief surged through her. It had been almost four months since she'd spoken with Tina and her niece, Ariel. It had been over two years since she'd seen them. She shouldn't get too excited. Saturday was Phaedra Natsui's wedding. Devon would be on the run from dawn until God-only-knew-when. Her first conversation with Tina and Ariel would be a short one.

At least she was getting to talk to them. Sometimes the weight of her memories of those happy days when she could hop on a plane and visit her sister was unbearable. She longed to feel safe again. To sleep one night without fear.

"There is some good news," Warren told her. "We're transferring your things from your condo in Santa Fe to your apartment here. They should arrive within the week."

"Great," she replied halfheartedly. She had clothes and office stuff WITSEC had sent after she'd left Houston. The clothes were too heavy to wear here, and since she couldn't work in accounting, the disks and software weren't of much use. Worse, they'd just take up space in her small studio.

"WITSEC rigged it to have your condo go into foreclosure. That way we can remove your belongs and sell the place without attracting too much attention."

"Good. I can use the money." Wait, she thought, remembering the disaster in Santa Fe. "Don't transfer the money here. I think that may be the way they found me last time."

"I doubt it. We do double blind transfers."

"I don't care. Keep the money for now."

"You owe WITSEC for the cosmetic surgery."

"Fine," she said with sarcasm. "Deduct that amount. Then let the rest sit. I don't want to take any unnecessary chances."

"Okay. It's your call."

She hung up and went back to draping the serving tables. A few minutes later, her telephone rang again. "Call me back on a secure line."

Devon wandered into the house and hoped no one noticed. Chad's sisters were too busy draping chairs and chatting about their children to pay attention to her. She called Warren, and he rattled off the number WITSEC had called to give her references.

"That's not the number of our office," she said, a frission of alarm waltzing across the back of her neck. "I guess it could be Eddie's cell phone."

"Christ! Lemme get back to you."

She gave him the number on the kitchen telephone, then hung up. She wondered how reliable WITSEC was. Someone inside the system might be leaking info to her former bosses. If she'd known then what she knew now, she would have anonymously contacted the FBI, left PowerTec, and found a new job. Then she would still have her life, her family.

The phone rang a few minutes later, and she answered it before the first ring was over.

"It's a cell phone number," Warren told her, his voice brusque. "It belongs to Chad Langston."

Devon wasn't surprised. Chad was interested in her, and he had access to Eddie's records.

"What do you know about Langston?"

"Not much." She explained what she knew about Chad Langston

Warren was silent for a moment. "I'll run a background check on him."

It was less than an hour later when Warren called again and had her use the secure line.

"This sucks," Warren said. "Langston was with Delta Force during the Gulf War."

"So?"

"So! So they are the best of the best. It's a multiservice unit that culls the top guys from all the branches of the military for Special Ops. You know, covert operations."

"What does that have to do with me?"

"Not only can he survive behind enemy lines with nothing, but he knows how to use all sorts of high tech equipment. He can find out a lot about you that a regular guy couldn't. He did research for DARPA after his military tour was over."

"DARPA?"

"It's the advanced research division of the Department of Defense. Top secret stuff. They employ the best scientists in every field. Not just any Delta Force guy works with them."

"Interesting."

Now she knew why she found Chad so attractive. He acted like a jock but a brilliant mind glimmered through. He'd gone to Stanford and had made Delta Force. She'd always found bright men incredibly attractive. Of course Chad took this to a new level. He was way sexier than most men she'd been drawn to.

Sexier than Tyler, she decided. A twinge of hurt pierced the armor she'd erected around her emotions. She tamped it down. Tyler had never really loved her or he wouldn't have found someone else so quickly.

She told herself to forget the past, forget how attractive Chad was. Concentrate on the clear and present danger. Her life depended upon it.

"Langston's going to figure out you aren't who you say you are in no time. You need to have a cover story ready or I'll have to relocate you."

Relocation. She honestly didn't think she could face another relocation. She loved Hawaii. The astounding beauty and the rich heritage of this place had captivated her. When the trial was over, she planned to return here to live.

If they moved her again, it would be months more before

she was allowed to speak to her sister. She honestly didn't think she could survive another relocation.

She told Warren, "I'll have a good cover story ready."

"Clue me in so I can backstop it."

"I'll call you later."

CHAPTER ELEVEN

CHAD PICKED UP the telephone on his desk. He expected his buddy, Rafe Kalama to be calling him back with the info on Devon Summers's DMV application. It wasn't Rafe on the phone. Instead he heard Archer Danson's terse voice.

"Yo, Langston call this number from a secure line." Danson rattled off a number and hung up.

"I'll be back in a minute," Chad told Ane as he left.

Across the street at the Ala Wai Boat Harbor, he used the public phone booth to call Danson. Undoubtedly he was at a public telephone, too, so no one could trace their calls.

"We've got trouble," Danson announced the second he picked the telephone. "Big trouble."

"Okay. Shoot."

"I had another operative testing the device."

Chad wasn't surprised. The "device" which had yet to have a name was too revolutionary to leave the testing to one person.

"Like you, he was no longer in the military, out-of-the-loop," Danson continued. "Last night someone slit his throat and stole the device."

"Jesus! Any idea how they found him?"

"There's a leak at the DARPA. I've got an operative on it, but nothing much so far." Obviously frustrated, Danson huffed. "Where's your device?"

"At home." He didn't add that it was sitting on his night-stand where anyone could grab it, if they searched his house.

"Lock it up when you're not testing it."

"I have a safe," Chad replied. "If they have the tracking device, why would they bother to steal another?"

"It's like the drone."

"Son of a bitch! Why didn't you tell me?"

DARPA had developed the Predator drone in total secrecy. Only one set of plans for the unmanned aerial vehicle had existed. It was tested in total secrecy. When DARPA revealed it, the military was astonished. The Predator became a huge success, saving untold numbers of lives.

"Langston, you worked at DARPA. I assumed you would know this device is every bit as revolutionary as the drone."

"I expected it to have flaws," Chad admitted, "and to be years in the testing."

"This is the final round of tests."

"Are the plans safe?"

"Absolutely. Couldn't be safer. But whoever took the tracker may want to disassemble one to see how it's set up while leaving the other intact. If that's the case, they'll go after yours."

"Makes sense. Any idea who 'they' are?"

"Terrorists probably, but I could be wrong. Could be a rogue military group."

Chad took that to mean the CIA. Friction between the Central Intelligence Division and the Defense Department ran high.

"They could only know about me from the payroll records. Right?"

"Yes. Your military service file has been deleted from the deactivated database. The only record is in the payroll department. It shows you're a private at Fort Hood."

"I guess that would throw them off track. To be safe, forget paying me. I'll do it free. Just say it's my way of paying back the country."

"Great. I'll delete your name from the payroll and delete from the system the records of the payments we've already made," Danson told him with a smile in his voice. "I want you to watch your back just the way you did in Black Ops."

Chad resisted the urge to correct Danson. He'd performed a number of covert operations, but he'd been trained to call them Special Ops. Black Ops sounded like the CIA, when it was up to no good.

"There wasn't any need to kill my operative in order to get the device. It was done for sport or something."

"Uh-oh." Chad wondered if he knew the guy. He was probably ex-military, too. Danson wouldn't tell him, but if he watched the news, he might find out.

Chad hung up, cursing himself. Years in laid-back Hawaii had blunted his well-honed instincts. He couldn't blame Danson for not warning him. He knew DARPA didn't go to outside sources for testing often. He needed to hunker down into military mode again.

Think danger.

Think death.

If he didn't, he could be the next guy with his throat slit.

By the time Chad returned to his office, Rafe had called. Chad could have hacked into the DMV database himself, but it was cleaner to have a policeman log in his badge number and get the information. Since the police routinely checked DMV records, there was little chance the inquiry would ever be noticed.

He dialed Rafe's cell, and his friend answered immediately. "Can you talk?"

"Sure. I'm just filling out paperwork. Here's what was on the driver's license application Devon Summers filled out."

Chad jotted down the info, then asked, "What's the date on the application?"

He listened, thinking Devon had lied to them. She had been in Honolulu a full month longer than she'd told them. What had she been doing?

He thought about the way Devon had come out of nowhere to apply for a job, when she undoubtedly could have gotten a job at one of the resort hotels for more money. Why? Had she known his office was opposite Walt's? Could she be after the second device?

If Devon Summers was after him, she had more talent than most. She had him believing she didn't give a damn about him. He thought about what Keke had said. Sometimes playing hard-to-get worked wonders. Female operatives were often much more successful than men because they had a gift for deception.

He thought about Danson's warning. *Watch your back.* One man had already been killed. That should justify what he was about to do.

It took him a few minutes on his computer to remember exactly how to access the major credit reporting agencies. It was illegal, of course, but it could be done. DARPA and other government agencies did it to check on terrorists and drug kingpins who usually paid for everything in cash, people who didn't have credit histories like hardworking Americans.

"Hey, what do you know," he muttered under his breath.

There was Devon Lynn Summers. Charge accounts at Marshall Fields and Bonwit Tellers. A car loan on a Beamer. An American Express Card. A Visa. A student loan that had been paid off several years ago.

Conscious of not breaking the law for any longer than possible, he exited the program and shut down his computer. She had an excellent credit history—back there—but she hadn't done anything here. Why not?

THE FIRST DAY of the show was almost over, and Brock managed to smile at the group clustered around his Gull Wing, but his gut was churning like a snake pit. Three times as many people were crowded around the caper-green Gull Wing across the way from him. Horst was standing beside Jordan, preening as if he owned the one-of-a-kind car.

Shit! What if Jordan sold the Gull Wing to Horst? Brock wouldn't allow that. He wanted that car as much as he'd wanted anything in his entire life.

His cell phone vibrated, and he pulled it off his belt. It was Operative 77, the up-and-coming agent he'd sent after the gadget DARPA had developed. He walked away from his

Gull Wing toward an open space where he could talk without being overheard.

"What's happening?" he asked.

"I've got it."

"Great. Did you..."

"Numero Uno, I took care of things like you told me to."

Perfect! This was the kind of operative he liked. Someone who did exactly what he was told. Not a fuckup like the woman who blew it in Santa Fe. What's more, the guy was smart enough not to say he'd slit someone's throat while they were talking on cell phones.

"Got anything else for me?" 77 asked.

Brock pivoted and watched Jordan laugh at something Horst had said. "Not right now, but maybe later. Hand deliver the device to Obelisk on Monday."

Brock strolled back to his car cheered by the news. With this new gadget in his possession, he could write his own ticket at Obelisk.

His phone vibrated again and he pulled it off his belt. Kilmer Cassidy, the CEO of Obelisk, was on the line. What did the prick want now?

"Anything on that Robbins woman?" Cassidy asked for the hundredth time since the bitch had disappeared.

"I'm working on it."

"No progress at all?"

Brock detested the way Cassidy talked down to him as if he were some flunky. "We've eliminated several states. I'm working on the others."

"How?"

"Checking new DMV records."

"WITSEC gives every witness a new birth certificate and social security card. They must get a driver's license on their own. Right?"

"Exactly. I'm relying on AgeComp to tell us if she's altered her appearance," Brock replied, referring to the age-progression software that had been developed to change the appearances of missing children as they grew older. Cassidy had heard all this before, but the greedy cocksucker had nothing better to do than harass Brock and check the offshore accounts.

"What if she's in some big city where she doesn't need a car?"

"That's always a possibility, but a remote one." He explained—yet again—how he'd figured Samantha Robbins was out west. "The only city where she wouldn't need a car is San Francisco. WITSEC usually puts witnesses in less charming spots."

"Santa Fe has plenty of charm."

"True, but—"

"I say we tap her sister's phone. I've said so all along. Do it."

Cassidy hung up before Brock could reply. He cursed under his breath. Wire tapping the sister's telephone probably wouldn't help. Unless Samantha let something drop that would tell them where she was, they could spend eons listening and get nothing. Worse, they might be caught.

Every listening device—no matter how sophisticated— emitted a tiny electronic signal. He would bet his life WITSEC had their special software program monitoring the sister's telephone. He needed to come up with a better plan. The key to finding someone was in their habits. You could change a lot about a person, but habits stayed constant.

BY THE TIME Devon finished the last chair and said goodbye to Keke and her sisters, it was almost eight o'clock. If Chad had returned home, he hadn't come out to see them. She drove across town, thinking about him, her eyes on the rearview mirror to see if she were being followed.

Watching, all instincts alert, she checked the cars behind her, beside her, and even those in front of her. Experience had shown trouble could come from any direction, from out of nowhere. When you least expected it.

She had a cover story ready. Would Chad buy it? He was intelligent, and she wasn't a very good actress. She was better now than before, Devon silently admitted. Being in WITSEC had transformed her into a person she no longer knew.

A person she didn't like or trust.

The cell phone in her pocket vibrated. Her shoulders jerked back as if she'd received a shock. She had another phone in her purse, but since she'd been here, she'd received only a few calls—days apart. All of them had been from Warren. She fumbled in her pocket and pulled out the cell phone.

"Where are you?" Warren asked.

"I'm on South King Street on my way to get Zach. He's still at the office."

"Meet me at King Kamehameha's statue."

"Do I have time to pick up Zach?"

"No."

Suddenly she heard the dial tone. Cold prickled her scalp and sweat dappled the back of her shoulders. Something was wrong.

She parked her rusted-out Toyota at the Federal Building near the Aliiolani Hale, the State Supreme Court building. The building's stunning architecture had surprised Devon, when she'd first seen it. Instead of being built of coral, the way many of the original buildings were, this one was a Spanish-California design. She supposed it was a testament to the way the island had succumbed to foreign influences over the years.

In a square facing King Street stood King Kamehameha's statue. The black and gold monument of the imposing warrior-chief who united the islands was remarkable for its feathered cloak and tall spear. During the day, tourists flocked to the area to have their picture taken. It was dusk now, and a few Japanese tourists lingered, garlands of cameras around their necks.

She didn't immediately spot Warren, but she'd met him here often enough to know he would let her wander around for a few minutes before he casually joined her. She strolled through the area, alert for anyone she'd seen somewhere else. The people seemed to be a tour group from Japan. They scuttled across the street to visit the Iolani Palace, which in contrast to the Aliiolani Hale, was a Victoria monument complete with a Coronation Bandshell.

From her left, a shifting shadow caught her attention. Her ability to synthesize as much information as possible in seconds had become a survival skill. Warren, she realized, and her tense muscles relaxed.

"It's getting too dark to look at the palace," she whispered to him.

"S'okay," he replied. "I checked. It's a Nippon-Paradise Tour that's running late. No one in the group is a threat to you."

Warren was thorough. She would give him that. He wasn't as friendly as Derek, but he took his job seriously.

"WITSEC just alerted me," he told her, his voice low even though there wasn't anyone within earshot. "Someone accessed your DMV records."

She drew in a deep hitching breath. When she'd been warned someone was trying to access her records in Santa Fe, it had been the harbinger of trouble. More than trouble. Romero's throat had been slit, and the poor man had bled to death just for being her friend.

No matter what Curt Masterson had claimed, Devon believed Rutherford and Ames had obtained confidential information on her, either by paying off someone inside WITSEC or hiring a top-notch hacker.

"DMV records are fairly secure."

"Define fairly," she relied, bitterness burning in her tone. Once she would have believed him, but her experience in Santa Fe had proved how vulnerable she was.

"It takes a police ID number, usually a badge number to get the info. Cops need it for traffic violations."

"Great. All it would take would be a legit number to access the database."

"True, but it isn't all that easy. The officer has to put down the reason. Officer Rafer Kamala went into the DMV records two hours ago. The reason he gave was 'illegal parking.' That's common downtown."

"I *never* park illegally. I haven't gotten a ticket," she said, her mouth suddenly dry with apprehension. "You warned me to be careful."

He studied her for a long moment as if trying to decide if she were telling the truth. "Positive?"

"Absolutely."

They had reached the end of the walkway and had turned back. They moved along in silence for a few minutes. Devon watched the people around them, while appearing not to do so. No one seemed interested, but she'd learned the hard way that looks could be deceiving.

"With a name like Kamala, I'd say the cop is from the islands. Wonder where he went to school?"

She saw where he was going with this. "You think he knows Chad Langston."

"It wouldn't surprise me. The islands are tight. An 'us' and 'them' attitude prevails. 'Them' being—"

"The tourists."

"Right. I've been here seven years. I'm not a tourist, but I'm not quite accepted yet."

"I understand."

Warren stared down at the pavement for a moment before lifting his gaze to meet hers. "Look, we've done our best to protect you," he said, his tone apologetic for the first time since she'd known him. "We even did something we've rarely done to make Devon Summers a real person. We created a credit history for you."

She knew this wasn't standard policy. WITSEC gave everyone a new identity but it was up to the individual to get credit. Without a previous history, it was difficult. Masterson had done it for her because he wanted Devon Summers to appear to be a real person—should anyone check.

"I know. I don't mean to sound ungrateful...but I'm frightened. You see, this is beginning to feel like Santa Fe all over again."

The image of Romero flashed through her mind. She stared at the statue, then looked back at Warren. "I don't want anyone else to die. I don't want to leave, either."

"You said you had a plan. Run it by me now, or I'm relocating you ASAP."

CHAPTER TWELVE

KEKE SAW CHAD walking across the grass to where she sat with a group of parents watching their children play soccer.

"Hey, it's great you could make it," she said.

Chad took the seat beside her on the first rung of the bleachers. "I can't stay, but I want Lui to know I stopped by."

Keke smiled at her brother. Chad usually came to the games, and she knew it was because their father had been too busy to attend Chad's games when he was little. Managing the Turtle Bay Resort had been demanding. Paul was under the same stress, although her husband came to a game at least once a month.

"The coach just took Lui out. I'm sure he'll put him back in soon. He's one of the best players." Like you were, she wanted to add, but didn't. Chad felt responsible for the family. She didn't want to put more pressure on him by calling attention to how much like him Lui was.

Lui glanced toward the bleachers and saw his uncle. He gave a short little wave, too big a boy now to wave wildly at Chad. He would have six months ago, she thought. Time was passing much too quickly. Soon her babies would be grown.

"How'd it go after I left this morning?" her brother asked.

He wasn't looking at her. He was staring at the field. She had the feeling he was distracted.

"I went home early to take the kids to the dentist. They're getting fluoride treatments. Nola called to say they finished the chairs."

"Great." He looked around. "Where's Mei?"

Keke tipped her head toward the grassy area behind the soccer field. "She's with the younger children over there, playing tag. Susi Kameha is watching them."

Just then Mei looked over, spotted her uncle, and came scampering across the grass.

"You're in for it," Keke said with a laugh.

"I don't mind." Chad looked at her. "Has Lui's grandmother been to any of his games?"

"No. She's too busy volunteering with the Society to Preserve Hawaii's Native Plants and Flowers."

Chad didn't comment, but Keke knew what he was thinking. Their mother would never have missed a game. Paul's mother came each Wednesday to dinner. Once a month she had them for Sunday lunch. That was all the time she had for her grandchildren.

Mei bounded up to Chad, her little arm's outstretched. "Unka Chad, Unka Chad." She planted a smacking kiss on his cheek.

"Pehea oe?" How are you?

"Maikai." Fine.

Mei inclined her head coyly and gazed up at Chad with adoring blue eyes. Where did she learn to flirt? Keke wondered. Must be too much television.

"Want to see a nice doggy?" Chad asked.

"Yeah! Yeah!"

Keke asked, "Did you get a dog?"

Chad shook his head. "It's Devon's golden retriever. Let's go see Zach."

Keke stood, glancing quickly to the field to be certain Lui was still on the sidelines. Chad swooped up Mei and hoisted her onto his shoulders. They walked across the freshly mowed turf to the parking lot.

Keke saw a large honey-blond golden retriever with its head out the window of Chad's gleaming black Porsche. Her brother was getting too close—too fast—to this woman.

"Nice doggy," Chad said as they approached the car.

Keke saw the dog's tail whipping through the air. He was a handsome dog, she thought, regretting that Paul was allergic. Her children wouldn't be growing up with dogs and cats the way she had.

"Nice doggy," mimicked Mei.

Chad guided her small hand to the top of the retriever's head. "Pet him like this." He helped Mei pet the dog, then released her hand. Mei continued to stroke the dog. "His name is Zach."

"Nice Zash. Nice Zash." Mei gazed at Keke. "Mommy can we get a doggy like Zash?"

Mei knew the answer, but like most kids, she kept asking. "No, sweetie. Pets make Daddy sick. We don't want Daddy sick. Do we?"

Mei averted her head, her way of pouting. Keke knew it was difficult to understand, when most families had multiple pets and you had none. Maybe they could get a bird.

A tinkling noise announced the arrival of the ice-cream truck that came at half time. Mei squirmed in Chad's arms, and he set her down.

"Here's money for an ice cream." He pulled a five-dollar bill from his money clip. "Keep the change."

With round, gleaming eyes, Mei grabbed the bill. She started to charge off to join the line forming at the truck but stopped. She ran back to Chad, her arms raised. She gave him a quick smooch.

"Luv you, Unka Chad."

"Love you, honey," he replied.

She scampered off, and Keke thought, once again, what a great father her brother would make. Chad showed no signs of settling down, but he seemed unusually taken with Devon. Maybe she was "the one."

Keke hoped not. Devon was beautiful and sharp, but there was a remoteness about her. Keke couldn't see her sitting around all day at a *luau*, talking story with friends and family.

"What's with the dog?" she asked.

"Devon didn't come back to the office. She's probably tied up getting this wedding back on track. Eddie wanted to go home. I left Devon a note saying I had Zach with me."

"Without asking her?" Keke was surprised. This wasn't like her brother, but then there was something about Devon Summers that made him behave in uncharacteristic ways.

"I thought I was doing her a favor."

He sounds defensive, she decided as she watched him stroking the retriever's head through the open car window. Keke wasn't sure what to say. She pretended to be checking on Mei in the ice-cream line.

"You spent time with Devon," Chad said, the timbre of his voice changing. "What do you think of her?"

I think she has your number—big time. "Honestly?"

The harsh lines bracketing his lips softened. *"Hele. Hele."* Go on. Go on.

"I like Devon. She's intelligent and gorgeous, but there's something about her that's...distant or guarded or—I don't know. She's different."

Chad nodded rather solemnly, she thought.

"I can't help thinking about what Ane said," she said.

"Like Pele's ghost, Devon is going to disappear."

She knew Chad didn't put much stock in island lore. Oh, no. He was too much a man of the world now, but in the back of his mind, what their mother had taught them had to still be there. There was always a kernel of truth in those myths. Keke had a powerful premonition.

Devon wouldn't be with them long.

IT WAS NEARLY NINE-THIRTY when Rory came down to the beach to get Chad. He wasn't surprised to hear Devon Summers was at the door.

"Send her down here," he told Rory.

He'd deliberately taken Zach so Devon would have to come here to get her dog. He tossed the stick into the surf, and Zach bounded into the ocean. It was dark, but a hunter's moon flooded the sugar-fine beach with pale light. Chad had been standing in the dark and throwing the stick for Zach for the last twenty minutes.

The whole time his mind had been on Devon. He wanted to get her alone. He needed to talk to her and get a feel for what was going on inside that pretty head. She'd lied about when she'd arrived and lied about where she lived.

What else had she lied about? If she had nothing to hide, why hadn't she told the truth? What was she up to? Why was she working for a small outfit like Eddie's? He couldn't help remembering the way Eddie had been conned by the woman who'd held Shelby's position. Devon had a much more powerful job with a lot of latitude to sign bills and work with vendors.

Vendor kickbacks for business were a fact of life in Hawaii. Devon was probably too new to realize this, but it wouldn't take long. Knowing Eddie's nature, Devon must have sized him up already and knew she could take advantage of him if she wanted. He wondered—yet again—if he'd made a mistake by encouraging Eddie to hire Devon.

Devon walked across the pool area and spotted Chad at the water's edge. Some force stronger than her anger kept her from asking him what the hell he thought he was doing by taking her dog.

She watched Zach hurl himself with reckless abandon into the breaking surf, pursuing a stick. Chad had yet to notice her approaching, and she paused for a moment. Remember how much is at stake, she told herself.

Her stomach contracted. She hadn't eaten, but it was more than that. She'd been apprehensive since she'd returned to the office and read Chad's note. It had said he had taken Zach home, since she'd been working so late.

Why hadn't he just walked Zach and left him at the office? She had a key. There would have been no problem getting Zach after everyone had left. She was certain Chad was up to something. He'd been digging into her past, causing trouble.

Don't let your anxiety show and make Chad more suspicious, she cautioned herself. What was important was to implement the plan she had to handle Chad Langston. It had been difficult to convince Warren that this would work, but he'd agreed to let her try. It was worth the chance, if she could avoid another relocation.

She was on the grass now, heading toward the beach. Zach emerged from the surf, water sluicing off his coat. He was happy here, too. If WITSEC forced her to relocate, Zach might not be allowed to go with her this time.

"Hello, there," she called, carefully modulating her voice to keep anger out of her tone.

Chad turned toward her. He had on a pale blue T-shirt that read: Island Divers with a map of the islands underneath. His company, she presumed as she tried not to notice how the well-washed cotton fit snugly over the hard planes of his chest. Unconsciously her eyes dropped lower to the board shorts he wore low on his hips. The all-male bulge was outlined by the fabric.

She jerked her eyes back to his face, hoping the dim moonlight hadn't revealed her close inspection of his ripped bod. He offered her a brash grin that said he'd noticed and women always adored him. With her next heartbeat, she reminded herself this wasn't some *GQ* bod. This man was dangerous—especially to her.

She stopped at the edge of the grass. Zach bounded up to her, tail whipping the air, and dropped the stick at her feet.

"Hey, where've you been?" Chad walked up to her.

"Running around like crazy. We've got a big wedding right here this weekend. Remember?" Zach nuzzled her hand, and she petted his wet head.

"Hope you didn't mind my taking Zach," Chad said, his voice full of good-old-boy charm.

She had to remind herself this man was cleverer than he appeared. He might seem helpful, but he'd been investigating her.

"I'm glad you took Zach. It looks like he's having fun. I didn't think I would be so long," she explained, hoping her breathlessness would be attributed to her walk down to the beach, not her apprehension at weaving yet another lie.

He stared at her a moment, his eyes a little hard to read in the moonlight. "I didn't know what to feed him. Rory cooked him a steak."

Great. She'd bought Zach as a puppy, and he'd always eaten kibble. This was his first steak. No doubt the big lummox adored it and would turn up his nose at the dry stuff now. Zach picked up the stick and plopped it at her feet.

"He loves retrieving in the surf," Chad told her.

"He loves retrieving, period." She picked up the sandy stick and heaved it toward the star studded sky. "Go, boy!"

Zach galloped across the sand and plunged into the surf. Her breath stalled in her throat. Could he see the stick? What if he kept swimming out to sea and drowned?

"Is it too dark for him to find it?" she asked Chad.

"No problem. There's enough moonlight."

He moved closer and she resisted the urge to back up. She kept her eyes on the ocean where Zach was swimming like a shark, head above the water, no splashing.

"See how the waves are sparkling?" Chad asked.

There was an intimate pitch to his voice that she deliberately ignored. "Yes. It's beautiful."

"According to island lore, when the water sparkles like that it's the *menehunes* dancing on the waves."

"Really?" She found island tales intriguing, part of what made Hawaii so unique. She wanted to settle here—if she could live through the trial.

Chad gazed down at her. Seeing her in the moonlight caused his pulse to lurch, jumpstarting his body. He forced himself to remember she was a liar, and he'd lured her out here for a reason.

"Have you eaten?" What he wanted to ask is why she'd lied, but he couldn't without revealing he'd been checking on her.

She hesitated. "No, but I'll catch—"

"I've got tons of food. You know how it is with a twenty-year old male in the house."

"I don't want to put you to any trouble."

"No trouble. Besides it'll give Rory time to wash down Zach and towel him off before he gets into your car."

She laughed, but it sounded forced to Chad. He studied the full curve of her slightly parted lips. Aw, hell, did he ever want to kiss her, but he checked the impulse in time. This woman was trouble.

Devon watched Zach splash out of the surf, head held high. He pranced over to them, so proud of retrieving the stick that it made her smile.

"Good boy," she told him.

The stick clamped firmly in his mouth, Zach shook hard. Droplets of water splattered both of them, and they shared a laugh.

"Come on," Chad touched her arm and led her toward the house. Zach trotted along behind them.

Be careful of this woman, Chad thought. She's the type men can't resist. He had to admit that he not only found her attractive, but her aura of mystery added to her appeal. Most women were disappointingly easy to figure out. Not Devon.

"Rory," Chad called when they were closer to the house.

"Yeah?" Rory poked his head out of a second story window.

"Would you wash down Zach while we eat?"

"Sure."

Devon gazed at the fabulous house. Light poured from soaring glass windows that showcased vaulted ceilings rising two stories into the night sky. From here it appeared to be a small hotel. It certainly wasn't like any home Devon had visited, even the pseudo-Tudor mansions Rutherford and Ames had built in Houston.

Rory ran down and called, "Come on, Zach. This way to the shower."

From the furious wagging of Zach's tail, Devon could tell the dog was crazy about Rory. They headed off toward the corner of the house where Devon assumed an outside shower was located.

"You ought to let Zach come here instead of leaving him in the office. Zach's a young dog. He needs exercise. Rory will take of him."

"Is Rory your son?"

He chuckled. "No. Rory's father died in Desert Storm. Rob was a good friend of mine. When Rory became too much for his mother to handle, she let him move to Honolulu with me. He finished high school here and is now taking classes at UH."

"And surfs."

"Well, sure. This is Hawaii. Rory came from Indiana. He has a lot of catching up to do."

They walked into the black and white high tech kitchen where Devon had used the telephone earlier in the day. Her entire apartment could fit in this kitchen, she thought. Above the island in the center of the kitchen was a very long surf-board.

Chad caught her staring upward and said, "It's Duke's long board."

She nodded, vaguely aware of a legendary surfer named Duke. There had been so much she had tried to learn about Hawaii in just a short time that the name didn't completely register.

"Surfing was a sport of Hawaiians going back to ancient times," Chad told her as if he were reading her mind. "It was almost a lost art in the 1920s when America discovered Hawaii. Duke Kahanumoku was surfing off Waikiki at the time on that long board I bought. Tourists were fascinated by his ability to ride the waves. He became famous."

"And surfing took off," she added.

"You bet. Duke wouldn't know the sport now," he replied with a sentimental glance upward at the wooden long board.

"Boards are shorter. Surfers are into big waves like the ones on the North Shore, not coasters like those on Waikiki."

"Interesting," she said, noticing his change of expression and not knowing what to make of it.

"Why don't I have Rory swing by the office and pick up Zach after classes? He could return him to the office in time for him to go home with you."

Pretty soon Zach would like Rory better than her, Devon decided with a pang of jealousy. Maybe it was for the best. If she had to run and leave Zach behind, she wanted him to have a good home.

CHAPTER THIRTEEN

DEVON TRIED HARD to keep her reluctance out of her voice. "I'd be grateful if Rory could take care of Zach. I'd pay—"

"Forget paying Rory. I pay him to look after the house, which is a total no-brainer. He'll take care of Zach for nothing. He's crazy about the dog."

This was exactly what she feared. She needed Zach in her life in a way she couldn't explain to anyone who'd never been all alone in the world—except for a dog. Now that animal, who had no idea how much he meant to her, was about to be taken away by a young guy with surfing and babes and God-only-knew-what else on his mind.

Zach was all she had, but she needed to be willing to let him go—for his sake. If she had to run, or was killed, she wanted to know he was safe and loved.

"Steak or fish?" Chad asked.

She hadn't noticed him approach the refrigerator. "Fish, if it's not too much trouble."

"No problem. I have fresh *opakapaka*. Pink snapper native to the islands. Ever tried it?"

"No, but I'm game." She tried to sound casual and friendly, but not too friendly. For her plan to work, she needed him to trust her. So far she hadn't done anything but give him the cold shoulder. He'd be even more suspicious than he already was, if she did an abrupt about-face.

"What can I do to help?" she asked.

"The dishes are in the cabinet to the right of the sink. The silver is in the middle drawer. Set the table out on the terrace."

She did as she was told, thankful to have something to do other than look at him. There was a small terrace off the kitchen with a round table and four chairs. From this angle Devon couldn't see the pool, but there was a spectacular view of the sea and Diamond Head.

Chad brushed the barbecue grill with olive oil. "So the fish won't stick," he explained over his shoulder to Devon as she set the table. "If you're not careful *opakapaka* falls apart."

"I've seen it on menus, but I've never had it."

"Do you eat out a lot?"

"No, not really." She could have added that she couldn't afford it, but she suspected Chad already knew she was broke.

Rory came around the corner with Zach. "He's all clean, but I think I should blow him dry."

"That isn't necessary," she said, but Rory was already headed inside.

"Let him," Chad said. "It'll keep him off the Internet for a while."

Devon laughed. "Table's set. What else can I do?"

He put on the fish and checked his wristwatch. "Five minutes per side should be just right. I'm sure we've got veggies."

She followed him to a huge refrigerator. He swung the door open and she saw it was more than just well-stocked. It would have taken some major rearranging to wedge in anything else. She thought of the minifridge in her studio apartment. It was full, too, but it was loaded with yogurt and cottage cheese. Chad's seemed to have lots of junk food.

He pulled open a lower compartment and took out a bag of broccoli. "You can see who does the shopping."

"Rory."

"Yeah. He would live on macaroni and cheese and frozen pizza, if I let him."

She took the bag. "Let me wash this."

"Good idea. I'll get the wine."

He disappeared down the short hall off the kitchen. She wouldn't be surprised if he had a real wine cellar. After all, he could fit two hundred people in his living room. She rinsed the broccoli under the tap, wondering if she could pull this off.

"Far Niethe or Chalk Hill?" Chad asked from behind her.

"Either is fine."

Being in his kitchen and preparing a meal had an intimate feel to it Devon hadn't anticipated. What she was going to do made her ashamed of herself, but she had no choice. If she didn't come up with a reasonable explanation to satisfy Chad, Warren would relocate her.

"Here's a bowl for the broccoli." Chad handed her a ceramic bowl with a lid.

His arm brushed hers. She heard her own quick intake of breath and instantly looked away, torn by conflicting emotions. Why did she have to be so attracted to a man who was dangerous to her?

"Why are blond jokes so short?" she asked, going for her old fallback, a joke to relieve tension.

"I give."

"So men can remember them."

Chad chuckled, a deep husky sound. Again she looked away, praying she could pull this off.

"Time to flip the fish," he told her. "Zap the broccoli in the microwave. Two minutes max."

"Yessir!" She saluted.

Chad smiled to himself. He doubted Devon was after the DARPA gadget. She'd been here all day. If she'd looked, she would have found it. In military mode now, well aware one man had died, he'd put the device in his safe. And he was watching his back.

A few minutes later, they were seated at the table. Chad poured them both a glass of the Far Niethe chardonnay. They ate in silence for a few minutes.

"You know what I find interesting about the *menehunes?*"

Devon's question took him by surprise. Had she been here long enough to know much about the *menehunes?*

"I'll bite. What?"

"They're little people like the leprechauns in Ireland."

"Is that right?" He'd heard of leprechauns, sure, but he wasn't that familiar with Irish myths.

"Leprechauns and *menehunes* are pranksters. Imagine two islands halfway around the world from each other. Hawaiians couldn't have known about Ireland's 'little people' yet a lore evolved that's surprisingly similar."

"Interesting." He drank a little wine, studying her. "I wouldn't have thought you'd been here long enough to know much about the *menehunes.*"

She brushed back a lock of hair that had fallen across her cheek in a way he found incredibly provocative. "I couldn't sleep one night. I went online and read several articles."

"Not much you can't find on the Internet."

"So true. God bless the Internet."

Chad saw Devon had almost finished her fish. Unless he missed his bet, she was going to plead a busy schedule and be out of here soon. Here goes nothing. "When you didn't come back to work, I decided to go by your place and see if I could put Zach in your yard or something."

"You didn't have to go to all that trouble," she said without a flicker of hesitation.

"The address on your application is Mailboxes in Paradise."

She arched one delicate brow. "It is?"

Chad let her words linger in the balmy air. Damn she was good. Her expression was convincingly puzzled.

"I must have transposed a digit when I wrote it down."

He honestly couldn't tell if she was lying or not. He usually had a feel, a sixth sense about these things. Not this time, not with this woman.

"I don't have a yard. It's a tiny studio no bigger than this terrace. That's why it's so great to be able to take Zach to work with me."

Interesting, Chad thought. She managed to casually toss some info at him without telling him where she lived.

"Did you have a bigger place in Chicago?" he asked, deciding not to press her and see what happened.

"There was a courtyard, but mostly I walked him. If I was having a busy day, I called Pawsabilities, and they walked him."

It was odd really and quite disturbing, Devon thought. Lies fell from her lips with awesome ease. The lies would become second nature. Derek, her first handler, had assured her of this. The ability to blithely lie had finally kicked in.

Self-preservation.

If she didn't lie, they would get her. And Rutherford and Ames would win. Her parents had taught her good triumphed over evil. Those two were not getting away with cheating the government and killing people.

"Do you have family back there?" he asked an assessing glint in his eyes.

"My parents are dead." She might have said this a little too brightly because it was the truth. "My sister lives in Florida. She has a little girl, Ariel, who is seven."

She listened as he told her with obvious pride about his three sisters and their children. She could tell he sincerely loved them. It made her long even more to see her sister. She'd been very close to Tina even though they'd lived in different states. What she wouldn't give to see Tina and Ariel.

When he finished, she stood up, saying, "Let me help you clear up. Then I've gotta run. Tomorrow will be crazy with all the last-minute details. You have no idea how hysterical brides can get."

He didn't say anything until they'd cleared the table. His piercing blue eyes leveled at her, he asked, "How long were you in Hawaii before you found a job?"

She'd been asked this question during the interview. She had told what Derek had called an "unnecessary lie." *The fewer lies you tell, the less likely you'll get caught.* He'd given her this advice many times, but an unnecessary lie had slipped from her lips. She could have blamed it on Chad's distracting presence, but she didn't. She was the one responsible.

Chad must know the truth from her DMV application. She had to handle this very carefully. She kept her voice level despite his inquisitive stare.

"I came here two months ago. I needed some downtime. I found an apartment I could afford and a car that runs most of the time. I just hung out, testing various beaches."

"Which was your favorite?"

Boy oh boy, this guy simply never gave up.

"Punaluu. It's not crowded and the swimming is fantastic," she replied. She hadn't really lazed her days away on the inviting sand. She'd familiarized herself with the island, keeping in mind that she'd had to run once. She might need to again.

"Why did you tell Eddie you'd only been here a month?"

She tried for a contrite look. "I didn't want him to think I was a loser who'd been hunting for a job for weeks and weeks."

His brows drew together. "Weren't you offered a job at one of the big hotels?"

"I didn't apply to any of the large resorts," she replied truthfully.

"Why not? With your experience—"

"I've worked for the Four Seasons. Too corporate." She mustered the smile that usually worked wonders on men. "Everything is by the book. No room for creativity."

Now this was an utter lie. She hadn't applied to any of the large hotels because Warren had been concerned some visitor might be a person she'd known in the past. She doubted anyone would recognize her now, but Warren had insisted. Also larger offices were likely to be on higher floors with only one way out—a death trap.

"Bury yourself in working class Honolulu," had been Warren's order. She'd taken the extra precaution of selecting a ground floor office with two exits.

Three beats of silence. She couldn't tell what he was thinking. She decided if she added anything more, she would sound defensive.

"Do you have a home phone?" he asked.

Her green eyes fixed him with a somber gaze. "No. I just use my cell. Later, you know, when I'm making more money, I guess I'll get a regular phone."

He nodded thoughtfully. "Do you live alone?"

She'd anticipated this question. Anyone who'd bothered to check her DMV application and knew she didn't have a home phone number must have checked to see if she'd applied for electrical service. She had but she'd used another name.

"I have a roommate," she hedged, thinking of Zach. She glanced at her watch. "It's getting late. I'd better go. Zach must be dry by now."

He stared at her for a long moment. One finger under her chin, he lifted her face to the light, taking her by surprise. Her heart seemed to soar into her throat. Only a scant inch separated their lips.

"Devon, just where do you live?"

She gazed into his eyes without wavering. "I prefer not to discuss this."

"Why not?"

"Let's just say I moved here to get away from certain things. I want to maintain a very low profile."

Chad measured her for a moment, wondering just what she meant. Her explanations for his other questions had seemed reasonable. He thought she was telling the truth, but why wouldn't she give her address?

"Okay, I respect your right to privacy. Just answer one question."

She nodded a bit tentatively, he thought.

"Are you wanted for some type of criminal activity?"

"Of course not!"

The mortified expression on her face convinced him in a second. "Sorry, but I couldn't help wondering. Why else would you be so secretive?"

"It's personal," she told him in a tremulous voice. "I haven't done *anything* illegal. There's someone I would rather never see again."

"Gotcha." He should have guessed. A lover, an ex—there was a man in Devon's life who'd made her miserable enough to leave her home and move thousands of miles away.

"Thanks," she whispered.

His finger roamed the curve of her cheek. She wanted to pull away, but too much was at stake. She told him, "I'd like to be friends."

He rolled his shoulders as if stretching a tight muscle. The snug-fitting T-shirt pulled taut across the well-defined contours of his chest. She would bet her life no woman had asked to be just his friend.

He was standing so close that she had to fight the urge to run. His hand slipped under her chin, forcing her to look directly into his eyes again. Even in the muted light on the terrace, it was impossible to miss the raw sensuality in his gaze.

Friends. Chad groaned inwardly. Just what Keke had suggested. The hyena theory. S'okay, it might work for some guys, but it wasn't his style. He'd been trying but it made him as frustrated as hell.

"Sweetheart, I've got three sisters and all their friends. I don't need another friend."

She opened her mouth to reply, but before a word could slip out, he lowered his mouth to hers. He slid his strong fingers into the hair at the base of her neck and held her head in place. His tongue touched hers, and an unexpected surge of pleasure nearly buckled her knees.

He pulled her close, his powerful body molding against her smaller frame with shocking sensuality. She allowed herself to be thoroughly kissed. It was part of the plan, wasn't it? Get him to like her, believe her.

He moved back as if to say something. Instead his lips brushed her ear, and she had to stifle a moan of pleasure. He tickled the soft lobe with his tongue.

"I understand you're trying to put a bad relationship behind you. I can wait. Just don't think of me as a friend."

Suddenly her body seemed weak, and a strange excitement

was building within her despite knowing this was wrong, dangerous. What he could do to her without half trying was amazing.

His lips met hers again. The caress of his mouth, the solid feel of his body, pressing into softness stoked a primal urge to kiss him back. His hands scaled down her ribs, slid to her waist for a moment, and came to rest on her buttocks. He held her firmly against his erection.

"Here's Zach," Rory called as he bounded out of the house, the retriever at his side.

Devon pulled away, grateful for the interruption. Mission accomplished, she told herself. Chad had bought her explanation.

She would have to hold him at bay. With luck, someone else would capture his interest. She would need to be careful. She couldn't afford to let him get close. She was already responsible for one man's death. She refused to cause another senseless murder.

BROCK LEANED CLOSER to Jordan Walsh. They were in a booth at Tuscan Steak, his favorite restaurant in fun house Miami. Others might be trendier or have better known chefs, but the steak here was the best in town. He was on his third Knockando and Jordan was sipping her second Black Dahlia. She was getting a little tipsy, he decided. As soon as they ordered, he would broach the subject of selling the Gull Wing.

"I always have the New York strip," he told her.

"Too big for me. I'll take the petit filet rare."

"Wine?"

"That would be lovely."

Brock ordered an expensive '89 Chateau Margaux with confidence. After all, it paid to make a good impression and he could tell Jordan was impressed.

Let that asshole Horst Trensen IV eat his heart out. He'd hogged Jordan all day. Trensen had been blown away when

Brock had walked over and reminded Jordan that he would meet her in the lobby at eight.

"How'd you enjoy your first show?" Brock asked after the waiter had taken their orders.

"Exciting. Very exciting. My feet are killing me."

"It's a lot of work. It gets rougher the longer you're on the circuit."

"I can just imagine." She took a sip of her martini with those pouty lips. "I like it, though. I've always wanted to have a one-of-a-kind car."

That makes two of us. He took a peek at her tits just visible at the neckline of the moss-green dress she was wearing. He could taste them. Just wait until he got her up to his room.

"Do you think you'll sell your Gull Wing?" he asked.

"Why would I do that? I want to buy another special car. Did you see the crowd? I had more people than anyone."

"I thought you might get bored doing shows."

"I love the shows. How else could I meet interesting men like you?"

He could see that he was going to have to have his new agent, Operative 77, take care of this broad—after he'd had some fun with her.

CHAPTER FOURTEEN

BY THE TIME BROCK brought Jordan up to his room, he was half in the bag. Three Scotches and the wine put him over his limit. Over Jordan's, too. He had absolutely no trouble getting her up here.

Thank God she hadn't wanted to take in South Beach's infamous club scene. Strobe lights and techno music always put him in a foul mood. He had no use for degenerates with easy money and nothing better to do than stay up all night dancing.

"Fucking A," he muttered under his breath.

The message light on his telephone console was blinking. Who in hell would be calling him? Operative 77 had already contacted him, and Brock didn't have any ongoing projects that would merit a call unless there had been a security breach and Obelisk needed him.

"Just a minute," he told Jordan. "Let me pick up this message."

"I'll fix us a nightcap."

She trundled off toward the bar, her sexy legs none too steady on those spiked heels. He smiled to himself, imagining her buck naked in bed.

"It's Cassidy. Call me immediately," said the voice mail.

Call him now? It couldn't be a security breach. Obelisk's CFO always handled those problems. Cassidy was merely a face man. The message had been left two hours ago. It was late, but Brock knew better than to ignore the prick's call.

He grabbed the handheld phone and walked out onto the

balcony so he would have some privacy. Cassidy answered on the first ring.

"About the Robbins woman," Cassidy said the minute Brock identified himself. "Did you check name stew?"

"Of course," Brock said as calmly as possible. What a piss off. Name stew was lists of names from book clubs, magazines, DVD Web sites, political parties, churches—you name it. He kept track of name stew with a special soft ware program, and Cassidy knew it. This was just his way of jerking Brock's chain.

He was suddenly hit by a gut-wrenching thought. Maybe Cassidy wasn't giving him a hard time. Cassidy reported to a group of wealthy men who were behind Obelisk. Their names were supposed to be top secret, but Brock knew exactly who they were. When he returned to his office, he would check the reverse ID he had on Cassidy's telephone and see who he'd spoken with lately.

"If you check newer subscriptions to *Vanity Fair* and the *Smithsonian,* you might find her."

"And *Dog Fancy.* When she was in Santa Fe, she was also taking a dog magazine. I checked them. Nothing yet." Cassidy was such a dumb-fuck. "Anything else?"

"This has gone on too long. I want that tap installed immediately. I double-checked Robbins's phone records from Houston. She spoke to her sister twice a week during the last few years. She's calling her now. Get on it."

"I have a better idea. I'll explain when I return." Brock hung up, something he would never have done a month ago, a week ago, even yesterday. But now he had the top secret device. He'd stored it in the small safe in the closet along with his computer. He hadn't had a chance to test it yet.

Meanwhile he had conceived a brilliant, foolproof plan to find the bitch.

"What's going on out there?" Jordan asked.

He turned, smiling. She'd taken off her shoes and had a snifter of Le Paradis cognac in each had. The woman had expensive tastes. He didn't mind as long as she sold him the Gull Wing.

"A business call. Not important." He took the snifter from her extended hand. "Isn't this a great view?"

Jordan sidled up to him, a little bleary-eyed. He hoped she didn't pass out before he got her in bed.

"I have the same view from my room. It's awesome."

He swigged his cognac to kill a caustic remark. Sometimes she was just a little too uppity. The thought of Operative 77 slitting her throat warmed his stomach like the fine cognac.

Brock gazed at the view. Directly below was the Delano's long rectangular pool. A couple was fucking doggy style on a chaise. That's why he hated SoBe. No class. Wannabe models by the hundreds, drag queens, exiled dictators, drug addicts and Eurotrash.

He preferred Coral Gables, the bastion of WASP power until the Cuban invasion. Now even Coral Gables was more South American than American. A friggin' shame.

The Biltmore, the crown jewel of Coral Gables, was his kind of hotel. It had been designed by the same team who created the Waldorf-Astoria. An architectural triumph frequented by classy people with impeccable backgrounds.

Like a glistening silver ribbon, the beach beyond the swimming pool caught the moonlight. Waves tumbled onto the shore like dice. That's what he was doing.

Rolling the dice.

He wanted Kilmer Cassidy's big corner office and the leggy blond secretary who undoubtedly serviced him on that black leather sofa. Cassidy was just another suit. In contrast Brock had the cunning instincts of a predatory animal. Obelisk was a secret agency funded with money misdirected from military projects and controlled by a pack of thieves who were already wealthy. Brock could run the operation better than Cassidy.

Jordan interrupted his thoughts. "I've got a view for you that's better than the one you're looking at."

He turned and saw she'd slipped out of her dress. She was

standing next to him in a green thong and a lacy push-up bra that matched her dress. He was hot and achingly hard before he could draw a breath. She turned and flashed her perfect ass. It had a small tattoo of a black widow spider.

Brock almost belted out a roaring laugh. This broad was totally clueless. She probably thought she was some femme fatale. What he could teach her about death! He caressed her smooth ass with his fingertips.

He dumped their snifters of cognac in the potted palm and ripped off the small swatch of fabric that passed for panties. Quick as a snake, her fingers were inside his pants. She clamped her hand around his cock and pumped him hard. He screwed her, standing up on the balcony.

BROCK WOKE UP the next day. It felt as if someone had tried to take off the top of his head with a chainsaw. Sunlight blinded him and all the white in the room only made it worse. For a second, he didn't remember where he was.

Ugh. The Delano with all its white walls, white drapes, white furniture. White. White. White. No wonder his head ached. This would never happen at the Biltmore.

"Jordan," he mumbled, suddenly recalling raw sex on the balcony. Where was she?

He was naked in bed. Alone. He braved a glance around the room but saw no evidence Jordan had ever been there.

His gaze fell on the digital clock on the nightstand. Shit! It couldn't be one o'clock. Could it?

This was the final day of the car show. It would close at three and the cars would be loaded for shipping. He had to shower and shave and get across town in traffic that was constantly gridlocked.

He swung his legs to the floor, and his stomach took a sickening upward lurch. He stumbled across the whitewashed floor to the bathroom, his head spinning, and vomited. He collapsed to his knees in front of the toilet, sweat drenching his body.

"No wonder they pronounce Knockando *No Can Do*. Three scotches puts you on your ass."

He grabbed a washcloth, wet it and crawled on all fours back to the bed. He lay there for almost an hour, the cool washcloth over his eyes. He'd never had a hangover this bad.

"Never mix the grape and the grain," he recalled his father warning him. Sick bastard had been a major boozer. Jack Daniel's straight up. A bottle a night. The blowhard probably knew what he was talking about.

Brock wondered how Jordan was doing. It gave him a perverse sense of pleasure to imagine her suffering the way he was. She was great in bed. Majorly kinky.

"Wait a minute."

He didn't actually remember her in bed. His last memory was pounding into her body as he had her backed up against the wall of the balcony. They probably had progressed to the bed, but he didn't remember it.

"Shit!"

He hated not being in control. How could he have let it happen?

THERE WAS A TERSE MESSAGE for Brock from Kilmer Cassidy, when he returned to his office in the underground bunker at Obelisk. He was still queasy from yesterday's hangover. He doubted he could ever drink single malt Scotch again.

By the time he'd gotten his act together and arrived at the convention center, the show was over and the cars were being loaded into transport trucks. Jordan's one-of-a-kind Gull Wing was already gone. She wasn't around, either. He still intended to get his hands on her car, but first he had to deal with Cassidy.

If he'd tested the DoD device, Brock could tell off the prick, but he'd had to load up his cars and get them safely back to their warehouse in Washington. By the time he did, it was late, and he was too beat to test anything.

Brock shivered as he shrugged into his microfiber jacket

and gloves. Sometimes the need to cool the hyper-sensitive equipment was a pain in the ass. When he had Cassidy's office, he could wear thousand-dollar suits instead of a dull gray jacket.

He stalled, not wanting to see Cassidy, and checked his messages. Nothing important. He took out the handheld device and put it in his desk drawer and locked it. He plugged in his laptop to the flat screen monitor and Ergonomic keyboard.

He preferred working on the laptop to any of the computers in the room. The laptop had all the info the other computers had—and more. He plugged in the reverse caller ID and accessed Kilmer Cassidy's records.

With a special software program he'd designed, he compared hundreds of calls from Cassidy's office and came up with a list of names in minutes. Most were Obelisk employees. None were from any of the coven of wealthy jerk-offs who actually owned Obelisk.

Smiling to himself, Brock accessed Cassidy's cell phone records. Bingo. Six calls to retired General Bashford Olofson. Bash to his buddies. The former army officer had made a fortune after his retirement by supplying mercenary soldiers to train Third World armies.

Then Bash had concocted a more lucrative scheme—divert funds from legitimate military projects to Obelisk. It was set up to appear to be a super secret government organization devoted to combating terrorism. In the post 9/11 era, the cloak of government secrecy was sacred. Obelisk employees signed confidentiality agreements, believing they were working for an elite arm of Homeland Security.

Olofson was the one prompting Cassidy to put the heat on to find the Robbins bitch. The general had ties to PowerTec executives Rutherford and Ames. They were weak sisters who would roll over on Olofson if Samantha Robbins wasn't taken care of properly.

Brock decided to go to the general directly as soon as he'd

tested the DoD's new infrared device rather than confront Cassidy. The revolutionary gadget would fascinate the general. Brock's innovative idea of how to deal with the bitch would assure him of Olofson's backing to take over Kilmer Cassidy's position.

He switched off the reverse caller ID and stroked a few keys on his computer to bring up the internal records of Mid-Atlantic Bell. Jordan hadn't said where she lived, but if she kept her car in Falls Church, chances were she lived in Mid-Atlantic's territory.

No Jordan Walsh was listed, but there were four J. Walshes in the greater Metro area. He didn't have time to check them all now. He hit Print and generated the information for future reference.

He spent the next hour in Cassidy's office explaining what was essentially a simple plan with no flaws. Cassidy liked to nitpick. Brock humored him while he admired the view from the corner office. Soon it would be his.

"This had better work," Cassidy told him. "Last time you fucked up. The boys aren't happy."

"The boys" led by Olofson had gotten wealthy by funneling money to Obelisk. From there the funds went to purchase military equipment. It was then sold to the highest bidder.

Third World countries that couldn't develop their own weapons paid top dollar. Terrorist cells forked over gold. Drug cartels handed over bags of already laundered cash for items they wanted. The money these sales generated went into offshore or Swiss accounts, making "the boys" even richer.

Only three people at Obelisk knew the secret: himself, Cassidy and CFO Harold Nolan. To protect the project, they had needed top-notch security. It had been necessary to hire Brock and cut him in with a minuscule portion of the profits to keep their dirty little scheme under wraps.

Once Brock would have frowned on trafficking in military weapons to America's enemies. Not anymore. Morality was relative. Someone was going to make the sale. If Obelisk handled it, Brock and Cassidy and "the boys" profited.

Had Brock stayed at the Defense Department he would be still making less than six figures. He wouldn't have the town-house in Georgetown or his most prized possessions, his cars. Once he was CEO, Brock's take from the cash cow would bring him staggering wealth.

"You hear me?" Cassidy said, snapping Brock back to their conversation.

"Don't worry," he assured Cassidy. "She'll talk. There's always a limit to human endurance."

Cassidy grunted unenthusiastically. Brock left his office, set to implement the plan. This would require two operatives. Number 77 was his first choice. He liked the way 77 had carried out the mission.

The second operative was harder to pick. Brock went through his computer files. After much deliberation, he selected a kid handling negotiations with drug lords in Colombia. The cartels there were ruthless. They'd shoot down a commercial airliner just to whack one person.

Operative 251 had been commended several times by trusted men in the field. He was a trained sniper who used a .50 caliber rifle. That meant 251 had to be accurate from three-quarters of a mile away.

Not only did a sniper have to be an expert shot, but he had to be extremely patient. He usually had to lie in wait for hours at a time to hit the targeted person. This job would take patience.

Brock liked this guy on paper. He would need to meet him in person to be certain. It would take a little time to find him in whatever godforsaken part of Colombia he was working and fly him here. Cassidy would give him a ration of shit over the delay, but Brock didn't care. He needed the right team for this job.

He used his laptop to type in a message to Operative 251 to contact Brock ASAP. Even if the kid was in the jungle, he would check in, using his battery-powered laptop, when the DoD satellite passed over Colombia. Brock expected to hear from him soon.

He almost called the J. Walshes listed in the Metro area, but decided if he did, he would be compelled to ask Jordan out tonight. His time would be better spent waiting for 251's call.

He ran reverse ID programs on the other Obelisk employees, a routine security measure. The secretive nature of the project meant as few employees as possible were hired. They all seemed to buy the antiterrorism bit. Paying them way above what they normally could earn ensured a certain loyalty in this economy. But you never knew when some smartass like Samantha Robbins would become suspicious and contact the authorities.

While he waited for the computer to run through the numbers, Brock took out the device Operative 77 had stolen. It resembled a handheld GPS, but it had several interesting buttons on it. He knew it must access the DoD satellite and require a laser scan of an authorized thumbprint.

No wait.

This was DARPA's latest gizmo. It would scan the iris. The man was dead. Brock wasn't going to be able to test this.

He pondered the situation for half an hour, then decided to try backdooring it. His iris was in the DoD database, and his security clearance was the highest. With a few keystrokes, he told the DoD satellite to let him in.

He put his eye up to the small screen and punched the on button. Bingo! He was in. It was almost too easy. Their security sucked. He put in the coordinates for Cairo where it was the middle of the night.

Pinpricks of red light coalesced on the screen just like regular infrared. It didn't tell him a damn thing. He hit the Zoom button to zero in on the American Embassy. Pinpricks of red light appeared.

"Interesting."

They could isolate images in a city packed with heat generating objects. That was a step forward. A mile forward actually. He pressed the ID button.

Bovine.

A cow or a bull? Couldn't be. Cairo was a sea of unwashed humanity with some of the dirtiest, most disgusting animals on the planet, but the only animals at the American Embassy were bomb sniffing dogs.

He double-checked the coordinates and hit Zoom again. He stared at the screen, his stomach beginning to have that debilitating hungover feeling again.

Bovine.

He thought about it for a moment and decided there could be a reasonable explanation. Some Arab with a camel had entered the compound. With security being what it was these days, it didn't seem likely.

Brock looked up some info on his laptop, then entered the coordinates for the El-Hijra Mosque. Evening prayers were long over, but there were always men hanging around the mosques.

The handheld showed about a dozen separate pinpricks of light. That was about right for this hour, he decided. He zoomed in on one.

Canine.

What? Dogs were not allowed in mosques. On the off-chance there was a mutt there, Brock zoomed in on another figure.

Canine.

What a piss-off! This thing was a long, long way from being perfected. He couldn't waltz into General Olofson's office, and claim to have the Holy Grail of nighttime surveillance.

The weight of all his forty-one years slammed down on his shoulders. He slumped back in his chair and stared at the so-called revolutionary device.

CHAPTER FIFTEEN

"DON'T WORRY ABOUT THE CALL being traced," Warren told her. "We've installed special equipment on your sister's line. We'll know if anyone is monitoring her telephone."

Devon nodded and dialed her sister's number for the first time in months. They were sitting in Warren's office and using a special cell phone Warren had flown to Honolulu for Devon to use once. The next time she called, it would be on a different telephone.

Tina answered with an excited "Hello" on the second ring. Devon wasn't surprised. The Federal Marshals would have told Tina to expect the call.

"It's me," Devon said, tears welling up in her eyes unexpectedly.

"How *are* you?"

One hot tear rolled down her cheek. Just the sound of her sister's voice after not hearing it all these months cracked the emotional armor she'd built around herself after Santa Fe. "I'm fine," she managed to say after an edgy silence. "Just fine."

"We had your favorite—German chocolate cake—on your birthday," Tina told her, the threat of tears now in her voice. "Ariel blew out the candles for you."

"I'll bet she was cute," Devon responded, being as upbeat as she could. She'd spent her birthday in the WITSEC safe house. If anyone there knew about her birthday, they hadn't mentioned it.

"You should see Ariel. She's growing up so fast. She'll be eight next month."

"That's hard to believe."

Devon wished she could ask her sister to send Ariel's picture to WITSEC, but she knew it would be useless. No pictures. No personal items. Ever. She was lucky to have Zach with her. Only Masterson's clout had made it possible.

"Steve received a big promotion," her sister said. "There's a chance we'll be moving."

"Moving? Where?"

This tenuous telephone link was all she had of her sister. She'd been to her sister's home many times. She could picture Tina there. In an odd way it was comforting to be able to visualize her sister in familiar surroundings. If they moved, Devon wouldn't be able to "see" Tina in the same way.

"Well, you know Steve. He wants a bigger house with a media room. We've been looking in Boca Raton."

"Nice area." Devon could just picture her brother-in-law in a palatial home. A successful member of a venture capital team, Steve Layton was easily impressed by the trappings of wealth. No doubt he gave Tina a hard time over Devon's situation.

"There are better schools in Boca for Ariel. She's taken up horseback riding, you know."

"Really?" Devon didn't know, but then they hadn't been in touch in months.

"Yes. Hunter-jumpers. There's an excellent instructor at the Flintridge Equestrian Academy. Ariel could work with her every day, if we lived nearby."

Devon listened as Tina chattered on about Ariel and Steve and life in suburbia. She was happy for her sister. This was the way the world was meant to be—a normal existence.

"You're doing okay?" Apparently her sister had finally run out of family news.

"I'm much better than I was."

They both knew the rules. Devon couldn't discuss her job

or the weather or anything about her present situation. Even if the phone wasn't tapped, there was always the possibility someone might try to force information out of Tina.

She wanted to tell Tina all about Hawaii. Like many people who lived in the East, Tina went to the Bahamas or the Caribbean to vacation, not Hawaii. But saying anything about where she was could get her thrown out of WITSEC. No matter how desperately she wanted to share this magnificent island with her sister, Devon couldn't.

In truth, there wasn't anything of any relevance Devon could tell her sister about herself. Her comments had to be limited to boring comments like: I'm feeling fine. The weather was off-limits. So was her job. Even if she made friends, they couldn't be mentioned by name.

Her life was a big nothing. All she was supposed to do was listen to her sister talk about her own life. Once this would have depressed Devon, but not now. Just hearing her sister's voice was enough.

KEKE STOOD AT THE BAR set up near the infinity pool. The cocktail party following Phaedra Nitsui's wedding had lasted nearly an hour and a half. There were three other bars set up on the grounds, but Keke had done the work of two bartenders at this station. She'd had Rory at her side, pouring wine and champagne. He was learning to bartend so he could get a job at one of the trendy Waikiki clubs.

Guests were now midway through dinner so business was light. She and Rory were stacking glasses in the trays to be picked up by Royal Palms Rentals. Shelby bounced up, smiling, and chattering.

"Know why the wedding party, like, always dresses in the same awesome outfits?" Shelby asked both of them, but her eyes were on Rory.

Keke resisted the urge to tell Shelby this was no way to flirt. Guys were not obsessed with wedding trivia the way Shelby was.

"I give," Rory replied.

Shelby looked at her, and Keke shrugged.

"It goes back to Roman times. They, like, thought evil spirits attended weddings, *soooo* looking for trouble. People dressed alike confused them, and they flew off."

"I get it," Rory said unenthusiastically.

Shelby leaned against the bar, gazing at Rory. "That's why brides wear veils. Then the evil spirits can't see them."

"As if," Rory sneered.

"It's *sooo* totally awesome that superstitions from *waaay* back are still, like, with us today."

"Aren't you supposed to be doing something for Devon?" Keke asked. Devon had been everywhere, calm, but handling a million details.

"She's helping put the fresh flowers on the wedding cake. I'm supposed to get the bride's bouquet from the woman who catches it. I have to rush it down to Hazuriku's and have it freeze-dried."

"Freeze-dried?" Rory asked. "What for?"

"It's, like, the latest. You can save them forever. They don't look all dried out or *soooo* phony like the silk flower duplicates some brides have made. The bouquet stays, like, exactly the way it is today."

Rory grunted and shook his head. "Let's see how Rudy's doing."

Shelby trotted off with Rory to see how Chad's black swan was faring in the pond filled with red canna leaves. Another waste of money, Keke thought. The whole wedding had been over the top.

The exotic scent of Hawaii's native plumeria had been overwhelmed by a special machine that wafted the smell of roses into the yard. A suggestion of a breeze had rustled the palms all evening. When it blew in her direction, the air became heavy and cloying.

Nothing could detract from the astonishing beauty of the site, she decided, her eyes drifting to the ocean. A lover's moon hung low in the star-filled sky and gave the sea a magical luster. Ribbons of sea foam glistened on the sand. Like a handful of diamonds thrown on to the water, the waves sparkled.

Keke could almost hear her mother saying, "It's the *menehunes* dancing." She couldn't help wonder what her mother would think if she could see Chad's home. They'd grown up as a typical middle class family. They'd never lacked for anything, but they hadn't been indulged, either.

Chad had always been a little different. He'd excelled at school without even trying. Most of his friends thought of him as a surfer, but Keke had always known her brother harbored secret ambitions. In his sophomore year in high school, Chad had sent away for several college catalogs—not just any catalogs—ones from top schools like Yale and Stanford. He'd been the only student from the North Shore to win a scholarship to Stanford.

Her brother becoming successful wasn't a shock to Keke. What did surprise her was his return to Hawaii. When he'd joined Special Forces after college, she believed he would never come home again, but she'd been wrong.

Keke saw Chad sitting at a table across the lawn. Naturally he'd been invited to the wedding, and not just because it was his house. He was one of the more successful businessmen in the islands. He didn't know the bride personally, but he was acquainted with Senator Inoye, her uncle.

The woman next to Chad appeared to be flirting with him. Keke couldn't help being proud of her brother. Chad was handsome, but in a tuxedo, he was devastating. Even so, Keke thought tuxedos were too warm, too formal for Hawaii.

The pretty brunette seated beside Chad would have trouble interesting him. Since early this morning, when they'd begun setting up, Chad had covertly watched Devon. Most people wouldn't have noticed, but Keke knew her brother well. Devon had his number, all right.

Keke admired the woman's take-charge efficiency, but she did *not* want to see her brother hurt. Until this morning, the thought had never occurred to Keke. Chad always seemed so invincible. But Keke's sixth sense had kicked in, telling her Chad was in trouble this time. She had no idea how to help him except to hang around and watch. If Chad needed her, she'd be there.

Her mother had always said everyone had an Achilles' heel. She couldn't help wondering if Devon would be his. Just then, Chad looked up and caught her staring at him. She waved, thankful he didn't know what she was thinking.

Chad rose and walked across the grass over to the bar. "Whew! That's a load off my mind. The food was great—just great."

"You were worried about the food?" Keke couldn't imagine her brother caring one hoot about what he ate. Here was a man who'd lived behind enemy lines on MREs.

"Eddie had never used Trade Winds Catering. I didn't want him to be embarrassed if the company didn't meet expectations."

She nodded dubiously. "You were worried about Devon pulling this off. Weren't you?"

"Yeah. But Devon really did a great job." There was more than just a hint of pride in his tone.

"The caterer was Lori's legacy," she pointed out.

"True, but getting this wedding together on such short notice is impressive."

Keke nodded, not quite willing to give Devon any more accolades. Her brother was already too taken with the woman.

FROM THE POND where Rudy was gliding in endless circles through thousands of red canna leaves, Devon watched the bride and groom cut the cake. Thank God, the day was almost over. It had gone better than she could ever have imagined, considering the event had been done almost entirely at the last minute. Tomorrow was Monday and Aloha Weddings was closed. She planned to sleep in, then take Zach to a remote beach to let him run and swim.

"Everyone's raving about the food, the decorations, the band."

She nearly jumped at the sound of Chad's voice. How had he come up behind her without her knowing? She must be so tired that she'd let her guard down.

She ventured a glance at him, looming beside her. He had a bod that looked good in anything, but did wonders for a tuxedo. He was smiling at her, and she couldn't help smiling back. He had the most extraordinary eyes, she decided. The incandescent blue of the water off Waikiki.

She wondered what he thought of the backless lavender dress she'd impulsively bought for this wedding. When she'd discovered how many prominent people were going to attend, she'd wanted to make a good impression. Don't kid yourself, she thought. Chad is the one you wanted to impress.

"I had a lot of assistance with this wedding," Devon told him. "Your sisters, Rory, everyone was a tremendous help. Thanks for everything."

Chad shrugged as if to say: No big deal. But his help had been very important. She didn't want anyone to realize she had no experience planning weddings. After tonight, people would believe she was an expert.

"Let's dance."

She imagined herself in his arms and almost shivered. "I don't think it's appropriate for me to—"

He'd taken her hand and was leading her toward the dance floor that had been put down in the middle of the yard. Bite Me, the band well-known for its rock tunes, was beginning to play a slow song.

She wanted an excuse to get out of dancing—she honestly did—but nothing came to mind. He swept her into his arms. Chad pulled her close and deftly spun her into the center of the crowd. It was almost impossible to move much on the tightly packed dance floor.

Devon looked across his shoulder at the other dancers and told herself this would be over in a matter of minutes. She could make it through one waltz. She kept herself rigid in his arms, only moving slightly to the beat of the music.

His warm hand was on the small of her back. His thumb slowly rubbed her bare skin. The motion forced her to relax even while it sent prickles of awareness up her spine.

She could feel each separate beat of her heart against her breastbone. Every one was louder, stronger. Time for a joke, she thought. Defuse the sexual tension.

"Did you hear about the blonde who had two dogs?"

He angled his head down, his compelling eyes gazing into hers.

"They were named Rolex and Timex."

"Why?" he asked with a raised eyebrow.

"Hul-lo! They're watchdogs."

A charged silence arced between them, then Chad commented, "You tell jokes at odd times."

"They just pop into my head."

Chad decided Devon was nervous, and he wondered what had happened with the man she was hiding from. Had he physically abused her? It was possible, but given Devon's assertive personality, he didn't think that was the case. He intended to find out what had gone on, but first he had to get close to her.

He pressed the hard contours of his chest against the lush fullness of hers. The softness of her body against his sent a surge of desire mingled with tenderness through him. When he caught the bastard who'd turned Devon into such a wary woman, he would make the jerk sorry he'd ever been born.

He moved his hand up her bare back, fluffed her hair aside and caressed her nape. Devon's eyelashes fluttered, a golden fringe against her green eyes. He smiled down at her, and something approaching a genuine smile curved her lips.

A shaft of light from the DJ's ongoing light show lit up Devon's eyes. She blinked, and in that instant Chad saw a slice of blue iris. Then her contact settled into place again.

I'll be damned, he thought. She's wearing colored contact lenses. Why?

The last strains of the waltz ended, but Chad didn't release Devon. He wanted to shake the truth out of her but knew that wouldn't get him the answers he wanted. An old boyfriend could be after her, but why would colored contacts be necessary?

Maybe it was a fashion thing. Growing up with sisters had taught him how far women would go to be fashionable. But his gut instinct told him something more was wrong than Devon was admitting.

Devon groaned inwardly as the band began to play another slow tune. She tried to casually pull away from Chad, but he tightened his grip and moved to the music. She had no choice except to dance with him.

His hand slowly roved up and down her bare back, stroking her skin with his bare fingertips. The seemingly casual movement left her breathless.

The couple next to them bumped into Devon and stepped on her foot. "Ouch!"

"You okay?" Chad asked.

"Yes. It's too crowded to dance." Devon thought this was a great excuse to get away from Chad. "Remind me to order a bigger dance floor the next time we have a wedding this large." She hobbled away, limping slightly even though her foot was fine.

Chad caught up with her in the side yard just off the kitchen. "Is your foot hurt?" he asked, although he was pretty sure she was using it as an excuse to get away from him.

"It's a little sore. That's all."

He stepped in front of her, and she stopped. He took her arms and pulled her against him. Suddenly he was acutely aware of the enveloping darkness of the side yard, the chatter of guests in the distance, the diffused light filtering through the palms. But he had her alone.

"Please don't do this," she whispered.

"Shh! It's nothing but a kiss."

"Last night was a mistake."

Chad shook his head. "It was a beginning. You know it. Admit it."

She shook her head, sending her floss of golden hair fluttering across her bare shoulders.

"If Rory hadn't come out with Zach—"

"I would have slapped you."

Chad threw back his head and laughed. "Yeah, right."

He lowered his mouth to hers. She went rigid in his arms for just a second, then with a sigh almost lost in the night air, she brushed her lips against his. Chad almost lost it.

He'd thought all day about that kiss last night. He'd been waiting to kiss her again, to see if he'd imagined the intense chemistry between them. He hadn't. It was tangible, potent.

Devon meant to push him away, but before she realized what she was doing, she was *kissing* him. He returned the kiss as he tunneled his fingers through her hair. The feel of his tongue mating with hers, his strong fingers on the back of her head, distracted her.

All she could think about was this moment, this kiss.

She rose up on tiptoe, mesmerized by the slow, sure way his tongue filled her mouth, then retreated, only to return again. It was a languid, deliberate kiss meant to arouse, and her body responded. Her loins contracted in anticipation.

She slipped her hands under the panels of his jacket and caressed the ripped bod beneath. He was rock-hard—all leashed power. She'd wanted to touch his magnificent chest from the first moment she'd seen him.

Last night she'd had a taste of what making love to him would be like. She'd never been kissed with such focused intensity. Now, running her hands over his powerful back muscles, she knew it would be a once-in-a-lifetime experience.

He moved his hips against hers, his erection pressing into her belly. Oh, my. How fantastic it would be to make love to him. Her insides seemed to melt, the heat centered between her thighs.

A warning bell rang somewhere in the back of her brain.

How easy it would be to surrender to passion. If she didn't stop right now, there would be no turning back. She would have another man involved in her life. She couldn't do this to him.

Somehow she managed to break the kiss. "I have work to do before the bride and groom get in the limo." She sounded as if she'd been running a marathon.

She brushed past him, her skirt slapping his knees. She sprinted through the darkness into the kitchen where a horde of caterers were cleaning up. She looked back, but Chad hadn't followed her.

She didn't know if she was relieved or disappointed.

CHAPTER SIXTEEN

IT WAS AFTER MIDNIGHT by the time Devon had taken Zach out of the service area of Chad's home and had driven back to her apartment. At this time of night, it would be easy to let down her guard, but she remained hyper-vigilant. Nothing on the street seemed threatening. No one loitering, pretending to be waiting for a bus. No one walking a dog. No suspicious vehicles.

There was a van way down the street. She decided to drive by it rather than head for her parking space behind her building. No one was in the van as she passed it. Aloha Flowers and Leis was painted on the side. It didn't appear to be the type of van Derek had warned her about.

She drove around the block and went into the apartment building's parking lot. Her assigned space was vacant. She parked and carefully surveyed the shadows before getting out with Zach.

Her studio faced the courtyard where a lone palm was surrounded by scarlet bougainvillea that prevented her door from being seen from the street. There was only one entrance to her apartment, but a window at the rear could be used as an exit in an emergency.

She'd checked to make certain she hadn't been followed home. Now she stopped and casually looked over her shoulder to double-check. No one was around. Even the kid in the apartment opposite hers had turned off his boom box.

She slipped the key into the lock. With a click that echoed across the courtyard, the door opened. The lamp on the table had a cell that automatically switched on the light when the sun went down. From the door she could see no one was in the room.

That left the bathroom and the closet.

She pulled the Sig Saur 225 that she'd bought on the street out of her straw bag as she walked into her studio apartment. It held nine bullets—eight in the magazine and one in the chamber. She would have liked more firepower, but that would have meant a bigger weapon and it would be obvious she was carrying a gun.

A quick look assured her that no one was inside the bathroom. The closet couldn't conceal anything more than her meager wardrobe, but she checked it anyway—just in case.

"We're safe," she told Zach, "for now."

He wagged his tail, seeming to understand. Devon slipped off her shoes and inspected the blister on her instep. It was puffy and filled with fluid. She hadn't wanted to waste money, so she hadn't purchased Band-Aids or Neosporin. Instead she'd splurged on the lavender dress.

"The blister can wait until tomorrow," she said to Zach as she bent down to pull off the sofa's cushions to make it into a bed.

A firm knock hit her like a jolt of electricity. She tiptoed to the door and peered out the peephole, thankful she'd replaced the outside light with a higher watt bulb. Warren was standing there, a box under each arm.

She opened the door, saying in a low voice, "What's going on?"

"Your things from Santa Fe arrived." He walked inside and set both boxes on the kitchen counter.

"It couldn't wait until tomorrow?"

"No. I'm off to DC for a WITSEC field training exercise. A continuing ed thing."

"How'd you know I was home?"

"I was down the street watching."

She cursed her own stupidity. When she'd driven along the

street, she'd checked for occupied cars, but she hadn't noticed any. "I should have—"

"I'm in the van parked halfway down the block."

"Aloha Leis and Flowers?"

"Good. At least you spotted it."

"There wasn't anyone inside."

"You've got to look for magnetic mat signs that can easily be changed or removed. Tricked out vans with extended wheel bases. Windows on the sides that are so black you can't see into them and find the video equipment."

"They trained me to check for those things, but I didn't notice—"

"Come with me to get the rest of your stuff, and I'll show you what you missed."

She slipped into flip-flops, followed him out of the studio, and down the dark street, Zach at her heels.

Warren pointed to the spotlights on the roof of the van. "See those spotlights on the roof and the extra lights on this van?"

"Yes. More lights than usual."

"Except for expensive tricked-out vans, it's not normal. It's a red flag. The spots on the roof are really microwave transceivers linked to the computer in the back. The other lights are collection dishes for directional microphones."

Devon looked more closely at the van. Back in Santa Fe, Derek had warned her about special surveillance vans like this, but she'd never seen one until now.

"If they—somehow—track you here, they may have doubts about your identity, since you look different. They'll observe you until they're positive."

A frission of alarm prickled the fine hairs across the back of her neck. Despite his reassurances, Warren wasn't certain she was safe.

"All they have to do is lift a fingerprint," she said.

"Your fingerprints have been removed from every database."

"I was fingerprinted at PowerTec."

"Those were altered."

"Before Rutherford and Ames could make a copy?"

"That's what I'm told." Warren's voice sounded strained. He opened the front door of the van. "Take the two smaller boxes. I'll carry the larger one."

End of discussion, she thought. I'm on my own. Once the idea would have frightened her, but not now. It was much better not to rely on anyone except herself.

"When are you coming back?" she asked.

"In a week. Any problems call the 800 number or contact the FBI field office here. You've memorized the numbers, right?"

"Of course." She didn't want to remember what had happened the last time she'd called the 800 number, then tried to contact the FBI. If it happened again, she was running—not calling. She had cash and phony ID hidden and ready to use.

They walked in silence the rest of the way to her apartment, stopping once to let Zach lift his leg on a hibiscus bush. Inside they placed the boxes in the corner near the closet.

"Are you positive Chad Langston bought your story?" Warren asked.

She prayed her eyes didn't reveal what had happened tonight. "Absolutely."

"I'll take your word for it, but I'll discuss the situation with Masterson. He may want to move you anyway."

"Please discourage him. You don't know how hard it is to start over. I won't be able to call my sister again for months."

"I realize it's difficult." His voice, usually flint against steel, now seemed sympathetic. "I'll do my best. Just promise me you can handle Langston."

"I can handle him as long as you've backstopped my story."

"Don't worry. I fixed everything."

Without another word, Warren walked out and closed the door.

"How am I going to get rid of Chad?" she asked herself.

The hot kiss in the side yard proved how vulnerable she was. She'd ached with need and had almost given in to it. She'd been kissed by a fair number of men over the years, but none of them did it with the same intensity, the same passion. If she responded to a couple of kisses, what would a night in his bed be like?

Don't even think about it.

BROCK WAITED two long days until his contact at the DoD came back from vacation and called him.

"You idiot! You had me send a kick-ass agent after a worthless gadget that's still in the developmental stages."

"No way!" His source sounded genuinely shocked. "DARPA's about to put it into production just as soon as these final tests are complete."

"I'm telling you the thing isn't worth shit!"

"Th-there's got to be some mistake. Archer Danson himself is heading up the project."

"You've been snowballed."

Two beats of silence. "Maybe something went wrong with the one you have. Your agent could have damaged it in transit."

Brock snorted his disgust.

"There's got to be one, maybe two, more. Danson wouldn't leave all the testing to just one person. I'll check on it and get back to you."

Brock slammed down the receiver. He stared at the liquid plasma TV screen. Solar flares had wreaked havoc with the satellites. Several were out. Electricity was down in Sweden.

"Who cares?" he asked out loud.

He picked up the telephone again and dialed Jordan's number. He'd tracked her home address to a condo complex in McLean, Virginia. He'd left several messages on her machine, but she hadn't returned his calls.

After the seventh ring, Jordan's sultry voice came on the line, delivering the same message he'd heard before. "Hi, there. It's Jordan. I'm out having fun or working hard so I can afford to have fun. After the beep, leave a message. I'll get right back to you."

"Where is the bitch?"

Could she be deliberately not returning his calls? It was possible, he silently conceded. He didn't remember all of what had happened between them. Maybe he'd done something...or she'd done something embarrassing.

Perhaps he should leave a less formal message. Something romantic like "thinking about you." No. "Missing you" would be more romantic. Women went for that bullshit.

Line seven rang, the number his operatives used. The only call he was expecting was from 251. The operative hadn't used the uplink to the satellites in two days. The way his luck was going, 251 had been murdered by the drug lords.

"Numero Uno."

"Operative 251 here." The rasp in his voice reminded Brock of a chain smoker. He hated smokers because the habit owned them. They left their posts to smoke, jeopardizing missions.

"Do you smoke?"

"No. It's not allowed. You should know that."

Jesus! The guy had some nerve. He didn't sound the least bit impressed to have Brock call him.

"We need to meet in person," Brock told him.

251 didn't hesitate. "San Pedro, Belize. The Mayan Princess on Ambergis Caye this Friday."

"Wait a minute." Brock didn't like someone else calling the shots. "Costa Rica."

"No. Belize. I'll register under the name of Scott Andrews."

Brock weighed his alternatives. He was tempted to tell him to fuck off and die. But no one was as good as this guy, and Brock needed the best for his plan to succeed.

"Why Belize?" Brock asked.

"I've got business there."

"Gottcha." That explained a lot. Central America was a haven for drug smugglers. No doubt 251 needed to be there as part of his project.

Obelisk was a rigidly compartmentalized operation. Members of some teams didn't know other teams existed—or what they were doing. Checks and balances. Even Brock, who knew more than anyone, wasn't sure what 251 was actually doing in Colombia. He assumed the kid was selling military equipment diverted from military projects to drug lords.

Brock agreed to the meeting, saying he would contact him at the Mayan Princess. He hung up, a little uneasy. He was breaking one of his rules. Never meet an operative in person.

He reminded himself that he didn't have a choice. His number one priority was killing Samantha Robbins. He couldn't risk another debacle like Santa Fe. If he intended to take over Cassidy's position, he had to whack the bitch.

He tried Jordan again. Her damn machine kicked on, but this time the message said she was away on business and would return calls from the road.

Brock had bigger fish to fry than some dumb twit who didn't call him back. He would take care of her later. He needed to find someone to take his place when he moved into Cassidy's position.

"You've been way too smart on this," he said out loud.

In keeping his operation a one-man-show, Brock hadn't trained his replacement. No one had any idea how to run the sensitive, super-secret equipment. Most of it wouldn't be hard to learn, but deciding who could be trusted to head security, was another matter.

A big problem.

Anyone who took over his job had to know exactly what Obelisk was doing. It wasn't the first time the thought had occurred to him, but only now did he appreciate how difficult this was going to be. Virtually all of the personnel at Obelisk were operating under the illusion that they were doing a patriotic service to help America.

It was better to go to the outside, Brock decided. A disgruntled worker at the Pentagon or CIA would be ideal. Someone like him, a guy who wasn't being given the credit he was due, a guy who wasn't being paid enough.

A lot of guys fit the profile. He just had to do a little research.

CHAPTER SEVENTEEN

CHAD LEFT RORY to put the house back together on Monday morning and drove into town. He'd used the infrared gadget Danson had given him to track Devon after she'd left the wedding. He'd told himself he was testing the device, but in the bright light of the island sun the next morning, he couldn't kid himself.

Devon Summers captivated him in a way no other woman ever had. After what he'd seen last night, he was even more intrigued.

And suspicious.

On the infrared screen, he'd watched her return home. The GPS coordinates told him exactly where she lived. That was the information he wanted, and he'd almost turned off the tracker when a person came to her door.

At midnight?

Why, he'd wondered.

He'd kept watching, unwilling to admit he was actually jealous. The device didn't tell him if Devon's visitor was a man or a woman, but he was betting on a man. He'd waited to see if the man was spending the night. Curiously they both had come out with Zach and went to a vehicle parked down the street.

The device didn't tell him exactly what they were doing, but it appeared that they had removed something, then returned to Devon's apartment. It appeared to have been done purposely so darkness concealed them.

She'd seemed sincere about moving here to get away from

a troubled relationship. Now he wondered if—despite her denial—she could be involved in some illegal activity like drugs. She might not be out to bilk Eddie, but she was wearing contacts to disguise her blue eyes, and she refused to give out personal information.

He planned to find out what she was up to.

First, he had to contact Danson. DARPA should know their gadget had a flaw, if the murdered man testing it hadn't already told them. He found a pay phone on King Street and called Archer Danson.

As usual, Danson said he would contact from a secure line. While he waited, he bought a packet of crackseed and a bottle of Surf's Up water from the Stop N Go Minimart.

He'd been snacking on Hawaii's version of trail mix since he was a kid. In ancient times, Chinese warriors had carried bits of dried, salted plum to eat when food wasn't available. Shanghaied sailors had brought the treat to the islands where it became a popular snack.

The pay phone rang and Chad tossed back a handful of crackseed and washed it down with some water before answering on the third ring.

"You have something to report?" Danson asked.

"The device is sound as far as I can tell, except it has problems when objects are on the water. A small boat with people aboard will show on the screen as a watercraft. For some reason it doesn't pick up humans or animals onboard."

"Christ! No one else mentioned this." Danson grunted the way he often did when he was thinking. "You're sure?"

"Positive. I've tried it in several different situations."

"I'll have the engineers get on it."

"Do you want this one back?"

"No. Keep testing. Remember to watch your back. Report anything suspicious."

For a moment Chad was tempted to tell Danson about Devon and ask him to run a check. He decided that wasn't the best way to handle the situation. He needed to investigate her himself. He wasn't being arrogant, but he had plenty of experience when he'd been with Delta Force. Besides he had a personal interest in the situation.

DEVON STARED at the three boxes from her office in Houston. They'd been transferred to Santa Fe when WITSEC had sent her there. She'd shoved them into a closet, hoping one day she could go back to her old life and would need some of the financial books and computer disks.

Where was she going to put them now? Unlike her place in Santa Fe, this studio didn't have a closet big enough to store all the boxes. She should throw them out. It didn't seem likely she would ever return to a financial career.

"What's wrong with you? Stop being so pessimistic."

Zach cocked his head and gazed up at her. She remembered her promise to take him to the beach. She decided to leave the office stuff stacked in the corner, and unpack the clothes. She wanted to save her winter coat and a few suits.

Eventually Rutherford and Ames would come to trial. If it was winter, she would want heavier things. She also considered the possibility she might be forced to run and need a warm wardrobe. She began to sort through the clothes, selecting a few. The others she would drop off at the Salvation Army on her way to the beach with Zach.

She was halfway through the clothes, when she heard a knock at the door. Cold fear prickled her skin. Who could it be? Warren was the only one who knew where she lived, and he was gone.

Zach was wagging his tail, but then, he was a golden retriever who thought everyone was his friend. Approaching the door without making a sound she decided it was probably a neighbor or a Jehovah's Witness. She peered out the peephole.

Chad Langston.

Oh, my God! How had he found her? She thought she'd taken every precaution.

Devon considered pretending she wasn't home, but decided against it. A man like Chad would be persistent. She might as well face him now. She swung open the door and tried for a surprised smile to hide her anger. A busybody like Chad could get her killed.

"Good morning," Chad greeted her.

She couldn't force herself to be flirtatious. She motioned for him to come inside. Naturally Zach rubbed Chad's long legs, begging to be petted.

"How did you find me?"

Chad looked up from stroking Zach's head. "I planted a location transmitter under the bumper of your car."

She knew about the thumb-sized devices that could be hidden—unnoticed and difficult to find—on any vehicle. All it would take to track the transmitter's signal would be an FM receiver that could be bought at any electronics store. Considering Chad's Delta Force experience, this was a low-tech approach, but it had worked.

Her disheartened feeling at being so easily found morphed into something darker, uglier. She was angry with Chad, true, but more that that she was profoundly discouraged. Devices purchased at any electronics store had led Chad to her. What could Rutherford and Ames do with their unlimited funds?

In a way she was flattered that he'd taken the trouble to find her. In another way she was furious. He had a lot of nerve, but then that was probably why he was so successful. He didn't let anything get in the way of what he wanted.

"This place is a mess," she explained, stalling, wondering how to handle the situation. "I'm unpacking. A friend brought me some of my things late last night."

Chad eyed the boxes she was unpacking and the clothes strewn around the small studio. Relief clicked deep inside his chest. Devon wasn't up to anything illegal.

He wanted to ask why the delivery in the middle of the night, but that would expose his location transmitter story as a lie. No one could know about the DARPA tracking device.

He also wanted to ask if the friend was a man or woman, but didn't. He sensed her hostility and didn't want to alienate her more than he already had.

"This place doesn't look big enough for you to have a roommate," he commented as he stroked Zach's silky fur.

He didn't think she was going to answer. He was pushing his luck, but he couldn't help himself. He wanted her in a way that he'd never wanted a woman. Okay, okay, it was physical, but she intrigued him on many levels.

She was attracted to him, yet she kept holding him off. Something was wrong and he was here to find out what it was.

"You're petting my roommate," she said, her tone bitter.

He smiled inwardly. She hadn't quite told a lie, but she'd cleverly managed to evade the truth. Her reluctance to out-and-out lie told him a lot about her.

"You have electrical service, but your name isn't in their database."

For a second, he thought she was going to punch him. "Why are you checking on me?"

He stepped forward and brushed his knuckles against her cheek. She grabbed his wrist but didn't pull his hand away.

"I care about you, Devon. I know it's crazy because we don't know each other that well, but it's how I feel. I think you're in some kind of trouble. I can help."

His tone was so sweet, so sincere that it brought the sting of tears behind her eyes. No one could help her and she knew it, but she was touched that he wanted to try.

"You can help me by leaving me alone," she replied, pushing his hand away from her face. "Don't tell anyone where I live or anything you've learned about me."

He'd expected her to refuse help. After watching her at work, he'd seen the kind of independent woman she was. He plopped down on the sofa on top of a winter coat. "I'm not leaving here until you talk to me."

His response didn't surprise Devon. She'd been around him enough to realize he didn't know anything about not winning. She hated herself for what she was going to do, but she had her story ready.

She paced the small studio for a few minutes, pretending to be distraught. She finally sighed—not too dramatically she hoped—and walked over to the sofa. She removed a pile of sweaters intended for the Salvation Army and set them on the floor. She sat down as far away from Chad as possible on the small sofa that doubled as her bed.

"When I was working at the Four Seasons in Chicago, I coordinated a large corporation's Christmas party. It was before the dot-com meltdown so it was a lavish affair."

As she spoke, Devon made certain to look directly into Chad's eyes. Looking away or looking down was a tip-off that you were lying. She was, of course, but she'd rehearsed this story many times. She prayed she could pull it off.

"One of the guests was Nathan Albert. We were introduced and chatted briefly. That evening when I returned to my condo, exhausted, I found one hundred crystal vases filled with red roses. Each note had the same message: Beautiful roses for a beautiful lady. Nate had signed each note."

Chad watched Devon closely. Her gaze was steady and her voice showed little sign of emotion. She was good at holding her emotions in check, he decided. He had a troubling feeling he knew where this story was going.

"It took me a minute to remember who Nate was. It was shocking that he'd done something so over-the-top after meeting me for just a few minutes. I was a little put off."

"Some guys can't resist trying to impress women," Chad commented.

She nodded, slowly, thoughtfully. He seemed to be buying her story so far. "The next day, Nate called and asked me to dinner. I really didn't want to go but after all those roses...how could I say no? We went in Nate's limo to Tango, one of the nicest restaurants in the city. Naturally, we had the best table, and he was on a first-name basis with all the staff.

"I went out with him a few more times, but then I decided to cut it off. When he touched me, I cringed. I didn't like kissing him, and I knew soon he'd expect...more. Also, I suspected Nate had ties to the mob. I made a few excuses when he phoned. Then he called and simply said he was picking me up at seven. I was angry, but I went out with him, intending to explain that I couldn't see him anymore."

Chad knew this guy wasn't taking no for an answer. Devon was a woman no man would want to lose, but a reasonable guy would have let her go at this point.

"Nate said he'd made up his mind. I belonged with him." She looked away and tried for a grim expression. "I had no say in the matter. I told him to drop dead. I walked out of the restaurant and took a cab home.

"I didn't hear anything for over a week. Then my best friend called from the hospital. Two men had pulled her off the street and had beaten her up. Next time, they promised to kill her. They said for her to give me a message: Nate was the best thing that would ever happen to me."

She paused here and swallowed hard. "The following day, a courier brought me a package. Inside were telephoto shots of my sister, Tina, and my niece, Ariel. No message. Just the photos. I understood what he meant. Nate knew where my sister lived, and if I didn't cooperate, she was next."

The bastard, Chad thought, the image of his own sisters in his mind. If anyone ever harmed them, he knew without a doubt he would kill him.

"Naturally, I went to the police. There was nothing they could do. Pictures were just pictures."

"What about your friend? Those goons who beat her up and used Nate's name."

"She changed her story, said she couldn't remember what happened." Devon shrugged. "I can't blame her. She was in pretty bad shape. Next time, they might kill her. She moved back to Sioux City and refused to take any of my calls."

Chad heard the sadness in her voice and knew this must have been more difficult than he could possibly imagine. "Did you have anyone who could help you?"

"Not really. I had friends, and ex-boyfriends, but no one as close as Melissa. Even if there had been someone, I couldn't jeopardize anyone else's life. I tried to get a restraining order, but the police said Nate would have to threaten me or do something first."

Chad waited for Devon to continue. When she didn't, he prompted, "What happened?"

"I had no choice but to see Nate until I could figure out what to do. I didn't want anything to happen to my sister." She shuddered and drew in a sharp breath, a move she'd practiced in front of the mirror dozens of times. "It meant sleeping with him, but it bought me time. I researched how to disappear and create a new identity."

He imagined Devon forcing herself to submit to this creep. He could see the prick pawing her lush breasts and shoving himself between her thighs. Something deep in his gut clenched, the way it had when he'd been behind enemy lines during Desert Storm. He knew he was going to have to slit the throat of an Iraqi guard. He couldn't shoot without jeopardizing the mission and exposing his team's position.

It was kill or be killed then.

This was different. Nathan Albert was no threat to him, but he wanted to put a knife through the guy's heart for what he'd done to Devon. All of this flashed through his mind in a second. With it came the realization that she meant even more to him than he'd admitted to himself.

He was ready to kill for her.

"Nate, the conceited ass, never suspected a thing. He showered me with gifts, and I accepted them. I never told him how important my sister and niece were to me. In fact I subtly implied the opposite. All the while, I prepared to run, but it took me almost a year."

There was an odd twinge in her voice, and she stopped for

a moment. Chad waited, not wanting to interrupt her chain of thought.

"I converted cash to money orders and forwarded them to Portland where I intended to move. I took the train to Philadelphia and New York to hock the jewelry and furs Nate had given me. The money went to Portland. When I had liquidated all I could without alerting Nate, I bought a one-way plane ticket from Indianapolis to London and left."

"What about your sister?"

"I'd told Tina. She and my niece stayed the summer on a private island in the Caribbean. Nate sent someone to question my brother-in-law, but I don't think he believed they knew where I'd gone because we'd been down to Nate's penthouse in South Beach several times, and I'd never gone to see my sister. He didn't think we were very close."

Chad nodded, thinking there were a dozen ways the jerk could track Devon unless she'd taken elaborate measures to cover her tracks.

"I left when I knew Nate was going to be in the Caymans for a week so I'd have a head start. I took only a few things. My computer, a few family pictures and some clothes. I didn't leave a note or anything."

"What about your job?"

"I told them I had a sick aunt in Phoenix. Then I flew from Indianapolis to London."

"You must have gotten a passport in a different name," Chad commented.

Devon shook her head, a smile of pride curving her lips. "I wanted Nate to think I was somewhere in Europe."

Clever, Chad thought. Very clever. Portland was halfway around the world. "You must have gotten a new passport to get back to the States."

Again Devon shook her head. "With all the terrorist activity, I couldn't risk getting caught with a phony passport. I'd figured out a way to get back without leaving a trail or getting a new passport."

Chad stared at her, more than a little amazed. He could think of a few ways of entering the country without going through immigration, but he was trained in covert operations. She wasn't.

CHAPTER EIGHTEEN

WHENEVER POSSIBLE, face-to-face contact was the best way to ensure the operative totally understood the mission and would carry out orders, but Brock had always taken extreme measures to remain anonymous. His handle was "Numero Uno" but none of his field operatives ever saw his face. If they didn't see him, he could never be identified.

He'd sent the operatives to Santa Fe without meeting with them in person. Now he realized what a big mistake he'd made. Had he met them, Brock felt confident he would have realized what a loose cannon the woman was. He wouldn't have been forced to spend all these months searching for Samantha Robbins.

Brock flew from Miami to Belize with a group of scuba divers. He pretended to be just another diver interested in diving the Blue Hole. Eons ago a huge underwater sinkhole almost five hundred feet deep had formed off the coast of what for years had been British Honduras but was now Belize.

The Blue Hole ranked right up there on a diver's must-see list. The Great Barrier Reef. The Molikini Crater. The Puerto Rican Trench—the deepest spot in the Atlantic Ocean. The Blue Hole.

Brock could talk the talk. He'd done the Great Barrier Reef, and he'd boned up on the others. It always paid to blend in with the crowd.

He took Mayan Air from Belize City to Caye Caulker. 251 was staying on the larger and more popular Ambergis Caye. Brock had decided it was better to have one quick assessment meeting with the guy and leave. He didn't need to hang around the same town with him.

He checked in to a B & B on Caye Caulker. The whole frigging island was a throwback to the seventies when Caye Caulker had been a haven for drop-out dopers. Belize had cleaned up the place a bit, but Brock would bet his life that a little money would buy you any controlled substance you wanted.

The Blue Fin B & B was painted a soft coral with lime-green shutters. It reminded Brock of Key West. All twelve rooms had been booked by the scuba diving group he'd flown in with from Miami. Brock's room had a view of the Caribbean blue water and the waves crashing on the barrier reef a quarter of a mile away. Palms swayed in a refreshing breeze. Miles of white beach with very few people. It was picturesque—if you went for the tropics.

Give him a Gull Wing any day.

BROCK WAITED under the palms just a few feet from the water at Lilly's Restaurant next to the Mayan Princess Hotel. Ambergis Caye was more happening than Caye Caulker. More people. More hotels. More night life.

Not that Brock gave a fuck. He'd been forced to come here a day early so he could dive the Blue Hole. One rule of going undercover was to play the part. It would look suspicious if he hadn't gone diving.

He had to admit it, the underwater sinkhole made famous by Jacques Cousteau had been fascinating. On the surface the Blue Hole's water was sapphire-blue and stretched a thousand feet across. Beneath he'd dropped one hundred and thirty feet, then swam under a ledge. Stalactites and stalagmites riddled the walls. Prehistoric looking red sharks swarmed through the dark waters. The sharks would have intimidated some divers, but Brock had seen plenty of them at the Great Barrier Reef.

Brock glanced at his watch. 251 had three minutes left,

if he was on time. Brock had no use for agents who weren't punctual. Attention to details was important to a successful operation. What he had in mind had to be executed flawlessly.

He gazed at the clusters of people nearby. He'd told 251 to wear a swimming suit. That way the kid couldn't be wired. Not that he thought 251 would tape their conversation, but it always paid to be cautious, especially when this operative was going to be able to identify him.

Trouble was—everyone was in a bathing suit. He'd hoped to spot 251 as he approached and observe him. Sometimes the little, unconscious things people did told him a lot.

He remembered meeting Samantha Robbins for the first time in TriTech's offices. The first thing he'd noticed—other than she was attractive—was that she could read a sheet of paper on a desk even if it was facing away from her.

He scanned the area again. People were in couples or groups—no single men. A twosome caught his attention. A blonde with tits like Jordan's and a tall, tanned guy with shoulder-length dreadlocks that bounced as he walked. The top section of his dark brown hair had been bleached blond by the sun.

Another rich kid with nothing better to do than hang out in Belize.

The two kissed, a lip-lock that lasted a full minute, then the guy patted her on the butt. She sashayed down the beach, and the kid walked over to him and dropped into the chair across from Brock.

"Numero Uno."

The kid said it with total conviction. How could he know? There were three other men sitting alone at Lilly's.

Stunned, Brock nodded. "Let's walk up the beach."

"Let me get a beer first." The kid signaled the waitress. "A Belikin."

While they waited for the local brew, Brock asked where

An Important Message from the Editors

Dear Reader,

Because you've chosen to read one of our fine romance novels, we'd like to say "thank you!" And, as a **special** way to thank you, we've selected <u>two more</u> of the books you love so well **plus** an exciting Mystery Gift to send you — absolutely <u>FREE</u>!

Please enjoy them with our compliments...

Pam Powers

Lift here

Peel off seal and place inside...

How to validate your Editor's
"Thank You"
FREE GIFT

1. Peel off gift seal from front cover. Place it in space provided at right. This automatically entitles you to receive 2 FREE BOOKS and a fabulous mystery gift.

2. Send back this card and you'll get 2 brand-new *Romance* novels. These books have a cover price of $5.99 or more each in the U.S. and $6.99 or more each in Canada, but they are yours to keep absolutely free.

3. There's no catch. You're under no obligation to buy anything. We charge nothing—ZERO—for your first shipment. And you don't have to make any minimum number of purchases— not even one!

4. The fact is, thousands of readers enjoy receiving their books by mail from The Reader Service. They enjoy the convenience of home delivery...they like getting the best new novels at discount prices BEFORE they're available in stores... and they love their Heart to Heart subscriber newsletter featuring author news, horoscopes, recipes, book reviews and much more!

5. We hope that after receiving your free books you'll want to remain a subscriber. But the choice is yours— to continue or cancel, any time at all! So why not take us up on our invitation, with no risk of any kind. You'll be glad you did!

GET A *Free* MYSTERY GIFT...

SURPRISE MYSTERY GIFT COULD BE YOURS **FREE** AS A SPECIAL "THANK YOU" FROM THE EDITORS

The Reader Service — Here's How It Works:

251 had been diving. That way, if anyone was listening, it would sound like a normal conversation.

"I was out at Shark Ray Alley. Swimming with the sharks. There's nothing like it." He flashed a smile that probably made women drop their panties.

"Nurse sharks and reef sharks. They're not dangerous."

"You never know."

"I was out at the Blue Hole with the red sharks."

The waitress delivered the bottle of Belikin. The kid paid her and left a hefty tip. A waste of money, Brock thought. The kid rose and swigged the beer as they headed up the beach. Brock wasn't sure what to make of 251.

"You wanted to see me?"

"Yeah." Brock wasn't ready to discuss the plan with him yet. He wasn't sure this was the right agent for the job.

"Why did you ask to meet in Belize? Something to do with your current assignment?" Brock didn't expect much of an answer. Whatever 251 was working on was compartmentalized and top secret.

"Nah. I wanted to come to Belize to see my parents."

Christ! The kid had hauled his ass down here just so he could visit a couple of retirees.

Since English was the national language, Belize attracted a lot of older Americans. The weather, the cost of living and the cheap real estate added to Belize's appeal.

He could just imagine the kid's parents. Farmers from Kansas or some other nowhere state who thought they'd died and gone to heaven.

"You're not staying with your folks?"

The kid drained the beer and rubbed his temple with the cool bottle. "I spent a couple of days with them."

"Where's their place?

251 gave him a curious look. "I guess my jacket's buried pretty deep."

A jacket was the intelligence file Obelisk gathered on every employee. Brock had the information and had secretly copied every file to his laptop. Compartmentalization meant he didn't know exactly what all the operatives were doing, but he knew all about their backgrounds.

"My family belongs to the Mennonite Church. They have a dairy farm at Spanish Lookout in Western Belize."

Shit! Religious fanatics distantly related to Pennsylvania's Amish. He hadn't read that anywhere in the jacket he'd studied. His gut roiled with the sudden realization that he might not have all of the information on everyone at Obelisk.

Brrp-brrp.

"That's your cell phone."

Still hammered by the unexpected insight, Brock fumbled with the cell phone clipped to the waist of his khaki shorts. It was his source at the Pentagon.

"I've gotta take this."

"I'll wait for you at Wet Willie's." He pointed down a long pier where a thatched roof hut bar was perched on the end.

Brock watched as 251 sauntered down the pier. "Yeah?"

"There's another DARPA night vision device being tested in Hawaii."

"Give me the details."

Brock listened while his source explained. That gadget was essential if he was going to go to Olofson about taking over Cassidy's job. But first he needed to whack Samantha Robbins.

He hung up and slowly walked out onto the pier. Sea grass lined Belize's shore. Long piers lined with chaise lounges and nearly nude sunbathers extended out from the hotels. People swam off the docks and slipped into bars like Wet Willie's for a drink.

Brock tried to make up his mind about 251. He needed the Robbins bitch taken out immediately, but it would require two operatives to handle the job. He couldn't send one of them after the DARPA widget until she was permanently out of the picture.

It worried him that he might not be getting all the info on

people. It wasn't a good sign. Someone didn't trust him. What he needed to do was prove himself by killing Samantha Robbins.

He found 251 sitting outside Wet Willie's, a bottle of Belikin in one hand, his legs dangling over the end of the pier.

"Uno, look at that stingray. Has a six-foot wing span at least."

Amazing, Brock decided. Wet Willie's was crammed full of people getting a jump on happy hour, waves crashing on the reef not far away, and dive boats returning for the day loaded with people. Despite the distracting noise 251 had heard him coming and knew who he was without looking.

Brock sat down beside him and pretended to be interested in the stingrays gliding through the clear water.

The kid turned to him. "Just because I was raised a Mennonite doesn't mean I'm not the best operative around. Ask anyone who's worked with me."

"I have. You seem to be tops in the field." He emphasized "seem to be" to keep the punk from being so cocky.

"I'm the best because of the strict way I was brought up. Life as a Mennonite is like being in the military—except for all the praying."

Christ! Just what Brock wanted to hear. He was a firm believer that a military background best prepared operatives for fieldwork. They took orders without questions.

"Look," Brock told the kid, "I need an operative who blends in, not someone who sticks out. This is a very sensitive, top secret assignment."

"Gotcha." The kid stood up. "Meet me for dinner at Caliente's at seven."

Before Brock could answer, the kid was gone.

CALIENTE'S WAS A WATERFRONT cantina down the beach from the Mayan Princess. Brock walked into the cantina and sat at the bar. He scanned the crowded room, but 251 hadn't arrived yet.

Rather than return to Caye Caulker, Brock had walked the streets of San Pedro. It hadn't taken much time to cover the three unpaved streets and duck into the shops.

He supposed tourists found the place charming, but Brock was too worried to be interested in Mayan arts and crafts. Like a knife, the thought that he wasn't being given total access to Obelisk files stabbed repeatedly at his thoughts.

Who would have the authority to do such a thing? Only Cassidy. Brock was positive Cassidy wouldn't have done it without encouragement from General Olofson and "the boys."

Why?

If it had been info about money, Brock would have understood. But he was in charge of security. He should know everything about everyone in the field—not their assignments that were compartmentalized—but their backgrounds were crucial to security. How else could he check up on operatives?

It was possible that he'd read 251's jacket too fast and overlooked the Mennonite business, but he doubted it. Normally he'd check his laptop immediately, but he'd left it locked in the safe at his house. He hadn't thought there would be a secure place to store it here, and he'd been right. As soon as he returned, he would double-check 251's profile.

He glanced at his watch. Almost seven. He wasn't sure why the kid wanted to have dinner. Brock had already made up his mind. He was going to recruit his second choice.

It didn't hurt to have dinner with 251, he decided. Who knew? Someday he might have a job for him.

Brock ordered a Belikin, annoyed because the kid was late. Mennonites must not have proper respect for time, he decided. But what did he know about Mennonites? Very little, but he'd learn more as soon as he returned to his office.

A group of people jammed their way into the bar, laughing and talking. The kid wasn't among them. Brock sipped his beer. Drinking beer wasn't his thing, but from the looks of the bottles lining the wall, rum and tequila ruled in Belize.

It didn't matter. After that night with Jordan and the killer hangover, Brock doubted he would be drinking Scotch again soon.

He picked up his beer and decided to check outside for 251. There were tables on the sand a few steps down from the bar. None of them appeared to be occupied by a lone male, but perhaps he couldn't see them all.

As he rose, the nerdy kid with the short butterscotch-colored hair and wire-rimmed glasses at the far end of the long bar caught his eye. The loser was attempting to chat up the girl on the barstool next to him. Lots of luck.

Then it hit him. It was 251. His short hair and stoop-shouldered posture along with the glasses had transformed him completely. He'd been in the bar the entire time. Brock couldn't help smiling. The kid had wanted to show him how he could alter his appearance.

He wanted the job. Brock admired that in an operative. If they were hungry, they obeyed orders without question. He'd been right all along. This was the guy to pair with 77.

Samantha Robbins was as good as dead.

The kid looked up, realized he'd been made, said something to the girl and came over to Brock. Not only had his appearance changed, but the way 251 carried himself had also been transformed. He shambled along, stoop-shouldered, rather than sauntered the way he had when Brock had first seen him.

No one would bother to look twice at this guy.

"Good thing I tipped the guy five bucks to hold our table," said 251. "I thought you were never going to figure out who I was."

The punk was cocky, but this time Brock couldn't fault him. He was good, and Brock needed him more than he was willing to admit.

"We're eating down the beach at Jambel Jerk," said 251. "It's noisy on their roof deck. No one will hear you tell me about my new assignment."

Brock followed the kid down the steps to the sand. He mentally went over his story to convince 251 to whack the bitch without arousing any suspicions.

Brock waited until they were seated on the rooftop deck and had ordered jerk lobster. To Brock, Belize was a supreme bore, but they had great cheap lobster and he liked the Caribbean influence in their food.

"This is a sensitive mission. It's being directed from the highest level in the government." Brock deliberately made it sound as if the president himself had authorized this operation.

The waitress delivered their Belikins, but didn't try to flirt with 251 the way she undoubtedly would have had he still looked the way he had this afternoon.

Brock wiped the ice-cold brown bottle with the napkin wrapped around the top of the bottle. "Why do they always put a napkin on the bottle?"

"The caps tend to rust. You're supposed to wipe it off before you drink." 251 wiped off his bottle and took a small sip, his mannerisms totally different than they had been this afternoon.

Brock kept his voice low. "This is an antiterrorism project."

From behind the wire-rimmed glasses, 251's eyes might have narrowed slightly. Since Brock didn't know what exactly 251 had been doing in Colombia, he didn't know what line they'd fed 251. Patriotism was the usual angle.

"We've discovered a sleeper cell in the States. You're familiar with sleepers?"

"Sure. They're programmed by Al Qaeda or whoever and lie in wait until they're given the signal to attack."

"Exactly, but what's unusual about this cell is that it's headed by a woman."

"What's unusual about that? We've seen suicide bombers who are women."

"This woman is an American citizen."

The kid whistled softly into his beer bottle.

"The order from the top is to kill her before she causes thousands to die."

CHAPTER NINETEEN

DEVON STOOD BESIDE CHAD on the North Shore and watched the surf pummel the beach while Zach romped along the water's edge. The retriever had the good sense not to plunge into the dangerous surf.

"I surfed here almost every day when I was growing up," Chad told her.

"Impressive," Devon replied, and she meant it. The surf here was awesome—some of the biggest waves she'd ever seen. They crashed onto the beach with frightening intensity.

Chad had insisted on taking her for a drive after she'd told him the story she'd concocted about Nate Albert. He was a real person—his name supplied by Warren—the story was pure fiction. Her overwhelming sense of guilt hadn't subsided one bit during the long drive up here.

She watched Zach playing tag with the waves as they raced up on the shore and reminded herself why she'd fabricated such an outrageous tale. Staying here with Zach had become terribly important to her—more important than telling the truth. Once she wouldn't have believed this, but her time in WITSEC had taught her to do anything and everything she could to protect herself.

"What are you thinking?" Chad unexpectedly asked.

She stared at the powerful waves for a moment, then turned to him. "Will you do me a favor?"

He pushed his shades to the top of his head, and his eyes met hers. The intensity in his expression astounded her.

"What's the favor?"

"I want you to forget about me. Go on with your life as if you'd never met me."

He put his large hand on her shoulder. His touch calmed her, took a bit of the darkness away somehow. It was a dangerous feeling. To rely on him could be fatal—for him, for her.

"I can't forget about you. I can't just walk away. I already...care about you." He drew her into his arms. "You know that. Don't you?"

It was all she could do not to give in to her emotions and rest her head on his sturdy shoulder. "This is way too fast. I can't do this."

"Do what?" he asked, his lips against the hair on the top of her head.

"I have to be careful."

"You said Nate Albertson is in federal prison."

"That doesn't mean he won't send one of his henchmen after me." She forced herself to pull out of his arms. "I don't want you involved."

"I can take care of myself," he replied as he led her down the beach toward a bench. "I was in Delta Force."

On the way up to the North Shore, Chad had told her about himself. No doubt he was a highly trained man who was far better able to protect himself than Romero had been. Still, Rutherford and Ames could afford a top-notch hit team like the one they sent to Santa Fe. Chad might not even see them coming.

Zach bounded up to them, his exuberance forcing her to smile. "Good boy." He had a stick in his mouth that he'd found somewhere on the beach. She tossed it high in the air but away from the water. She didn't want him in the treacherous surf.

"There was a man," she told him as they sat down on the wooden bench, "a friend who had a gallery next to where I worked."

Chad's eyes roved over her in silent appraisal, and she wondered if he was asking himself why she hadn't mentioned this earlier. She'd wanted to tell as few lies as possible. She'd told him that she'd been working in a gallery in Portland when a hit team had come to kill her. Basically she'd re-hashed the Santa Fe story including the part about the two cell phones, but she hadn't mentioned Romero's death. She'd claimed she'd gotten away and had driven south to Santa Barbara where she was able to crew on a sailboat bound for Hawaii.

This jibed with her explanation of how she'd escaped Nate Albert by flying to London, hitchhiking to the south of France and hiring on as crew on a boat sailing to Florida. Chad had remarked that this was an ingenious way of getting back into the country. Airports had extremely tight security since 9/11 but yacht harbors had lax customs check points.

"What about the man?" Chad prompted.

"They killed him." She exhaled, hard. "Slit his throat."

"I'm sorry." He ran his fingers along the curve of her cheek. "I know you're worried about me, but—"

"Don't you *get* it? He died because he befriended me. I don't want to put you at risk. If they—"

"They?"

Careful, she warned herself. She'd been thinking of Ru-therford and Ames and had said "they." Slow down. Watch what you say. "Remember, I told you the hit team was an or-dinary looking couple from the Midwest. They weren't what I would have expected. Who knows what the next team will look like?"

His eyes raked her face, their blue depths gleaming with an inner light that was almost frightening. Tenderness replaced the fearsome intensity in his expression. "We're in this *together.*"

She'd been alone and lonely for so long with only Zach for comfort. To know someone cared touched her in a very unexpected way. She wanted to wrap her arms around him and cradle him against her breasts. To keep him safe. It was an irrational, maternal instinct she realized, but she couldn't help herself.

We're in this together.

He didn't have a clue about what was really happening. Devon was tempted to warn him, but there was so much about him she didn't know, and she couldn't risk getting tossed out of WITSEC. She had no choice but to stick with the story she'd fabricated.

Zach pranced up to her, the stick in his jaws. She took her time extracting it from his mouth while she tried to decide what to do about Chad. She threw the sand-coated stick as far down the beach as she could.

Chad reached over and threaded a tendril of her hair through his fingers. His eyes never left hers as he played with her hair. Unrelenting determination in his voice, he repeated, "We're in this together."

Chest swelling emotion welled up inside her. She couldn't look into his eyes any longer. She was afraid he would see through the web of lies. He leaned down and she almost sighed as his lips hovered over hers.

"Don't," she managed to murmur.

"You don't want me to kiss you?"

"No. I don't." Even to Devon, her voice sounded pathetically unconvincing.

"If I recall...you kissed me big-time last night."

She hadn't forgotten, not for a second, not even when she'd been spinning the tale about Nate Albert. Her entire body had been taut with anticipation since he'd walked into her apartment. Encouraging him was dangerous for both of them.

Tell a joke, her mind ordered. Defuse the situation.

"Know what God said after creating Eve?"

Chad frowned at her.

"Practice makes perfect."

He shook his head. "Very funny. You joke to get out of tight spots."

She couldn't deny it. Jokes relieved tension. She'd learned that as a young child when her parents had been fighting.

He took her face in the palms of his hands and tilted it upward until she was forced to look into his eyes. In their smoldering depths she saw something she couldn't name. Ever so slowly he drew her to him.

She knew she shouldn't do this. Kissing him only encouraged feelings of intimacy. His we're-in-this-together attitude would only increase if she allowed him to get close to her like this. She tried to pull away, but his powerful arms anchored her in place.

His lips touched hers and longing rose, swift and overwhelming. Devon admitted the truth to herself. She wanted this man. It wasn't just, sex, either, she realized with shattering clarity. She needed much, much...more from him.

He teased her lips apart and nudged his tongue into her mouth. Her pulse went berserk, throbbing heat invading the sweet spot between her thighs. She clung to him, savoring the male scent of his body, the salt air dancing around them, the trace of woodsy aftershave.

His hand inched up her rib cage and cradled her breast. He stroked the nipple with his thumb until it was a taut bead straining against the sheer fabric of her sundress. She arched against his rock-hard, inescapably masculine frame and furrowed her fingers through his hair.

She molded her body against his and kissed him, not even *thinking* about holding back. Passion surged through her and she knew she didn't have the willpower to resist him. She'd known she had a sensual side, but her physical reaction to other men had never been this intense.

He pulled back a scant inch. His heavy-lidded eyes gazed down at her. "You see? All it takes is a kiss." His warm breath stirred her hair. "And we're ready to go."

There was no point in denying it. Unwilling to trust her voice, she merely nodded.

"I don't think a public beach is a very good spot."

"No, it's not," she agreed.

"Let's go to my place."

BROCK STARED AT 251'S FILE. There was nothing in the jacket about the agent's Mennonite background. It listed his parents as Martha and David Norton. Place of birth: Belize City, Belize, Central America.

Did another more comprehensive file exist somewhere else at Obelisk? If it was stored in an electronic format, Brock would know about it. But if it was in an old-fashioned paper file—it could be anywhere in the building.

Cassidy's office was the most likely spot. As CEO he should have information on everyone. Brock had never found Cassidy to be particularly clever. Why would he hide 251's religious background? It didn't make sense.

While he mulled over the puzzle, Brock logged on to ref-desk.com and looked up the Mennonites in Belize. They were distant relatives of the Pennsylvania Amish who had moved to Mexico in the 1900s. They were devoted pacifists who rejected any form of taxation. In the 1950s the Mexican government tried to make them join the Social Security network. The whole group packed up and moved to Belize.

Unlike the Pennsylvania Amish, the Mennonites in Belize didn't reject modern equipment. None of that horse and buggy crap some people found quaint. The Mennonites in Belize were very successful farmers and produced most of the country's dairy products. The small but influential group was wealthy compared to their countrymen.

Brock read a little more but didn't find anything online that gave him the slightest clue about why 251's Mennonite background wasn't in his file. Brock knew he was going to have to get into Cassidy's office and see if he had paper files that hadn't been scanned into the security system.

There wasn't any reason Brock could see not to go ahead with his plan. Tomorrow 251 would be back in this country. 77 had already been prepped on the mission.

"Samantha Robbins is as good as dead."

His words echoed through his office. With the bitch out of

the way, he could send 77 after the DARPA device some jerk was testing in Hawaii.

"Speaking of bitches." He picked up the telephone and called Jordan Walsh. The bitch hadn't returned a single one of his phone calls. Who did she think she was? The damn answering machine picked up, and he slammed the receiver down.

Maybe he should just go over to her place tonight. The message didn't say she was traveling. He assumed she would be home. He didn't care about Jordan Walsh blowing him off—but he did care about her Gull Wing. He intended to have that car.

Brock killed the rest of the afternoon running security checks on Obelisk executives. No one but Cassidy seemed to be in contact with Bash Olofson. It occurred to Brock that Olofson might have files on Obelisk operatives. Brock had never tried to get into his computer.

"Too risky."

If he were caught breaking into Olofson's house, it would be the end of his career. He had no doubt the general would have him killed. Brock liked to get into computers directly. He had no trouble accessing the Obelisk executives' terminals because they were in the building.

He could send the general an e-mail greeting card and use some other general's name so Olofson would be sure to open it. Most people didn't yet realize that worms could be embedded in those cutesy online cards. The worm wouldn't destroy files. It would relay them to another computer.

Brock would have to purchase a computer and use a false name. There was always the chance the worm would be discovered. He didn't want it traced back to him.

That evening he went to Jordan's condo. No lights were on and no one answered the bell. He slipped a note under the front door.

Call me. I miss you.

He wanted to go to his warehouse and detail his cars, but night was the only time he could safely search Cassidy's office. He drove back to Obelisk, parked in his spot and checked his watch. The security guards patrolled the building every thirty-seven minutes.

Brock slipped into the building and took the backstairs to Cassidy's twelfth-floor office. He had keys to every office in the building, even though the only other set of keys was supposed to be in the security guard's office. He slid the key in the lock and the door clicked open. Brock slipped inside and shut it quietly behind him.

He turned on the special military flashlight. It was longer and thinner than a standard flashlight, but gave off tremendous light. He checked his watch. In thirty-one minutes the guard would make rounds and check this office. He had to be out by then.

It didn't take half that long. Cassidy had nothing of interest hidden in his office. Nothing. Where was the file?

CHAPTER TWENTY

CHAD WAS HALFWAY BACK to his house when his cell phone rang. He wasn't in the mood to be interrupted, but the caller ID indicated Ane was trying to reach him. She rarely called so he decided this must be important.

With a smile to Devon, he answered, *"Lil eha?"* What's happening?

"The police need you at Kewalo Basin. A little boy disappeared. They think he may have fallen in."

"I'm on my way."

Chad hit the end button and cursed under his breath. Just his luck. Devon had finally warmed up to him, and he had to leave her.

"I have a contract with HPD," he told Devon. "I do underwater forensics for them. A kid fell into the water at the Kewalo Basin."

"Kewalo Basin. Isn't that where the fishing fleet is based?"

"Right. But there are lots of children around the docks. They wait for the fleet to come in and help out or take home fish too damaged to sell."

Devon sighed so softly that he might not have heard except his head was tilted toward her. "That poor mother. She must be frantic."

"If the kid's been underwater for more than a few minutes, he's gone." It disturbed him to say it, but from experience, he knew this was true. "Children drown without a sound and without much splashing."

"Unlike adults who yell for help and flail around in the water. Right?"

"Absolutely. Kewalo Basin is an extremely busy place. A child in the water might not have been noticed."

"Won't the police send divers down?"

"Trust me. Fishermen searched the minute the mother alerted them. By the time the police arrive, it'll be treated as a crime scene."

"This sounds like an accident, not a crime."

He could hear the emotion in her voice and knew she was empathizing with the mother. Devon had a soft side she rarely allowed people to see. She would be a great mother. Where had that thought come from? he asked himself.

"Look, the islands are surrounded by water," he said. "It wouldn't be the first time a parent tossed in a kid who was already dead."

"You mean...to cover up child abuse?"

"Exactly. Once it was police policy to bring up the body and collect evidence on the surface. Now they send down underwater forensic experts like me. I locate the body, take photos and measurements and thoroughly examine the area. I'll be the one to put the body in a plastic mesh bag so the water can drain when it's on land."

Devon covered her eyes with one hand for a moment. "Sounds like grim work. How did you get into it?"

"I always loved the water. Part of Delta Force training is the same course they give navy SEALs. I took underwater investigation classes when I was in the service. When I got out, I started Underwater Investigations. I work primarily for insurance companies when they need to verify a cause of death that occurred in the water."

"Shelby told me you worked on the Laci Peterson case."

Chad smiled to himself. So she'd been asking Shelby about him. The airhead didn't know much, but it pleased him that Devon had asked. Actually, it pleased him a lot more than he would have believed.

"Laci's parents called me in, but the police had already sent down a team of underwater experts. There wasn't much I could add."

"I guess she and her baby were badly decomposed."

"You bet. The water there is very cold, but she was under a long time. Here with the water so warm decomposition is extremely rapid."

"How do you know if they drowned or if they died elsewhere and were thrown into the water?"

"First I check the victim's mouth. If there's sand or seaweed in it, I'm fairly certain the person was alive and breathing when he hit the water. Foam at the mouth is another sign. It's mucus secreted from the trachea when water is inhaled." Chad drove off Kunia Drive onto Highway 1. "Sometimes I can't tell. The coroner has to autopsy the body. He looks for small tears or hemorrhages on the lungs."

"Interesting," Devon said, her voice low.

They drove in silence for a few minutes. He turned off the highway onto city streets. A slug fest. No question about it. Honolulu had traffic problems as bad as those on the mainland.

"You can let me off at the corner," Devon said. "Zach and I will walk home."

An oddly primitive warning sounded in his brain. Now that he knew she was in danger, he didn't want her to be alone.

As if reading his mind, she said, "I'll be careful. This way you can get to Kewalo Basin faster. The child's mother must be going out of her mind with worry."

He knew she was right, and he also realized he couldn't be with her every moment of the day. "I don't know how long this is going to take. I'll call you. Maybe we can get together later. It'll depend on how long I have to be underwater."

She nodded slightly and he hoped she wasn't going to change her mind. He brought the Porsche to a halt at the curb in a loading zone. Devon got out. Her skirt hiked up for a moment and gave him a glimpse of her long, slim legs. Zach hopped out of the back.

"Thanks for showing me the North Shore."

"See you later." Chad watched them walk up the street until they disappeared around the corner. As usual Devon had subtly checked the people nearby.

He'd been right to try to get close to her. Devon was too frightened to allow many people into her life. But now that he had persuaded her to open up, he was going to be part of her life. They had chemistry going for them, but more than that, Chad related to Devon in a special way. He saw something of himself in her. They shared the same independent streak.

Chad drove to Kewalo Basin and parked beside a police cruiser. In the trunk of his car he kept his gear. The water in Hawaii was so warm a wet suit wasn't necessary, but he needed his dive vest and regulator. He had a special face mask with an earpiece and a speaker. When he was conducting an underwater investigation, he had to be able to contact officers on the shore. He also used an underwater camera and a waterproof recorder to document his findings.

"*Aikane!*" Buddy! His friend, Rafe greeted him. "Good news! The kid didn't fall in the water. He and a cousin wandered into the video arcade down the street."

"Great. The last thing I want is to search for a drowned child."

He chatted with Rafe while he repacked his gear in the trunk of his car.

"Hey, thanks for getting that info from the DMV for me."

"No problem. Did it help?"

"You bet."

They said goodbye and Chad climbed into his car. He revved the engine to kick on the air conditioning. He tried Devon's number on his cell, but she didn't answer.

She wasn't in trouble, was she?

He drove to his office, telling himself that he couldn't worry about her every second of the day. It didn't seem likely that Nate Albert would send a hit team from behind bars, but stranger things had happened. Obviously Devon thought it was a real possibility. She'd taken elaborate measures to ensure her safety.

He checked the cars around him to make certain no one was following him. He needed to shift into readiness mode. One man had already died while testing the DARPA gadget. Albert had killed Devon's friend while trying to get to her.

When he arrived at his office building, he looked in Aloha Yachts and Weddings to see if Devon had come here. No one was inside. They were closed Monday and Tuesday, but Eddie sometimes came in to catch up on paperwork.

"Any calls?" Chad asked Ane as he walked into his office.

With a smug smile, Ane said, "I told you so."

"Okay. What did you tell me?"

"The murder in Turks and Caicos would be solved."

He stopped in his tracks. "Really? How?"

"One of the crew members went to the police and admitted he'd lied. The captain and the wife weren't onboard the yacht all afternoon. They'd paid the crew to give them an alibi."

"Why would the guy suddenly confess?"

"Tom Holden from Fidelity Insurance said the crew member discovered he has colon cancer. He didn't want to die with this on his conscience. Mr. Holden has e-mailed you the final report. The wife and the yacht captain are living together in Boston. The police there eked a confession out of Mrs. Townsend. The captain punctured the air hose with the bang stick and held Robert Townsend down until he drowned. The wife was onshore nearby."

"*Hoopono.*" Justice. He walked over to his desk and found a few messages, but nothing from Devon. He tried her cell again. Still no answer.

He booted up his computer and checked a few facts of her story. *Liquid Fix,* the boat Devon claimed to have crewed on, had sailed from St. Tropez to Key Largo, Florida. Devon Summers had been listed as a crew member on that voyage.

He'd been in Key Largo several times when he'd left the military and had been doing testing for DARPA. It was a haven for rich people with yachts the size of ocean liners. There wasn't a customs office there. The harbor master kept a roster of incoming ships and their crew. The information didn't go to the main computer customs used to run background checks for possible terrorists because all the harbor master recorded was the names and citizenship status.

"Ingenious," he said under his breath, "and dangerous." He hoped to hell that Homeland Security was on to this.

Nate Albert would have been able to hire a hacker to break into the U.S. Customs master computer and check for Devon's name. It would have been entered into the computer as she flew in from abroad. He wasn't clever enough to check the numerous private yacht harbors.

He used Google to look up Nate Albert. A little over three months ago, Albert had been sentenced to six years in federal prison for racketeering. They'd nailed him for bootlegging cigarettes from Canada. Chad bet the prick was involved in drugs and prostitution, but bootlegging cigarettes was the only thing they could prove. He knew the Feds did that a lot. It helped get known criminals out of circulation.

He felt like a major skank for checking up on Devon, but his training wouldn't allow him to not verify a few facts. He'd believed her when she'd told him the story. The only thing that had bothered him was Devon using her own name. She'd pointed out that Albert had found her when she'd been living under another name. She didn't think he'd expect her to use her real name.

Okay, maybe. But it still troubled him.

Devon had a power and depth to her that other women he'd known didn't have. It came as a shock for him to realize he wanted to settle down with Devon. He'd never thought much about starting a family. His sisters and their children had seemed to be family enough.

Until now. Until Devon.

His cell phone rang. It was Devon. She'd been at the Salvation Army dropping off the clothing. He made arrangements to pick her up in an hour.

"*Pono!*" Careful, Ane said as he walked out the door. "She's *pilikia*." Trouble.

DEVON STOOD AT THE SHORE where the waves were breaking at her feet and watched Zach romp in the water, retrieving a tennis ball Chad had tossed for him. Chad had picked her up more than an hour ago and had brought her to his home.

She didn't know what she was feeling. She realized she cared about him—even without really spending time with him—more than she had Tyler. How had that happened so quickly?

You're lonely.

A chill settled over her as she watched Zach frolic in the surf with Chad. She'd allowed a man into her life, someone who might easily die because of her. What was she thinking?

Something in her couldn't bring herself to let Chad go. She tried to examine her emotions, but she decided that being in WITSEC had changed her. Not only was she more cautious, but she was emotionally exhausted. She needed him in a way she'd never needed another person before, and it frightened her.

"Come on in," Chad called. "The water's warm."

She was wearing a red bikini that she'd bought on sale when she'd first arrived in Honolulu. She walked into the surf, and discovered he was right. The sun had set in a splash of crimson, leaving the sea burnished with a golden glow. She stopped beside Chad.

Her eyes drifted over his powerful body, which did wonders for the green Hawaiian print swimming trunks. She couldn't seem to force herself to look away. The magnetism he generated was almost a living, tangible thing.

Chad examined every inch of her expressive face. Her full lower lip added to her sensual appeal. But even in the dim light he could see how hiding, always being on guard was wearing her down. The determined set of her jaw, the spray of lines just beginning to form at the corners of her eyes spoke of fears unuttered, unshared. He wanted to be part of her life and to somehow make her world right again.

He slipped his arm around Devon's tiny waist. Parting her lips, she tilted her head toward him inviting his kiss. His mouth met hers and he took a moment to caress that full lower lip with his tongue. She moaned softly and furrowed her fingers through his hair.

The balmy night was warm, but Devon's body was even warmer. Its heat unfurled rapidly from where lush breasts were pillowed against his chest. He wanted to see those breasts without a stitch of clothing on them. He wanted to kiss them, brand them with his mouth.

Aw, hell. He wanted to kiss every inch of her gorgeous bod. For now he contented himself with letting his tongue mate with hers and running his hand down her smooth back. He inched his fingers beneath the red fabric across her cute bottom.

She twined her legs around his and arched her body so her pelvis was against his penis. His pulse skyrocketed and he had a full-blown erection in a heartbeat. He'd never been so painfully hard in his whole damn life.

And he'd never wanted a woman more. Not just for sex. He wanted her on many levels.

He cupped her bottom with his hand and pushed her against his penis. She moaned softly, her arms now curled around his neck.

"Maybe we should go inside," he whispered.

"Okay."

He picked her up and carried her out of the water. His body was so masculine, so comforting. Zach trotted after them. "Here," she whispered when they were near the chaises around the swimming pool. Rory was in Kaui for a surfing competition. No one else was around.

"Works for me."

He gently laid her down and stretched out beside her, his breath stirring the wispy hair along her temple.

"Oh, my," she whispered as his lips found the sensitive spot at the curve of her neck.

Her breath came out in a soft rush and with it came a debilitating flash of intuition. Even as he kissed her, she was shattered by a sense of loss. This would end. She would lose him, and the overwhelming power of the loss brought tears to her eyes.

She would be alone again.

Chad raised his head just long enough to catch a flicker of something cross her face. "Darling, what's the matter?"

She shrugged, lifting both shoulders off the chaise in a way that seemed as if she were getting set to run.

"We're in this together," he told her. With the back of his knuckles, he caressed her cheek. His eyes searched her face as if there was nothing—or no one—more precious on the earth.

He put his hands on either side of her face and bent down to kiss her. His lips were soft, moist, undemanding. The glint in his eyes made her feel like the most precious thing in the world. Her dread eased, and she allowed her fears to flow out of her like a receding tide.

Live in the moment. All you have is here and now.

She gazed into matchless eyes and knew all the hell she'd been through was worth this moment, this man. With trembling arms, she circled his neck, and whispered, "Make love to me."

"I was planning on it." His voice was husky.

For a moment, she experienced a stab of guilt for telling him such an elaborate lie, but she couldn't chance confiding in him. The only chance she had for a future with this man was staying in the program. She'd detected a note of suspicion in Warren's voice when he'd asked her what she'd been doing. Nothing.

Oh, yeah, and Diamond Head was just another hill.

He untied the top of her bikini and tossed it over her shoulder. Out of the corner of her eye, she saw Zach nose it, then trot away to where he'd dropped the tennis ball.

He reverently ran his warm hands over her breasts and her nipples tightened at his touch. She gazed out at the sparkling water and knew the *menehunes* were dancing on the waves, smiling at them. She took a happy breath and inhaled the heady fragrance of plumeria floating on the balmy air. The stars had popped out, in that sudden way they do in the tropics, and winked down at them.

He lowered his head and gently kissed first one breast and then the other. The raspy prickling of an emerging beard tantalized her sensitive breasts. He drew one turgid nipple into his mouth and gently sucked. Her pulse went haywire and moist heat built between her thighs. She shifted beneath him, striving to feel his erection where she needed it the most.

He stood up and in one swift motion dropped his swim trunks. His penis jutted out from his powerful body. Her stomach fluttered, and she heard herself sigh. He was drop-dead gorgeous, the moonlight silvering the pale skin that hadn't been exposed to sunlight.

She reached up and cradled the full weight of his sex in her hand. One finger traced the ridge of his penis until she reached the rounded velvet tip. Her hand glided up and down the turgid length of his sex, squeezing hard as she stroked.

"Hold it, babe. Aren't you forgetting something? Drop the rest of your bikini."

She let go of him and shimmied out of her wet bikini bottom.

"You're fantastic, Devon," he whispered as he grabbed her.

He lowered her back onto the chaise, taking the brunt of his weight on his forearms. He kissed her again, this time more insistently, his erection prodding her belly. He slowly eased one hand downward until it found the moist curls between her thighs.

Hot and wet, she was more than ready. "Hurry, hurry."

He stroked her for a minute, fondling the slick nub. He inserted one finger deep inside her, and she cried out for a second. He withdrew his finger, then entered her again this time with two fingers. She slowly moved against his hand.

He pulled his hand away and nudged her legs apart with his knee. The tip of his shaft began to probe her. He inched forward, gently rocking his hips and pressing inside her. She felt her body stretch, giving to accommodate his size. She arched upward as he thrust into her, hot and hard.

A growl came from deep in his chest, but it reverberated through her entire body. She quivered and her heart thundered in her ears.

She let herself go, and threw her legs around his hips. "Oh, Chad. Oh, my God."

Almost immediately a flood of pure pleasure rushed through her. It crested with a rush of erotic sensation that kicked up her spine and slammed into her brain like a handful of sparkling stars. It took a minute to catch her breath and realize Chad hadn't yet climaxed. She stayed with him, intent on giving him as much pleasure as he'd given her.

He came a few minutes later. Moisture sheathed their bodies, and Devon felt strangely languid, almost boneless.

Breathing like a marathon runner, Chad rolled to the side to take his weight off her. "I'm crazy about you, Devon. Crazy about you."

CHAPTER TWENTY-ONE

BROCK HAD ABSOLUTELY no luck in finding another set of files. He'd electronically checked every computer at Obelisk. That left Olofson's computer. He'd e-mailed the general a greeting card with an embedded worm. It instructed the computer to download all the general's files to the new computer Brock had purchased, using cash and a fake name so it could never be traced back to him.

"What crap," Brock muttered. The general had so much stuff on his computer it would take days to sift through all the info. He tried searching for 251's name but didn't get a hit. It was possible the info was in code. After all, General Olofson had once headed up army intelligence.

His telephone rang, the line his agents used to contact him. He picked up the receiver. "Numero Uno."

"251 here. I just landed at Dulles."

"Great. Tomorrow I'll arrange a meeting with 77, your partner on this."

"I'm going to need equipment."

Brock knew he meant a sharpshooter's rifle and a night vision scope. Airport security being so tight these days, 251 wouldn't have brought his weapon with him. "Make a list of what you need. I'll take care of it."

"I'll call you in the morning."

"Don't use a cell phone."

"You don't have to tell me that."

Brock hung up, a smile on his face. Samantha Robbins was

as good as his. He'd have a little chat with the bitch, then let 251 take over.

He tried Jordan Walsh again. It had been two days since he'd left the note. Now he was more than just angry. A blinding hot jolt of rage hammered him every time he thought about her. No woman had ever ignored him like this. Jordan's damn machine picked up. He slammed down the receiver.

After a few minutes thinking over the situation, Brock called one of his local operatives. The jerk was practically worthless, but this assignment didn't require much brains.

"It's Numero Uno. I've got a job for you. I want Jordan Walsh's condo staked out. Call me the minute she shows up."

The guy took down Jordan's address and the cell phone number Brock was currently using. Tonight he wanted to go to the warehouse and detail his cars. Those babies needed a little loving.

CHAD COULDN'T CONVINCE Devon to move in with him. Since they first made love, they had spent every night together, but Devon insisted on going home early each morning. She claimed she needed to be independent. Chad thought her relationship with Nate Albert had made her a little distrustful of all men. It would take time for it to ease, and he had to face the fact that she might never get over it completely.

If he and Devon were going to have a future together, something had to be done. What? He wasn't sure how to handle the situation. Warning a guy like Albert to leave Devon alone would be like waving a red flag at a bull. It might just lead Albert to Devon.

He wondered if Archer Danson could help him. Maybe he could contact an inmate at the same prison and have the man talk to Albert. He could feel him out and see if the creep was still after Devon.

He put in a call to Danson, then went to the pay phone near the marina to wait for his call. On the way out of his office, he waved to Devon from across the courtyard. He didn't even think about telling her what he was going to do. He didn't want to have to explain his relationship with DARPA.

The phone rang a few minutes later. "Danson, I need a favor."

"Okay," he replied slowly. "What kind of favor?"

"There's a wise guy from Chicago named Nathan Albert. He's sitting in federal prison in Illinois for bootlegging cigarettes in from Canada. I need a fellow inmate to talk to him."

"I hope you know what you're getting into. Chicago wise guys are just about the most ruthless."

"I just want to see if he's still after Devon Summers."

"I take it you're involved with this woman."

"That's right. I need to find out if she has anything to fear from him now. He tried to kill her once already for leaving him."

A long pause. "What if he *is* still after her?"

"Good question." Chad glanced down the street and saw Keke parking her car. Great. She would wonder what he was doing on a public telephone—if she saw him. He turned away, hoping Keke wouldn't spot him. "I don't have to do anything right now unless Albert has sent someone after Devon. He's just starting a six year sentence."

"Which means three years with good behavior."

"Great."

"Don't do anything that will jeopardize your safety or get you into trouble. If there's a problem, get back to me. I can put you in touch with people..."

"Right." He knew Danson meant assassins who killed for the money but weren't affiliated with the mob.

Danson asked for a little more information and said, "I should have an answer for you tomorrow. The next day at the latest."

"Any word on the person who murdered the other agent testing for you?"

Danson grunted. "We've got a few leads. I'll keep you posted if there's anything you should know. Meanwhile watch your back."

Chad hung up and slowly turned around. His sister stood across the street waving at him.

"Hi, there!" Keke called.

Chad walked toward her with what he hoped was a relaxed smile. He hadn't spoken with her since he'd started spending so much time with Devon. Keke was far too perceptive where he was concerned. If he mentioned Devon, that would be it. Keke would be all over him.

Warning him.

Neither Keke nor Ane had warmed up to Devon. If they knew why she wore isolation like a shield, they wouldn't think the same way about Devon.

"Is there something wrong with your telephone?" Keke asked.

"Nah. A buddy who's still with Delta Force is hyper about security. No cell phones. No office phones that can be traced."

"Public phone calls can't be traced?"

"Yes, but they rarely are. They're swept clean every forty-eight hours by the phone company. Occasionally crooks get caught. Remember the Menendez brothers?"

They walked down the sidewalk toward the office, and Keke said, "Those rich kids in L.A. who shot their parents?"

"That's right. They claimed to have made a phone call from a public phone. The police were able to access the records before the sweep. That lie incriminated them."

"Speaking of incriminating." Keke stopped, shielded her eyes with her hand. "This morning I came in to drop off some stuff. Devon was going through Eddie's files and inputting data into her computer."

"She's probably bringing her files up-to-date. Lori left quite a mess."

"Why would she need his marine repair files? If you ask me, the woman is planning to embezzle funds. Remember how easily that other woman took Eddie. I don't want it to happen again."

Chad nodded saying, "Oh, Keke. I doubt that."

"You're hot for her so you can't see what's really happening."

"I'll check into it. I promise."

Keke huffed, not satisfied but obviously unwilling to argue any more with her brother.

"I'm picking up Shelby. Her car's in the shop. We're working a sunset cruise for Eddie tonight. Insurance Underwriters of America or something."

"Sounds exciting." He gave her a quick hug and a peck on the cheek. "See you later."

DEVON LOOKED UP from her computer and saw Chad standing in the doorway of Aloha's offices. Everyone had gone to work the sunset cruise except for Devon and Zach.

Her heart lifted at the sight of him. When he was around it seemed *possible* that she could lead a normal life. Warren was back from his WITSEC Continuing Ed course, and she was going to be able to call her sister on Saturday. Even better, Masterson had agreed not to relocate her because of Chad. Things seemed a little more in balance, less scary.

Zach jumped up and bounded over to him, his tail whipping through the air.

"Good boy, Zach." Chad paused to stroke the retriever's golden head. He looked up at her, his eyes a little more serious than usual. "What are you working on?"

"An Excel spreadsheet. I'm working up a cost analysis of the business."

"Eddie asked you to do that?"

"No," she admitted, "but we don't have a wedding this weekend so I thought I would put together some numbers."

He rose, walked over to her desk and kissed her lightly on the cheek. He studied the material she had up on the screen. Devon shifted uncomfortably. Her accounting background helped her analyze the data and organize it in sophisticated charts and comparison columns.

"Impressive."

She gazed up at him. "Eddie's not charging enough for some of his services. A few vendors are double billing him."

"I suspected as much. You have to be careful how you handle Eddie. He's got enough pride for two men. He won't want a woman telling him how to run his business."

"Don't worry. I plan to stay under the radar screen. I'm raising some of the prices on certain wedding categories to start. I'll speak to the vendors and demand credit for the duplicate billings."

"Atta girl. Good thinking."

There was something off in the way he was looking at her, his tone of voice. She shouldn't have used her accounting skills to analyze Eddie's business, but she hadn't been able to help herself. Her gut instinct from day one was Eddie wasn't very good at managing his business. He was a sweet man who'd been good enough to hire her. He deserved her help.

BROCK HAD KEPT surveillance on Jordan Walsh's condo for three days now. She hadn't turned up. He'd had the neighbors questioned, but apparently Jordan had only recently bought the place. None of them knew her, but a few recalled an attractive redhead.

Attractive?

A knockout with Bugatti tits.

He wished he'd asked more questions about her business. She'd mentioned what had sounded like a Web site. If he knew more, he could find her right now. Whatever Jordan did, she traveled a lot.

The St. Louis Auto Show was coming up in a week. He went online to see if she'd registered the caper-green Gull Wing. She had.

Bingo!

He would offer her an obscene amount of money for the car. If she didn't take it, he would have her killed and deal with her estate. Maybe he should prepare a bill of sale—force her to sign it—if she wouldn't willingly. Then kill her.

Brock stared at the liquid plasma satellite screen on one wall of his office, thinking. He zoomed in on L.A., shining in the morning light after a night of rain had washed it clean. Palms, magnolias, bright red bottlebrushes gleamed while high-rises sparkled. Like snakes slithering through the jungle, traffic barely moved.

Served the suckers right. Too much sunshine and good weather.

Brock had never killed anyone, but he'd ordered numerous whacks for Obelisk. Most of the hits were in Third World countries where no one asked many questions. A murdered woman with an expensive car in St. Louis might not be his best idea.

He would have to get a gun after he'd flown into town. A cardinal rule of jobs like this was to buy a gun that couldn't possibly be traced back to you. Dump it immediately after using it. Tricky.

Talk to her in St. Louis. Take her out—have someone else do it—in D.C. where crime wasn't any big deal. Good plan, he decided.

He left for his second meeting with agents 251 and 77. They met on the Georgetown campus. The operatives had hip, loose-fitting clothes so they could hide a weapon. Backpacks hid rounds of ammo and other equipment. Here they blended in perfectly. Brock thought his tweed jacket made him look like one of the professors.

"You've got everything you need?" he asked.

Agent 77 nodded, but 251 said, "We could use extra cash just in case."

Brock smiled to himself. No question about it, 251 was sharp. Brock had anticipated this and had gotten more cash. If anything went wrong, you didn't want to be using a credit card that could be traced.

"Use the pay phones. If you have to use a cell, ditch it immediately."

"Right," they both said a split second apart.

He handed them the high definition aerial photographs he'd downloaded from the DoD satellite less than an hour ago. They were concealed in a textbook on Freud called *A State of Mind*. Brock thought it made a nice touch.

"Call me when you've located the bitch."

"Right," they again agreed.

"Any questions?"

251 said, "When I've finished, she'll be better off dead."

The words hit Brock like a sucker punch to the gut. *Better off dead.* He'd thought the same thing—only he wanted to be the one to make Samantha Robbins wish she was dead.

"Don't kill her," Brock warned them. "I have to debrief her."

251 shrugged, saying, "Like she would hesitate before killing innocent Americans."

"That's just it," Brock replied, concern filling his voice. No telling what 251 might do in the name of justice. "She may know of other sleeper cells out there. I *must* be the one to debrief her."

251 shrugged again. "We're outta here."

CHAPTER TWENTY-TWO

TWO DAYS LATER, Devon came to work and waved to Chad, who was already in his office. As usual, she'd spent the night with him, but she'd gone home to change. She would like to live with Chad. It felt safer there. The gates, towering walls and the high-tech security system made her feel secure. It was an illusion, of course. She knew that a determined hit team would have no problem killing her.

She kept her apartment because Warren couldn't know about her relationship with Chad. If he did, Masterson would relocate her rather than chance Chad discovering her true identity.

At times guilt, like a vise cinching her chest, made her regret her relationship with Chad. What if he were killed because of her? With his background, he could defend himself better than most men. She kept telling him she had a premonition that Albert's men were getting closer—just so he would keep up his guard.

But she couldn't bring herself to break off the relationship. He'd come to mean the world to her. God willing, when this was over, she would return here, and they could have a future together.

"You'll never, like, believe what happened," Shelby said as Devon walked into the office, Zach at her heels.

"I give. What?"

"Saturday's wedding is canceled. The groom has cold feet." Shelby tsked. "As if! This has been planned for almost two years."

Devon nodded. Everything was lined up for this event. With the wedding canceled, there wouldn't be much to do day after tomorrow except cocktail cruises for conventioneers. She wasn't involved in the sunset cruises; she worked strictly on weddings. Several were coming up and she had a lot of work to do on them. This would give her extra time.

"Shelby, call around and see if we can sell the flowers and food to other vendors. Cut the prices to the bone to unload as much as you can. I'd like to see the bride get back *some* of her money."

"She'd ordered, like, tons of tulips. They symbolize love, you know."

Devon hadn't known, but she had realized how hideously expensive the flowers had been. Tulips weren't grown here and had to be flown in, using special refrigerated containers.

The average wedding in America cost about thirty-five thousand dollars. This wedding was just over one hundred thousand dollars. At this point everything was paid for, and the bride would be lucky to recoup a quarter of what she'd spent.

The cell phone in Devon's purse rang, and she went to her desk before pulling it out. She didn't want Shelby to get a glimpse inside her purse and spot the second cell phone or the gun.

"Hello," she answered.

"I need to see you," Warren told her. "Are you free now to meet me?"

"I guess. Where?"

"Under the sperm whale at the Bishop Museum in, say, an hour."

Devon clicked the off button. Eddie hadn't come in yet. He was down at the docks helping overhaul one of his catamarans that had snapped its mast in a heavy wind. She wouldn't be missed.

"Shelby, could you watch Zach for a couple of hours?"

"Sure. I guess Rory's still in Kauai surfing."

Devon nodded. "He'll be back tonight. He'll start taking Zach again tomorrow."

It took her less than an hour to drive to the Bishop Museum and park. At this time of day, it was crowded with tourists, which was the reason Warren had chosen to meet here. No one would pay attention to them. The whole way over Devon had speculated on why he wanted to see her. Usually she would be concerned about her sister, but now she was worried he'd found out about Chad.

Relocation.

She would have to give up Chad and leave Zach behind. She honestly wondered if she could do it. At moments like this she thought she would rather die. But then Rutherford and Ames would go free. She had to be strong, stay the course.

Stiffening her resolve, she entered the building. Suspended from the ceiling was a fifty-five-foot-long skeleton of a sperm whale. She gazed up at it, awed, the way she had been the first time she'd come here.

Take heart, she told herself. *Don't always expect the worst.* Her life had new hope now. Maybe Warren had news about the trial. The minute it was scheduled, she planned to tell Chad the truth.

She wandered around the room with the milling tourists who had come to see the authentic Hawaiian artifacts from the islands pre-European days. Many people called the Bishop Museum "the Smithsonian of the Pacific." Devon understood why, but she couldn't concentrate on the interesting exhibits.

After what seemed hours, Warren walked in, dressed in Bermudas and a Hawaiian shirt only a tourist fresh off the plane would have bought. Obviously he'd dressed to blend in. He circled the room once before approaching her.

"Get aloada that whale," he said to her. "Big enough for ya?"

Devon played along. "I'm glad he didn't show up on Waikiki while I was in the water."

Warren led her away from a tour whose guide was giving the group an in-depth explanation of how natives had built and waterproofed the thatched huts. "Something has come up."

Fear ate through her like a corrosive acid. "What?"

Warren put his hand on her arm. "Your sister has been in an accident. Don't worry, she's okay, but you're not going to be able to talk to her this week."

She closed her eyes for a moment, her heart beating alarmingly fast. "What happened?"

Warren kept walking, moving away from anyone who might overhear even though their voices were barely above a whisper. "Hit and run as she came out of the mall. There was a witness, a young kid from Des Moines. He said it was an old man in a late-model Cadillac. Typical Florida accident. At a certain age licenses should be taken away."

She remembered so well the carefree brightness of Tina's smile. It was impossible to imagine her flat on her back and expressionless in a sterile hospital bed. The only time she'd seen Tina grim-faced had been when she was getting ready to have Ariel. Devon had held her hand, helped her breathe and count the way they'd learned in the Lamaze lessons. Tina's husband, Steven, had been too squeamish to do it. "Are you sure she's okay?"

"Positive. She sustained nothing more than a broken arm. That's a miracle, considering."

"Then why can't I call her?"

"She'll be in the hospital for at least two days for observation in case internal bleeding develops. That's not uncommon when a pedestrian is hit by a car. We can't plant an electronic sweeping device on a hospital phone on short notice. It takes a court order. By the time we get it, your sister will be home. As soon as she is, you may call her."

"Is there any chance Rutherford and Ames caused the accident?"

"No. The witness gave a good description of the old man and the car. The police may have found him by now."

Danger loomed on the horizon like a powerful hurricane. Her life was veering to the dark side again. Usually Warren was as sympathetic as an Auschwitz guard, but now he seemed compassionate. Devon suspected something was terribly wrong.

Warren led her to the entrance. "There is some good news. It looks as if the trial will be scheduled within the month."

"Cripes! I've been hearing the trial was going to be scheduled for almost two years."

"Now they're trying to juggle some dates. The attorney defending those two is some high profile guy from L.A. When they pin Mark Greagos down, we'll have a date."

Devon should have been relieved, but she wasn't. Her sister was in the hospital, and she was trapped here. What if Warren was wrong and internal bleeding caused her to die without Devon seeing her for the last time?

Without saying goodbye?

Without saying, "I love you, Tina. I'll never forget all the happy times we shared"?

"Do something fun this weekend. Go somewhere with Langston. Get your mind off this."

A wild flash of shock ripped through her. "You know about our relationship?"

Warren held the door, and they walked out of the museum into the bright sunlight. "Yes. I discussed it with Masterson. Chad Langston was an outstanding Special Ops guy. Masterson thinks it's added security."

"He's going to the Big Kahuna Surfing Competition in Kauai," she replied, making this up as she went. "Rory, the boy who's living with him, is competing. I could go with him."

"Do it. Just be sure to take your cell phone so I can keep in touch."

"Promise to call me with an update on my sister."

DEVON DROVE to a minimart off Alakea Street near the district court building. She could use a public telephone to call her brother-in-law to verify Tina's condition. The records would be erased in the next two days, but caller ID would show the area code, and Steve would know where she was. Instead she bought a universal prepaid phone card. Designed for visitors from foreign countries—mostly Japanese tourists bought them in Hawaii—the cards had no caller ID and couldn't be traced.

She purchased one good for an hour and went to a pay phone. She tried Tina's home telephone, but the answering machine picked up. Becoming a little frantic, she punched in the cell phone number Steve had when she'd been in Houston. Hopefully he still had the same number.

On the fourth ring, he answered, "Hello?"

His tone was hollow and anguished like a voice in a crypt. For a gut-cramping second the world froze, and she couldn't speak.

"Hello?" he repeated, irritated now.

"Steve, it's Devon. I heard about Tina. Is she all right?"

"Devon." He made it sound like a four-letter word.

They'd never really gotten along. Devon had always suspected he resented her early success. It had been a while before his career had taken off. Another reason Steven was cool to Devon was her close relationship with her sister. Steve liked to be the center of attention. He loved to recount his exploits on the football field at Florida State. Tina found this charming, but Devon thought it was immature.

"How is she?"

"Hanging on."

"What do you mean? I thought she just had a broken arm."

"For starters," he said, his voice as sharp as a new razor. "A broken pelvis and a ruptured spleen."

Warren had deliberately lied to her. She slumped against the wall of the phone booth. "Oh, my God."

"Ariel could be without a mother."

"What hospital is she in?" she asked, wondering how her niece was taking this.

"Miami-Dade Medical Center."

She asked, "How is Ariel doing?"

"She's at a friend's home. I'm not at the hospital. I'm next door getting coffee so I can stay awake through the night in case Tina wakes up."

The vehemence in his voice astonished Devon. He was angry and frightened, she decided. He was venting his emotions on her. Usually Steve was as sentimental as Attila the Hun. Until this moment, she had never realized how much he truly loved her sister. He was terrified Tina would die.

"Don't be angry with me," she said gently. "I'm as upset as you are."

"You caused this," he shot back. "Tina goes around all the time preoccupied because she's worried about you. She stepped off the curb without looking."

There wasn't any point arguing with him. "Please tell her to hang in there. I'm coming. And tell her I love her."

She hung up the telephone without waiting for a response. No doubt, Steve would have told her to butt out. They didn't need her.

CHAD STOOD at the Ala Wai Marina's pay phone and waited for Danson's call. Depending on what the informant had learned, Chad would have to make a decision. Or he could wait three years until Albert was paroled and decide then. Three years was a long time. The wise guy could get killed in prison, contract a fatal disease, or change his mind about Devon.

While he waited, Chad trained the DARPA gadget on a boat leaving the pleasure craft harbor. It still didn't register any humans on the vessel even though Chad could clearly see people.

The phone rang and he picked it up. "Hello."

"You owe me," Danson said. "I sent one of the federal prosecutors to talk to Nathan Albert. Prisoners are always looking for ways to knock time off their sentences. I thought

Albert would be more likely to talk to him than some lowlife con he considered beneath him."

"Good thinking."

"How well have you checked up on Devon Summers?"

The fine hairs across the back of his neck stood at attention. "The facts I checked were verified. Why?"

"Albert claims he doesn't know her. Said he had a long-time girlfriend in Chicago who came to see him every week. The visitor's log confirmed this. I checked with the attorney who prosecuted the case, and he said she was in court every day. She lived with Albert in a penthouse on Lakeshore Drive. She's staying there now."

The truth hit him like a knockout punch. Devon had lied. She'd thrown enough bullshit at him to bury the island. And he'd fallen for it.

Anger slithering through his veins like venom, he asked, "Any clue who she is? What she's up to?"

"Good question. She does have a work history in Chicago. She paid into Social Security until last year, which shows no payments."

"That's when she claimed to have been working in Portland under another name."

"I'd be very careful. My guess is Devon Summers is there to kill you and get the device you're testing."

CHAPTER TWENTY-THREE

CHAD STORMED ACROSS the street to Aloha's offices. "Where's Devon?"

At the sound of his voice Zach romped up to him to be petted. Chad didn't have time. He intended to get the truth out of Devon. No more lies.

Shelby arched one eyebrow and shook her head. "I don't, like, know."

"She must have told you something." He could see his angry voice was alarming Shelby, but he didn't care.

"She asked if I could, like, watch Zach for a couple of hours."

He grabbed the telephone on Devon's desk and punched in her cell number. It rang until voice mail picked up. He slammed down the receiver.

"No idea where she might have gone? What if you needed to get in touch with her?"

"Why would I, like, need to get in touch? She could call me."

Reasoning with Shelby was like explaining tax-exempt bonds to the homeless. "If she comes back, don't tell her I'm looking for her, but call me on my cell."

The airhead's doubtful expression told him that she'd grown closer to Devon than he'd thought.

"Don't tell. It's a surprise."

She giggled. "*Waay* cool."

"A *big* surprise." He stalked toward the office door.

"Oh, I forgot. Just before Devon left. She, like, got a phone call on her cell."

He spun around. "Do you happen to recall what she said?"

"Um." Shelby thought a moment. "Not much. I think she asked, where or maybe when. She left, like, right away."

Puzzled, he said, "Thanks. Don't forget about the surprise."

He hurried out the door and rushed over to his office. His cell phone was on his desk. Devon might have left him a message on his cell or office voice mail. She had no reason to think he'd discovered her pack of lies.

Frowning, Ane was guarding the office like a bouncer.

"Any calls?"

"A couple. Nothing important. I put the messages on your desk."

He went to his desk and checked the messages. Nothing from Devon. Nothing on his voice mail, either. Nothing on e-mail.

He hated to ask Ane, because she'd warned him Devon was *pilikia*—trouble. "Did you see Devon leave Eddie's office?" From her desk, Ane had a direct view of Aloha's front door.

She glared at him for a long moment, then replied in a voice as flat as old beer. "Let her go. Like Pele, she'll vanish."

He grabbed his cell and left the office, telling Ane to call him if she needed him. He didn't tell her to contact him should Devon return. He knew she wouldn't.

He should have listened to Ane and Keke. Their woman's intuition was stronger than his sixth sense. Devon Summers was *pilikia*. But now he was involved, and he was just plain too stubborn to quit. Aw, hell. It wasn't about being pigheaded. He was crazy about Devon.

Chad hopped in his Porsche to go to his place for his Special Ops bag, then to Devon's apartment. He doubted she was there, but he intended to search the place. Surely he could find some clue about who she really was.

He gunned the powerful engine and ripped out of his parking space behind the building, thinking. Danson believed Devon intended to kill him, but Chad had his doubts. If she was after the DARPA gadget, now safely stowed in his trouser pocket, she'd had plenty of opportunities to try to get it. She carried a Sig Saur in her purse for self-protection, she claimed. She could have held the gun to his head, demanded the device, then killed him.

Why hadn't she? For the life of him, he couldn't figure it out. He was missing something here. What? He thought it over, but it still didn't make sense. The answer had to be in her apartment.

DEVON STOOD in front of the locker she kept at the Aliiolani Bus Station. The facility was a bit run-down, but had an authentic, non-touristy feel to it lacking in other parts of Honolulu. It was a hub for day-workers who couldn't afford to live in Honolulu or even its less expensive suburbs. They lived "up country" and took buses to their jobs in the city.

She had left a small suitcase, a wig, clothes, phony ID—and cash in the locker. Santa Fe had taught her to be prepared to run in an instant. She'd been lucky that Romero had cash on him and a car. This time she had her own money—and a plan.

Devon knew her plan was fraught with risks. She needed to get to Miami, see her sister and return to Honolulu before Warren realized she'd left the city. She figured he wouldn't call her too often, if he thought she was with Chad. If he did, Warren wouldn't have any way of knowing where she was. Should she sound a little far away, he would assume the cell connection to Kauai wasn't so good. The outer islands didn't have as many cell towers and reception in some areas was iffy.

If Warren discovered she'd left the island for any reason—especially to return to a "danger zone"—a place where a WITSEC protectee had family or friends, it would be a "security violation." She would be immediately expelled from the program.

She would be on her own.

Devon had to take the chance. Nothing on earth would be worth letting her sister die without telling Tina that she was the best sister in the whole world. And how much she loved her.

She glanced around the bus station to make sure no one was watching as she slipped the Sig Saur and her Devon Summers ID into the locker. She would have to get another

gun in Miami—just in case. She didn't think Rutherford and
Ames were after her, but she had to be careful.

Once her things were safely inside the locker, she closed
the door and inserted a week's worth of quarters. That was as
much as the machine would take. She needed to return within
the week or the locker attendant would open the locker and
remove her things.

It was Thursday afternoon. She wouldn't be in Miami until
tomorrow. If all went according to plan, she would return on
Sunday. She would have seen her sister, and WITSEC
wouldn't know she'd left.

In the station's rest room, she changed into navy-blue board
shorts and a baby-blue T-shirt that exposed her midriff. She
loaded her two cell phones and new ID into a straw bag. She
tucked her long hair up into the cap of a wig with short brown
curls that appeared to have been styled with an egg beater.

Her reflection in the cracked mirror pleased her. "A tourist returning from a week in paradise."

She took the clothes she'd been wearing and put them in
the locker with the other things. Checking her watch, she
saw she had time to get to the travel agency to pay in cash for
the ticket she'd booked over the telephone. She could pick up
a few last minute items and make the necessary calls.

Lying had become second nature to her, but calling Chad
now with yet another fabricated story bothered Devon. Could
she do it without sounding so flustered Chad would know she
was lying? She decided to put it off until she'd picked up the
ticket and things.

And she needed to say goodbye to Zach—in case she
didn't make it back.

CHAD PARKED THE PORSCHE on the street behind Devon's
apartment. He got out of the car and walked around to the
back of the building. Devon's parking place wasn't occupied.
He tried her cell phone again. Voice mail picked up, but he
didn't bother leaving a message.

Had she gone to meet someone? Who?

He'd always enjoyed a good mystery, but not now. Not when he was so crazy about a woman. He thought about the moon shining down on the pillow, her hair fanned out across his pillow, the light filtering through the palms into his bedroom. The dewy look of her skin after they'd made love.

Devon had taken advantage of his feelings, pretending to care for him. It was all an act. She wanted something, either from him or...who knew? But her elaborate attempt to hide the truth indicated this was serious...maybe criminal.

You're about to commit a crime, he warned himself. Sure, he'd killed men, stolen military equipment and God-only-knows-what during the Gulf War when he'd been with Delta Force behind enemy lines.

This was different. He would have a helluva hard time explaining breaking into Devon Summers's apartment. He could end up in jail, his SAP/SARS security clearance revoked, his family publicly humiliated. It could even mean time in prison.

He'd weighed all these factors on his way out to the house to get his Special Ops bag. It contained a lot of special military equipment. Most of it was legal, but impossible to obtain. He'd gotten it through connections after he'd left the service and had gone to work testing for DARPA.

One item—the device he was going to use now—was illegal. A Lockaide was supposed to be available *only* to law enforcement for use in special drug bust cases where it was necessary to gain entrance to a building quickly without alerting the tenants.

He obtained it through military connections, thinking he might need it in his underwater forensic work. Often boats or cars submerged underwater had trunks or compartments with locks that needed to be opened quickly. He'd used it several times while working for the HPD.

He walked into the courtyard, shaded from the street by a scarlet bougainvillea, and glanced around. Hiphop music drifted out from the apartment across from Devon's. Everyone else seemed to be at work.

He knocked at her door and waited. Knocked again. He pulled the gunlike Lockaide out of his trouser pocket. The muzzle was a long pick. He inserted it into the lock and squeezed. With a clink, the lock released.

Chad stepped inside and pocketed the Lockaide. He looked around, taking a mental inventory of the room. There was a poster of Diamond Head on one wall and several small inexpensive prints on the other. A vase with a hibiscus—the state's flower—was on the coffee table.

No personal photographs anywhere. She'd spoken fondly of a sister and a niece, but there weren't any photos of them. Or anyone.

Actually there was nothing personal here unless he counted a bowl with Zach's name on it. That was the place to start. Look for memorabilia. It told a lot about a person.

He rifled through the credenza. Underwear, T-shirts and shorts. No photos or trophies or commemorative plaques or newspaper clippings. He didn't find any personal letters or greeting cards, either.

The kitchen held almost nothing except food and dishes. One drawer had a rent receipt along with a few coupons for cleaners and a pet groomer called Pawsitively Perfect.

The bathroom had towels and toiletries. Devon had far fewer cosmetics than his sisters, but money was tight, and Devon didn't wear much makeup.

That left the closet. Just clothes. He took the time to search pockets for notes or business cards. One had a cleaning receipt. There were a few purses and a hat. None of them revealed anything about the mysterious Devon Summers.

In the corner were the boxes she'd unloaded from the van that night. Some had been filled with the clothes he'd seen when he'd first visited. He expected to find more clothes. He opened the first box and discovered books and computer disks. The other boxes had even more books and more disks.

The disks had labels on them with small neat handwriting. He sorted through them but couldn't tell what they were without putting them into his computer.

He turned to the books. They were on statistics and accounting. Some of them looked like very advanced accounting—way beyond anything Chad could do. No wonder Devon whipped through Eddie's files and completed a sophisticated analysis of his business in one day.

"I'll be damned," he muttered under his breath.

Devon might have been working as a wedding planner, but she had an impressive financial background. Why would she hide it? Didn't make sense. Hell, nothing about this woman made sense.

He decided to check the flyleaf of every book. People often wrote their names or put bookplates there. He opened each one. Nothing.

He went back through them and shook each one in case a bookmark or business card or something had been stuck in one. The third book had a small slip of paper from what must have been an office pad.

From the desk of Samantha Robbins

Who in hell was Samantha Robbins? A friend? A colleague? Could it be Devon's real name?

He stared at it and tried to decide how old the paper was. It seemed new, but then it had been sandwiched between the pages of a book and hadn't oxidized. This apartment had yielded far fewer clues than he'd expected.

He'd known he was going to have to confront Devon and hear what she had to say, but he'd wanted to have some ammo in case she lied again. Now he'd lowered his personal standards and had broken the law. For nothing.

The cell phone in his pocket vibrated. He pulled it out, heading for the door. "Yes?" he said, his voice low.

"It's me, Shelby."

"What's happening ?" He peeked outside and saw the coast was clear. He slipped out of Samantha's apartment. "Did Devon call?"

"Well, no. Not exactly." The airhead was whispering. "Devon's here. She's taken Zach, like, outside to do his business. I wasn't sure if I should call."

Swear to God, Shelby couldn't tell chicken salad from chicken shit. "You did the right thing. Go out there and stall her. I'm on my way." Chad clicked the end button and sprinted toward his car.

He was halfway back to his office when his cell phone rang again. "I'm sorry I couldn't, like, stop Devon. She's left."

"Did she say where she was going?"

"Sorta."

"Where?"

"She said to tell Eddie her friend is sick. She'll be back when we open next week."

Chad thought about her apartment. It didn't seem as if she'd packed. But he could be wrong. So far everything he'd thought about this woman had been wrong.

"Devon said you and Rory would take care of Zach."

"Sure. Did she say or do anything else? Anything at all?"

"Well...I went to talk to her the way you said. She, like, had tears in her eyes. I heard her telling Zach that she'd never forget him."

Shit.

She wasn't coming back. She'd had tears in her eyes because she was saying goodbye to the dog she was crazy about.

"How long ago did she leave?"

"Aaaah....I'm not sure exactly. I had to take a call."

"More than five minutes?"

"I—I guess."

He phoned Ane. "Any calls?"

There was a long pause that he didn't like. "A message on your voice mail."

"Thanks. Would you transfer me to voice mail?"

A second later Devon's voice came on the line. "Hi, it's me, sweetie. Something's come up. Remember my friend who had to leave Chicago because Nate's men beat her up? Well, I found out she's sick. I need to go see her. I should be back Sunday...probably late." She sighed softly, the way she often did. "I love you."

The line went dead and Chad nearly threw the cell phone out the window. She'd never told him she loved him. What crap! Why say it now when she knew she wasn't coming back?

CHAPTER TWENTY-FOUR

BROCK STOOD in the Grand Ballroom of the Adam's Mark Hotel in St. Louis, where the reception for the auto show was being held. He nodded to a few of the Gull Wing owners he knew from previous car shows. Normally he would have shot the bull with them, but not tonight.

He was on a mission.

Finding Jordan Walsh was the only thing on his mind. He sipped a mineral water with lime. The thought of Scotch soured his stomach. Just thinking about Jordan turned his stomach, too. What a smart-ass bitch.

Just wait. She would get hers.

He scanned the room for the redhead, but didn't see her. It was early, though. Jordan would walk in any minute. He'd rehearsed over and over what he was going to say to her. Of course, he wouldn't let Jordan know how royally pissed he was. After all, she might willingly sell him the car.

Horst Trensen IV sauntered up to him with what appeared to be a Scotch in his hand. Trensen stopped beside Brock, and he smelled the odor of a Highland malt—probably Glenfiddich or Glenlivet. Brock's stomach went into a free-fall, then leveled off.

"Another show. Another show," the president of the Gull Wing Association said as if he were supremely bored.

Brock knew better. The association was Trensen's life. He'd always held some stupid-ass position, and now he'd risen to president. It was a three-year term. After that Trensen would join the powerful advisory board for five years.

When Brock retired and had the time, he intended to hold a position with the association himself.

"Have you seen Jordan Walsh?" Brock asked casually. "I noticed her Gull Wing in the program. It'll be displayed not far from mine."

Trensen's hooded gray eyes blinked. "Poor Jordan. Her workload is killing her. She had to scratch."

His words were like a knee to the groin. Scratched! How could the bitch do this to him? Another, more disturbing thought hit him. Had Trensen spoken with her? Probably just an e-mail to the association.

"When did you talk to her?" Brock asked, testing.

"This morning. That sweet thing is exhausted."

Fury knotted inside Brock's chest, and he struggled not to show it. Not to this pompous ass. Jordan hadn't returned his calls, but clearly, she'd been talking to Trensen. "What kind of business does she own?"

Trensen swigged his single malt before answering. "Didn't you have dinner with her in Miami?"

Brock was tempted to slug Trensen's stomach where it rolled slightly over his belt. "We didn't discuss business. It was cars and...you know," he said, implying sex.

Trensen didn't get the hint. "Jordan's special. She's built an Internet empire on ladies' lingerie."

"How much money can there be in undies? There's a Victoria's Secret in every mall. What department store doesn't have a huge underwear section?"

With a smug smile, Trensen took another sip of Scotch before leaning toward Brock and saying in a low voice, "Jordan makes most of her money in, you know, supplies to go along with the lingerie."

Brock got it. Vibrators. Sex toys.

"What's the name of her Web site?"

Trensen considered this for a moment. "XtremeX." He winked. "You're not going to believe the lingerie...and stuff."

Brock mustered a smile. "I'll bet."

"Gotta go," Trensen said. "The board wants me to go to dinner with them."

Brock walked to the window and gazed out at the lights illuminating the St. Louis arch. Unfuckingbelievable! The bitch had blown him off in favor of a prick who didn't have Brock's looks or his smarts.

Just wait. Just wait.

XtremeX. Now he knew how to find the bitch. A Web site could exist in cyberspace and be untraceable, but if it sold product there was a warehouse somewhere. If not, they had an office that dealt with vendors who shipped their products.

Jordan Walsh, it's all over.

Of course, Samantha Robbins was his first priority. But that situation was in hand. His agents were rolling. It wouldn't be long.

CHAD DROVE HIS PORSCHE back toward Devon's apartment. She would take the things that were important to her and some clothes. Why was she leaving? She couldn't possibly know he was on to her. She was running—unexpectedly— for some other reason.

He drove toward the back of Devon's apartment where she would park. Airhead Shelby had indicated Devon had at least a five-minute head start. If she wasn't already here, she would be here soon. Her car wasn't in her parking place. Chad found a spot up the street where he could see Devon when she drove in.

He resisted the urge to stare at his watch. When he left the service, he'd bought the Breitling Colt Ocean, which had been designed specifically for Special Forces. After what he judged to be five minutes he checked the Breitling. Dead on the money. Almost five minutes to the second.

Where was Devon?

The light dawned. Dumb shit! Why hadn't he realized it sooner? There hadn't been a suitcase in her apartment. She must have already packed it. She had to be on her way to the airport. Wait a minute! She claimed to have returned to America by sailing into a private yacht harbor. She could very well be leaving again the same way.

Somehow he doubted it. If she planned to use a boat as an escape route, Devon was too smart to have tipped her hand by telling him. He decided not to take a chance. While he drove through the snarled traffic to Honolulu International, he called Dave Keliliki, Ala Wai Harbor Master. Ala Wai was the only marina on Oahu that had yachts large enough to make the long voyage back to the mainland or to the South Pacific.

"Hey, *aikane.*" Chad greeted his friend. "Any yachts leaving port this afternoon for the States or SP?"

"Nah. There's a major squall out there. No one's sailing today. They'll have to hold off until tomorrow. More likely the next day. Why?"

"I'm looking for a friend. Could you give me the names of the boats scheduled to depart?"

There were only three of them. Chad thanked Dave and reached Eddie on his cell. He knew Eddie was nearby, working on a disabled Cat. Eddie could check to see if Devon had signed on to one of those crews.

"Eddie, do me a favor."

"Sure. What's up?"

"A couple of yachts, *Pipe Dream, Blarney,* and *Wind Spirit* are heading for destinations in the South Pacific. See if Devon is crewing on one of them."

"*Pono!*" Crazy. "Why would she do that?"

"I haven't got time to explain. Just trust me. Check those boats. If you find her, call me." He hung up without giving Eddie a chance to ask another question.

Chad parked in the airport lot. He prepared to board a plane with Devon if necessary. He left the Lockaide in the trunk of his car. It looked too much like a gun to get it though airport security. He'd need a bag, too. Security agents became suspicious of passengers traveling without luggage.

He took the special ops duffel and headed into the terminal. He stopped at the ATM. He always carried a fair amount of cash, but in this case, he might need more.

Honolulu's airport wasn't big compared to many cities on the mainland, but searching for Devon was going to be a bitch. He scanned the crowd lined up at the counters and those at the security check points. He didn't see her, but then, he didn't expect to. She could already be through the security check if she'd gone directly to the airport from Aloha's offices.

Chad stood in front of the departures board and analyzed the flights leaving in the next two hours. He skipped over the inter-island trips and concentrated on flights bound for the mainland. L.A., Chicago, Miami...*Miami*.

Something clicked in the back of his mind. How well he remembered the look on Devon's face as she explained that her brother-in-law, Steve, hadn't been able to go with Tina to the Lamaze sessions, when Devon's sister was pregnant. Devon had flown to Miami each weekend to help her sister. She'd been in the hospital room when her sister had delivered.

Something wistful in Devon's voice and fond expression convinced Chad this story had been true. He'd been deceived by this woman too many times to count, but he decided to trust his gut on this one. Since Devon had made up the Nathan Albert story, he had to assume she'd made up the friend, too. He was convinced her sister existed, and Devon truly loved her.

The Miami flight was already boarding. The only way he was going to get on it this late was with a first-class ticket. He raced to the first-class line and filled out a luggage tag from the counter for his duffel while the agent ticketed the two people ahead of him.

"Flight 1782 to Miami," he told the agent when it was finally his turn.

"I'm sorry sir," replied the perky attendant. "It's already boarding."

Chad knew he could charm just about any woman when

he tried. "It's an emergency. My mother's in the hospital in Miami." He held up the small special ops bag he was pretending was luggage. "I rushed here with little more than my toothbrush and a fresh shirt."

The attendant wavered and called over her supervisor, a middle-aged man who could've taken first, second and third in a chin contest. He eyed Chad, who tried for a hangdog expression. The supervisor nodded curtly and turned away.

Getting through security proved more difficult. Chad had to explain the DARPA gadget. He should have locked it in the safe at his house, but he'd forgotten. He didn't dare leave it in the Porsche. They were stolen way too often to risk it.

"It's a GPS," he told the security guard. "A brand-new one that just came on the market."

"I don't know. Looks...strange." He turned to another guard. "Harry, ever see a GPS like this?"

Harry, who didn't look more than fifteen, swaggered over. He took the device from the other guard and inspected it. Chad didn't pray often, but this was one of those times. If they confiscated it, he'd play hell explaining it to Danson.

Harry rolled his eyes. "Sure. See'm all the time."

Chad grabbed the gadget, raced down the hall toward the gate. He shoved it in his bag and handed the flight attendant his boarding pass.

"You just barely made it," she said.

Chad rushed down the jetway and into the plane. An attractive brunette with shoulder-length brown hair took his boarding pass. With a flirtatious smile, she directed him to first class.

"How's it goin'?" Chad asked, flirting back. He might need her help.

"Just great." She handed him back his boarding pass. "You're in 2-B."

While she was talking, Chad used his peripheral vision to check the main cabin. No sign of Devon's blond head. He would have to wait until they were airborne to really look.

He'd be screwed if she wasn't onboard—trapped on a nonstop flight to Miami.

DEVON SAT NEXT to the airplane's window and gazed out at the blue water. They'd taken off a half hour ago. She'd kept her nose buried in a romantic suspense novel by Meryl Sawyer. Normally *Lady Killer* would have held her attention, but conflicting emotions assailed her.

She had to see her sister, had to know Tina was better. Tina knew how much Devon loved her, but saying it in person—perhaps for the last time—was terribly important. They'd always been close, but now Devon felt a world away. It took so long to fly to Miami, by the time she arrived, it might be too late.

The knife of betrayal lanced through her. Warren Martin had lied. WITSEC had lied. They didn't want her to know the truth. Tina could die for all they cared. The only thing that mattered to them was keeping her safe until she could testify.

The young Fort Lauderdale couple seated next to her was kissing again. They were flying home after a honeymoon on Maui. They'd been so happy, so in love, when they'd introduced themselves that Devon's heart ached with something too deep for tears.

Saying goodbye to Zach had been difficult enough, but calling Chad had been wrenching. It was lucky he'd been out of the office. She might have broken down had she spoken to him. She'd blurted out the lie, then something completely unanticipated and unrehearsed.

I love you.

Until that very second, she hadn't admitted the truth to herself. Of course, she must have known it on some level, but leaving him—knowing she might never return—had made her realize exactly how she felt.

Devon hadn't treated him fairly. "We're in this together," he'd told her more than once. She should have trusted him with the truth. She hadn't because she thought WITSEC knew best, and she could trust them.

Wrong.

They were lying to her about her sister. No telling what had really gone down in Santa Fe. WITSEC might have known ahead of time or found out later and never told her. There was also the very real possibility—something she'd always suspected—that Rutherford and Ames had bought off a Federal Marshal to "take care" of her.

How vividly she remembered kindhearted Romero sprawled across the floor, his blood pooled around him. She missed him more than she could have imagined when she'd lived in Houston and had many friends. He had been her first friend after a long year of isolation, when she'd walked around, terrified of her own shadow.

Until we meet again, may God hold you in the palm of his hand.

The final line of the Irish Blessing unexpectedly popped into her head and she blinked back the sting of tears. Romero was up there, watching over her, telling Devon what she had to do. *Don't you let your concentration waver or you may end up dead.* There was always the chance this was a trap. She must to be ready.

"Miss, Miss." The flight attendant was trying to get her attention.

"Yes?" Devon responded.

"Come with me," the brunette said with a friendly smile.

Devon unfastened her seat belt and squeezed by the honeymooning couple. "Is there something wrong?"

The flight attendant whispered, "There are a couple of empty seats in first class. These kids will smooch all the way to Miami. You need a break."

"Thanks." Devon couldn't help smiling as she followed the attendant up the long aisle to the first-class cabin.

"Here you go." She indicated an empty seat.

Devon sat in it, fastened her belt and turned to introduce herself to the man next to her. He'd been gazing out the window when she'd sat down. She hoped he wouldn't be the talkative type. If he were, she would snuff it by burying her nose in *Lady Killer.*

"Hi, I'm—" The air siphoned from her lungs, and blood pounded in her ears like a drum.

Chad Langston. How on earth?

"Just who are you? Barbara Ashton is the name you used to get on this plane. You were Devon Summers in Honolulu."

Like a house of cards, all her lies collapsed around her. The caring man who'd made love to her so tenderly had vanished. There was nothing but hostility and barely leashed anger in Chad's voice.

How did he know? How had he found her? It didn't matter, she decided. She couldn't blame him for being furious. She'd allowed WITSEC to turn her into a liar.

"I don't blame you for being upset," she told him. "I can explain."

He crossed his powerful arms and glared at her. "Shoot."

She turned and checked the nearly full cabin. No one seemed to be paying attention to them, but they were awfully close. She whispered, "I'll have to tell you later when no one can hear us."

He continued to stare at her until the silence between them was as wide as the Pacific. Finally he unhooked his seat belt and stood. "Get up."

Only a total idiot would have questioned him. The Chad she knew had morphed into a half-tamed animal. Silly Shelby had told her stories about Chad killing men behind enemy lines. Devon hadn't believed her. Now she fully recognized his potential for violence.

She undid her seat belt and moved into the aisle to let him out. He stepped by her. His large hand latched around her wrist. He hauled her down the aisle.

"Where are we going?"

Without answering, he towed her forward and shoved her into the first-class rest room.

"You can't do this!" she cried as he stepped in with her.

"Don't worry," he said, each syllable etched with sarcasm. "Everyone will assume we're joining the Mile High Club."

He pushed her against the wall and grabbed her chin with his large hand. "Okay, we're in private. Talk."

CHAPTER TWENTY-FIVE

CHAD SAW FEAR in Devon's eyes, but he didn't give a damn. Yesterday, he wouldn't have believed it possible. He'd wanted to protect her, save her from the man stalking her. Build a life together.

Yeah, right.

He gazed at her delicate face and noticed her full lower lip tremble. This close he caught a whiff of the citrus scent she wore as it rose off her petal-soft skin. It was just the barest trace of fragrance—no big deal—but it was enough to set his nerves on edge. Unexpectedly, heat flushed his entire body.

What in hell?

How could this traitorous pang of desire hit him now? He clenched his eyes shut for a second, hoping to dispel the unwelcome sensation. His body had a more intimate plan. Her sexual magnetism had always aroused him.

"What's the matter, Devon?" he ripped out the words, reminding himself this woman had deceived him big time. *Don't be a sucker for her sex appeal.* "Can't you think of another lie?"

Devon stared into his furious face, a scant inch separating them. She was almost grateful he had her braced against the wall, his powerful body holding her in place. Her legs no longer seemed capable of supporting her.

Anguish seared her heart. Devon honestly wanted to tell him the truth. She'd been ashamed of herself for obeying WITSEC while they didn't give one hoot in hell about her. She'd wished she'd confided in Chad.

But this man was a stranger. His jaw was clenched so tight she could see a vein pulsing at the temple near his hairline. His virile appeal had turned unexpectedly menacing. Dangerous.

She couldn't decide what to tell him. At this point, Chad would refuse to believe her. He might very well call around to confirm her story. If Rutherford and Ames didn't know where she was, his questions could expose her.

Even as Chad's lips came down savagely on hers in a dark, primal response to contact with her body, he told himself to let this lying bitch go.

But his brain cells had taken a hike south. All he could think about were the nights they'd spent in his bed, making love for hours on end, Devon's naked body kissed by moonlight. The image caused an immediate, painful erection.

He wanted to sheath himself inside her again, feel the sweet rhythm of her body moving with his, touch her between her legs. Crowning the firm thrust of her breasts, he felt her nipples tighten beneath the midriff-baring T-shirt she wore. A surge of masculine pride swept through him. He could still get to the little liar.

And, he had to admit, his body still responded to hers. He was so achingly hard he throbbed with the need to possess her. Oh, yeah, inside her one last time.

With both hands, Devon pushed against his shoulders, but she couldn't budge him. His lips plundered hers and his tongue invaded her mouth with alarming intensity. His actions were raw, passionate. A challenge and a threat. As primitive as life or death.

Her response was the polar opposite. Her body ached for comfort the way a dying man prays for the end. Her mind was almost numb from the rigors of her ordeal. She longed for solace.

Damn it all to hell, she thought, acutely aware of her body reacting to his, but not in a comforting way. This was primal sex like minks in heat. She tried tensing every muscle. That helped, but her traitorous nipples still tingled.

A tremor rippled through her, and, despite her best efforts, she arched her hips so the brunt of his erection pressed into her belly. She needed him to make love to her again, but she wanted him to be the gentle, caring man she'd come to love. She had no idea why he was doing this. He was furious with her and somehow saw sex as a way of punishing her.

Maybe kissing him, reminding him of what they'd had, would soften him.

Chad had slanted his head to kiss her more fiercely, when he felt her rubbing against his penis. The little liar was using her body again. Even as he reveled in it, he hated her more than he'd hated any woman. Hey, he didn't hate women. He liked them, loved his sisters, liked their friends, and was still on good terms with his former girlfriends.

This woman was the exception that proved the rule. She'd taken advantage of the way he'd cared about her. Lied to him. Even said she loved him. And he hated her for it in a way that he'd never imaged he would hate a woman.

He shoved his hand up under the T-shirt that exposed her sexy midriff. The silky skin lured him upward ever so slowly so he could savor her soft skin while his mouth plundered hers for the last time. He arrived at the lacy cup holding the breast in place. He shoved aside the excuse for a demi-bra and fondled her lush softness.

His thumb teased the pebbled nipple until Devon purred. His body was humming, too, but he refused to acknowledge it. His erection begged for relief and he rammed it against her.

He released her breast and slid his hands downward along the bare skin of her midriff, feeling her for the last time—he promised himself. His hands edged beneath the elastic waist of her board shorts. He found the sweet curve of her bottom. He levered her upward until his penis was shoved into the apex of her thighs. He ground against her until she moaned with pleasure.

Devon wanted him to make love to her to make her forget her sister, Warren's lies, the death threat hanging over her.

Even if it meant Chad taking her standing up in a tiny airplane bathroom, Devon needed the closeness, the intimate connection to the man she once believed she loved.

A soft knock interrupted them and Chad pulled back. Devon slumped against the wall.

"Are you almost finished?" the flight attendant asked, her voice muffled by the door. "Another passenger needs the facilities."

"In a minute," Chad replied, his voice gruff.

"You've got a few seconds." His voice broke with huskiness, but the anger was still there—more intense than before. "I want the truth—now."

She had everything to lose, but she decided to risk it. "My name is Samantha Robbins. I was assistant to the CFO of PowerTec, a firm that supplies equipment to the military. I discovered they were shortchanging the government, skimming money and sending it offshore. I notified the FBI and they sent in an agent. She was killed and the FBI relocated me in the Witness Protection Program until the trial.

"What I told you about Oregon is true, but it happened in Santa Fe where I'd been relocated. I was lucky to escape with my life." She took a deep breath and straightened her clothes. "I'm going to Miami—violating WITSEC rules—because my sister has been in a serious accident."

She shoved by him and rammed open the lever on the rest room door. "Stay away from me."

Devon stormed through the first-class cabin, aware that most people were staring. She couldn't have cared less. Already she regretted telling the truth—even if it had been a very short version. She could be walking into a trap, and she'd just increased her chances of being discovered by confiding in a man who now hated her.

She'd seen loathing in his eyes, felt it in the brutal way his body had taken advantage of hers. She should have kept her mouth shut, but some part of her wanted him to know the truth. Then, no matter what happened, she wouldn't think of herself as a person who could tell lie after lie to the man she'd thought she loved.

Devon's words had detonated on impact. Chad's thoughts whirled like dervishes. Samantha Robbins. Witness Protection.

Suddenly it all made sense. The need to hide. Being forced to lie.

Why hadn't he thought of Witness Protection? He'd imagined all sorts of things—most of them illegal—when he'd learned she had lied to him. It had never occurred to him that she might have a legitimate reason.

Or was this just another clever story?

He stared at Devon's retreating back, slack-jawed. Many women would have broken under the weight of what had happened to Devon—assuming she was telling the truth. Instead of falling apart, she'd been a scrapper and had learned to protect herself amazingly well.

Truth or lie?

Usually Chad saw things clearly and didn't waver. Not since he'd met Devon. She had him going in circles. Should he believe her?

From the desk of Samantha Robbins

The slip of paper was still in his wallet. He didn't have to look at it. She must be telling the truth. Right?

He pulled out his shirt to conceal his painful erection. Aw hell, he would have blue balls for a week. What did it matter? he decided. He charged out of the rest room, rushed by the curious flight attendants, and saw Devon swish through the curtain separating first class and coach. He caught up with her in the darkened coach cabin where many passengers were watching a movie.

He touched the back of her arm. "Wait!"

"Leave me alone." She was whispering but there was vehemence in her tone that hadn't been there until now.

He pulled her into his arms and told her, "Don't make me

cause a scene. The flight attendants will have to report it to security. If you don't want anyone to know you've left Honolulu, come with me quietly."

"You bastard!" Her voice was low, but intense.

Chad kept his arm around her, his grip tight. He led her back to their seats in first class. He nudged her to the inside seat near the window so she couldn't get out without going by him.

He gave her a few minutes to calm down. Now this cabin was also dark, the only light coming from the movie screen up front. He signaled a flight attendant and ordered a gin and tonic for himself and a glass of champagne for Devon. When the drinks came, Devon took hers, gazing at him with suspicion.

He raised his glass. "To the truth."

She stared at him, her eyes wide, and he could see she was still freaked by what had happened in the rest room. She clinked her glass against his. "To the truth."

He took a swig of his drink, then set down his glass on the tray in front of him. He raised the armrest that divided their seats into two and scooted as close to her as he could get.

He kept his voice low, not wanting any of the other passengers to overhear him. "If you hadn't run, I would simply have asked you."

"Asked me what?"

"Why you'd made up the story about Nathan Albert. He has a girlfriend, all right. She's living in his Lakeshore Drive penthouse while he's serving time. She visits him every week."

"How do you know?"

He took her glass of champagne and set it on the tray beside his. With one finger, he tilted her head so he could see her eyes in the light from the screen. "I was trying to help you. I have a friend who has...contacts. I asked him to see if Nate Albert was still interested in you."

"What were you going to do if you found out he was still after me?"

"I'm not sure," he admitted. "I guess I'm a control freak.

I needed to know what we were dealing with, then I would have decided what I was going to do next."

He removed his finger from beneath her chin and took her small hand in his. "I was prepared to do whatever it took—even have him killed."

Devon closed her eyes. For a single, painful moment the truth assailed her. What had happened to her life? It had spun totally out of control because she'd tried to do the right thing. She'd gotten one man killed, and now, here was another man willing to have someone murdered for her.

"I would *never* have wanted you to order someone killed."

He squeezed her hand. "I believed your story. I thought Albert had slit one man's throat and you were in mortal danger."

"I'm so sorry." Her throat tightened, and it took a minute for her words to find their way through the barrier. "I might have gotten someone else killed. And made you do something—"

"I've done things in the past, behind enemy lines, that could only be justified in a time of war. I'm no stranger to death."

"Still for someone to die because I fabricated a story is reprehensible." Her breath drifted out on a quiet sigh. "I should have told you the truth that first night we spent together."

"I wish you had." His voice was more solemn than she'd ever heard it.

"I thought WITSEC knew best," she told him. "They're only interested in keeping me alive to testify." She explained how they'd concealed Tina's true condition from her.

"Oh, babe, that's awful." In the dimly lit cabin, she saw him frown, his eyes level beneath drawn brows. "Hit and run, huh? Did they catch the guy?"

"No, not yet."

He studied her face for a moment in the caring way he had when they'd been in Honolulu. Devon asked him, "What are you thinking?"

"It could be a trap. Tell me more about who's really after you."

She whispered into his ear and told him the story about Rutherford and Ames. She concluded with, "They're dangerous men who can afford the best of the best. They managed to find me in Santa Fe despite all the precautions the Federal Marshals took."

"I would think it would be extremely difficult to find someone who had expert help in reinvention herself." If she were really in Witness Protection, it would have been next to impossible to find her, he thought, again wondering if she were being honest with him.

"I suspect someone in WITSEC tipped them—or they managed to track my money from Houston to Santa Fe." She explained about buying the condo and gallery. "They've been sold now, but I won't let them transfer the money here in case that's how they found me last time."

"Smart move."

"I need to be very careful when I visit my sister. They—"

"*We* need to be very careful when *we* visit your sister," he countered, his voice low. "We're in this together."

CHAPTER TWENTY-SIX

DEVON STOOD at a pay phone outside The Golden Palms Motel near Miami International Airport. She was trying her brother-in-law's cell phone for the third time.

"He still isn't answering," she told Chad.

"At least you know Tina's been upgraded from critical to stable."

They'd called the hospital from the airport and had learned Tina's condition had improved slightly. With the new privacy laws, that's all the hospital could tell them.

"I think I should go over to the hospital now."

Chad put a restraining hand on her shoulder. "We agreed to take every precaution. You need to be disguised."

"And we should have guns."

"I told you. I know where to buy weapons."

After they'd landed, they had taken a taxi to Rent-A-Wreck, a car rental agency that offered nothing but ugly, battered cars. Chad had insisted they wouldn't be easy to spot in a car like their dented white Acura. They'd driven to a pink motel that rented rooms by the hour. Devon wasn't sure why it was called The Golden Palms. The only palm she'd seen was a fake one not more than two feet high in a pot just outside the registration office.

"Let's go," Chad said. "If we hurry, we can find two guns and buy clothes to disguise you. We should be able to see your sister after dark. That'll be perfect. If someone's watching the hospital, we should be able to slip by them."

"You really think this is a trap." Devon didn't want to believe it was true, yet she was well aware two people had already died. Rutherford and Ames wouldn't hesitate to hurt Tina to get to her.

"It pays to be cautious," Chad replied.

They piled into the dented Acura and drove to nearby Little Havana. She'd been there once years ago, when she'd visited her sister.

They parked on Calle Ocho, the main drag. Shops and cafés the size of pigeon holes lined the street where the signs were all in Spanish. The scent of café cubano, the strongest espresso she'd ever tasted, drifted out from the cafés and mingled with the rich smell of illegal Cuban cigars.

Salsa music pulsed from the shops and boom boxes sitting on the curbs. Nearby old men played dominos and chatted on the sidewalks, still reminiscing about the "good old days" in Cuba though they had been in Miami for almost fifty years.

"Stay here," Chad told her. "Lock the doors."

"No way. I'm coming with you."

He slanted her a look that said he was going to argue, but he didn't. She still couldn't tell if he truly believed her story or was merely going along to see what would happen. He was taking precautions, though. His actions told her that he cared, but she wished he would say something.

"Okay, but put on your shades and let me handle this."

She slipped on her sunglasses and stepped out of the car. Blistering heat shimmered off the sidewalk in waves. Hawaii was humid, but the trades made it pleasant. The heat here sapped all of her energy before she'd taken a few steps.

"How do you know where you're going?" she asked.

"I don't, but drug addicts have to support their habits. You deal or you steal. What you steal you've got to sell."

"Exactly. That's how I bought my Sig Saur. I went up a back alley in Chinatown. I could have bought a number of guns, including an AKC." She couldn't help being proud of herself. It had taken courage to walk down that dank alley and negotiate for a weapon.

He put his strong arm around her and pulled Devon flush

against his side. "Christ! I hate thinking of you wandering around in a place like that."

"Get over it. I'm prepared to do whatever it takes to survive."

"I know, babe. I know."

They walked down the one-way street until they were on the perimeter of Little Havana. Many of the shops here were boarded up. Others were illuminated by a single bulb at the end of a cord suspended from the ceiling.

"Land of *santeros*," Chad commented, referring to Cuban priests who practiced the same folk religion they had in Havana.

"I thought you hadn't spent much time in Miami."

"I've just passed through. My work was in the field, but we learned about the *santeria* in Delta Force. The Cubans have become a presence in Florida. It pays to know their traditions."

"My sister says it's legal for them to sacrifice a chicken." She wasn't particularly fond of chickens, but she couldn't imagine "sacrificing" any animal.

"Animal rights activists took them to the Supreme Court. They ruled it was part of their religion, like the Native Americans who are allowed to smoke peyote as part of their services."

Chad steered her around a corner and down a side street barely wide enough for a compact car. A few young punks clustered together, their dark eyes blazing—attitude with a capital A. *Marielitos,* she thought, recalling what Tina had told her. The first wave of Cuban refugees had been intellectuals, and many had gone on to great success in Miami.

The *Mariel* boat lift had given Castro the opportunity to empty out his prisons. The *marielitos* hadn't given up a life of crime just because they were now in the land of opportunity. Too many had honed their skills and passed them on to the next generation.

One gang member was bopping around in a circle, dancing to a beat only he could hear. The others leaned against the filthy wall, watching them. Chad strode forward, and Devon kept pace with him, thankful she had on the dark-haired wig. This was no place for a blonde.

Chad reached into his trouser pocket and pulled out a wad of twenty-dollar bills. Devon instantly saw the narrowed eyes, the shifting glances. They're going to jump him, she realized.

"I need a gun. Make that two guns."

"Well, bro." One punk swaggered forward, his English tinged with a Cuban accent. "Lemme help." He reached out for the money.

Chad pulled it back. "Let's see what you have."

A flash of his dark eyes forewarned Devon. He whipped out a switchblade and it flipped open, its razor-sharp blade catching a beam of sunlight. Chad shoved her out of the way, and she stumbled sideward, aware of the other men inching forward.

The punk lunged and Chad kicked so fast Devon almost didn't see his foot leave the ground. Chad's knee shot up between the man's thighs. The young tough doubled over, his body convulsing as if he'd been zapped with a jolt of electricity. Chad grabbed his wrist and twisted hard. The bone snapped, the sound not so much a crack as a gristly crunch. An agonized moan bounced off the nearby wall.

The knife fell to the asphalt with a *clink* that echoed along the narrow street. Chad bent over, plucked it off the ground. He jerked the punk to his feet and held the knife to his jugular. Chad's face contorted with an emotion too deep to be mere anger. "Ready to die?"

The kid clutched his balls with his good hand. *"Dios, mio. Dios mio."* My God. My God.

"I take that as a no," Chad said and the kid nodded, tears funneling down his cheeks.

Chad released him with a snort of disgust. The punk crumpled to the pavement, one hand flapping like a rag doll's while the other cradled his crotch.

Chad held the switchblade outward to the men who were

now huddled in a pack. "Are we going to do business or fight?"

"Whatcha' lookin for?" one of them asked.

"Sig Saur 225. Two of them."

Devon knew this wasn't the easiest gun to locate. Punks like this worshipped firepower. The 225 didn't hold as many rounds as they preferred, but the weapon was easy to conceal. Just right for Devon and Chad's purposes.

"Gimme five," the punk said. "I'll be back."

"We'll be down the street at El Diablo café," Chad said. "There's an extra fifty in it if you get the guns to me in half an hour."

Chad snapped his fingers at Devon as if she were his dog, but she didn't take offense. These men were into major macho stuff. They were afraid of Chad now, and he had to keep up the image.

When they were back on *Calle Ocho,* she asked, "Did you encourage that guy to fight with you on purpose?"

"You bet. It's law of the jungle. Go for the jugular. Show them who's strongest. If I hadn't, they would have jumped me and stolen my money."

"How could you be sure one of them wouldn't pull a gun and shoot you?"

He shrugged. "I couldn't but they're addicts interested in little more than their next fix."

Devon walked beside him and thought how lucky she'd been in Chinatown. The two junkies she'd approached had been so strung-out that they hadn't been capable of overpowering her and stealing what little money she'd had. For ten bucks, they'd directed her down the alley to a Chinese herb shop. The owner took the stolen guns, gave them money to buy drugs and resold the weapons for higher prices.

They turned into El Diablo, a sidewalk café Devon hadn't really noticed when they'd walked by the first time. A waitress built like a tombstone ambled out. *"Que?"* What?

"Dos *medianoches* y dos Coronas," Chad ordered in Spanish.

"You speak Spanish?" Devon asked.

He nodded. "It's very helpful if you spend much time in Special Forces."

She realized there was a great deal about him she didn't know. "How much time have you spent in Southern Florida?"

"Not a lot, but I was in the Everglades quite a bit doing some testing for the military."

Interesting, she thought, but she could tell by his closed expression that he wasn't going to discuss it further.

"Okay, so what did you order?"

"*Medianoches*. Ham and cheese sandwiches with pickles sliced lengthwise. I understand they were popular in Havana when people would stay out all night dancing at clubs. At dawn they would eat *medianoches* and go home."

The waitress delivered the sandwiches. Devon sampled one and found she liked it—she hadn't realized how little she'd eaten on the airplane. She'd been nervous about telling Chad the truth and so worried about her sister that she hadn't been able to eat.

"Your appetite is back," Chad commented. "Good. You'll need your strength if this goes south on us."

"I hope—"

The young punk who offered to get them guns rushed up, a backpack slung over one shoulder. "Check dis, dude."

Chad scooted their plates aside, and the kid put five Sig Saurs on the small table. He made no effort to hide what he was doing from the café or the street. Out of habit, Devon glanced around. There weren't any police in sight. She hadn't seen a single patrol car since entering Little Havana.

"I'm going to try Steve again," she said, standing.

She left Chad carefully examining the guns and went to the pay phone on the side of the café. Steve startled her by answering on the second ring.

"It's me, Devon."

"What do you want?" Steve sounded more exhausted, more irritable than he had the first time they'd spoken.

"I understand Tina's a little better."

"A bit. She has a long way to go."

"I need to see her."

"She's in ICU. One visitor at a time. I have to be with her."

"Couldn't you spare me a few minutes to see my sister?"

"It won't do any good. She's not conscious. You'll just be wasting your time."

"I've come a long way...risked a lot."

The long silence nearly split her eardrum.

"All right. Two minutes. That's all."

"This evening."

"I'll be here." Steven clicked off without another word.

"We're good to go," Chad told her when she returned to the table. "Two Sig Saurs and two extra clips each—just in case."

BROCK TRUDGED UP to Kilmer Cassidy's office. He'd returned to his bunker under Obelisk this morning after a late night flight from St. Louis. The show had been a hit, if you judged by crowds, but Brock had been angry and frustrated the whole time. Jordan had cozied up to Trensen, but she hadn't bothered to return his calls.

Why not? Had something bad happened in the Delano he didn't remember?

Nagged by that thought, he opened the door to Cassidy's office. The knock-out blonde who'd been hired as Cassidy's "secretary" greeted him with a perfunctory half smile and told him to go into Cassidy's office.

"What's the status on the Robbins woman?" Cassidy asked the second Brock came through the door.

"The trap's sprung," Brock assured him while he mentally took inventory of the office. He'd do some major redecorating when he moved in.

"Make it fast," Cassidy snapped. "I've gotten word they're about to set a trial date."

Brock battled the urge to tell the arrogant cocksucker that he'd known this for more than a week. "We'll have the bitch soon."

"I want to know the minute you do."

Brock waited for Cassidy to ask another question or bark an order, but the prick just glared at him. Cassidy's silence unnerved Brock. The sonofabitch always had so much to say. Brock thought about the missing file, and his inability to come up with any information on Olofson's computer. He had a hunch he was losing their trust. He shouldn't feel pressured. This was their fault for not listening when he gave them the heads-up on Samantha Robbins.

But Brock did feel pressure. The only way to get their trust back was obvious.

"Don't worry. Give me twenty-four hours. Then the Robbins bitch will wish she were dead."

"You're sure I can pass for a teenage boy?" Devon asked Chad.

"Absolutely."

After they had purchased the guns, they'd gone to Ekhard's and bought extra wide bandage tape and a Marlins baseball cap. Then they'd visited the mall and purchased tennis shoes that cost more than the average family made in a week. Baggy gangsta style jeans and an X RULES T-shirt completed the outfit.

Chad had clipped her dark, curly-haired wig short. With the baseball cap on backward and her breasts taped flat, Devon could pass for a boy, but she needed to keep on her dark glasses to disguise the feminine rise of her cheeks and her long eyelashes.

Chad had altered his appearance, too. He'd added pounds around the middle, hips and legs with a layer of insulation they'd found at a construction site. He, too, wore baggy pants and a Marlins T-shirt. He'd wrapped his head in a rank green do-rag that was now more brown than green. He walked hunkered over slightly, as if his weight and the backpack he had slung over his shoulder slowed him down.

The backpack held the contents of his duffel, a strange-looking flashlight, GPS and other things she hadn't recognized when he'd repacked the duffel before checking out of the fleabag motel. They were parked in the visitors' lot outside Miami-Dade Memorial Hospital.

"Remember about your gun," Chad said.

"Right."

They'd already agreed to double-check to see if the hospital was screening for weapons. If they weren't, they planned to keep them concealed in the pockets of their baggy jeans like gang members did. If the hospital had a metal detector, they would have to leave the guns in the trunk of the Rent-A-Wreck.

"All set?" Chad asked.

Devon nodded and leaned over to kiss his cheek.

"I'll check out the lobby for the metal detector and anyone who might be waiting for you. Then I'm going up to look around ICU. Give me ten minutes exactly. If I don't come back to get you, revert to Plan B."

Plan B. She would drive north to Atlanta and board a plane for Honolulu there. If the hospital was being watched, Rutherford and Ames might have the Miami Airport under surveillance.

He trailed his index finger up the curve of her throat, barely making contact, his eyes never leaving hers. With the breathtaking sweetness of a lover's kiss, his mouth met hers. She moved into his arms.

Please, she longed to say. *Don't let me go. Love me the way I love you.*

He pulled back and his eyes roved over her face in silent appraisal. "No heroics, Devon. Time it. If I'm not back in exactly ten minutes, get out of here."

CHAPTER TWENTY-SEVEN

IT WAS SEVEN MINUTES and eleven seconds later when Devon spotted Chad sauntering out the hospital's front door. She let out the breath she hadn't realized she'd been half-holding since he'd left.

She was going to be able to see Tina!

A few seconds later, Chad opened the car door and got in behind the steering wheel. "No metal detectors, but there are security cameras. Just in case someone reviews the tapes or is monitoring them, keep your head toward me when you walk to the elevator. I didn't see anyone watching the lobby, but we can't be too careful."

"I'm probably not in any danger. Right?"

"If they're really sophisticated, they're watching the hospital with night vision equipment from a distance. You'll be harder to spot, especially in a disguise. We have to operate at all times as if you're being stalked."

She nodded, knowing he was right. "What about ICU?"

"There's a security camera at the end of the hall and one at the nurses' station. Keep your head down. The cap and the glasses will conceal your face. You see your sister for as long as the ICU nurses allow you to stay. Then we deadhead for Atlanta."

She nodded her agreement. If anyone was watching the Miami Airport, they wouldn't find her.

His lips touched hers like a whisper, his mouth brushing hers, then pressing more firmly. The kiss didn't escalate into heated passion, the way their other kisses had. It seemed to be a pledge of something deeper, more meaningful.

Love welled up inside her. What would she have done without him? It wasn't just that he was an expert in surveillance and disguises. Having him with her made Devon less anxious, less panicky. Less likely to make a deadly mistake. With him at her side, the all-encompassing loneliness eased.

"I don't know what I would have done without you," she whispered. He kissed her again, and the sweetness of his kiss triggered an ache deep inside her. How did he feel? Did he truly believe she'd told him the truth? Did he love her?

"Let's roll."

They both stepped out of the wreck and sauntered toward the entrance, walking "the walk." Gangsta types—even Cubans in Miami—had an attitude that showed in the way they walked. It had taken Devon almost an hour of practice to get it down.

They ambled up to the entrance, and Devon checked the shadowy parking lot but detected nothing suspicious. Inside, she turned her head toward Chad and away from the security camera. They took the elevator to the second floor ICU.

"Let me do the talking," Chad said, his voice low as they stepped out of the elevator. "Keep your face away from the security camera over the nurses' station."

They walked toward a pod crammed with high-tech gear. Devon didn't spot the security camera, but she trusted Chad to know what to look for. Several nurses were sitting off to the side, monitoring patient information relayed from their rooms to the pod's computers.

The nurse on duty glanced up at them, then continued making notes on a chart. "Yes?"

Chad leaned over the counter in a way that would have intimidated many people. Evidently the nurse had seen a fair number of gang members and an unshaven six-foot-four guy in a filthy do-rag didn't bother her. Devon kept her head averted from where the security camera must be concealed among an array of equipment mounted on the walls.

"My friend's here to see Tina Layton," Chad told the nurse.

"Immediate family only," the nurse replied with a brief glance up at them.

"It's Tina's brother."

The nurse arched one eyebrow, clearly questioning this. "I'll need to check the records. Mr. Layton has power of attorney." She tapped a few keys on the computer in front of her.

Please, Steven, Devon silently prayed. Have me on the visitor's list.

"Well," the nurse said, obviously surprised. "Here you are—"

"It's okay to go in," Chad cut her off before the nurse said her name out loud.

"Yes, but Mr. Layton is with the patient. I'll have to let him know."

The nurse trotted down the hall to a door marked 2-C. A few seconds later Steven emerged. He'd aged considerably since she'd last seen him. His wheat-blond hair had crept upward another half inch. His skin was like a turtle's shell from hours on the golf course. Deep creases fanned out from the corners of his eyes and formed three horizontal lines across his brow.

"Samantha?" The shock in his voice pleased her. The disguise was working.

"It's me."

"She's still—" Steven's voice broke, and Devon knew he was seconds from crying.

"May I see Tina?"

"That's all right."

He eyed Chad with suspicion and didn't comment when Devon told him that Chad was her friend. "Only one person in ICU at a time."

"S'okay. I'll wait here." Chad gave her arm a silent gesture of reassurance.

"I'm going to slip in with you," Steven told her. "The nurses don't count me."

The animosity she'd heard over the telephone seemed to have vanished. She thought she understood. Steven was an only child whose parents had died several years ago. He didn't have anyone to help him. It was easy to be angry with Devon at a distance, but now he had someone to share this tragedy with him.

"I would never have recognized you," Steven said as he put his hand on the lever to open the door into the room.

"That's the idea. Forget I was here."

Steven knew she was in WITSEC. As her closest relative, Tina had been informed immediately, when the FBI removed her from Houston and turned her over to the Federal Marshals who ran WITSEC. Tina had never been told where her sister had been relocated or that she'd been moved a second time, so Steven didn't know anything, either. It was just as well. Devon had long ago decided her brother-in-law was a little weak. He would give her up in a heartbeat.

"Tina?" she called softly as she entered the room and halted. For a moment she couldn't believe it was her sister. Her face was like aged parchment, pale and dry. An oxygen clip pinched her turned-up nose. The lower part of her body was in some sort of contraption to stabilize her fractured pelvis.

There wasn't the slightest vestige of Tina's heartwarming smile. Only the curly lashes Devon had always envied and her Cupid's bow lips told Devon this was her sister. Fear seeped from every pore, hitting her with a mind-numbing punch as she grasped the seriousness of her sister's condition.

Critical.

She'd heard the term, known what it meant, but seeing Tina like this almost shattered her fragile self-control. She stood motionless in the middle of the room, gazing at her sister and silently acknowledging Tina might die.

Devon forced herself to move forward and kiss Tina's cool, dry cheek. She took her sister's right hand into both of hers. The other hand was attached to a frightening array of tubes and wires.

"It's me," she whispered in her ear. "It's Sammy."

No one but Tina had called her Sammy since grade school. It was too boyish, she'd decided the moment she'd discovered the opposite sex was good for something besides climbing trees with her.

"She doesn't hear you," Steven said. "I've been trying for two days."

Devon stroked her sister's hand. "I know, but I've heard it stimulates the brain. It might help her regain consciousness."

"Can't hurt."

"Tina, remember the time you locked me in Aunt Meg's steamer trunk? When you finally let me out, I made you swear to eat my veggies for a week."

Nothing.

"It's Sammy. It's Sammy," she whispered directly into Tina's ear. "Talk to me. I've missed you so."

The only sound was the annoying *plink-plink* of an IV attached to her sister's arm.

"What do the doctors say?" she asked.

"She should wake up, but they can't guarantee it."

Devon again whispered in her sister's ear. "Tina, remember our marmalade cat you named Moe? You swore it was a boy. Then Moe had six kittens, remember?"

Tina's left eye flickered.

"Did you see that?" she cried with excitement.

"Yeah. She moves her eyelids now and then. It doesn't mean anything."

Devon's heart lurched against the wall of her chest. She'd imagined a heart-to-heart talk with her sister—not this. She'd been unrealistic, of course. She should have known; she'd been told repeatedly Tina was unconscious.

"Tina," she whispered again. "Please. I haven't got long. I'm here. I love you. Steven loves you. So does Ariel. Wake up. Talk to us."

Nothing.

"Where's Ariel?" she asked.

"Still with friends."

"Perhaps if she spoke to—"

"No. I won't allow it. If worse comes to worst, I don't want Ariel to remember her mother like this."

Devon couldn't argue. Until now, she'd always carried a mental image of Tina's ceaseless smile. Seeing her this way would stay with Devon forever if her sister died.

Devon slipped into the hall to talk to Chad. He was turned so his back was to the security camera. He pulled Devon close to keep her out of range, as well.

"Tina's still in a coma," she whispered to him. "I've tried talking to her, but she isn't responding."

"It's been only forty-eight hours. It might be days..."

"I don't have that long."

"There's a red-eye tomorrow at midnight from Atlanta. That's the latest we can stay, if you want to return to Honolulu without anyone realizing where you've gone."

Two nurses rushed by them and charged into Tina's room. A wild flash of panic ripped through Devon. "She's dead."

"No," Chad assured her. "There wasn't a Code Blue alert."

Steven came out, his hands shoved into his pockets, his shoulders hunched over. "Tina's moaning. The nurses are checking her."

They waited in the austere hallway frozen in silent anticipation for a few agonizing minutes. No one came out of the room.

Finally Chad asked Steven, "Have the police located the driver who hit Tina?"

"No. I called them from the coffee shop about an hour ago." Steven shook his head, clearly disappointed. "No sign of the car."

"It's bound to have front end damage," Devon said.

"True," Steven agreed. "The witness gave a good description. A late model Lexus. Beige with Florida plates."

Devon glanced at Chad. She knew what he was thinking. After forty-eight hours the odds went down that a crime would be solved. An elderly man in a damaged Lexus shouldn't be this hard to find.

A nurse poked her head out the door. "She's asking for someone named Sammy."

Devon was momentarily speechless with surprise. *Thank you, God. Thank you.* Tina was asking for her.

She noticed Steven's bleak expression and choked back an elated cry. She grabbed Steven's hand, pulling him along with her. "She'll ask for you any second."

Inside, the nurse was adjusting the oxygen clip in Tina's nose.

"'Ammy." A low, guttural moan. "Sammy?"

Her sister's voice, a painful echo of the past when they'd been young. Happy. A thousand forgotten memories swept through her, in a second each was stamped with her sister's image. She couldn't control her spasmodic trembling. Tina was calling to her, the way she had when they'd been children.

A lifetime's memories of childhood days played through her mind. Her sister, her best friend. Unlike some sisters who were sibling rivals, they'd always cherished their relationship. Over the years, it had become a priceless source of inner strength. When Tina needed someone to help during child-birth, she'd turned to her sister.

Luck had deserted Devon back in Houston and hadn't been with her since. She'd been terrified her sister would be taken from her, as well. But Tina was speaking, calling her name. Didn't it mean she was getting better?

Holding raw emotion in check, Devon leaned over the bed. "I'm right here, Tina. Can you open your eyes?"

Tina's lids fluttered and she moaned again, louder this time. Her lids slowly lifted until they were at half-mast and revealed pain-glazed, unfocused blue eyes. A suffocating sen-sation tightened Devon's throat. If only she could take her sis-ter's pain away. Make it hers instead.

"M-M-Moe's...under...house. What's he...doin' there?"

Devon clutched her sister's hand, careful not to dislodge

the IV. "Moe's not a boy, remember? She's having kittens under the house."

"What the hell?" asked Steven.

"Sh! She's talking about a cat we had when we were kids."

"It's not uncommon," the nurse assured them. "She's reliving an event in the past. Now that she's conscious, she'll move forward in time."

Tina groaned again and tried to move but the contraption around her broken pelvis held her in place. "Kittens? Daddy...won't..."

"We can talk to Daddy, but I don't think he'll allow us to keep a kitten."

"I—I..."

A middle aged man with a stethoscope draped around his neck barged into the room. He wore an expensive suit a shade darker than his gray hair and had an arrogant air that made Devon bristle inwardly.

"Dr. Wells," the nurse said, her tone reverential. "The patient is regaining consciousness."

"Everyone out."

"I'm her—"

"Out!" he barked at Steven.

Devon followed Steven into the hall where Chad was waiting for her, his shoulder still braced against the wall, blocking the security camera.

"She's awake, but her mind is in the past."

"At least she's regained consciousness."

"I want Tina to know I'm here," Steven said. "I've been here the whole time."

Her brother-in-law's voice was whiney. Always self-centered and easily peeved, Steven was now exhausted and upset that Tina had asked for Devon instead of him. No matter what happened, coming here had been worth the risk. She'd helped the sister she loved and missed so much.

Dr. Wells emerged from Tina's room. "You're Mrs. Layton's family?"

They all nodded. The doctor didn't seem the least fazed to be confronted with a powerhouse in a do-rag and a person whose sexual orientation was questionable. This was Miami. There were enough weirdos around to give L.A. a run for its money.

"I've medicated Mrs. Layton. She'll sleep all night."

"But she just woke up," Devon protested. "Wouldn't—"

"Her body needs time to adjust to the pain. When we reduce the medication in the morning, she'll be more fully awake."

"She'll be able to talk to me?" Steven asked.

"I guarantee it. The worst is over." The doctor checked his watch, obviously anxious to leave. "Go home. Get a good night's sleep and come back in the morning."

BROCK BUFFED THE HOOD of his red Gull Wing. It was already gleaming so brightly in the warehouse lights that it could have blinded someone. He didn't care. It eased his tension to tend his babies.

The Gull Wing had been a hit in St. Louis, but the show had left him with a hollow feeling. His car was a sensation because Jordan's Gull Wing had been scratched. Being second best put him in an even worse mood than he'd been in lately.

He'd tried locating Jordan using the XtremeX Web site. It was connected to an anonymizer that encrypted e-mail and rerouted it through a variety of servers until it was impossible to tell where a message originated. This was illegal, of course, and told him the bitch was probably trafficking in drugs or porn. Why else would she cover her tracks in cyberspace?

The cell phone in his pocket vibrated. He'd kept it two days—a full day longer than he should have—because his operatives in Miami hadn't checked in yet today. He had to give them the new cell number before he could ditch this one.

"251, this had better be you," he said, his voice echoing in the large warehouse where he kept his cars.

"Numero Uno?"

"Right." He recognized 251's voice.

"We think Samantha Robbins visited her sister at the hospital tonight."

"Think? Shit! Don't you know?"

"The audio sounds like it."

Brock choked back a curse. He'd devised an elaborate plan to tail Tina Layton and hit—but not kill—her. He'd even arranged for 251 to pose as a vacationing kid from Des Moines to give a bogus description of the car and the driver. He knew word would get back through WITSEC to the bitch.

"What do the security cameras show?" 251 had paid off a night worker at the security company to make copies of the ICU tapes.

"Hard to say. You know security tapes."

Indeed Brock did. Most security camera tapes had no audio. They were often grainy and taken from an odd angle. Still, plenty of perps had been nailed with shots from security cameras.

"Copy what you've got to a disk and e-mail it to me at the office." Brock pitched the used lint-free wipe toward the trash bin in the corner. "Same with the audio. I'll enhance the video and get back to you. Go on standby mode." He instructed 251 to call him back on the agent's line at Obelisk or on the new cell number he gave him.

On the way back from the warehouse to his underground bunker at Obelisk, Brock drove by Jordan's apartment to kill time while 251 converted the tape. There was a single light on not far from the window facing the street. He parked in the loading zone and rang the bell. Nearly a minute passed and no one responded. He rang again. Nothing.

Shit!

He couldn't contact Jordan Walsh. He could highlight an ant on a leaf in the Amazon, but he couldn't find this woman.

In a huff, Brock drove to Obelisk and was waved through the security check point. Brock parked in his space and noted no other executives at the company were working late. Well, what did he expect? They were home counting their money and fucking their girlfriends.

Not that Brock cared.

When this was over, he would have something better than a broad. He would have a one-of-a-kind Gull Wing Mercedes. Who needed a woman?

In his office, Brock pulled on his microfiber jacket, then wriggled his fingers into the gloves. He smoothed the lightweight material across his palms and made sure his fingers were free to work on the computer.

He had AgCom on his computer. The age progression software had been developed to show abducted children as they grew older, employing digital imaging techniques. He could take the most washed-out or shadowy photograph and enhance it until it was *National Geographic* quality.

He'd used AgCom to compare a photograph of Samantha Robbins with women in Western states who had applied for driver's licenses. He hadn't found her, but that didn't mean it was AgCom's fault.

The whir of the incoming field line alerted him to what had to be 251's electronic transfer of the pictures of ICU taken by the security camera. The audio transcript captured by the parabolic mike would come through another system. It would be more difficult to analyze, but with the special enhancement equipment Obelisk had, Brock was sure to have a clear audio transcript by morning.

He peered at the incoming security tape. Miami-Dade Hospital couldn't have ID'd Godzilla with their security cameras. The tape showed a tall man—well over six feet—wearing a prison gang's do-rag around his head and a smaller male in his late teens.

He watched the tape as the twosome meandered with all the bravado gang members could muster toward the series of doors that led into individual ICU cubicles. Out came Steven Layton who greeted them.

What the fuck? Who were these jerk-offs?

This required a photo-analysis. He reversed the tape and froze it at the shot from the nurses' station. It was a full-frontal shot of the tall man, but the teenager wasn't facing the camera. What little of his face could be seen was shadowed by a Marlins ball cap and black-rimmed glasses.

He tapped a few keys, and AgCom converted the video to a still photograph. The computer would eliminate the security camera's distortions and lighten up the shadows. Every photograph could be reduced to pixels—pinpricks of light—millions of them. The special software sorted through the pixels and deciphered their relationship to other pixels.

In less than a minute, a clearer image appeared on the screen. It was still disappointing. The square-jawed tall man's features had improved slightly, and the shadows from the cap had been removed. But Brock still didn't have a clue who they were.

CHAPTER TWENTY-EIGHT

DEVON LAY SPRAWLED next to Chad on the faded floral print bedspread in the Celebrate! Miami Motel. They were the other side of the city from the Golden Palms; Chad insisted they change motels for security reasons. They still were driving the battered Acura, but Chad had switched license plates with an auto in a used car lot that was closed for the night.

She wanted to sleep, but her breasts were aching and sore after they'd removed the tape holding them flat. She couldn't feel sorry for herself, though. *Think about Tina.* She'd regained consciousness. With luck, tomorrow they would talk. It had been a lifetime since she'd been able to talk to her sister face-to-face. There was so much Devon wanted to tell Tina, and so little that she was allowed to say.

Next to her, Chad's arm twitched. He wasn't able to sleep, either, she realized. "You're worried, aren't you?"

He pulled her to him, and she bit the inside of her lip to keep from crying. His arm tightened protectively around her. "I know you need to see Tina tomorrow. I just don't like hanging around."

"And you don't like the police not being able to locate the driver of the car that hit Tina."

"Right. They should have been able to locate the old man by now."

"Maybe they have more important crimes."

"Police love no-brainers. It makes retirees and tourists feel safe. They've been working on this. Trust me."

"If this was a trap, no one made a move to get me."

"It was dark and you were well disguised. We'll change disguises before you visit Tina again."

Every instinct for self-preservation warned her that he was right, but somehow, she kept refusing to believe Rutherford and Ames were behind this. She didn't *want* it to be true, she silently conceded. She needed to see her sister without the panicky feeling that she was hanging over the edge of a dangerous precipice—and likely to die any second.

Traffic thrummed along even though it was almost three in the morning, the noise seeping through the cracks around the swamp cooler that wheezed and blew whiffs of chilled air over the bed. The odor of industrial strength disinfectant came from the bathroom. It didn't matter. Nothing mattered except Tina was getting better. Devon closed her eyes and was claimed by the deep, dreamless sleep of emotional exhaustion.

When she awakened, sunlight shafted through the break between the faded curtains. Chad was nearby; his hair buzzed so close to his skull that he was almost shaven clean.

"Hey, sleepyhead. Check this outfit. I picked it up while you were asleep." He held up a yellow and lilac print dress nearly leached of all color and a white wig tinged with blue.

"You're a grandmother," he informed her.

"Whatever." Devon boosted herself off the bed and hurried into the bathroom.

Her blond hair hung in matted hanks from wearing the wig. She found a comb and a disposable toothbrush in the dop-kit perched on the rim of the sink. She brushed her teeth and tugged the comb through her tangled hair.

She inspected the skin that had been beneath the duct tape. It was still scarlet and sore. Wearing a bra was going to hurt like hell. A small price to pay, she reminded herself.

What time was it?

She checked the tank watch with the wide rubber band Chad had given her as part of their gang disguise. Nearly noon! Tina would be awake.

She opened the door. "It's late. Tina has to be up by now."

"I called the hospital. Your sister has been upgraded to improved."

"Great. We've got to hurry."

"Not so fast. If they're watching the hospital, they'll have expected you long before now. We need to take our time, put on the new disguises, and go over late in the afternoon."

BROCK CALLED 251's cell again. He hated using cells but this situation was different. He'd expected the Robbins bitch to reappear at the hospital.

Nothing.

"Any sign of those two?" Brock asked when 251 picked up.

Late last night he'd relayed the information the AgCom analysis had provided and told them to watch for the tall man in the do-rag and the boy. Brock was positive the boy was Samantha Robbins in disguise. The identity of the man remained a mystery.

"Lots of coming and going at the hospital. No sign of those guys."

"Call me the second you spot them."

Brock gazed at the tall, overweight man on the computer screen. AgCom had refined the picture as many times as it could, removing all of the distortion. The computer had compared the image with the millions of bits of information stored in its data bank. It was a laborious task even for a computer that operated at top speed.

Finally the program converted the black-and-white photo to color. Beneath the do-rag the man's hair would be dark brown, almost black, like his eyebrows. His eyes were an intense shade of blue. His skin was tanned, indicating he spent considerable time in the sun.

The expression on the man's face troubled Brock. Maybe it was just an act, but the jerk radiated a certain ruthlessness that Brock didn't like. He could present a problem for his operatives.

It was an eerie sensation. He knew he was right although there was no way to confirm it. The guy might be a little overweight, but he could still cause a problem when they moved in to grab the bitch.

Who was he? A pro, or some sucker the Robbins woman had picked up along the way? Beautiful women had a way of doing that, he decided, thinking of Jordan Walsh.

It couldn't be a WITSEC agent. They would never allow a witness to enter the "danger zone." Weddings, funerals and ailing relatives were *verboten*. The bitch was AWOL.

Brock decided to run the man's photograph through Homeland Security's passport database. It was a slower program because HS didn't have the funds Obelisk did. He wasn't sure how long it would take, but chances were the dumb-fuck had a passport.

Brock studied the liquid plasma screen, currently on an uplink to the DoD satellite. He could watch the hospital, but he didn't have the advantage his operatives on the ground did. They could see into the hospital from a horizontal angle from across the street. He could only watch from directly above until the satellite moved and gave him a better angle.

A *ping-ping* from another computer told him the audio analysis was finally complete. His operatives had been recording conversations in Tina Layton's room with a parabolic microphone. Drug enforcement had developed the parabolic mike. Because it was employed from afar, it didn't require a judge's authorization the way a search warrant or a wire tap did. The parabolic system didn't provide as clear a tape as more sophisticated devices.

A fact that Kilmer Cassidy had warned him about.

He'd argued—successfully—that patients were too often moved in hospitals as was equipment. They couldn't count on sneaking in and relocating a bug in such a busy place. Now, he admitted, the risk might have been worth it.

Parabolics picked up the gurgle and burp of the machines in the hospital room, noise from the street, and every other sound imaginable. Drug enforcement had special agents who were trained to listen and interpret what was being said. They rarely had to contend with as much noise as was generated in a hospital, and junkies didn't whisper.

The printer kicked into action and spit out a printed version of what was on the audiotape. *It's me. It's Sammy.*

Bingo!

Sammy had to be a nickname for the Robbins woman. The bitch had come to visit her sister—just as he'd known she would. A good disguise had gotten her by his operatives. The bitch had nine lives, but she wasn't getting away from him this time. Samantha Robbins would appear again. When she did, his men would nab her.

Brock had planned to wait until his operatives had the broad in the secluded house he'd rented before he appeared on the scene. Considering what had happened last night, he decided to leave for Miami as soon as he could line up one of the Obelisk jets.

"I CAN'T WAIT," Devon told Chad. "I want to see Tina now."

"I know you do but you're much safer when the angle of the sun hits the building across the street. I've studied the area. If someone is watching for you, that's where they'll be."

"I guess you're right," she reluctantly agreed.

"Keep walking," he told her. Unlike yesterday, Devon now needed to master the hunkered-over walk of an elderly woman. "Your cane is fitted with a knife. Just twist the handle and it will come apart."

"I have the Sig Saur in my handbag"

"True, but you may not have time to get it out. And if someone jumps you, chances are they'll be wearing a Kevlar vest. It's bulletproof, but a knife will slash right through the material."

"What if they're not wearing Kevlar? Miami's pretty hot to put a vest under your shirt. Wearing it on top would call attention to the person."

"Good thinking. If they're not wearing a vest, even better. Go for the heart." He offered her his body. "Here, try it on me."

It took several tries before Devon could pull out the knife and effectively lunge at him. She was good, but he knew she wouldn't stand much of a chance with pros. She would be a distraction while he took care of them.

Chad had spent his time at the hospital analyzing the situation and deciding what he would do if he wanted to kill Devon. He'd watch the main entrance because it was the closest to ICU, and there was a reception desk there where visitors obtained information on patients. Opposite the entrance was a huge apartment building. That's where he would hide. The other buildings were medical offices, which would be more difficult to use without being discovered.

A sharpshooter could hit anyone going into the building, but Chad didn't think they would risk killing Devon at the hospital entrance. He was betting they would follow her and take her out someplace that they could get away from easily.

UNFUCKINGBELIEVABLE! All five of Obelisk's jets were being used. No doubt Cassidy had gone to Hilton Head to play golf. Another jet was en route to the Caymans where Obelisk had numerous offshore accounts. The others were on top secret assignments, but one was due back at eight. By the time it refueled and flew him to Miami, it would be ten o'clock. His operatives should have the bitch by then.

While he killed time, waiting for the jet to return, he drove by Jordan's condo. It was late afternoon, and he knew she wouldn't be home yet. He'd pressed softened wax into Jordan's front door. The expert locksmith Obelisk used had made him a key.

He parked his car down the street and watched the condo complex for a few minutes. No one came or left the building. It wasn't very large—only twelve units. Jordan's condo was on the top floor.

Brock left his car and walked to the building. He rang the buzzer by the J. Walsh nameplate. Nothing. He waited and rang again. Still, no answer.

He looked around to make certain no one was watching. He used the door key he'd had made to enter the building. Rather than risk meeting a tenant in the elevator, he raced up the stairs to the sixth floor.

There were two units on the penthouse level. Jordan's faced the street. The other was occupied by a retired dentist who spent most of the winter at his place on the "redneck Riviera" outside Mobile.

Brock rang Jordan's doorbell and waited. No one came to the door. He didn't expect her to be home, but it never hurt to be careful. He inserted the key in the lock and opened the door.

"What in hell?"

The living room was empty except for a card table with a lamp next to the windows facing the street. He checked the kitchen. Nothing in the fridge. The cabinets were empty. He looked in the bedroom and closets. Zilch.

A disturbing thought waltzed up his spine like a snake. He'd been set up.

CHAPTER TWENTY-NINE

DEVON STOOD BESIDE her sister. Steven was sitting on the other side of the bed in a chair that was pulled as close as possible to Tina.

"You should have been here earlier. Tina's sleeping now."

It was late afternoon and the angle of the sun was low. Chad believed this might prevent anyone watching from across the street from spotting her. Disguised as an old woman, complete with makeup that made her skin appear wrinkled, Devon had taken a taxi to the hospital. Chad had driven behind her in the wreck. He'd disguised himself as a hospital technician. Chad was wearing green scrubs, had a stethoscope draped around his neck, and had an ID badge he'd made up at a copy shop pinned to his chest.

"I couldn't get here any sooner," Devon told her brother-in-law.

He grunted. She could tell the animosity was back. Now that Tina's condition was improving, Steven didn't feel so vulnerable.

"What did the doctor say about her condition?"

Steven quirked an eyebrow. "Which doctor? She's got a dozen."

"Give me a rundown. I'd like to know what *all* of them thought."

"Bottom line, she's getting better. It'll take months and lots of physical therapy, but—"

"Tina's going to recover."

"Looks that way."

"I'm so thankful. I've prayed—"

"Know what bums me?" Steven asked with a frustrated scowl. "An old man didn't hit Tina. It was a young guy with a skull cap driving a Hummer."

"A Hummer? I thought—"

"The witness has disappeared. Supposedly he was from Des Moines, but the police haven't been able to locate him."

"How do you know all this? Did Tina—"

"She was awake earlier. The detective investigating the case came by. She told him about the Hummer and the kid driving it."

Suddenly her forehead felt tight and a dizzying tremor of panic gripped her. Chad was right. This was a trap. Tina had almost been killed—because of her. Even now, her sister was barely alive. It was her fault.

Despair and an overwhelming sense of defeat gripped her. She'd blotted out common sense with false hope. Rutherford and Ames had already ruthlessly murdered two people. Killing Tina wouldn't have meant a thing to them.

Devon realized she should walk out and let them kill her. Right now, she couldn't imagine how she could possibly escape without someone else dying because of her. Her sister. Ariel. Chad.

The trial, she thought. If only she could stay alive until then. From the stand, she could let the world know the price of telling the truth.

"S-Sammy?" her sister called in a voice almost too low to be heard.

"Tina. I'm here." She edged closer to the bed.

"W-w...where?"

Devon realized her sister didn't recognize her. She pointed to her own chest. "It's me. Sammy."

"Y-you're—"

Steven jumped to his feet, saying, "Don't talk. It takes too much out of you. Let her talk to you."

Devon took her sister's hand, thinking how much better

Tina looked. She was attached to more equipment than Devon cared to count, but they'd removed the oxygen clip and Tina's bed was slightly elevated so she no longer appeared to be flat on her back and totally out of it.

"I came, Tina, the minute I heard you were in the hospital." Devon gestured to her disguise. "You know it's almost impossible for me to get away, but it didn't matter. For you, I'd risk anything."

Tina's eyes were barely open, but tears seeped out of the corners. "I know. I've missed you so much."

Devon caught her brother-in-law's grimace. "Steven's been here the whole time. He's never left your side."

Tina rotated her head a notch. "I—I know. That's why I love...him."

"She's exhausted," Steven told her. "Maybe you should come back later—"

"I can't! I have to leave soon."

"D-don't...go," cried Tina, her voice not more than a whisper.

"Let me do the talking," Devon said. "There are things I need to tell you."

Steven eyed her warily, but Tina bobbed her head.

"I've heard the trial will be soon. After I testify, I hope my life returns to normal." She didn't add that Rutherford and Ames had arranged for Tina's accident or that they could still be a threat to Devon even from behind bars. "We can spend time together again—"

"W-w-wonder...ful. We need to see...each...other."

"Of course, and I want to be with Ariel."

Tina asked her husband, "Where is Ariel?"

"With the Overfelts. They took Ariel to the stable to ride her horse earlier today."

"Good." Tina moved her head to look directly at Devon. "Tell me...what's...happening."

What could Devon say? Nothing. She couldn't reveal anything about where she was living or any personal information that could lead someone to her. The discrepancy between her sister's account of the hit-and-run and the witness's story warned Devon to be extremely careful. This room could be bugged. Every word she uttered could be used to target and kill her.

"I'm happy," Devon told her sister with amazing honesty. "I have a new life." She smiled at Tina even though she wasn't positive her sister could actually see her clearly. Tina was heavily medicated and barely functioning. Still, this might be the only time they had for months to come. "I've met a man."

"W-w-what about Tyler?"

Naturally she'd told Tina about her affair with Tyler. She'd never mentioned him since she'd left Houston.

"Tyler married someone else."

"S-s-sorry..."

"Don't be. It was for the best. I've met a great guy. You're going to like him."

Steven's nose crinkled as if he'd smelled something rancid. Devon didn't pay any attention to him.

BROCK SAT IN THE BACK of the luxurious Sikorsky S-76 and studied Jordan's Web site. *Sex in a basket.* A cutesy pink basket filled with sex toys. *Major kink in a bag.* A lavender floral bag with a whip sticking out of it.

There wasn't a clue on the site that told him who Jordan Walsh was or where she lived. The key, of course, was the Gull Wing. He had a call into Mercedes to see if they had an address.

His cell phone vibrated and he pulled it out of his pocket. He'd been in the air over an hour. Judging from the endless stretch of darkness below, they were somewhere over South Carolina.

"Brock Hardesty," he answered in case it was someone from Stuttgart calling him about the Gull Wing.

"251 here."

"Have you got her?"

"No, but she's in with her sister. We can tell by the conversation."

"Is she still wearing the baseball cap?" Brock avoided using "disguise." The Sikorsky was a luxury helicopter that made little noise. He didn't want to chance having the pilot overhear him.

"Ah...we're not sure."

"Why not?"

"We didn't see her come into the hospital."

Shit! 251 might be the master of disguise, but he wasn't good at detecting them on others. "Was 77 monitoring the minicams?"

"Yes. He didn't spot her, either."

Brock's operatives had placed inexpensive video cameras at the secondary entrances. Designed for spying on kids or the nanny, these cameras fit in the palm of his hand. Battery powered, they could be easily hidden in the trees and were difficult to spot unless someone knew to look for them. Their transmission was relayed to the monitoring station set up in the apartment building across from the main entrance.

"One of you hustle up to ICU and find out what she looks like."

"I sent 77. He should be there by now."

"Who else is in the hospital room?"

"Just the husband."

"The next time I hear from you, I want you to tell me you have the bitch." He hung up without another word.

The image of the man in the do-rag played across Brock's mind. If the prick wasn't in the hospital room, he must be hanging around nearby. What was he up to?

The phone vibrated again before Brock could put it away. It was the classic car specialist Mercedes kept on their staff in Stuttgart.

"I'm Hans Ziegler," the man said in a clipped German accent. "You have a question about a Gull Wing."

"Yes. I'm a collector. I have a red '52 Gull Wing. I'm interested in acquiring a caper-green Gull Wing recently restored by Jordan Walsh."

"Vat color?"

"Green. Specifically caper-green. It's a one-of-a-kind Gull—"

"K-purr? Those little brown zings chefs use for garnish?"

"That's right."

"Not a Mercedes color."

"I know," he replied, trying not to sound too impatient. "This was a custom automobile. Jordan Walsh recently had it restored and Mercedes supplied the paint."

"Impossible! All vintage restorations come through my office. We never shipped caper-green paint because we don't have it. Never have. Never will."

Brock thanked Ziegler and hung up.

The bitch had deliberately tricked him. Why? Why?

He stared out the helicopter's window and thought about his night with Jordan Walsh. He'd blacked out from too much alcohol—something he'd never done before.

Was it possible Jordan had slipped something into his drink? He'd read about the date rape drug rohypnol, commonly called "roofies." Guys slipped the pills into drinks. The women continued to function, but couldn't remember anything the next morning.

What possible reason would Jordan have had for giving him a roofie?

The light dawned and he barked a laugh. The device DARPA was testing. That's what she'd been after. When he was out cold, she'd opened the safe—room safes were easy to crack—and removed the gadget. She'd substituted something that didn't function properly.

Who in hell was she working for?

CHAD WANDERED TOWARD ICU with a clipboard in his hand. He'd taken it off the counter in the maternity unit. In scrubs with a stethoscope around his neck, Chad didn't attract any attention.

His first mission had been to locate the ancillary cameras the hit team had put up at the other entrances to the hospital. There was one in the eaves over the ER entrance that Chad couldn't get to, but the others were in trees and bushes. He'd taken care not to have his picture appear on the screen and came at them from the side. He zapped them with Pam that he'd transferred into a small spray bottle.

The cameras were the inexpensive type easily purchased at any electronics store. A dash of Pam and the image produced became blurry. Anyone monitoring the system would blame it on the poor quality of the camera.

Chad walked by the ICU pod, his head turned so the security camera didn't pick him up. A man was coming out of Tina Layton's room. Chad opened a closet door marked Storage. It turned out to be bedding and linens.

The man hurried by without paying any attention to him, but Chad got a good look at the guy. Tall, bulky chest, sandy hair in a brush cut. Military, Chad decided, or ex-military like him. Men who'd been in the service tended to have a certain look. There was a cadence to their walk that came from drills and marching. This guy fit the profile exactly.

He closed the closet and walked off to the side to keep out of the security camera's range. He looked over his shoulder to see if anyone from the nurses' station was watching him. They weren't; he spritzed the camera with Pam.

Chad checked the nurses' pod again, then slipped into Tina's room. Devon's sister was asleep, and her husband was hunched down in a chair beside the bed. Devon opened her mouth to say something, but he silenced her with a finger over his lips. He nodded to Steven Layton, who didn't seem to recognize him, and pulled Devon into the hall.

"What was that man doing in here?" he asked.

"Wrong room. He was looking for Richard something."

He shuddered inwardly and braced himself for what he'd

known was coming since Devon had told him why she was flying to Miami. He whispered in her ear, "He's one of the hit team. They must be getting an audiofeed from the room. They didn't know what you looked like and came to find out."

"My sister says a young guy in a Hummer ran her down."

"Why am I not surprised? We go to Plan B."

She closed her eyes for a second and nodded. "I have to say goodbye to Tina."

"No, don't tell her that. Say you're going for coffee and you'll be back in ten minutes." When she agreed, he added, "There will be a taxi waiting for you at the side entrance near pediatrics. I'll follow you in the Acura."

CHAPTER THIRTY

KEKE KICKED OFF HER SHOES at her front door and raced into her home to answer the telephone. It was Ane on the line.

"Keke, is there something wrong?" the older woman asked, obviously troubled by Keke's urgent message.

"I'm not sure. I'm trying to find Chad. He didn't show up for our luau, and he didn't call. I thought maybe he mentioned something to you about going out of town on business."

"Noooo," Chad's assistant replied very slowly. "He isn't away on business. I schedule all his business appointments."

"Do you have any idea where he might have gone?"

"Have you tried that woman? Pele's ghost?"

"Eddie gave me Devon's number, and I called but no one's home." Keke peeked out the window to be certain the children were safe. "The last I saw him, Chad was using the marina's pay phone to call a friend from his Delta Force days. The guy had called him for something. Do you suppose Chad went somewhere to meet him?"

Ane didn't respond.

"Can you hear me?" Keke asked.

"Yes. I just don't like discussing Chad's *oihana.*"

"I wouldn't ask about my brother's business if I weren't worried. It's not like him to disappear when the family was having a luau."

"True," Ane agreed. "A friend didn't call Chad. He called someone. All Chad said was his name, then he hung up and left the office. I don't know what made me do it. I'm not usually such a *hana mau kino.*"

Oh, puleeze, Keke thought. Ane was queen of the *hana mau kinos*. Busybodies. She lived to mother Chad. That's why Keke had called her.

"I pressed the redial button on Chad's telephone. The number on the display was a Washington, D.C. area code. I hung up before it could ring. I looked out the window and saw Chad standing by the marina's pay phone."

Keke didn't know what to think. Her brother rarely lied, especially about something as seemingly trivial as a telephone call. "If I hit the redial button on his phone, would it still dial the number?"

"No. He returned to the office and made several calls. That number is gone."

"His Porsche isn't in his garage."

"Have you checked the airport lot? Maybe he decided to drop in on one of his dive shops on another island."

"I called them. No one's seen him, and they're not expecting him." Keke twisted a strand of hair around her finger. "I'll drive out to the airport. It shouldn't be hard to spot a black Porsche."

"Mark my words. He's with Pele's ghost. She's *pilikia*."

Keke loaded Mei and Lui in her Datsun and drove along Kalanianole Highway until she reached the turnoff for Honolulu International Airport. *Pilikia*. Trouble. She couldn't help feeling her brother was in trouble, and she wouldn't be surprised if Devon was involved.

Why would Chad lie about a call? Why wouldn't he have told someone that he couldn't make the luau? This wasn't like Chad, and it had her very worried.

"Isn't Grandmother coming to dinner?" Lui unexpectedly asked.

Cripes! Keke had completely forgotten. "Your father is taking us out."

"Goody," cried Mei. "Chuck E. Cheese!"

Keke wondered if Mother Nakamura would have a conniption. She'd been amazingly good-natured when she'd surprised them by showing up at the luau, but she hadn't eaten much. She'd sampled the fruit and rice dishes. The tender pork from the roasted pig hadn't made it onto her plate. Chuck E. Cheese should be a challenge for her.

Keke turned into the airport and waited in the line of cars, going to park. "Let's play a game," she told the children. "I'll give a dollar to the first one of you who sees uncle Chad's black car."

"The Porsche," Lui said.

Keke took a ticket from the machine and drove into the lot. If Chad had taken his favorite toy to the airport, he would have put it in the covered parking. She headed into the structure and methodically drove up and down each row. When she arrived at the top level, she decided this was a wild goose chase.

"It's not here," Mei said.

"Is Grandmother going to be waiting for us?" Lui asked.

Keke checked her watch. No doubt about it Mother Nakamura would be sitting on their porch in a huff. She drove out of the structure toward the booth where cars were lined up to pay.

"There it is! Right there!" cried Lui. "I get a dollar. I get a dollar." He poked his sister. "You lose."

Keke glanced around. "Where?"

"Next row over. See?"

Keke spotted a black Porsche but wasn't sure it was Chad's. She rounded the bend and went up the next row.

"See those wheels? It's Uncle Chad's Porsche."

Leave it to Lui to notice the custom chrome wheels Chad had had made for his Porsche. Keke put the car in park and walked around her brother's car. Judging by the coat of dust, the Porsche had been here for some time. Her intuition screamed something was really wrong. Chad usually took his SUV to the airport.

He must have left very unexpectedly.

CHAD IDLED AT THE CURB not far from the side exit near the pediatric unit. Fear traveled in a rippling wave up his back, to his neck, and clamped down on his temples like a vise. He wasn't afraid for himself, but if he wasn't careful Devon would be killed. He figured they had ten—fifteen minutes—tops to get away. Then the goons would realize Devon hadn't gone for coffee.

The yellow taxi pulled up, and a few seconds later Devon strolled out of the hospital. Going to Plan B, she'd ditched her old lady's clothes and was wearing black jeans and a black blouse. A backpack had replaced the worn handbag. In it she would have stowed the part of the cane that converted to a knife. Devon climbed into the cab, and it pulled away from the curb.

Chad followed several car lengths behind the taxi. The plan was to drive north and have the cab drop off Devon at a motel in North Miami Beach. Chad would pick her up and they would deadhead for Atlanta.

Chad checked the rearview mirror to see if anyone was following him. There were lots of headlights. It was still early enough to have plenty of cars on the road. An expert hit team would follow on a parallel street a block over, if the traffic was light, and be nearly impossible to spot. Since there were so many cars around, anyone following him would be in the rear.

He was counting on this team being only two, possibly three men. Hit teams who weren't "connected"—part of a mob operation—usually worked alone or in pairs. People tended not to notice two men together. More than that attracted unwanted attention.

Chad peered in the rearview mirror again. If the hit team had military training, they would be driving a van or a SUV. He was looking for a larger-than-normal luggage rack or lights on the roof that would conceal a camera with night vision and magnification capability, which could read a license plate two blocks away. He expected them to confirm Devon was Samantha Robbins and try to take her out with a single shot, either from a high-powered rifle or at close range with a hand gun.

They would leave something to make the hit appear to be drug-related. The last thing they would want was a murdered tourist that would have Miami in an uproar. But no one gave a damn about drug killings. They were a fact of life in Miami.

Chad was four cars behind the taxi. The screaming yellow cab was easy to keep his eye on. The traffic behind him that might be following Devon was more difficult. There weren't any vans or panel trucks in sight, but the world was full of SUVs. Apparently everyone needed a four-wheel drive to get them to Starbucks and the mall.

They were approaching the turnoff for Highway 826. Just before it was the Sherwood Inn, where the taxi was going to leave Devon. He planned to take 826 over to the toll road and shoot back up north to avoid the congestion around Fort Lauderdale and Boca Raton.

The traffic behind him had thinned. The only vehicle that looked familiar was a red Corvette. Hit men did not tool around in expensive cars witnesses would remember.

Expect the unexpected.

The Delta Force motto popped into his head. With it came a visceral warning. Something wasn't right.

The Corvette had been several cars back when they'd left the hospital. It still lagged several car lengths behind. It should have caught up. Most Corvette drivers would have flown by him already.

DEVON SAW THE SIGN for the Sherwood Inn up ahead. Almost there. With luck, they would make the Atlanta to Hawaii flight. She would be safe in Honolulu until the trial.

"Go to the back," she told the driver. "Number sixty-seven."

Chad had told her to wait in front of this room where she wouldn't be seen from the street. She glanced at the meter to the right of the Haitian driver who'd tried to engage her in conversation earlier. She hadn't meant to be rude, but she couldn't talk. She kept seeing her sister and Romero.

The men after her would stop at nothing.

The taxi's air-conditioning was on the fritz or so the driver claimed. She suspected he kept it off to save on the gas he used. The windows were rolled down. It was hot and her skin was clammy. One good thing about the wreck was its air-conditioning worked.

She pulled a wad of bills out of her wallet, intending to leave him a nice tip. The knife that had been part of the cane was on top of her things in the backpack near the wallet. The knife had a special sheath over the blade so she could still use it after she'd left the cane in the hospital rest room. She pulled it off, careful not to cut herself on the razor-sharp blade, and moved the Sig Saur beside it. After the driver let her out, it would be several minutes before Chad appeared. She wasn't taking any chances.

The taxi pulled into the parking space in front of number sixty-seven. The security lights were on but they weren't very bright. Dark shadows formed in several places nearby. She was reassured by the number of cars in the lot. At least there were people around.

A lipstick-red Corvette drove into the space next to the cab. Behind the wheel was a woman with long, dark hair. The flashy sports car reminded her of Tyler's midnight-blue Corvette.

It seemed like another lifetime. A life that belonged to another person.

The cabdriver glanced over his shoulder at Devon, his white teeth gleaming against his dark skin. "That'll be—"

Pop! A dull cracking sound reverberated through the taxi. The driver scrunched sideways as if picking up something from the seat. A long second ticked by.

"Are you okay?" Devon asked.

No response. Devon leaned forward. Oh, Jesus, no! Blood was streaming from a small hole in the side of his head.

She realized the woman in the Corvette had used a gun with a silencer. She hit the floor and jerked on the drawstring of her backpack for the gun or the knife. A hulking silhouette loomed beside the taxi's back door opposite where she was hunkered down.

"Get out of the car," ordered a male voice.

Stalling, she didn't answer. Chad couldn't be far away. She'd looked over her shoulder twice in the cab and had spotted the Acura. Surely he would be here in a minute.

"I said get out of the car."

She recognized the voice of the man who'd come into her sister's room. From his bulked-up shadow, she guessed he was wearing a Kevlar vest as well as a woman's wig. If she used the gun, it would have to be a shot to the head. Was she good enough to kill him before he shot her? Until WITSEC, she'd never fired a gun. Now she wished she'd spent more time at the range.

Where *was* Chad?

The back door of the taxi near her feet swung open. The shadows prevented her from clearly seeing his face, but she could tell it was a man in a woman's wig. He had a long-barreled gun in his left hand. A special silencer, she decided. With the tiniest pop, the gun had killed the man. People in the motel wouldn't be awakened by shots from this gun.

"Get out or I'll haul you out!" he ordered, his voice low, yet undeniably threatening.

She jerked her knees closer to her body and hunched around the backpack, her hand inside closing over the knife's handle. "Go ahead. Shoot me, but I'm not moving."

"I'm not going to shoot you." His voice was deep, crusty and radiated ruthlessness. "You have something that belongs to my friend. He wants to talk to you."

What on earth? She didn't have anything. Now that she'd been relocated twice Zach and some clothes were all she possessed. "You've got the wrong person. This is a mistake."

"You're Samantha Robbins."

Buying time, she didn't respond. Surely Chad would come

along any second. Then it hit her. Chad should have been here by now.

A keening cry of agony too deep for tears welled up in her throat. She'd known this would happen. She was the kiss of death—literally. They'd murdered Chad. She choked back her emotion. She didn't have time for sentiment now.

The FBI agent, Romero, the taxi driver and now Chad. Her sister almost became another victim. The flame of vengeance burned in her gut.

"Who wants to talk to me?" she managed to say, a plan forming in her mind.

"A friend. He just wants to ask you a few questions."

"About what?"

A blast of static erupted from the taxi's radio. "Where are you, Xavier? Report in. Report in."

Poor Xavier, she thought. He'd probably come by boat from Haiti, believing he'd find a better life in America. Her heart lurched madly with something too intense, too painful to be mere anger.

Devon didn't care anymore. She would take this ruthless killer with her. Or die trying.

He lunged forward, grabbed her ankles, and dragged her out of the car in one swift movement. She banged the back of her head against the car and hit the pavement. White-hot pain shot through her skull, and for a moment, she couldn't focus.

He grabbed her hair and jerked her head backward. The dimly lit parking lot whirlpooled before her eyes.

Strong arms snaked around her midriff and hauled her upright, pinning her hand in her backpack while she dangled, her toes barely touching the ground.

"Gimme the gun."

"I-it's in my backpack." She tried to sound as if tears were about to gush. The opposite was true. A strange calmness now accompanied the anger burning with astonishing intensity.

One scream could bring help, but she might not get a

chance to kill this bastard. Chad's face flashed across her mind. He had so much to offer the world, yet they'd snuffed out his life without hesitation. She decided against screaming, and her vision suddenly cleared.

"Gimme your gun," he repeated, his sour breath on her face.

"I-it's in m-my...pack"

He released her, but kept his gun pressed against her ribs. "Throw it down on the ground."

Her hand still on the knife, she fished in the backpack, pretending to be searching for the gun. She dropped the gun onto the pavement along with the backpack. In the same instant, she hurled herself at him, heaving her weight at the arm holding the weapon. With her other hand, she rammed the base of her palm against his nose. He reeled sideways with a furious grunt, then staggered two steps forward, waving the gun.

She aimed the blade just under his breastbone. Using the full weight of her body, she shoved the knife into the cushy Kevlar. "This is for Chad."

Without a sound, he doubled over and crumpled to the ground. Blood spurted from the wound and hit the taxi's door like a gusher. The metallic odor of fresh blood permeated the humid air.

Hands trembling, she searched his pockets and found several thousand dollars in cash and a wallet with a Florida driver's license. She yanked the wig off his head, picked up his gun, and tossed everything into her backpack.

Head aching but pumped with adrenaline, she opened the trunk of the Corvette. Duct tape and a flashlight. She'd hoped to find tools. She needed to switch the Corvette's license plate with one of the cars in the motel lot.

On the front seat, she found a tiny plastic packet of white powder. Cocaine, she thought. She picked it up with a tissue and took it over to the dead man. She tucked it into his pocket. Removing the bloody knife was trickier. It had lodged against a bone. She pulled hard and it released with a gristly crunch.

A sweep of headlights blasted the area. She stayed low, telling herself she wasn't surprised. It was amazing no one had come along before now. From this angle between the cars, they couldn't be seen unless they drove down this far. She was prepared to open the passenger door of the Corvette, leap in, and speed away. She assumed the keys were still in the car because they hadn't been in the killer's pocket.

The set of headlights veered right, the car pulled into a space up front, and she heard what sounded like college boys half-drunk getting out of the auto. Apparently they were trying to decide who had the room key. She waited while they went inside and wiped the blood off the knife using the hit man's trouser cuffs.

The boys stumbled into their room. She hunkered down and removed the Corvette's plates with the knife. Nearby was a Lexus with Florida plates. She switched those with the Corvette's plates.

She was behind the wheel, ready to drive north. Wipe your prints off the taxi, a voice in her head told her. She scrambled out of the car and over to the cab. It took several minutes to remove her prints.

She climbed into the sports car again, fired up the powerful engine, and put it in reverse. A single beam of light glared at her from the rearview mirror, blinding her. She jerked her head to the side to avoid the spotlight.

The hit man was part of a team. His partner had come to investigate.

She slammed her fist against the leather-wrapped steering wheel. "You're not killing me, you son of a bitch!"

CHAPTER THIRTY-ONE

DEVON SPUN AROUND, shading her eyes from the blinding light with one hand. The man was standing behind the rear fender. Light glinted off the barrel of the gun he was holding. Her head throbbed so much it made it difficult to concentrate. A whimper caught in her throat.

The car was already in Reverse, she reminded herself. She braved a quick peek over her shoulder. The killer had moved to the right so he was no longer directly behind the car.

She slammed her foot down on the accelerator and gunned the engine while she spun the wheel. The Corvette rocketed backward, tires screeching.

Thunk!

The man hit the pavement and rolled on his side. Devon had sideswiped the Chevy next to the Vette as she'd tried to run over the man. She slammed on the brakes to avoid ramming into any other cars parked behind her. She jarred to a stop that whiplashed her aching skull. The headlights illuminated the figure sprawled on the blacktop. She shoved the car into Drive, ready to finish off the bastard.

In one fluid motion, he leaped to his feet, the gun trained on her. Lord have mercy! It wasn't a hit man after all.

It was Chad.

"It's me," she yelled. "Don't shoot."

"Devon?"

She pressed on the lever to lower the window. "Get in the car."

"Hey! What's going on?" yelled a man who'd come to the door of one of the motel rooms. "You hit my car."

Glancing around, Chad rushed to the Corvette. He opened the car door, tossed in his duffel, and dropped into the passenger seat.

"Hey! Come back here," the man hollered.

"Quick! Head back into Miami," Chad told her.

She floored it, and the Corvette fishtailed. They strafed the bumper of another car as they peeled out of the motel lot.

"Where were you?" she cried, the car barreling down the street.

"The jerk driving this Vette shot out my tires. He'd called the police on his cell phone to report a drunken driver—behind the wheel of the Acura. They came along seconds after he drove off. I had to pass a field sobriety test. I ran as fast as I could to get here."

She glanced sideways at him. His look sent a tremor through her.

"I thought—" her voice cracked with emotion she'd kept suppressed after she believed he'd died "—they'd killed you."

He brushed her cheek with the pad of his thumb. "And I thought they'd gotten you."

"It was close. I used the knife the way you taught me." She quickly explained what had happened.

"I'm proud of you," he said, his voice husky.

"I'm proud of me, too. I didn't know I could do it," she told him with a cold shiver. "Before tonight, I thought I would have frozen or panicked and been killed."

"You're tough or you wouldn't have made it this far."

"Maybe, but you'd think I would feel some sort of remorse for killing a man. But after seeing Romero and knowing what happened to Tina, I didn't care—especially when I thought they'd killed you, too."

"I understand. When I was with Delta Force, they told us that once you accept you're as good as dead, you can function. It's surprising what you can accomplish if you're not focused on your own survival."

His words sank in and she nodded. "That's how it was.

Total calmness came over me." She thought a moment. "What about now? Are we okay?"

"We have to assume there's a second man out there. This Vette's too flashy to be their primary vehicle."

"You're right." She checked the rearview mirror to see if they were being followed.

"Slow down. We don't want the police to pick us up."

Devon eased off the accelerator, and her nerves began to quiver. The reality of what had happened settled in. She'd been a heartbeat from death. Without a second thought, she'd plunged a knife into a man's heart.

What had she become?

Once she'd been average—okay, a high-achiever, but no one special—now a hit team was after her, and she'd murdered a man. When she'd called the FBI, she'd never imagined a life on the run, fear a constant companion. How could this be the price of justice in America?

Who was Samantha Robbins? Devon hadn't been that woman for so long. With each identity change, she'd lost part of herself. She was no longer the woman she'd once been. Seeing Tina had helped, but only temporarily. She'd killed a man—something she would never have thought possible.

Face it, she silently admonished herself. You're lost in Oz.

"Are you okay?" she asked. "I bumped into you with the car."

"You didn't hit me. Delta Force taught us to drop and roll. Nine times out of ten that gets you out of harm's way. I'm fine."

"If I'd run over you...well, I don't know...I might have—"

"Forget it. Your reactions were quick. Had it been one of them, running over him was a great idea."

A thought hit her. "Chad, the man I killed claimed I had something that belonged to his friend. That man wanted to *talk* to me. The guy with the gun could have killed me on the spot, the way he murdered the cabdriver, but he didn't."

"Maybe he didn't want your body to be found there."

"I don't know. I found duct tape in the trunk of this car. I think he was planning to kidnap me."

After a long moment of silence, Chad said, "He wasn't going to put you into the trunk of this Vette. The space isn't big enough."

"Pull off at the next side street," Chad told her.

"Why?"

"If I were in charge of this operation, I would have a tracking device on this car...just in case."

She hung a right turn into a low income residential neighborhood. She pulled to the curb behind a Ford pickup. Chad climbed out, his high-powered flashlight in hand. She waited, feeling the knot forming on the back of her head.

How would this all end?

She couldn't imagine a good outcome. Still, something in her wanted to believe that justice would prevail. But right now, it seemed as if the forces of evil had the upper hand.

Chad returned to the passenger seat, a tiny buttonlike thing in his hand.

"What's that?" she asked.

"A location transmitter."

"Like the one you used to track me."

A beat of silence, then, "It was under the back bumper just where I would have put it had I wanted to keep tabs on my car. Why bother to crawl under the vehicle to hide it in some obscure place, if you don't think anyone would look for it?"

"Right. So toss it out the window."

A low chuckle rumbled from his chest. "No. They're tracking us. I don't want them to realize we know it. Head east toward Calle Ocho."

"Little Havana? At this time of night?"

He squeezed her shoulder with his hand. Its warmth seeped through her blouse, reassuring her. He kissed her lightly on the cheek. His thoughts were elsewhere, she could tell, but the gesture unexpectedly touched her. Less than an hour ago, she'd believed she'd lost him forever. She never expected to see him again, feel his hand on her arm, the touch of his lips on her cheek.

"We'll sell this Vette. We'll take the cash and—"

"I forgot to tell you. The guy I knifed had over three thousand dollars on him."

Chad's laughter reverberated through the interior of the small sports car. "Way to go, babe. Way to go."

BROCK LANDED in the Sikorsky at the Jet-Away private aircraft terminal. He should have heard something by now, he decided. He punched the autodial on his stolen cell phone. He would have to jettison it sometime today, but the idea disturbed him. His contact wasn't in the area. He wouldn't have a new cell phone.

"Gotcha, dude." It was 251's voice.

"What's happening?" Brock asked, doing his best to keep his frustration out of his voice.

"I'm close. Wait out front. I'll pick you up."

Brock pressed the 'end' button, a troubled feeling shrouding him. The missing jacket on 251, Jordan's duplicity, the pressure from Kilmer Cassidy. Too many stressors to be coincidence.

Something was wrong.

Troubled, he walked to the front of the small, private terminal to wait for his operative. The Robbins bitch was good, he privately conceded. She'd eluded one of the best hit teams around, but this time his men had her nailed.

A few minutes later a United Florists Van pulled up. Brock recognized the hub for the microcamera on top, disguised as an air vent. He leaped into the passenger seat.

"Give me an update."

The quick intake of breath told Brock that he had a problem.

"77 is dead."

He expelled a long, audible breath. "Dead? What happened?"

The kid stared straight ahead and didn't say anything for a few seconds. "She killed him."

"What the fuck are you telling me?"

"I don't know how exactly, but she managed to plunge a knife into his heart."

Shit! His world was going to hell. A house of cards collapsing—and no way to stop it. He let the words register as 251 kept driving. Something in his brain clicked. An image of the ruthless man with the bitch played across his mind with starling clarity.

"What happened to the guy with her?"

Another agonizing beat of silence. "He walked away from the police."

"Start over and tell me the whole story." Brock ground out the words. How was he ever going to explain the death of a top agent to Kilmer Cassidy?

"Like I told you. The parabolic mike picked up the Robbins woman when she went into her sister's room. Since we hadn't seen her come into the hospital, I knew she was in a different disguise. I sent 77 to see what she looked like."

"How was she dressed?"

"Like an old lady. 77 said she *really* looked the part."

"I'm sure she did." Of all the women Brock had come up against, the Robbins bitch was proving to be the toughest. For a moment he thought of Jordan Walsh, but right now, this was his top priority. Jordan would have to wait her turn.

"About this time, I notice how blurry several of our secondary cameras were. I figure the guy in the do-rag had tampered with them. I told 77 to watch the Pediatrics entrance. Lots of parents come in and out there. It's easy to slip by."

Brock didn't like the pride he detected in this kid's voice. *Pride goeth before a fall.* That was in the Bible, or maybe Shakespeare came up with it. Whatever. It fit.

"I got lucky. She came out—in regular clothes and hopped in a cab. I had 77 follow her in the Corvette. The guy she was with was following in an Acura."

Brock had let 251 talk him into a red Corvette for this operation. A Vette in Miami, especially South Beach, fit in better than the surveillance van they were in now. Obelisk had plenty of money, but Cassidy would pitch a shit fit over the loss of an expensive sports car.

"Seventy-seven said he could immobilize the punk following her by shooting out his tires and reporting him as a drunk driver. I was hanging back in the van until 77 nabbed her and called me in. Then it was off to the safe house to interrogate her. A minor traffic accident delayed me just a few minutes."

Shit! There was always an unpredictable factor in every operation. A fender bender blew this one apart.

"I rushed to the motel. Seventy-seven was dead on the ground, a vicious knife wound in his chest."

"She didn't do it. Had to be the asshole in the do-rag."

"I don't know. Women are..."

Brock battled the urge to spring out of his seat and strangle the fucker. Mennonite parents. A stellar background with Obelisk. Big fucking deal.

"Good news," his dip shit operative told Brock. "We've got a location transmitter on the Corvette."

Brock stared out at the lights dappling Miami's skyline. "Where are they headed?"

"South toward Key Largo. From there they can hire a fast boat to take them to Texas or New Orleans or the Bahamas."

"Anywhere," Brock said, amazed at his own bitterness. "The bitch could be going anywhere."

"CAN WE STOP for a minute?" Devon cried. The weight of her backpack strapped to her shoulders was compounded by the contents of Chad's duffel, which they'd crammed inside the backpack. Every time he rounded a curve, her head pounded and she thought she might fall off the Honda.

Chad slowed the motorcycle they'd traded the Corvette for in Calle Ocho and came to a stop near a copse of trees. They were on Highway 41 East heading through Shark Alley in the Everglades.

"What's wrong?" Chad asked.

"Let me shift a few things," she said, reluctant to admit how much her head was bothering her.

"I'll wear the backpack," Chad said. "I should have put it on in the first place. I just wanted to feel your boobs against my back."

Devon managed to laugh. The headache blotted out almost everything.

He took the backpack. "This is nothing compared to what I had to carry in Delta Force."

"You know I haven't had a chance to tell you how I feel about you," he said.

She nodded. They'd been on the run, never stopping for a minute until now.

"You mean the world to me. When I told you that we were in this together, I instinctively realized how important you'd become in my life. No matter what happens, I'm here because I care about you."

She smiled, but inside she wished he'd said he loved her. "I don't want anything to happen to you because of me."

"It won't. We're in this together. Keep that uppermost in your mind."

"It's a long way to Pensacola," she said, knowing now was not the time to say she loved him. "I might have a better plan."

Their original idea was to cut through the Everglades to the west coast of Florida and drive north to Pensacola where Chad could hook up with a buddy at the Naval Air Station. They'd planted the location transmitter on a car full of fraternity guys who were driving to the Keys. The second hit man was probably following that car. He wouldn't suspect they were north and west.

"Okay. What's your plan?"

"I thoroughly researched how to get back into this country—if I ever had to leave—yet not be in the security system's computer records."

"The private yacht idea was ingenious."

"Same thing with a private plane. Private terminals are small and often shut down at night. No one monitors security the way regular airports do. We should hit Naples in the morning, right?"

"Looks that way."

"Let's hire a plane to fly us out of Florida."

THE MOTORCYCLE SPUTTERED and hiccuped. Devon held on to Chad's waist as tightly as she could, considering the bulky backpack separating them like a block of cement.

"We're out of gas," Chad told her.

The Honda wheezed to a stop. She swung her leg off the back and stretched. It felt so good to be standing. She glanced at the gas gauge.

"It says half full."

"The dial hasn't moved since we left Calle Ocho. What do you expect? Those guys were thrilled to trade a beat-up motorcycle for a Corvette. Who said the gauges worked?"

"They took the Corvette to a chop shop, didn't they?"

"Absolutely. They figured it was stolen, but the trade was worth more than any of them could make in a month or longer. They chopped it last night rather than get caught with a stolen car."

Chad fumbled through his gear that was in the backpack. Devon sniffed the air. The Everglades had the same smell the rain forest in Hawaii had. The loamy scent of decaying plants and moist earth. The sun was seeping over the horizon, a lemon-orange glow lighting the Everglades by degrees. Cicadas were tuning up in the sawgrass. The world was waking up to a new day.

Please don't let this be our last day on earth.

Chad had set a lightweight pair of binoculars aside. She picked them up and watched the night hawks still patrolling overhead in what was left of the night sky, feasting on insects before retiring to sleep during the heat of the day. Cormorants, Ospreys and red-tailed hawks were winging up from the stands of trees. There were other birds, too. Devon profoundly regretted not being able to recognize them.

Life was too short. She wished she'd taken more time to observe the world around her. Less time for numbers.

She watched a nearby heron spear a fish with his bill. A terrapin, moss growing on his helmetlike back, clambered along the shore and plopped into the swamp. Devon would have sworn she'd heard the turtle sigh when he hit the water. Just watching the animals made her head feel better.

"Here. It's better than nothing." Chad tossed her a bottle of mosquito spray. "Bugs aren't terrible at this time of year, but your bod's prime meat."

She tried for a laugh, but it came out more like a croak. She slathered on the cream, the odor of Deet hitting her full-force. Chad was tinkering with some gadget that he'd hastily shoved into the backpack.

"It's about three miles to the Miccosukee Indian Village, according to this. We'll have to walk the bike there for gas."

"What is the Indian Village?"

"A tourist trap. The Miccosukee were trail Indians who eluded the U.S. government's Removal Act to ship them West."

"When did this happen?" Devon knew a little about Florida's history from her sister, but Tina had never mentioned this tribe.

"Mid-1800s. They settled here. Over the years they had the smarts to turn it into a tourist attraction."

"So the airboats will be skimming across the Everglades in a couple of hours."

"You got that right."

She wondered where the birds, and bobcats, and the endangered Florida panthers hid when the hordes of tourists raced across the Everglades. They used airboats to stay above the vines that grew in the water and could entangle a propeller. She empathized. She'd learned what it was like to live constantly in danger, always hiding.

"I've been thinking," Chad said as he began to push the motorcycle along the road. "The guy you killed knew your name. He thought you had something his friend wanted."

"Yes. That's what he said, but I can't imagine what he meant." She put her hand on the bike to help balance it. "I have so little it's frightening. WITSEC makes you leave everything behind. Luckily I was able to persuade the supervisor to allow me to bring Zach."

Chad was silent for a moment. The only sound was the crunch of the gravel beneath the wheels of the motorcycle as they pushed it along the shoulder of the road.

"What about all those books and disks in your apartment?"

Chad didn't bother to explain how he knew about them. Devon guessed he must have entered her place and searched her things.

"It's stuff I might use if I get the chance to go back to my real life in the world of finance."

Chad pondered her response for a minute, pushing the motorcycle forward and keeping his eyes on the road. At this hour, few cars had passed them on the Tamiami Trail, linking Shark Alley to the Indian Village.

"Were any of those files downloaded from the PowerTec system?"

"One," she admitted. "It was a proprietary file with financial info I shouldn't have had access to, but I copied it off Ted Rutherford's computer."

"Why?"

"I was suspicious. By then I knew PowerTec was skimping on military software, putting our troops in danger, and skimming money. I looked for the money trail but it wasn't in that file. I was going to download other files, but I didn't find the right opportunity."

"How did you get into the file? Wasn't it secured?"

"Yes. But I knew Rutherford's password. I'd looked over his shoulder once, when he was typing in his password. But no one would have realized I copied that file."

Chad cocked his head and gazed at her intently. "Yes, they would have. It's expensive, but it's worth it. A keystroke logger will tell you exactly what has gone on with your computer. It'll record every activity. If you copied a file, they knew about it."

"I don't think so. I copied the file more than a week before the FBI agent was killed."

"That only means they weren't on top of their game. The keystroke logger has to be analyzed. It takes a pro, which means a day or more, depending on how much you used the computer. By the time they knew you had the info, WITSEC had relocated you."

"They want the information I copied." Devon shook her head. "I can't imagine why. I showed it to the FBI agent they killed, and she didn't think it was important. She was an expert."

"Maybe she missed something."

Devon shrugged and swatted at a no-see-um munching on her arm. "Have you ever heard of a company called Obelisk? They do a lot with the military. They visited PowerTec. I noticed that name on the disk. When I went to D.C. on business, I couldn't find their offices."

Chad was silent for a moment. "The guys from Obelisk. Were they former military officers? Could you tell?"

"They could have been. I overheard this guy Hardesty say he once worked for the Department of Defense."

"Soon as we get to a safe spot, I'm going to have a friend run a check on them."

They rolled the bike into the gas station and filled it. "We can't use your credit cards," Chad warned. "They'll know where we are by the purchases."

"I know. I doubt they've ID'd me, but I don't want to chance it. We're going to need more cash than we've got, if we're going to fly home on a private plane."

CHAPTER THIRTY-TWO

BRR-ING BRR-ING. The telephone on the nightstand next to Keke awakened her with a jolt. She waited for Paul to answer the phone before remembering he'd gone to Taiwan on a buying trip with his uncle.

Brr-ing brr-ing. Telephone calls in the middle of the night always frightened Keke, ever since the Highway Patrol had called to tell them about her father's fatal car accident. She reached for the phone, praying Paul was all right. He traveled to the Orient twice a year; every time he went, she worried.

"Hello?"

"Hey, sis. It's me."

"Chad? Where are you?"

"I need you to do something for me."

His tone sent a ripple of anxiety through her entire body. "What's going on?"

"I need you to send nine thousand nine hundred dollars to the America Express office in Naples, Florida. Don't make it any larger. Go over ten thousand dollars, and it has to be reported. Large cash transfers make the Feds think it's drug money."

Keke hadn't known this, but it didn't surprise her that Chad did. He'd walked on the wild side more than he'd ever told his family. "I've got it. Nine thousand and nine hundred dollars."

"Put it in the name of Barbara Ashton."

"Who's she?"

"A friend."

Keke had heard about many of his friends, but she didn't recall him mentioning this woman. "Why don't you go to American Express yourself? They'll give you a cash advance against your credit card."

"I don't want to do that."

She flinched at the dark undertone in his voice. "You're in some kind of trouble, aren't you?"

"I'm fine. If you get me the money, I can be home late tonight."

"You're with that woman." Frustration with his evasiveness added to the fear gripping her. "She's gotten you into trouble."

"Keke, trust me. Everything will be okay. Just wire me the money."

He was with Pele's ghost but he wouldn't admit it. Keke had realized Devon was trouble since the moment she'd met the woman.

"It'll take me a day or so to raise that much cash."

"No, it won't. I'm going to give you the combination of my safe. You remember where it is, don't you?"

"Behind the painting outside your master bathroom."

"Right. I keep plenty of cash in it. That way if I have to leave suddenly, I don't have to bother stopping to get money."

Keke jotted down the safe's combination on the pad next to the telephone. This was a very troubling request. Chad had access to unlimited funds through his bank or credit cards. The Porsche. This call. Now, she was *positive* he was involved in something dangerous. If he couldn't discuss it over the telephone, there must be a good reason. Keke loved him—more than her other siblings—she admitted. She had to do everything in her power to help him.

"Keke could you be at American Express when it opens?"

Keke sucked in her breath, thinking of two children, lunches, carpools. She tried to keep the quaver out of her voice. "I'll be there."

He repeated the name of the woman who would pick up

the money and the address of the America Express office in Naples. Then he added, "Keke, don't tell anyone I called or say anything about the money."

"Everyone knows I'm looking for you. I called around when you didn't show up for the luau."

"Say you heard from me, and I'm out of town investigating an accident. I should be home tonight."

"Call me the minute you get in. No matter how late it is."

Chad hung up the telephone and turned to Devon. "It'll be four hours until American Express opens in Honolulu. That means we'll need to wait about five hours to pick up the money."

"It's really beautiful here. We could see if we can spot some interesting birds with your binoculars while we wait."

He had been using the telephone at the Corkscrew Swamp Sanctuary, a preserve run by the Audubon Society. It had a boardwalk trail that wound through stands of trees. Pools with water lilies had formed in the shallow water seeping up everywhere from the ground. Nearby a baby alligator was basking in the sun.

"Let me make a call, then we'll go for a walk."

While Chad picked up the phone again, Devon drifted over to a group of impressive looking trees and read the plaque. Bald cypress. The trees were over five hundred years old. Amazing.

Chad waited by the payphone for Danson to call him from a secure line. He debated how much to tell Danson about Devon.

"Good news," Danson said when he called back a few minutes later. "The engineers worked out the bug. You'll be able to tell what's on a boat now. I'll overnight a new device to you."

"Okay. I'm in Florida right now. I expect to be home late tonight."

"What are you doing there?"

"It's a long story."

"Is the device safe?"

"Yes." It was in the backpack slung over his shoulder. "I was wondering if you know of a company called Obelisk."

"Where did you hear about them?" His voice held a challenge.

"A friend was working at PowerTec and met Kilmer Cassidy and Brock Hardesty."

"Jesus H. Christ. With friends like that your buddy doesn't need an enemy. PowerTec's executives are about to be indicted. The Obelisk guys are just as shady. It's a front for Bash Olofson."

"Great." The general was notorious among military men for supplying mercenary soldiers to Third World countries. Once a man left the military, Bash had a job for him that paid a lot more than he'd made in the service. Olofson also provided countries with weapons. Many experts thought the armaments had disappeared from military bases.

"Bash isn't directly involved in Obelisk. He's too cagey. The government's been after him for years. They haven't been able to prove anything."

"What about Cassidy and Hardesty?"

"Nothing on them, either—that I know about."

Chad glanced at Devon who was at the far end of the boardwalk admiring a snowy egret. "If you had information that could crack their organization, who would you take it to?"

"You have the goods on Bash Olofson?" Disbelief etched every syllable.

"It's possible. I'm not sure yet. I'm worried it'll get into the wrong hands."

"Be careful. Those guys will do *anything* to protect themselves."

No shit! Chad thought a moment before asking, "Did your agent find out anything about who killed to get the other device?"

"A little. I'm still working on it." Danson laughed, a sound that could take chalk off a blackboard. "Don't you think you'd better level with me? Why did you really call?

It took Chad just a split second to make up his mind about what to tell Danson. "Remember I asked you to get to Nathan Albert?"

"Sure. About a girlfriend who never existed."

"Devon made up the story to protect herself. She's in the Witness Protection Program because she worked at Power-Tec."

"I'm familiar with the case. An FBI agent was murdered while investigating."

"Devon may have a computer disk with important information on it that may impact the case."

Danson let out a low whistle. "If the Obelisk guys even *think* she has the goods on them, she's a dead woman."

Chad took a few minutes to tell him about the hit in Santa Fe and the near miss last night. "She thinks it's Rutherford and Ames from PowerTec."

"I'm betting it's Olofson's group. The FBI has the noose pretty tight around the PowerTec guys. It's hard to believe they could have contacted a hit team. Give me an hour. I'll call you back at this number."

AFTER SCHMOOZING the security guards, Brock trudged up the stairs to Kilmer Cassidy's office. He could have taken the elevator, but he wanted to delay this meeting. He was in deep shit and he knew it. He went into the CEO's office, and his secretary greeted him with a cool nod. There was a young punk with spiked hair sitting in the reception area. Brock thought he might have to wait, but the blonde waved him in.

Cassidy was on the telephone. "Here he is now. I'll debrief him and get right back to you." He paused while the general said something. "I think Tango Charlie was brilliant. Our only choice."

Tango Charlie. Cassidy had to be talking to Olofson. Bash lived to talk in code. Brock had always found it annoying.

Cassidy hung up, and Brock remained standing, expecting to be offered a seat. He wasn't.

"What the fuck happened? You claimed this was a fool-proof plan."

"The bitch has a pro with her. He stabbed to death one of my best agents."

Cassidy didn't blink at the news of the murder. "Do the Miami police have any reason to think we're involved?"

"None. I set it up perfectly. They believe it was a drug deal gone bad."

Anger lit Cassidy's eyes. "So where's the woman now?"

Brock didn't go into details about the wild-goose chase down to Key West where they'd found the locator in some frat boy's car. "The pro got lucky. He managed to sneak away with her."

"How could he? You were supposed to have an agent seconds behind him in another car."

"He got hung up by a traffic accident. By the time he arrived, they were gone."

"Alpha Bravo isn't a happy camper," Cassidy said with a sly grin. "This news will really piss him off."

Brock knew the shit would hit the fan when he'd reported in late last night. Alpha Bravo, as General Olofson like to call himself, wanted the bitch interrogated, then killed. Brock had muffed it twice.

"I'm close," Brock informed Cassidy. "A photograph of the pro helping her is on the computer being analyzed. We have two dozen near matches." Actually it was more like fifty near matches, but Brock didn't want to give Cassidy more ammo. "You know how slow the Homeland Security software is. I'll have an exact match, but it'll probably take the rest of the day."

The computer would compare the near matches to the photo from the security camera. It used data such as the number of blue pixels per eye compared with black pixels. Every iris had a certain number of black dots in them, a telling characteristic. Eyebrows and angles of cheek bones could also be analyzed. A match would be found.

"It's too late," Cassidy informed him, his tone smug. "We've gotten you help."

"Help?" Brock couldn't keep the fury out of his voice. "I don't need help. I've headed security for—"

"That's the problem. You've been down in that bunker too long and not in the field enough." Cassidy tapped the intercom on his desk with a manicured index finger. "Tiffany, send in Kyle."

The fine hairs at the base of Brock's skull prickled to attention. His instincts had been dead-on. Something was wrong and had been for some time. The punk kid he'd seen in the reception area earlier sauntered into the room.

"Brock, this is Kyle Kramer. He's going to be your assistant."

Cassidy completed the introduction, and Brock almost lost it. The punk with the GenX name and spiked hair was going to be snooping through his files. Getting in his way.

"Kyle is General Olofson's nephew. He's worked overseas for the last two years. He has the highest security clearance."

So? Big deal, Brock thought. He was still a kid compared with the kind of experience Brock had.

"Kyle, tell Mr. Hardesty what you've found so far."

So far? Unfuckingbelievable! The punk had already been nosing through his files. How could that be?

Kyle consulted his Blackberry. "There's a reverse ID on every phone in the building. Mr. Hardesty has a software program that tells him exactly who called."

Brock struggled to keep his voice level. "That's just good security."

"Your personal computer has proprietary information on it. The info is never supposed to leave the building," Cassidy said.

How the fuck could he know that? Only by checking his PC. "I work at home and on the road," Brock replied, although he knew it was a weak excuse Cassidy wouldn't accept. "I keep it totally secure. It's with me or in a safe."

"Problem is," Kyle said, "there's a keystroke logger on your laptop."

"No way!"

Like the worm he'd installed on Bash's machine in an on-line greeting card, the spy could be anywhere in the world.

"Kyle's right. Someone installed a logger on your computer. Now they have information on Obelisk that we never wanted to leave the building."

Brock nearly doubled over, his mind numb with shock and disbelief. He couldn't imagine worse news. Not even the theft or destruction of his cars could compare. This was an intolerable security breach. Brock would have ordered a fuck-up like this to be killed.

What could he possibly do?

The best defense is a good offense, Brock reminded himself. "When did you check my computer?"

"This morning while you were debriefing the security guards about who'd been in the building over the weekend."

Cassidy's reply hit Brock like a sucker punch to the gut. Every Monday morning, he checked with security to see who'd been in the building during the weekend. He liked to do it in person. That way the guards felt more loyal to him. He wasn't just some asshole suit who took them for granted.

The debriefing took less than fifteen minutes and wouldn't take that long, except Brock liked the bonding bit where he had coffee with the guys. That meant the punk had entered his office and checked his computer in record time.

"How'd you get into my office?" Brock snapped.

"I let him in," Cassidy replied. "Too many botched missions. Now we know why. Someone's tracking you, and it isn't anyone at Obelisk."

The image of a knockout redhead with Bugatti tits flashed into his mind.

"Any idea how someone got to your computer?" Cassidy snapped.

Jordan Walsh.

He'd thought she'd been after the DARPA gadget. But no. The bitch had wanted to infiltrate Obelisk.

"There was an incident," Brock began, scrambling to formulate an explanation so Obelisk would investigate Jordan Walsh and excuse his transgressions. "When I was in Miami for a car show, I met a woman."

Cassidy's knowing smile irritated Brock and made him more uneasy.

"Jordan Walsh was showing a one-of-a-kind Gull Wing. We went out to dinner to discuss the possibility of her selling the car to me. After eating, I didn't feel all that well. I went to my room and fell asleep. I didn't wake up until noon the next day. I had a killer headache. I mean it was bad—"

"Was this woman near your PC?" Cassidy asked.

"Yes. She brought me some literature on her Gull Wing. My laptop was in the room safe along with a special device being developed by DARPA."

"Oh?" Cassidy said, clearly taken by surprise.

Brock instantly realized Cassidy didn't know a thing about the gadget because Brock had never used his computer to discuss it. He went on to explain about the device, embellishing on its potential and his part in trying to obtain it for Obelisk. Anything to save his bacon. He finished, adding, "The woman must have pocketed my key and come into the room while I was asleep."

"Wouldn't you have heard her come into the room and break into the safe?"

This from the punk.

"I'm sure Jordan Walsh slipped me something like a roofie that would knock me out. I didn't hear a thing. I slept until midafternoon the following day."

"Roofie? What are you talking about?"

Brock opened his mouth, but the punk explained it to Cassidy. Brock listened, deciding the kid had used the date rape drug before or he wouldn't know so much about it.

Cassidy pondered his explanation for a few seconds. "She cracked the safe and installed the keystroke logger. How would she do that without knowing your password?"

"It can be done," Kyle assured him. "There's a special logger that can be installed without turning on the computer. It invades the system the next time the authorized person logs on."

"Who the hell does this woman work for?" Cassidy asked.

They debated the situation and decided Walsh was with the CIA. They'd been trying to link General Olofson to a stolen armament ring for years. Nothing in Obelisk's records would incriminate the general, but they could be fried.

"I'll investigate," Brock said.

"No, you won't!" Cassidy paced across the room to the window. "Kyle will handle it." He spun around and pointed a finger at Brock. "You find Samantha Robbins and take her out." He dropped his arm. "Otherwise, you're out—and I mean out."

Brock knew they intended to kill him even if he whacked the bitch for them. He was O-U-T. And he knew it. His brilliant mind was already hatching a plan.

CHAPTER THIRTY-THREE

THE PAY PHONE at the Corkscrew Swamp Sanctuary rang a little over an hour later. Chad grabbed the receiver.

"Langston?"

"Yes."

"I've got some bad news."

Fear mushroomed inside Chad, beginning as a vague sense of anxiety. It intensified as he rested his shoulder against the wall next to the pay phone and gazed at Devon. She was at the far end of the wooden platform that overlooked the sanctuary. Her remarkable profile was half-hidden by the binoculars she was using.

"Last night Rutherford and Ames were killed in a private plane crash outside of Houston."

His stomach contracted, then twisted like a piece of wire. These men would stop at nothing. It was a miracle Devon had managed to kill one of them. "They were murdered."

"The authorities say it looks like mechanical failure, but they won't know until there's a complete investigation."

"I'm not buying it. Olofson and his buddies at Obelisk—"

"You're probably right. Word in the federal prosecutor's office is that Rutherford was going to cut a deal. Dunno what exactly, but I suspect Olofson and his gang got wind of it."

"Wouldn't be hard. Those prosecutors don't make squat. For enough money, you can buy all the info you want."

"You have to assume they're going after Devon next. If she

has hard evidence to link them to the crime, they won't be safe until they're rid of her."

"True." Chad was truly afraid for the first time in his life. These men were determined and resourceful. They'd managed to kill Rutherford and Ames even though they were under surveillance by the FBI. Chad wasn't sure he could protect Devon.

"If you're right about the disk, they'll insist on getting it before they kill her."

"That'll rule out a sniper. They'll grab her the way they tried to in Miami."

"But first they've got to find her. You have a head start. Get back to Honolulu and find that disk. Call me the minute you do."

"How will that help Devon?" Chad couldn't keep the sarcasm out of his tone.

There was a long moment of strained silence. Finally Danson said, "I'm going to give you some information you *must* keep to yourself. You cannot tell Devon or anyone. Agreed?"

"What choice do I have? Of course, I agree."

"I know a lot more about Obelisk than I told you." There was a serrated edge to Danson's voice now.

Aw, hell, Chad thought. Here it comes.

"One of my agents managed to infiltrate their organization. Between what we have and what the federal prosecutor uncovered during their investigation of PowerTec, the Secretary of Defense himself is ready to charge them with treason."

"Why would you be involved?" Chad asked. "DARPA is into development, not security."

"I suspected Obelisk was after the device. What I found uncovered a lot more. Problem is—we can't tie Olofson to any of it."

"You think the disk Devon has will incriminate the general."

"Absolutely. The federal prosecutor discovered the murdered FBI agent had checked that disk."

"Right, and she told Devon that there wasn't anything useful on it."

"She lied. Apparently the woman tried to blackmail Olofson. That's why she was killed. Later they discovered Devon had the original disk. All they'd taken from the dead woman was a copy."

"Holy shit! Devon's been holding a hand grenade without the pin all this time."

"She didn't have any idea?"

"Nope. She believed the FBI agent when the woman said the disk was worthless. She threw it in with some of her things."

"Amazing. If only she'd known."

"What can I tell her?"

"Just let her know the disk is really valuable. Don't mention anything else. It's top secret."

"Okay," Chad reluctantly agreed.

"Another agency has been monitoring Olofson's telephone calls."

Chad decided the other "agency" was the CIA. This was not encouraging. Even with the FBI and CIA involved, they still couldn't nail Olofson.

"He talks in code but I understand it's easy to tell what he means. He's been calling Kilmer Cassidy and putting pressure on him to get something, then get rid of the person."

With pulse pounding certainty Chad knew Devon was the person. "I'll get you the disk, then I'm going to ground with Devon until the trial."

"I doubt that will be necessary. Some of the illegal arms sales have been to terrorists. After 9/11 the government has extraordinary powers. They can arrest and hold these creeps indefinitely. They've waited, hoping to get Olofson."

"Sounds like a plan." Chad thought a moment. "How am I going to get the disk to you?"

"I'll send a courier for it."

Chad slowly hung up. Would finding the disk be enough to save Devon?

"YOU'VE FINALLY GOT SOMETHING." Kyle pointed at the computer screen that was trying to match the do-rag guy's photo with driver's license photographs.

"Look," he did his level best to sound like he accepted Kyle as a talented assistant with a lot to offer. After all, he was Bash Olofson's nephew. The general had no children of his own. His sister had two daughters and this son. The heir apparent, Brock thought. Might as well kiss ass.

"Our software is state-of-the-art. Homeland Security's sucks. They're underfunded. That's why this search took so long."

"I know," Kyle replied. "Do I look stupid?"

Brock was tempted to tell him the truth. Instead he pointed to the computer screen. It replaced the "Match Found" text with a rundown of Chad Langston of Honolulu, Hawaii. His DMV profile didn't tell Brock much.

"Would WITSEC have relocated Samantha Robbins in Hawaii?" Kyle asked.

Good question, Brock thought, but didn't give the twerp the satisfaction of saying so. "I doubt it. The next step is to run his name through our computers. Unlike Homeland Security, we'll have answers immediately. I developed the software myself."

"Way to go," Kyle replied, but he didn't sound very impressed.

Less than a minute later information on Chad Langston filled the computer screen.

"Wow! This is rad," Kyle said.

Chad Langston had been Phi Beta Kappa at Stanford. He'd been a colonel in the ROTC there and had gone on to serve in the army. He'd been selected for Delta Force.

"What's Delta Force?" Kyle asked.

The kid had no military experience. Obviously his uncle had him in the financial end of the business. "Delta Force is a special unit that takes the best from all branches of the service, puts them together in special ops and assigns them covert duty. They're highly trained and experts at firearms as well as field intelligence."

"Commandos," Kyle commented. "Trained killers."

More information scrolled across the screen. Brock ventured a sideways glance and saw Kyle was impressed with the program Brock had developed.

"Langston served in the Gulf War, then went to work for the Defense Department," Kyle said. "Doesn't say what he did."

"That means it was top secret and classified. We can find out if we think it's important."

More lines of text filled the screen. They silently read each bit of information. Brock mentally scrambled to piece it together. They were *not* dealing with an ordinary guy.

"He's an underwater forensic expert," Kyle said. "He owns a number of dive shops in the islands."

"Let's check his net worth." Brock tapped a few keys.

"Well, I'll be jiggered," Kyle said. "He's a millionaire. So what's he doing helping that woman?"

"Good question," Brock replied before he could stop himself.

"Maybe he racked up that kind of money from helping desperate people," Kyle said. "She could be paying him."

"Possibly." He gazed at the punk. "What would you look at next?"

"Credit card activity," he said without hesitation. "Let's see if we can track him by his purchases."

It was a good answer but Brock instinctively knew this man wouldn't leave a trail that would be easy to trace.

"He bought a ticket to Miami on American Airlines," the kid said. "There's no other activity on any of his cards after that. He must have suspected we would try to track him. I'm surprised he even put the airline ticket on his card."

"Paying in cash these days makes airlines suspicious," Brock told the punk.

"Gotcha." He leaned closer to the computer screen. "Let's

check the airlines to see if he used that ticket or exchanged it for another ticket to a different place."

Kyle hacked into every airline's central database. Nothing.

"He's still in Florida," Kyle concluded. "Or he's driven to another state. He hasn't returned to Hawaii."

"Don't be too sure. This guy could have phony ID."

Kyle rocked back in his chair and studied the computer screen. "If she isn't paying him to help her, what's the link between them? Why would some rich guy try to help her?"

"The woman's the bomb. A real looker. Could be that simple. Sex."

"Then she was living in Honolulu," Kyle responded. "That's where we'll find the disk."

The word "disk" had never been used at Obelisk. From the moment they'd discovered Rutherford's file had been copied, they all were under orders to never mention it. Obviously the kid had inside info to know about the missing disk.

"I thought killing the FBI agent who had the disk was the right move to protect your uncle. Who would have imagined the woman would have given the original back to the Robbins bitch?"

"I guess she didn't want Samantha Robbins to look at the disk again and see it had been altered or it was a blank."

Brock realized his first miscalculation in a series of miscalculations had begun with the FBI agent. She'd tried to hold up Bash and the rest of the group for cash. Killing her seemed prudent. Trouble was—women were unpredictable. Who would give back an original disk loaded with incriminating info?

Who would slit a guy's throat unnecessarily? he thought, remembering the fuck-up in Santa Fe. Who would be clever enough to elude the police by driving to Colorado the way Samantha had? Who would pretend to be a Gull Wing buff like Jordan Walsh?

Women were born to make men's lives hell. You could never predict what they might do.

"What next?" Kyle asked.

Brock was pleased that the punk didn't know where to go
next with this case. "Let's see if Langston has family. They'll
know more about him and the bitch. They'll know when he's
coming home or where he is."

"What if the woman isn't with him?"

Brock couldn't swallow his laugh. He chuckled, then said,
"Do you know we all die with our eyes open?"

Kyle edged away from him, a subtle movement, but Brock
noticed. "No. I wasn't aware of that."

"It's true. There are ways of making men—even those as
tough as Langston—talk." Brock pushed back from his desk.
"I'm going to Honolulu."

"I'm coming with you."

Brock would have argued, but the kid was Olofson's heir
apparent. He intended to gain the general's support through
the know-it-all punk.

KEKE SAT UP UNTIL THREE in the morning, expecting Chad to
call and say he was home—and safe. She checked the telephone
again—in case the call had kicked into the message center.

Nothing.

If only Paul were here, she thought. He would know what
to do. She called Chad's home again, but no one picked up
the telephone. No wonder. Rory had flown to Huntington
Beach, California for a surfing contest.

Would Chad have returned to Honolulu and not have called
her?

He promised, she thought. Chad wasn't one to go back on
his word. Something niggled at the corner of her mind. If he'd
come home, his Porsche would be gone from the airport lot.

She wanted to check but the children were asleep. She
couldn't leave them. She didn't want to awaken her two sisters and frighten them. Keke decided she had two choices. She
could take the children to the airport to check on Chad's car
or she could call Mother Nakamura.

Waking the children wasn't an option, she decided. Lui

asked too many questions. He would want to know why they were going to the airport again in the dead of night. Lui would report the whole incident to Paul. She wasn't sure she wanted her husband to know about Chad's problems.

Paul came from a different culture. Families stood shoulder to shoulder and troubles were shared. Chad was different.

He was a man with secrets. His life in the military was something he never discussed. There was a lot Chad didn't talk about. His dark side frightened her.

She bit the bullet and called Mother Nakamura. "I'm so sorry to bother you. I have to go out. I need someone to stay with the children."

"Oh?" Paul's mother sounded groggy. Well, it was very late. Mother Nakamura had suffered through a luau and Chuck E. Cheese. No doubt she was alarmed by this call shortly before dawn.

"It's an emergency. My brother needs me. I don't want to awaken the children. Could you please come over?"

Paul's mother agreed and half an hour later appeared in a sweat suit at their front door.

Keke kissed both her cheeks with genuine sincerity for the first time. "Thank you. Thank you."

Keke drove like a demon to the airport. She grabbed a ticket from the dispenser and drove into the parking lot. She turned left, then right to get to the spot where Chad had parked his Porsche.

It had vanished.

She stared at the empty space, fear gathering force like a tornado. Why hadn't he called? He had to be in terrible trouble.

Wait a minute.

He could have just arrived. She tried his cell but it kicked over to voice mail. She didn't leave a message. She called Chad's home. Voice mail again. She phoned the message center to see if he'd left her a message. Nothing.

CHAPTER THIRTY-FOUR

CHAD SAT BESIDE DEVON on the sofa that converted to a bed in her small apartment. They'd returned an hour ago, drove directly to her place, and found the disk. They'd inserted it in the lap top they'd purchased in Naples while waiting for American Express to open.

"I don't see anything on this disk that would incriminate Obelisk," Devon said.

"Trust me. It's here. It could be encrypted. It's also possible the info is hidden in a screen within a screen. That's how most kiddy porn sites are set up. It'll take more expertise than we have to tell."

"I don't know. The FBI agent told me the disk was worthless. Judging from what I see, I'd she was correct."

Chad cursed under his breath. Devon had no idea the FBI agent had been murdered because the information on this tape made her resort to blackmail, and Chad couldn't tell her.

When Devon had asked about his conversation with Danson, Chad glossed over parts of the story. Afterward, there were questions in her eyes, but she'd kept silent. She was too intelligent not to realize he hadn't told her everything.

"Let's make a copy of this disk and put it somewhere safe." He held up the silver disk. "Then I'm going to call my friend to make arrangements to pick up this one."

"Speaking of picking up things, I need to get Zach. He's supposed to be at Paws N Claws at nine to have his coat trimmed."

"We'll go out to my place now. I have a safe where we can store a copy of the disk." He stretched out his long legs before him. Even though he'd slept for most of the long plane ride, Chad was still tired. It was mental exhaustion, he knew. It came because he was so concerned for Devon's safety. "Zach should be fine. Rory didn't leave until almost midnight."

A tinkling sound told them Devon's cell phone in her purse was ringing. She always kept two in her purse, but only gave out one number. She'd turned it off when she'd left Honolulu, and she hadn't turned it on again until they'd climbed into Chad's Porsche a short time ago. In Florida, she'd needed to stay totally focused. Chad's sister had called several times and left voice messages asking about Chad. Warren had called also. She pulled the cell phone out of her purse. She flipped it open and checked the caller ID.

"It's Warren," she told Chad.

"Stick with our story. We were in Kauai. Cell reception there is iffy."

She checked her watch. Nearly six in the morning. "Why would he call at this hour?"

"He's tried to get you before. Now he's worried."

She was still furious that WITSEC and Warren in particular had concealed the seriousness of Tina's condition. But no matter how deceptive WITSEC was, they were some protection. Her experience in Florida had told her just how vicious—and conniving—these killers could be.

"Hello?" Devon tried to sound groggy as if the call had awakened her.

"I've been trying to reach you. Where—"

"I was in Kauai. The service is iffy there. What's happening?"

"I've got news for you."

"Really?" She already knew what he was going to say. Rutherford and Ames were dead.

"Rutherford and Ames were killed in a plane crash."

"Oh, my God!" She hoped she sounded shocked. "How did it happen?"

"Mechanical failure. You know how small planes are."

Her only experience with small planes was the Citation they'd hired to fly them back to Honolulu. It had been sleek and streamlined, the captain a professional. She hadn't worried about it going down.

Rutherford and Ames often traveled in private planes, which were common in Texas. Ames even had a Bell Ranger jet helicopter. Chad suspected the jet had been sabotaged to get rid of the men. She didn't doubt his assessment.

"What does this mean for me?" she asked.

"That's part of the reason I called. Masterson said to tell you to hold tight for a week."

"Then what happens?"

"With Rutherford and Ames out of the picture, there won't be a trial. Masterson wants to talk to you, then you'll be free to return to Houston."

"I'll be out of WITSEC."

"Right. You won't need our protection."

She'd already known WITSEC had no idea about the threat from Obelisk. Or maybe they did and didn't care. Unless she was a government witness, she wasn't valuable to them.

KEKE DROPPED THE KIDS off at school and went by Chad's home, but no one answered the bell. She used the key he'd given her to get in. She'd had the key for nearly two years—for emergencies. This was the second time she'd used it. The first time Chad had sent her for the money. Then Rory had been down at the beach with Devon's retriever.

Rory was gone now, the house eerily silent. She tiptoed up the stairs to see if Chad's bed had been slept in. It hadn't. There wasn't a crumb on the kitchen counters. Chad was back in Honolulu, but he hadn't come home. Disturbed, yet feeling guilty for entering his house without permission, Keke quickly left.

She drove to Chad's office. Since he was back, he would come here or at least check in with Ane.

"Have you heard from my brother?" Keke asked as she sailed into the office.

"No, but he doesn't have any appointments scheduled."

Keke sank into the chair next to Ane's desk. "I'm really worried."

"Hakina matata." Not to worry. "Chad can take care of himself."

Keke wanted to tell Ane about the strange request for money and the missing Porsche, but she'd promised Chad she wouldn't discuss this with anyone. An unexpected thought popped into her mind. Maybe Chad hadn't returned. Someone could have stolen his Porsche. It happened all the time and expensive sports cars were particularly vulnerable.

"Have you seen Devon this morning?" she asked, knowing Ane could spot everyone going into Aloha from her desk.

"No, but they're closed today. Remember?"

"That's right. I—"

A noise behind Keke made her turn. Two men were walking into the office. One was older with dark hair and slightly bulbous brown eyes. The other man was younger with spiked hair slathered with gel. Both were wearing lightweight sports jackets, an oddity in Honolulu even in a business setting. The heat and humidity called for shirtsleeves.

"Mornin'," said the older man. "We're looking for Chad Langston."

"He's not in right now," Ane responded.

"Are you expecting him soon? This is important."

There was an arrogant air about the man that annoyed Keke, and she didn't care for the way the younger guy was looking around, sizing up the office. Chad drove a Porsche and had a home in the pricey Kahala area, but his office wasn't impressive. She suspected Chad hadn't moved to more luxurious quarters in order to stay close to his best friend. Eddie couldn't afford a swank building.

Ane picked up her pen and poised it over a message pad. "He'll be checking in. If you'll leave your name and—"

"I'm Brock Hardesty." He pulled a well-worn leather wallet out of his pocket and flipped it open to reveal a shiny badge and a photo ID. "Federal Bureau of Investigation."

FBI? What could they want with Chad? More than a little uneasy, Keke wondered what was bothering her. Brock Hardesty or the feeling she'd had all weekend that her brother was in real trouble.

Hardesty nodded toward the younger man. "This is Special Agent Kramer."

"I'm going to need to take a closer look at your identification," Ane said.

Hardesty handed her the wallet. The photograph was superimposed with a hologram and looked official to Keke.

Hardesty handed Ane a business card. "There's an 800 number for the Bureau. Call them. They'll verify that we're here on official business."

"What type of business?" Keke asked while Ane picked up the telephone and began punching numbers.

"Who are you?" Agent Kramer asked.

"Keke Nakamura. Chad is my brother."

Agent Kramer's eyes shifted just slightly to the older man. Obviously he was in charge.

Hardesty asked, "Do you work for your brother?"

"No. I just dropped by to see him."

"Then you are expecting him?"

Keke hesitated, torn about how much to say. If Chad had gotten into trouble the FBI might be able to help him. On the other hand, he could be involved in something that would get him into trouble with the FBI. Loyalty kept her from blurting out anything.

Ane put down the telephone, and said to Keke, "FBI headquarters transferred me to the verification department. The number on his ID matches their description of Mr. Hardesty. They confirm he's here on official business, but they wouldn't say what exactly."

Hardesty reached for his wallet. "Headquarters can't discuss an ongoing investigation."

"When are you expecting your brother?" Agent Kramer asked.

"I wasn't expecting him exactly. I dropped by, thinking he would be here."

Hardesty's eyes narrowed, and he was silent for a moment. "When was the last time either of you spoke to or saw Chad Langston?"

"Thursday afternoon," Ane responded immediately, and Keke nodded.

"Has anyone heard from him since then?" Kramer asked.

Keke felt her throat closing up. She honestly didn't know what to say except Chad had told her to tell people he was working on a case. "He called me and said he was working on an underwater forensics case."

Ane didn't know this. When they'd last spoken, Keke hadn't heard from Chad, but the older woman's expression didn't give anything away.

"What day did he call?" Kramer asked just a little too quickly.

"Saturday, I think."

"You don't know?" Kramer asked.

"There's a lot going on at my house. I have two little ones and my husband is out of town. Chad called to explain why he missed a family luau. I only spoke to him for a moment."

Hardesty quirked one brow. "Where was he?"

"I'm not sure," she hedged. "We hardly talked."

"You're going to have to do better than that." Hardesty stared hard at her, his eyes bulging even more.

Keke glared back at him. She didn't like this man and had no intention of telling him more until she knew it was the right thing to do. "What do you mean?"

Hardesty tilted his head almost imperceptibly toward Kramer. The younger man reached into the pocket of his jacket and pulled out a palm-sized photograph. "We have reason to believe your brother is with this woman."

Keke and Ane examined the small photograph. A suffocating sensation gripped Keke's throat. It was a grainy picture and the woman's features were slightly different, but there was no mistaking Devon Summers. Her reaction must have showed on her face.

"I see you recognize her," Hardesty said with a triumphant smile.

"Pele's ghost," Ane said with uncharacteristic bitterness.

The woman had been trouble from the get-go, but Keke kept silent, not knowing if what she might say would help or hurt her brother.

"Ghost?" Hardesty said. "I beg your pardon."

"It's an island superstition," Keke replied. "A woman appears out of nowhere with a dog at her side. She's supposed to be the reincarnation of the island goddess, Pele."

"Yeah? Well, Samantha Robbins is no goddess," Kramer informed them, his tone bordering on hostile. "She's murdered two men."

"Slit one man's throat," Hardesty added. "Stabbed the other in the heart. Her latest victim was killed Saturday night in Miami."

"*Lani.*" Heavens. Ane slowly shook her head, suddenly looking much older.

Miami, Keke thought, how far was that from Naples? She wasn't sure.

"We have reason to believe your brother is with this woman," Agent Kramer said.

Hardesty quickly added, "Under her influence."

Chad? Under someone's influence. Keke almost laughed in his face. But then she remembered the strange way Chad had acted since Devon had come into his life. *The bigger they are; the harder they fall.*

Suddenly Keke remembered Devon's retriever. He hadn't been at the house this morning. She supposed Rory could have left him with a surfing buddy before he took off, but considering Chad's Porsche had been moved, Keke decided Devon had been with him. They'd taken the dog.

"Anything you can tell us will help your brother." Hardesty said, his soothing tone not quite ringing true.

"You've seen this woman, haven't you?" Kramer asked.

Ane looked at Keke, who didn't say a word, then at Hardesty. The older woman slowly nodded. "It's Devon Summers."

Hardesty barked a laugh. "Her real name is Samantha Robbins. She was wanted for questioning in the death of an FBI agent in Houston. She disappeared and turned up in Santa Fe as Lindsay Wallace."

Kramer added, "That's where she slit the throat of an innocent gallery owner. The guy lived long enough to write in his own blood that Lindsay had killed him."

Keke's stomach did a back flip. It was all she could do to keep from gasping. It was impossible for her to believe that Chad could have fallen for a cold-blooded killer. Not only was he too smart, but her brother was an honorable man. He'd never condone ruthless murder.

"You said this ghost-woman appeared with a dog," Hardesty directed his question to Ane. "A golden retriever?"

Ane jerked her head to nod. Keke could see Ane was breaking into sobs. Chad was like a son to her. She thought he hung the moon, but Keke knew better. He had a dark side honed by his years in Delta Force.

Hardesty's eyes locked on Keke's. "That dog's bloody paw prints were all around the body in Santa Fe. He was with her when she killed the art dealer."

Zach's sweet face flashed across Keke's mind. She saw him in Chad's Porsche at the soccer field not so long ago. Along with the memory came the image of her daughter, petting the retriever. *Nice Zash. Nice Zash.* Mei's words echoed in her brain.

Keke knew she'd been silent long enough. She had to consider her children, her husband, and even Mother Nakamura. By concealing the truth, the authorities might charge her with "aiding and abetting" or something. She loved her brother, but she had to tell the truth. She owed it to her family.

"Chad called me late Saturday night. He asked me to wire him money."

"So he did contact you."

The cold edge of irony chilled Hardesty's voice. Keke honestly wanted to slap him. Couldn't he imagine how difficult it was to turn on someone who loved and trusted you?

"Where did you send the money?" Kramer asked.

Keke told them the details of the wire transfer. They asked if Chad had called her since returning, and she could truthfully say she hadn't heard from him.

"His Porsche isn't at the airport. He didn't go home. I checked."

"Do you know where Devon Summers lives?" Kramer asked.

Keke shook her head. "No, but she works across the way at Aloha Yachts and Weddings. Her address should be in the personnel file. They're closed—"

"I have a key to the office," Ane volunteered.

CHAPTER THIRTY-FIVE

BROCK STOOD on the sidewalk, sweat pouring from beneath his armpits, dripping down his back and running through the hair on his chest. Seeping from his balls. His entire body itched from perspiration. He glanced at the punk kid, gratified to see he was miserable, too.

What choice did they have?

Their weapons were jammed into the waistbands of their trousers at their backs and concealed by the lightweight sports coats. Taking them off wasn't an option. Honolulu was loaded with tourists who would freak at seeing men wearing guns. Besides it had taken some doing to arrange for an Obelisk operative to have guns waiting on short notice when the company's private jet had deposited them on the humid island.

"Are you *sure* you wrote down the correct address?" Brock battled to keep his voice level.

Kyle Kramer stared up at the sign Mailboxes in Paradise. "Positive."

Brock thought about it for a minute, then laughed.

"What the fuck is so funny?"

Brock lifted the back of his collar to release some heat. "The Robbins bitch. She's smarter than anyone gave her credit for. We have a cell phone number that can't be traced and an address that leads nowhere."

Suddenly he was reminded of Jordan Walsh. She'd set him up for the fall of his career. If he didn't pull this off, he could kiss his ass goodbye.

Negative thinking wasn't his style, he reminded himself.

He was clever and cunning. He had a plan to outsmart everyone, including General Olofson. To set his plan in motion, he
first had to get the disk and kill Samantha Robbins.

"I don't think Keke Nakamura was lying," Brock added.
"She told us all she knew. We read the personnel file. This is
the address she wrote down."

"What about the Porsche?" Kyle replied. "We could uplink to the satellite and do a grid search for the car."

One of the many satellites in geosynchronous orbits above
the earth could zero in on Honolulu. It could scan block by
block in a grid pattern and magnify everything within the area
to search for the vehicle. There couldn't be that many black
Porsches around. Trouble was, the more populated an area,
the more difficult a space-based search became. With so many
indoor parking structures where the Porsche could be, it might
waste valuable time.

Brock said, "It's a long shot. Let's check Langston's home
first."

They climbed into the Lexus they'd rented. Kramer drove
them through Waikiki along Kalakaua Avenue. The area had
undergone a revitalization project since Brock had last been
here in ninety-nine. High end stores like Gucci and Chanel
had replaced T-shirt shops. Dramatic Hawaiian art—from
murals to bronzes—were prominently displayed. An
improvement, but Brock barely noticed.

Where was the bitch?

One of his local operatives had arranged for him to use a
yacht moored in the harbor. It wasn't ideal, but it was the best
that could be done on short notice. He assumed they would
have to interrogate the woman. She'd fought too hard to give
up the disk easily. He anticipated torturing her to see if there
were any copies of the disk floating around.

He mulled over the situation for a moment. Maybe the boat
was a great idea. Killing was fun but dead bodies were prob-
lematic. They would take her out to sea and dump her. If they
weighted down the body, she might never be found.

The thought gave him the first rush he'd had in days. He relished the opportunity to look the bitch in the eye. To make her pay for all the trouble she'd caused him.

CHAD WALKED into his office with Devon at his side. It was midmorning, and they'd picked up Zach at his house, switched from the Porsche to his Grand Cherokee, and had taken Zach to be groomed. Chad had insisted to going to breakfast after dropping off the dog. Ke Iki Hale was a little out-of-the-way, but he thought the spectacular view of the sugary sand beach and the rolling waves would ease a bit of the tension.

It worked; Devon seemed more relaxed. There was nothing to be done now. He had the disk tucked inside the case of the DoD device he was still testing. The copy was in his safe at home. He'd contacted Danson who said his agent was already on a DoD jet and would be in Honolulu by late afternoon. He assumed the agent would bring the improved gadget to test.

"How's it going?" Chad greeted Ane.

The older woman stared at him as if she'd never seen him before.

"Are you okay?" he asked.

She bobbed her head. *"Kupono."* Fine.

"Any messages?"

"Call Keke." Ane croaked out the words.

"Christ! I was supposed to call her when we got in last night," he said to Devon. "With everything going on I forgot."

"I'm going to go in to the office and do a little work," Devon said.

They walked over to his desk, and he whispered, "I think you should stay here." He didn't want to let her out of his sight until Olofson and his cronies were in jail.

"I'm just across the way. I have a lot to do. I can't just sit around here."

He thought about it for a moment. "I'm going to call your

cell phone." He pulled his cell phone out of the small black leather zipper case where he kept the DoD gadget and the disk. He punched autodial.

She reached into her purse and pulled out the phone that was ringing. She pushed "talk."

"Leave it on," he told her. "That way I can hear if anything's happening."

"Okay." She dropped it into the pocket of her sundress and kissed him lightly on the cheek. "See you later."

Chad watched Devon leave, thinking how much he loved her. He smiled to himself. He couldn't believe he was actually thinking about settling down. He'd assumed that his nieces and nephews would be substitutes for his own children. He'd changed his mind. He wanted his own family with Devon.

What did she want, other than staying alive? He could have asked her while they'd been waiting for the money to come into Naples, but he hadn't. There had to be a man back in Houston who was waiting for her. He'd felt he would be taking unfair advantage of the situation if he pressed her now while she was in danger.

Tremendous stress like this created a false sense of intimacy. He needed Devon to decide if she wanted him and a life here in Hawaii. Given she'd been away for almost a year and a half, it might take her some time to know her true feelings.

One thing was certain. He would have to get used to calling her Samantha. Did she go by Samantha, he wondered? Maybe friends called her Sam. There was so much he didn't know.

He picked up the telephone to call his sister and noticed Ane was still on the telephone. She'd made a call shortly after they'd come into the office. He was too far away to hear what she was saying. She was probably ordering office supplies or something. He punched the second line on his phone and made the call he was dreading.

It still wasn't safe to tell his sister the truth. He hated lying—especially to her.

KEKE'S CELL PHONE RANG as she was leaving Chinatown, heading home. Caller ID told her it was Chad. Guilt surged through her. She took a moment to steady herself. She'd done the right thing. Protecting her family had been her only option.

"Hello, Chad."

"Sorry I didn't call. We got in late—"

"Where are you?"

"At the office."

Keke knew Ane must have called the FBI agent the second Chad walked in. That's what they'd agreed to do. Let the pros handle Devon and Chad. It was easy to say, but now, knowing her brother might be arrested, Keke's eyes filled with tears.

"Thanks for wiring the money. My friend told me she received it."

"G-glad to help." She made herself ask, "Were you with Devon?"

"Yes. We were in Kauai."

How could he lie like this? Devon Summers had murdered a man in Miami. Chad must have been with her—or at least known about it.

"I know you don't like her, Keke. You would if you knew her."

She couldn't make herself say a word. Her brother had lost it, truly lost it.

"I love her," he said, his voice low. "When I see you, I'll explain all about the money."

"I'm not far. I'm coming over now."

Keke hung up and pulled to the curb to steady her nerves. She'd ratted on her brother. The least she could do was be there when they arrested him. She would have to get an attorney, post bail. Who knew what other help he would need?

"YOU KNOW," Brock told Kyle. "I knew those women would come through."

They were standing on the deck of the *Blarney,* the fifty foot DeFever motorboat their local rep had secured for them. It was moored at the end of a gangway in Ali Wai yacht basin. There was an unoccupied boat on one side of the *Blarney,* the other side was open water. Across from them was a boat that was for sale. No one was on it, either.

After checking out Langston's mansion—there must be big bucks in dive shops—and finding no one home, they'd come here. That's when the hog mama, Ane, had called. Devon and Chad had turned up. Devon was in an office by herself.

How lucky could he get? The bitch was less than a block away. Finally things were going right.

DEVON STARED at the computer screen. She had a big wedding coming up the following weekend. It wasn't as large as the extravaganza at Chad's, but there were going to be almost as many people. It was being held on Eddie's newest yacht, *Long Tall Sally.* The dingy, *Short Fat Fanny* was going to be filled with doves. At sunset, they would be released, circle the boat once, then fly toward Diamondhead. It was an expensive gimmick, and she hoped it worked.

A man with spiked hair and a sports coat walked through the open door.

"I'm sorry. We're closed. I'm just catching up on some paperwork."

"This will only take a minute."

He reached toward the small of his back. A second later she saw the gun. She knew she should have gone by her locker and picked up her own gun.

"Don't," she cried.

"Too late, babe."

He shoved a towel in her face. It was rank with a chemical-like smell. She tried to push it off her nose, but the room began to blur, then faded to black.

CHAD LOOKED UP and saw Keke coming into his office. His sister looked as if she hadn't slept in days. Was one of the children sick?

"Keke, is everything okay?"

Keke looked at Ane. The older woman shuffled through her desk without greeting Keke. A warning voice whispered in his head. Something was wrong.

Keke sank into the chair beside his desk. The same blue eyes he saw in the mirror every morning were blurred with tears. More alarm bells began to ring. Keke rarely cried.

"Are the kids all right?" he asked.

Keke nodded, tears cresting in her eyes. "I'm sorry. I had no choice. Believe me."

Chad jumped out of his chair and came around to where his sister was sitting. He hunkered down beside her so they were eye level. "Tell me what's going on."

She wept out loud, rocking back and forth in the chair. Chad tried to hug her, but she pushed him away. She turned and asked Ane, "W-where are they?"

Ane's voice was barely a whisper. "I called them."

"What's going on?" he asked. "What are you talking about?"

For a moment no one said anything. Keke's body was racked with silent sobs. Ane kept rumbling through her desk drawer, never looking at them.

"Th-the FBI," Keke said, tears seeping down her cheeks. "They were here."

It took a second for the words to register. FBI. Here? "What did they want?"

Keke squeezed her eyes shut but tears kept leaking down her face.

Ane said, "They're after Devon. She killed—"

Chad jumped to his feet and grabbed his cell phone. It was

on the desk next to his computer terminal. He held it up to his ear but heard nothing.

"Devon! Devon!"

"She killed an FBI agent and two innocent men," Keke said.

"No, she didn't." Chad dashed for the door. "She's in the Witness Protection program. Those weren't FBI agents. They're a hit team."

The door to Devon's office was shut but unlocked. No one was inside. The back door was ajar.

CHAPTER THIRTY-SIX

BROCK GAZED at the unconscious woman Kyle had carried into the yacht's main cabin. She didn't look like much, he thought. Slim. Blonde. How could one woman have caused so much trouble?

"The ether should wear off in about ten minutes," Kyle said.

Ether, the forgotten drug, Brock thought. Once it had been the anesthetic of choice for hospitals doing surgery, but it had been replaced by newer medications. He'd found it handy over the years. It could be carried in a small vial and poured onto a washcloth to sedate someone in a matter of seconds.

Kyle had carried the bitch here, pretending she was drunk and needed help getting back to their boat. Luck was with them once again. Kyle hadn't met anyone as he'd hauled her to the yacht.

"Did you check her purse to see if the disk was in it?" Brock asked.

"It wasn't there. You don't honestly think she'd walk around with it in her bag, do you?"

Brock shrugged. "With women, you never know."

The woman moaned almost inaudibly. Brock leaned forward. This bitch had been nothing but trouble since the first day he'd been introduced to her at PowerTec. His gut instinct had told him then this bitch would cause endless problems.

How right he'd been.

Too bad Cassidy and Olofson hadn't listened to him. No.

They'd waited until the FBI called in an agent to check out their books before they believed him.

He should have gotten credit for figuring it out, but no. He'd suffered endless blame for the problems this woman had caused. He was going to relish every minute this bitch suffered.

Devon blinked and the world around her whirled. She closed her eyes again, willing her brain to make things level. Where was she?

Her office. The man with the spiked hair.

She sat bolt upright. The spiked hair guy was gazing at her from a chair opposite her.

"Feeling better?" asked a nearby voice.

Devon turned and saw a short man with dark brown eyes on the sofa next to her. A quick scan of the room told her that they were on a boat. Where was Chad? Couldn't he hear any of this on her cell phone? It should be acting like an open microphone.

"Where am I?" she asked.

"On a boat." The man's words sounded terse as if he'd ground them out a syllable at a time.

"I remember you," she said. "Brock Hardesty with Obelisk."

CHAD HEARD THE WORDS "on a boat." How far could they be? he wondered. He'd checked on Devon only a few minutes ago. She'd been keyboarding on her computer.

"Chad, what do you mean? Is Devon a protected witness?"

"Absolutely. Those men weren't from the FBI. They're going to kill her."

He barely heard his sister's sob. He knew Devon was on a boat, and she had to be nearby. Not enough time had elapsed for anyone to have taken her very far. Her cell phone was still transmitting. The DoD gadget, he thought.

"Chad, I'm sorry. I thought—"

He barged by Keke. The only way he could find Devon

was with the DARPA device. If she was in the harbor, he could scan each boat and see where people were. Of course, there was a problem. The device might pick up people as dogs or boats or mechanical objects. Still, it was his best option.

He pulled the scanner out of the leather pouch.

"I want to help," Keke said.

"Call the local FBI office. Ask for Warren. Tell him some men impersonating FBI agents have kidnapped Devon."

He dashed out of the office to get the Beretta he kept on the seat of his SUV. On the way out, he passed a redhead. She was probably going into Aloha. People never expected them to be closed Monday and Tuesday.

"WE'VE COME FOR THE DISK," the kid with the spiked hair told Devon. For emphasis, he aimed a gun at her temple.

"I haven't got it."

"You know where it is."

Devon didn't see any point in denying it. "I looked at the disk and didn't see anything interesting on it."

"It's encrypted."

"What's on it that's so important? Look at all the people who have died because of it."

The kid said, "We're asking the questions here."

She cleared her throat, pretending to be on the verge of tears. "If I'm going to die over it, I have a right to know."

She was stalling. Surely Chad would be here shortly. The kid still held a gun. Brock probably had one, as well.

Brock scanned her face critically. "Smart gal like you should have been able to break the encryption."

"Or get someone to do if for you," the kid added. "You had it long enough."

"I didn't know it was valuable. The agent the FBI sent to PowerTec said it was worthless."

"She knew it was worth a fortune. Just before the FBI went to investigate PowerTec, the company hired experts to remove the confidential material. We didn't check the key-stroke logger on Rutherford's machine soon enough. You'd made a copy, but you'd disappeared."

"I had this all wrong," she admitted. "I thought Rutherford and Ames were after me."

"Pussies. Both of them. Rutherford was cutting a deal with the prosecutors."

"That's why you arranged for the plane accident."

"It was easier than sending a team after them. Besides, fewer questions are asked if there's an accident."

Devon hadn't cared for Rutherford and Ames, but they had families, wives, children, parents. A death impacted so many people.

"What's on the disk that is worth so many killings?" If she kept them talking, Chad would have more time to find her.

The kid said, "Don't tell her."

Brock rolled his eyes and stared up at the boat's teak ceiling. "Why not? She'll be better off dead so she might as well know what she died for."

The kid shrugged. "It's your show."

"The disk has information on Obelisk, the men running it, links to our sources in the military. It also shows where the money is stashed."

"The Cayman Islands. I learned that much when I was at PowerTec."

"It doesn't really matter where the money is. Who's getting the money is what's important. Some of our highest military leaders are profiting from the scheme."

"I called the FBI because I could see from PowerTec's records that they were cheating the government. Short orders. Inferior parts."

"You don't know the half of it." He spoke without a hint of boastfulness. "Now where's the disk?"

Her mind had been scrambling over what to say. She didn't want to send them to Chad's office. His secretary could get hurt. She didn't want to give them the copy in Chad's safe, either. If anything happened to her, she wanted the truth to come out.

"It's in a safety deposit box at First Honolulu Bank." It sounded logical to her. Where would a woman on the run hide a disk? She did have a deposit box there, but it had extra cash in case she needed to disappear.

Brock studied her for a moment. "Did you make any copies?"

"Nope."

"Don't believe her," the kid said. "Get the truth out of her."

Brock nodded. "Let's get the disk first. Then we can have a little fun. We don't want to walk into the bank with a bloody mess on our hands."

"Good thinking."

Where was Chad? He should have found her by now. It was a long trip to the bank. With luck she would have an opportunity to get away from them.

Running in a zigzag pattern was her best bet. WITSEC had told her that even an expert shot hits a moving target less than fifty percent of the time.

"Ahoy there! Permission to board," called a woman.

"Who the hell is that?" Brock asked. "Take a peek through the blinds."

All the blinds were down throughout the vessel. Evidently they didn't want anyone who happened by to look in.

The kid peered through the miniblinds. "It's a redhead. A real looker."

"Get rid of her."

The kid headed for the door.

"No. Wait a minute. Ask her name."

The kid stuck his head out and asked her name.

"Jordan Walsh."

Brock couldn't help smiling. The two women who'd made his life miserable were with him now. Killing two women and dumping them at sea was going to be the ultimate high.

Wait a minute! How did the bitch find him?

"Let her in."

Devon watched as a stunning redhead in yellow shorts and a lime green blouse walked in. She had Chad's device in her hand. How had she gotten it away from him? Had she killed him for it?

"Hello, Brock," she said with an alluring smile.

"How'd you find me?" He didn't sound the least bit thrilled to see her.

"I brought a little present for you." She held up the test gadget. "Infrared locator. It works great in the day and even better at night."

"Worthless piece of shit. I had one and it didn't work."

"That's because I disabled it."

"And you installed a keystroke logger on my PC."

"Just keeping track of things. " She blessed Brock with a sweet smile.

"Who do you work for?" He snarled out the words.

"Bash Olofson."

"Bullshit!"

"He's testing you. Bash has been unhappy with Cassidy for some time."

"Figures." He turned to the kid. "Do you know her?"

"No, but I've been in the Middle East for the last two years. Sounds like Uncle Bash. He's always complaining about Cassidy. He sent me to learn your job so you can take over for him."

Unfuckingbelievable, he thought. This whole time he thought he was going to get the axe because he'd lost Samantha Robbins twice.

Kaboom! The boat rocked hard and a shuddering sound rumbled up from the engine room.

Brock asked, "What the hell was that?"

"An explosion," Jordan said.

The kid added, "I smell fire. We'd better get out of here."

"Jesus! Just what I don't need." He pulled out his gun and pointed it at Devon. "No funny business."

Devon saw this as a chance to get away. She stepped out of the boat. People were running down the gangway to see what had happened.

Jordan said, "Better put the guns away. Cops will be all over this place."

Brock and Kyle shoved their weapons into their waistbands. Brock grabbed Devon's wrist in a death grip.

People were rushing up, asking, "What happened?"

"Probably a propane leak from the stove," offered an old salt who looked as if he'd been around water his whole life.

"We've got to go," Brock said.

The harbor master was speeding their way in a red boat. With this many people around, now was the time to make a break for it. Jordan winked at her. Suddenly Devon knew Chad must have used his diving expertise and caused the explosion.

Kyle led them up the gangway with Devon and Jordan walking on either side of Brock. Jordan stumbled and went down to her knees. Brock gave her his arm for support. Jordan started to rise, then suddenly tugged at Brock's arm.

Devon got the picture. She threw her weight against his side. She kneed him in the groin, and he dropped her wrist. She jumped off the gangway into the water. Swimming as fast as she could, she hid under the gangway.

There was an air pocket up top. They could probably shoot through the boards, but she doubted they would chance it with so many people around. A hand grabbed her ankle. She kicked hard, aiming for his crotch. It took her a second to realize it was Chad. She was right. He had been under the boat, planting the explosives.

Shots rang out. Chad pulled her under the water. They shared his equipment to get air and swim toward the restaurant area. Even under the water, they heard the wail of police sirens. They surfaced and in the distance saw police and an ambulance.

"Oh, my goodness. I hope Jordan didn't get shot."

"It looks like a man on the gurney. From his size, I'd say it's Hardesty."

"You're right. I see Jordan's red hair."

They pulled themselves out of the water. Chad peeled off his mask and fins while Devon tried to catch her breath.

"You set the explosion, didn't you?"

He smiled at her. "Piece of cake. During the Gulf War, I sabotaged a lot of Iraqi boats. I didn't want to sink it. I just wanted to create a diversion. I sent Jordan in first to make sure you weren't dead. When she didn't immediately come out, I knew it was a go."

"Who is Jordan?"

"She's a special investigator for the Department of Defense. They've been trying to crack the Obelisk deal for some time."

Jordan spotted them and came running over. "It's over. Hardesty's badly wounded. I doubt if he'll make it."

"Who shot him?" Devon asked.

Jordan smiled. "I did. With his own gun."

"She's a crack shot," added Chad.

"It's over. It's really over?" Devon asked.

Chad wrapped his arms around Devon and held her tight. "Yes, sweetheart. It's over."

"Gotta go," Jordan said. "I want to get the disk back to Washington."

"Goodbye," Devon said. "And thank you."

Walking off Jordan said, "Just make sure I get an invitation to the wedding."

"What wedding?"

He smiled his trademark meltdown smile. "Ours. Will you marry me?"

"Of course, but I warn you. I want several children."

"Do you want to wait a bit? Go home to Houston and see—"

"This is my home now, my life. I'd planned to return here

when things were over. There's nothing in Houston for me. Wherever you are, that's where I want to be."

"If you'd wanted to move back to Texas, I would have gone with you. I love you, Devon. Never doubt it."

* * * * *

*Turn the page for a look
at the next exciting book from
Meryl Sawyer...
HALF PAST DEAD
coming from HQN Books in November 2005*

"A KILLER INSTINCT separates a winner from a loser."

Texas Hold-Em was the man's favorite television show. If he wasn't home to see it, he recorded the program. Most contestants on the game were fair. He would grant them that much. If he played with them, the suckers would find out they didn't have killer instincts.

He knew he would never play *Texas Hold-Em* on TV. His world was too important to devote so much time to the poker circuit. A pity. People would have no clue what they'd missed.

The man's attention was diverted from thoughts of *Texas Hold-Em* by the task at hand. He trudged through Mississippi's waist-high underbrush in the dense forest of second growth pine. He'd driven into the area on his four-wheel drive, using one of the dozens of overgrown logging roads in the area. He'd passed several hunting shacks hidden behind the dense brush. Like a carpet, cushy pine needles put a slight bounce in his step, despite the limp body he lugged over one shoulder.

He'd never killed anyone before, but he'd known it was inevitable. He accepted the risk the way he accepted a great many hazards. What else could be expected when he lived a double life? Risk brought a rush that ranked right up there with sex or money. He'd come to crave it like a schedule two narcotic.

This snoop on his back had forced him to play his hand, and his killer instinct had kicked in. Dump the body in the woods. By the time it was discovered, decomposition would have set in, and the authorities would have trouble identifying the corpse.

He pitched the woman into the thicket. The carcass snapped some branches on its way down, a dry, brittle sound in the darkness. A *whump* told him the body hit the ground, and he heaved a sigh of relief. Maggots and spring rain would take care of the evidence. What more could he want?

He chuckled, the thick foliage muffling his laughter. The changing tides of destiny never failed to amuse him. "The force" had guided his entire life. It wouldn't desert him now.

Some secrets were carried to the grave—where they belonged. Dead men, dead women no longer have the power to reveal your secrets. The power was his and always had been.

CHAPTER ONE

Three Months Later

KAITLIN WELLS loved sunrise, a time of hope, of promise. A new beginning. Kat hadn't seen the sun come up for three years, seven months and forty-two days. But she never missed a sunset.

She trained her gaze on the meadow in the distance. Buzzards spiraled on outstretched wings, circling lower and lower to feast on some creature she couldn't see. It was probably a squirrel or a rabbit in the last throes of death.

On the horizon the sun sulked in a spring sky that was a bleak shade of gray. Trees loomed like sentinels, guarding the top of the ridge, dark silhouettes backlit by a sun that would blister the earth in another month.

A clanging sound behind Kat recalled home to her mind. She could almost hear children kicking cans and yelling at each other. Almost smell chicken frying in cast-iron pans. Almost see the sidewalks banked by azalea bushes laden with pink blossoms.

Almost.

Back home in Twin Oaks, day drifted lazily into night. Here, darkness fell with eerie swiftness. The sun had dropped behind the ridge now, and less than half of the orb was still visible.

"Hey! What the hell do you think you're doin'?"

She ignored the guard's voice behind her and didn't jump off the toilet. The image of home slipped out of her head like a fleeting dream, but she kept her eyes on the horizon beyond the barred window. The light of the dying sun glinted off the razor wire strung along the concrete wall, but Kat hardly noticed. She refused to miss the sunset. It was the only thing in her life with the power to lift her soul out of a very dark place, if only for a few seconds.

Whack!

The guard's nightstick slammed against the back of her thighs. She'd been expecting the blow. The pain shooting down her legs didn't bother Kat. Nothing could hurt her now.

"I asked what you're doin'," the guard repeated.

"Watching the sunset."

"You've got company. A newbie."

She'd realized having the small cell to herself wouldn't last. Like all prisons, the Danville Federal Correction Institution was overcrowded. There were at least two inmates in every cell and sometimes three or four.

With a metallic click, the cell door slammed shut, but Kat didn't bother to turn around. The sun had vanished, leaving a spectral-gray twilight. Out of nowhere appeared a skull-like moon. Its pale light intensified with each passing second.

"Which bunk should I take?"

The timid voice grated on Kat's nerves like shards of glass. She hopped off the toilet and looked at the new arrival. Red hair flowed over her shoulders like molten lava. Well, prison shampoo would zap its shine. The woman was probably in her twenties, but didn't look much older than fifteen. Her brown eyes were bloodshot and puffy from crying.

"Use the top bunk."

The woman tossed her bag onto the upper bunk and stuck out her hand. "I'm Abby Lester."

She made no move to shake hands. "Kat Wells." She dropped onto the lower bunk and picked up the book she'd checked out of the prison's library. It didn't pay to be friendly with other inmates, especially a newbie. New arrivals were encouraged to snitch. They often made up things just to get a pack of cigarettes or a Hershey bar. Kat had learned this the hard way and paid the price—a month in solitary confinement.

"I shouldn't be locked up." Abby's voice was barely above a whisper.

Kat didn't take her eyes off the page. She knew Abby was going to insist she was innocent. Everyone in the joint claimed they were innocent. If they confessed their guilt, there had been a really good reason why they'd committed a crime.

"I didn't know my boyfriend was going to rob the post office. He never said a thing about it. Honest. I was just waiting for him in the car."

Kat didn't respond. She tried to concentrate on Steinbeck's words. She'd read *Of Mice and Men* when she'd been preparing to go to college. She had sobbed at the end, but this time she knew she wouldn't cry.

"My mother's using her retirement money to find me another attorney. He'll get me a new trial," Abby said, her voice choked with tears.

Abby's mother loved her.

Kat's lungs turned to stone, and for a moment she couldn't breathe. She closed her eyes then quickly opened them. Steinbeck's words were slightly blurred.

Thank God her father hadn't lived to see her in prison. Unlike her mother, he would have come to visit every chance he could. Her mother hadn't written even one letter. Other inmates received care packages from home, but Kat's mother and sister couldn't be bothered.

"IT'S JUST A FORMALITY, you know. The council has to vote on the new chief of police."

Justin Radner nodded slightly at Tyson Peebles, mayor of Twin Oaks. He was the first black mayor of the small town where Justin had grown up. Although Peebles was seven years older, he and Justin had a lot in common. Both had been star players on the Harrington High football team. They'd each been offered a much coveted athletic scholarship to Ole Miss. Tyson had gone on to become one of the university's top stars. From there he'd been drafted by the Steelers and had played four years in the NFL, until a tackle after the whistle nearly paralyzed him.

Justin had refused the Ole Miss scholarship and accepted one from Duke instead. Ole Miss was *the* football school in the South. No one in their right mind turned down Ole Miss. Occasionally Justin wondered how different his life might have been had he stayed in his home state.

Filpo Johnson rocked back in his chair beside Justin and puffed on a Cuban cigar. "Thar's not much crime here, truth to tell. Kids 'n drugs, mostly."

Even though he was black, Filpo loved to play the white cracker. Justin wasn't fooled. Filpo headed the city council, and he had a mind as sharp as a new razor. Filpo had graduated from the school of hard knocks, and now ran several successful businesses on the "north side," where most of the black people lived.

"The Lucky Seven docks at Tanner's Landing. It's in the unincorporated area where we have a contract to provide fire and police services." Peebles spread his hands wide and smiled. "They have their own security. We don't have to worry about them."

The riverboat was owned by a syndicate controlled by New Orleans mob money. Twin Oaks had been a dying town until gambling hit the Mississippi. Justin bet half the town was employed at the floating casino or relied on it in some way. He got Mayor Peeble's message. Let the Lucky Seven handle its own problems.

"There are five of us on the council," Filpo drawled in a voice like warm honey. "Buck Mason will vote no."

For a gut-cramping second, the world froze. Buck Mason on the city council? Since when? No way in hell would Mason vote for him. He still blamed Justin for his daughter's death, though they'd broken up months before Verity died.

Filpo added, "Mason's got it in for you big-time."

"Now you're scaring me."

Filpo chuckled, then added, "Just warning you, my man."

Justin shrugged, then stood up, saying, "You have my cell number."

He strode out of city hall. Along the way, Justin passed the mayor's secretary. She quickly averted her head and pretended to study some papers on the desk. Once she'd been all over him, but that had been when he'd been a football star. And Verity had been alive.

Justin walked into the morning sunlight. The town square, like so many others in the South, featured a bronze statue of a Confederate soldier with a musket. Massive pecan trees planted after the First World War shaded the square and bright pink azalea bushes lined the walks, their blossoms swaying in a breeze scented with honeysuckle.

A vague memory invaded his thoughts as he gazed from the top of the city hall steps. He was a kid again, standing beside his mother. Men in white—some on horseback, others walking—paraded around the square. He clutched his mother's hand, asking, "Ghosts?" She'd hesitated a moment before responding that these were just men pretending to be ghosts. She'd swiftly marched him away from the square.

Years later, he'd learned he'd witnessed the last legally sanctioned KKK march in Twin Oaks. Times had changed, he decided, starting down the steps. In a town that had roughly the same number of blacks and whites, Twin Oaks now had a black mayor and a black president of the city council.

He seriously doubted that meant folks around here were any less prejudiced. They just learned to hide it better. Twin Oaks was half an hour and thirty years away from Natchez. He hadn't been home since his mother's funeral, but he knew change came with agonizing slowness to small Southern towns.

Prejudice was something he would have to deal with when he became chief of police. Yessir. He knew he'd be offered the job. After Duke, he'd enlisted in the army where he'd been selected to be a ranger. After the military, he'd joined the New Orleans Police Department. He would still be there if a drug bust hadn't gone bad and a bullet damn near killed him.

He'd returned fire and taken out Buster Albright. Buster's brother, Lucas, had sworn to get Justin. The court had sentenced Lucas to ten years in jail. Justin knew Lucas wouldn't cool off in prison. One day the man would come gunning for him.

Twin Oaks wasn't going to find another guy with his credentials, Justin decided. Despite Buck Mason, the mayor and the city council might not like him, but they would hire him. Kicking himself, he walked to his Silverado. Why in hell had he returned?

The answer was simple, he decided. Twin Oaks was in his blood. He could move, but he could never really leave this place behind. The town was small enough to have that old-fashioned feeling even though it had grown in recent years, and everyone didn't know each other the way they had when he'd lived here.

Justin revved the engine and drove out to Shady Acres Trailer Village. What a joke. A dozen single-wides that had been there since the seventies did not make a village. It was a half step from living in your car.

The original owner had entertained grandiose ideas. A fancy wrought-iron arch typical of New Orleans soared above the entrance. It had rusted and pieces had been broken off or been scavenged. Several majestic oaks with swags of moss were clustered around the entry. Beyond the trees, battered cars and muddy pickups were parked near ramshackle trailers.

"Here goes nothing," he muttered under his breath as he stopped in front of the trailer he'd called home for the first seventeen years of his life. His mother had tried her damnedest to make the single-wide look like a real home. The white picket fence she'd painted every spring hadn't been touched since she'd died two years ago.

Justin stepped out of the Silverado. His boots hit the dirt with a thunk and dust billowed up to his ankles. Whoever was renting the trailer didn't appear to be home. Justin eased aside the gate dangling from one rusting hinge and walked up to the door. Wood-slat steps with weeds jutting through the gaps led up to the makeshift porch.

Justin could see himself sitting on the steps, eating a mayo sandwich on white bread. His mother had never allowed weeds to sprout through the gaps, but even she couldn't keep out the snakes who liked the coolness during blistering summer heat. He'd dropped pebbles between the slats to see if any snakes were coiled below. The plunk had told him if he'd hit dirt or a snake.

He shook off the memory and knocked. A country tune blasted from the rear of the trailer park. With it came a gust of wind and the scent of rabbit stew. He wondered how many rabbits he'd shot and brought home for his mother to cook, when they hadn't had enough money to do more than pay the rent on the trailer.

No one came to the door. He tried the knob, but it was locked. He walked down the wooden steps and went around to the rear of the trailer. The garden his mother had tended, even when she'd been so eaten up by cancer that she could barely walk, had been taken over by weeds and wild onions.

He didn't get it. He honestly didn't. From the moment he'd joined the army and began making money, he'd tried to persuade his mother to move to a nicer place. To the end, she'd insisted this was her home.

"I'm glad you can't see it now, Ma," he whispered to himself. "The place is a disaster."

Justin's reflections were interrupted by the buzz of his cell phone in his pocket.

"Radner," he answered.

"You're in," Peebles told him. "Only Buck Mason didn't vote for you."

Why am I not surprised? "Great. When do you want me to start?"

"Tomorrow."

"I'll need a few days to clean up things in New Orleans and to find a place here."

"Make it fast. Kids hunting squirrels found a body in the unincorporated area. Dougherty says it's been in the woods for some time, but you know he isn't up to a murder investigation."

Tom Dougherty had been on the police force for as long as Justin could remember. He was a nice guy, but he was about as bright as Alaska in winter.

"Any idea who the victim is?" Justin asked, kicking himself for the rush he felt. Someone was dead. He shouldn't be excited, but he was. He'd assumed returning to Twin Oaks would mean nothing but routine police work.

"No. Dougherty says there aren't any missing person reports."

"He should check neighboring jurisdictions."

"From what Dougherty says we could have our first homicide in...what? Eleven years? The last one was when what's-his-name shot his partner during an argument over their hogs."

"Maybe I'd better take a look before they contaminate the crime scene."

"Good idea. I'll call Dougherty and let him know you're coming."

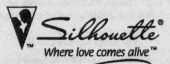